OF MAGES, CLAW, AND SHADOW

CHRISTOPHER D. SCHMITZ

TREESHAKER BOOKS

Copyright © 2025 by Christopher D. Schmitz

All rights reserved.

No portion of this book may be reproduced in any form without written permission from the publisher or author, except as permitted by U.S. copyright law.

Stay up to date on the world of Arcadeax... you'll get access to a bunch of special freebies, bonus content, and the author's newsletter. You can unsubscribe at any time.
To get access to this exclusive group, just follow this link:

https://www.subscribepage.com/duelist

and add your email to be added immediately!

Fables and Lorecaft

Many authors have dedicated fan groups online. After publishing nearly 100 stories I wanted to build a place allowing me opportunities to engage with readers and engage more meaningfully than even my newsletter does.

Enter *Legends and Lorecraft*.

In an industry where publishers, platforms, production costs, and promotional fees eat up most of the revenue authors make from books, subscription services help creators writing. Folks often tell me "I love supporting writers," and this provides a way for them to contribute to a sustainable space for them to shape the future of my writing (whether they're a paid subscriber or free.) Consider joining my readers community. Unlike the big publishers, *it is focused on putting readers first!* Members get early access to beta and alpha read projects I'm working on (which means they'll sometimes see early drafts—even before a story is done,) and there are tons of insider bonuses, plus amazing exclusives.

Take the first step towards adventure:

https://www.authorchristopherdschmitz.com/community

Introduction

The *Curse of the Fey Duelist* series has a strange-seeming numbering structure. Book 0 and any short stories with a number valued at lower than 1 are recommended to read *after* reading book 1, *A Kiss of Daggers*. Readers can choose to read in whatever order they want, but they were written with the intention of reading the story of Remy's attempts to become a hero *before* reading about his checkered past.

The series is numbered to place the books chronologically, but the recommended reading order is Book 1 first, and then Book 0 and prequels. Then read Book 2, and beyond.

- The Infernal Wars
- Tempus Exterminus. Dawn of the Mavens
- Fomorian Wars, Creation of the Aegis Bastion
- The Teind Sacrifices Seal the Black Gate. Wulflock gives the Unseelie Coire Ansic to Queen Mab
- Wulflock's Disappearance & Rise of Successors
- Akasha and Aicher
- Rhadachena rises to power and oppresses certain Unseelie
- Pendragon is cast out by Oberon. Cataclysm is averted. The Teind ceases, gates sealed & upheld by Oberon's might
- Aderyn Corff assassinates Queen Maeve of the Briar Court
- The Iron Bridge is created blocking Solstox
- Remy Reaton becomes a Duelist
- Fianna's Lycans Rise

~Timeline of Arcadeax~

Prologue

Two years ago...

A grizzled human stood upon the crossing over the Solstox Crossing. Hot daylight rained down upon him, causing sweat to bead at his brow and run down his beard and dreadlocks. He bent and clutched a fistful of iron shards and then yelled at his kinsmen.

"Faster, you dogs," Oddur insisted, wiping the sweat from his hairline. If the man had a whip, he might have cracked it. Instead, his gaze swept across the men and women of his tribe.

He and his clan considered themselves warriors, and had little use for tools and farming implements, however they had commandeered a number of wheelbarrows from area farms in the Selvages, the lands outlining either side of the Solstox Canyons which divided the Seelie and Unseelie regions of Arcadeax.

Oddur glanced at a woman collecting metal shards near the center of the bridge. Her tangled knots of hair drooped nearly to the ground as she retrieved pieces of broken, blackened iron and tossed them into the handcart. "Too much! That's too much," Oddur yelled at her. "We must not take it all or we'll provide a safe passage for the fey... They know this bridge is despoiled, riddled with toxic iron."

The human female nodded and then scattered the handful of metal ingots as if a farmer sowing seed. She moved further to the outskirts of the poisoned bridge. A human and traitorous aes sidhe once spoiled the plans of the unseelie queen here, thwarting her hopes of reigniting the old war between the Winter and Summer courts.

Spanning the distance across the chasm, bridges were the only effective way to cross an army from one side to the next without invading the Arcadeaxn faewylds. The wildfey watched the selvages, but allowed the Winter and Summer forces to use the strip of land on either side of the Canyons; it was also the entry point to their lands in the north. On the western side, a garrison of troops from the Summer Courts monitored the region against Unseelie invasion. Bridges spanning Solstox were rarely used... especially the toxic one known as The Iron Bridge.

Behind them, the Canol Lár fortress, abandoned since the Infernal Wars, stood upon a butte at the center of the ravine. Its form colored by haze and distance so it looked more like a mirage or a shadow of an older world. Working as quickly as possible to avoid detection, the remaining humans finished lading their wheelbarrows and signaled to their leader that their carts were full.

Oddur turned to face East, the Unseelie realm. Two figures stood at the furthest reaches, refusing to cross the threshold of the cursed trestle. He knew at least one of them was aes sidhe, a spell-casting member of the elven species. *There's no way we could have snuck onto the bridge under the watchful eye of the Summer garrison without arcane intervention.*

He did not know who the other figure was. The hulking brute had arrived sometime while the work was being performed. With that now completed, the human jogged in their direction to complete the transaction.

Humans were not native to Arcadeax, the land of the tuatha, the various fey peoples of the realm. However, many sons and daughters of Adam had existed in these lands for as long as there had been records.

Oddur slowed and crossed the last of the distance at a walk. He eyed the figure next to the black cloaked spellcaster. Oddur was larger than the dark aes sidhe; humans were typically physically superior, at least in many respects. They generally put on more muscle and were thicker across the chest and neck. On average, mankind was perhaps ten percent bulkier than elves, though the sidhe race had many other strengths to make up for any difference.

The creature next to the albino elf Oddur knew only as Hymdreiddiech stood taller and more muscular than even Oddur by a noticeable factor, and Oddur was the strongest of his clan, the Fianna's Fian Bairn tribe.

What looked like a red, burned boot-print puckered the olive skin of the orc's face. The flesh blistered at the edges of the foot-shaped marking. Oddur knew what must've made the disfigurement: iron. Fey creatures harmed by iron knew little but ceaseless pain. The metal burned when it inflicted its damage, and the agony of it never ceased. It never healed—was never forgotten.

The marking had a slight tread pattern visible. Oddur had heard the story of who this orc was, and how he'd earned such a wound.

Syrmerware Kathwesion was a notorious orcish slave taker. He'd become famous for running gangs of hunters in the Unseelie, *human hunters*.

More recently, rumor had it that Redcomb, the powrie champion, had given him this wound. Powries, or redcaps, were diminutive and vicious little creatures who refused to come to heel under Queen Rhagathena, the spider who sat on Winter's Rime Throne. They were also one of the few types of fey who could touch iron, and that made them dangerous. Few tuatha dared mess with a redcap. Possessing iron may have been illegal, but powries generally kept a low profile and were not populous enough to bother with beyond placing a royal bounty on them. Despite the reward, few ever risked so severe an injury by claiming one.

Syrmerware Kathwesion scowled at Oddur when he halted, keeping three steps away and remaining on the bridge. Oddur had heard rumors that the fey felt the presence of the iron upon the bridge. It had been described to him like the heat of a sunburn, and although the discomfort of it left when any tuatha departed the bridge, the experience was severe enough that fey avoided it.

The orc grumbled something below his breath which Oddur felt sure was an insult, and Oddur held the orc's gaze, endured the slaver's hate. The human's eyes lingered on the metal brand hanging on a thong at the slaver's neck. It was a nasty thing meant to mark the flesh of those he'd claimed as property.

Hatred between the two was mutual. *How many of my people has this monster pressed into service? I am glad that* he *now wears a mark, as well.*

Syrmerware Kathwesion joked, "This is the great Oddur? You don't look like much. I can see why the Fian Faolchú hold sway over all Fianna." The orc fingered his metal brand as if contemplating snatching the man and burning his flesh with the slaver's sigil. "Maybe someday, I'll find you unawares and on my side of the bridge?"

Oddur's nose wrinkled as he bared his teeth. "You'd be surprised at what I'm capable of."

"And still you come to barter with the forces of Winter?"

The human sneered. "Fuck you. If you want this iron so bad, how about I give you some?" Oddur threw a bit of iron slag at the orc. It bounced off Syrmerware Kathwesion's face inside the foot-shaped scar.

Snarling, Syrmerware Kathwesion reeled and clutched his face, though the pain had not been from the force of the blow. "You insolent, little meat-bag! I'll peel the skin from your bones!"

"You and what army?" Oddur challenged. "The way I hear it, you and your kind are practically an endangered species. Rumor has it someone fed the whole Demonsbreak iron riddled meat and wiped you all out."

The orc stiffened and set one foot onto the bridge. Oddur brandished the remaining pieces of iron and made Syrmerware Kathwesion think better of it.

"I will remember this, Oddur of the Fian Bairn. Someday, you and I will settle this, and I will cross your name off my list," growled the orc.

"Why not right now?" Oddur splayed his arms wide in challenge.

Syrmerware Kathwesion's nostrils flared. "You are merely number three... I'll not waste my time on you... yet."

"I'm not number one? I guess I'll have to work harder... Maybe if I kill a few more orcs. Who's ahead of me, then? Redcomb the Powrie and who else?"

"Aderyn Corff," growled the orc. His words vibrated with bitterness.

"Neither the redcap nor the Queenslayer are here, though, are they? And neither is Rhagathena, but *I am*, slave taker!" He cast the iron back onto the bridge. "I'll even fight you on the soil of the Selvages if you like." Some kind of power rumbled through his voice and Oddur's lip curled while his deep, amber eyes narrowed with intensity.

"Enough!" hissed Hymdreiddiech. "You test the patience of the Black Maven."

The elven spell caster's tone silenced the quarrelsome pair. Oddur saw something in the elf's eyes: something beyond the raw hatred and malice. He noted a weariness in them. *So, the elf is masking our presence with magic, after all. No wonder he insisted we harvest the ore with haste; an arcane veil this large must take a toll on him.*

"We have gathered the amount you requested," Oddur promised, waving a hand toward the humans and their forbidden cargo. "Do you have what you promised me?"

The Black Maven, a color chosen as a mockery of Lord Oberon's Maven Council stationed at Suíochán Naséan, or the Radiant Tower. Calithilon the White led the wizards' council and only a few knew that Hymdreiddiech even existed, let alone that he had set himself up as the secret antithesis to the circle of mavens.

"You shall deliver the ore to my agents in the Seelie lands," said Hymdreiddiech. "He will exchange the iron for your precious silvered weapons."

Hymdreiddiech stared at Oddur from beneath his dark cloak and then the Black Maven repeated his last statement, but spoke the words in the olde tongue. [My agent will exchange the iron for weapons of silver.] The olde tongue was the language of magic. It was impossible to speak falsely when using it; the mystic forces of Arcadeax itself ensured compliance.

"You... You want the iron delivered to the Seelie side of the bridge?" That much confused the human who had assumed the iron was bound for Hulda Thorne, or possibly Arctig Maen, the seat of the Winter court. He'd assumed that was the reason for Syrmerware Kathwesion's presence. Oddur was not well informed on news from the Queen Rhagathena's capitol, but even he knew that Oberon had sent emissaries to the royal wedding when the Spider Queen allied herself with the head of the orcish tribal collective known as the Demonsbreak.

"The Seelie," he repeated. "This metal was always bound for a greater destiny. It was not collected in vain," said Hymdreiddiech.

Oddur half bowed at the waist, agreeing to the maven's terms, but bristled inside. He'd heard of the Lightstarved, a group of enslaved humans and other creatures who were forced to collect and work the iron. Had their numbers not been depleted in recent bouts of war, including the incident that seeded the bridge with iron, as well as upon the great southern wall that separated Winter and Summer from the Fomorian Empire, Hymdreiddiech might have had no need to contract Oddur's people.

The Fian Bairn leader glared at the slave taker. Mostly it was Syrmerware Kathwesion's hunters who had stolen these people... But now was not the time or place to settle that grudge. First, Oddur had to get his own house in order.

"And what is the orc's part in this agreement?" asked the human.

Hymdreiddiech tilted his head. "His role is... unrelated to our business and entirely separate." The maven turned to the orc. "You have news from Arctig Maen?"

"Your queen has accomplished what she promised you. What you seek is now yours."

Oddur's ears itched for more, but additional news did not seem forthcoming. Instead, Hymdreiddiech merely grinned. "Excellent, then I must go. I have business in Faery Cairn and must be present for a rite at Oberon's court. Some child is supposed to carry the Dagda's Blessing," he said disdainfully before glaring at the human. "My diversion spell will end in a few minutes. I suggest you depart with the iron before that time."

And then the elf seemed to shimmer and then disappear. Whatever magic he'd used, Oddur's eyes had pierced the glamor of it, though just for a moment, the albino's form changed. If any creatures in Arcadeax knew shapeshifting, the Fianna were among them... And Oddur noted that Hymdreiddiech's pale skin and hair had changed. His eyes, too, had altered.

Oddur contemplated it momentarily and then turned his attention back to his enemy. The orc.

With no mediator present, they were free to kill each other without intervention. *Can I kill the bastard before Oberon's guards spot us?*

Oddur bit his lip and decided against it. Judging by his posture, the orc had done likewise.

"The Demonsbreak orc clans may be dismantled, but it is not dead," threatened Syrmerware Kathwesion. "It is more alive than ever before—and some day we shall have that fight you want so badly. I promise you that, Ddiymadferth."

"I welcome the day," Oddur said in a low tone. Like a wolven growl, the words rumbled in his chest. And then the two parted ways, heading opposite directions.

Chapter One

Remy knew he was dreaming. That didn't make reliving the memory any easier to deal with, though. In some ways, it made it worse. Every sense, every synapse in his brain, seemed to recreate that day with painstaking detail.

The day his best friend, and the best elf he ever knew, died at his feet. *Died because of my refusal to back down.*

Thoranmir Shelton stood upon the dais, the fighting platform, and crossed blades with Fuerian Vastra. The crowd cheered the murderous elf with a reputation of violence, and Fuerian found every excuse for it while dueling. A thunderous crowd roared with excitement when Thoranmir cut Fuerian, drawing first blood... But the wicked elf demanded satisfaction—exploited the rules. It was his right as a duelist to escalate the conflict past first blood and demand the duel end with one of them dead.

The more experienced Fuerian toyed with Thoranmir, running him through with his blade and killing him while maintaining hard eye contact with Remy: the human who took the Vastran lord's fiancé, publicly humiliating him. If Fuerian had not lost his status as heir of the Vastra family to his cousin, a related contender, the embarrassment might have threatened the clan's status as méith within Oberon's court.

Dream Fuerian glared at the human and hissed, "Ddiymadferth." Then he looked at Jaira and growled, "Whore of Adam." And then Fuerian ripped his blade free. Blood splattered across Anya's face, slicking Thoranimir's crippled sister.

Remy stood at the edge of the fighting platform and remembered. *This was not exactly how it happened... It's more how I felt when it happened.* "Anya was in the stands, not down here. She was too far away to have been bloodied."

The sudden levity helped him escape the trappings of emotion and think logically.

Remy looked at Anya. The dark-skinned she-elf was confined to her wheelchair for as long as Remy had known her, but he knew she'd long ago lost her legs. That accident had somehow bolstered her abilities and made her one of the most powerful aithermancers in the region. If pressed, she could even access the aither, the astral realm of spirit and thought, without the use of equipment, an irony since she could not travel normally without her akasha powered locomotive machine. It taxed her to do it, but it was possible.

In the time since losing Thoranmir, Remy had become a close surrogate. He knew he'd become like a brother to her, replacing the one she had lost... even though they would both admit that Thoranmir was irreplaceable.

Despite being a cold-blooded killer, Fuerian was protected by many layers of legal protocol. He had murdered Thoranmir but done it completely by the rules.

The dream reasserted itself. As the angry elf pushed his way past the dreaming Remy, he growled at him. "The Frith Duine will take you yet, ddiymadferth."

Fuerian spat the last word, and something shifted in Remy's hearing. He reached up and clutched his ear, feeling only pain. Remy pulled away his hand and found it slicked with blood.

"No, no, no," Remy chanted like a mantra. His dream transformed. This was the same dream he'd had the night before Thoranmir died, and which had come occasionally since. That first night Fuerian had offered to give Remy back his past life, complete with all the information that had been wiped from his mind by the poison of the faewyld's Aphay tree which he'd eaten from when he was young.

Fuerian had promised he could also provide passage back to his home realm, the realm of man, insisting it was where humans belonged. Fuerian promised that if Remy refused, he would earn only pain and suffering in this realm. Remaining in Arcadeax would result in Remy's death.

Still clutching where his ear had been cut from his head, Remy turned and ran, fleeing the horde of angry elves that amassed around him. They were Frith Duine, and the human hating mob had promised to cleanse Arcadeax of all ddiymadferth... of *humans*.

As traumatic as all his memories of his upbringing in the unseelie had been—his work as the royal assassin known as Aderyn Corff—this dream was the thing that rocked Remy to his core.

"It's not real. It's not real," Remy insisted as he sprinted toward his small home on the outskirts of Cathair Dé.

The dream took a turn from its last iteration. Unlike before, when Jaira protected her and Remy's half-elf changeling children from the Frith Duine, there were no children this time. This time around, their first child had not yet been born.

Dream Jaira burst suddenly into flames. The original dream had also ended in fire, albeit differently resolved.

Remy sprinted for the she-elf, but by the time he arrived, there was nothing left but bone and ash. An ethereal voice wafted through Remy's mind, the voice of Jaira's father. *None of this would have happened if that human had listened to me and left you alone.*

Nestled amongst the cinder, Remy spotted the hard, scaled, spherical object. It was a dragon's egg. He didn't know how he knew to identify it, but he recognized it all the same.

And then he felt the grips of rough hands as they took him. A he-elf sliced his other ear free. Remy watched the man, the Frith Duine leader, string his prize upon a lanyard next to so many others as he completed his macabre necklace.

This time, Remy did not fight. *Let them take me!*

The enemies shook him violently, and Remy gasped, rocketing back into his body and leaving the fallen dream world behind much like a mind reconnecting with flesh after a fouled egwyl meddwl trip. Something he'd done before; he vowed to never eat the spirit-walking fungus again.

Clutching his ears, he woke to find Jaira shaking him.

"Remy, Remy? What's wrong?" She laid a hand on his chest to soothe him.

Remy blinked, still reconciling his dream with the reality of his bed.

Jaira used her other hand and gently, but firmly, dragged Remy's hands away from his ears, which he found very much attached. "You were yelling as if you were hurt."

He embraced her, holding her close. "Night terrors. I saw him. Thoranmir."

Jaira gave him a melancholy smile. "I thank Danu every night for what he did—Thoranmir's actions saved me. If not for Thoranmir, I might be dead."

Remy squinted in the dark, making out his wife's features in the low light. Not that Remy couldn't imagine Thoranmir making such an extreme sacrifice, but that was not how he had remembered it.

She clarified, "If Thoranmir had not brought you to Cathair Dé, that creature that kidnapped me would have never been stopped—or perhaps the troll would have gotten me at the bridge, which might be preferable to the *other* alternative, my last name becoming Vastra in a forced marriage."

Remy laid a finger upon her jaw and caressed her face, understanding her meaning. It was about more than just Thoranmir's actions in the fighting circle.

Jaira and Remy had been married in a tiny ceremony many months ago, before moving into the cottage provided by Harhassus Morgansteen.

The marriage hadn't entirely been a secret, but the union had been kept fairly quiet. Because of the family's standing as a prominent méith house of the Summer Court. Remy still had his own last name, though Jaira expressed her desire for them to share a surname.

She laid her head across Remy's chest and he stroked her hair, gently caressing the pointed tips of her ears where they poked through her locks. The tangle glowed in the moonlight. Jaira kissed his chest with soft, slow motions. And then she kept going down.

"I—I'm not sure that—"

Jaira shushed him and then kept going, showing him how much comfort she offered. Or at least, how much she could distract him from his melancholy. She fumbled at the drawstring of her lover's pants and Remy helped remove them, suddenly eager for more.

Moments later, the heat of the flames in Remy's dream was a mere afterthought, replaced by an altogether different fire.

South of Daonra Dlúth

Large wheels crunched the gravel beneath the burnished wood and steel trim of the strong-box carriage. Unassuming, yet somehow pristinely ornate, the vehicle ambled along a backwoods road.

A team of regal horses drew the wagon, which boasted four soldiers at the front and four in the back.

The driver, an older sidhe with deep laugh lines, leaned back in his seat and grinned at his younger apprentice, who sat abreast of him. "Best tuck that color away." He reached over to the younger elf and tugged the elf's lapel into place so that it hid the tunic he wore beneath, a brilliant purple color and clothing of the style only worn by the royal house staff.

Seated atop the roof behind the driver, two archers sat crossed legged, wary of threats. They, too, had disguised their regular uniforms for a more plainclothes appearance. The same went for the troops before and after the transport.

"Nothing like a leisurely ride through the countryside," the driver explained to the younger he-elf, who blinked. Flin knew he was unseasoned by comparison, but he resented the elder Taol's tendency to talk down to him.

"I still don't understand the need for all this secrecy," said the younger elf. "I'd feel better if we traveled with a full complement of soldiers plus a team of Solais Cloaks from the Tower."

Shrugging, the driver stared into the sky. "Lord Oberon gets what Lord Oberon wants... But I think the answer is very logical: it's not always *him* making the decisions. Every few years, he takes a holiday from Faery Caern and they hold the Saol Nua feast in some remote location as the royalty vacations. Everyone always says the Mavens started the trend, but I think it's been at Queen Titania's insistence. Every so often, Oberon needs to regain her favor, I suspect, if the king means to continue in his dalliances."

Flin squinted at the driver. "Dalliances?"

Belly laughing, the older sidhe slapped his knee. "Don't tell me you haven't heard the rumors at court? Ain't like they're new."

"I'm not exactly at court. Neither are you. We're just servants, Taol."

Flustered, Taol spat as he held the reins, "Well, of course not, Flin. Even so, we hear whisperings in the corners of the palace... gossip of the court. But I'm certain Oberon's dalliances are more than mere rumors. Far too many halfbreed changelings in the court to account for anything else."

The older elf laughed again as Flin arched an eyebrow. "You mean you didn't know that Oberon has a habit of sneaking off to the mortal realms of Adam—and maybe others—and, *you know?*" He made a lewd, hip thrusting gesture. "I know people say that the ddiymadferth are horny for the sidhe, but Oberon's late night activities might prove we got it all backward."

"No wonder Titania always looks so pissed."

"At any given time, she's got to share space with at least three of her husband's bastard half breeds and pretend she knows nothing about them." Taol shrugged. "But *we* all know. Just don't let Titania hear you whispering about it."

The younger elf followed the older one's gaze and spotted the bird circling a loop overhead. "I'd be angry, too, I suppose."

Teasing Flin, Taol nudged him with an elbow. "You've got to get yourself a young lass of your own first, before you try empathizing with the cucks, my boy."

"I guess *you* would know," Flin jested, drawing a surprised look and chortling boom from the older sidhe. His surprised laughter verged on a cough.

Before his amusement died down, the crow that had been circling them in the sky landed on the edge of the roof and pecked the carriage three times in rapid succession.

"Shoo, bird," the kid called, waving a hand at it.

In response, it rapped again with its beak.

"Bad luck to disturb a crow," said Taol. "Don't you know the legend of Aderyn Corff?"

Flin furrowed his brow. "No?"

"The Corpse Bird. He was a famous assassin working for Rhagathena in the Winter Court. Some tuatha say that he is Remy Keaton, the houseless duelist from Cathair Dé."

"That's crazy," he said. "I follow all the duelist standings. Remy is a human."

Taol shrugged. "Be that as it may, I'm just reporting what I know. Anyway, Aderyn Corff, the Corpse Bird, was Queen Rhagathena's private killer. Tricked into a vow, or something like that, when he was young. The bird marked his targets—crows are smart, you see—and it followed whomever Aderyn Corff was sent to kill. But the story goes that this was no ordinary bird... Some say the bird was the spirit of the Dagda himself, or maybe it was Lugh or Taranis... I dunno. I'm not a religious fey."

"Right," the younger elf said, finally scaring off the bird as he lunged for it. The crow took flight and spiraled away, high and out of sight.

Both elves watched it go. "Shouldn'a done that. Bad luck," Taol repeated.

Flin gesticulated that he had no fear. "I'm far more interested in what we're carrying in the locked carriage than unseelie folklore."

The younger elf held Taol's gaze. As the driver, he'd been there to see that the doors were locked properly and would've gotten a peek inside.

After several moments, Taol sighed. "All right, boy. I don't suppose there's much harm in knowing. We set out straight from Faery Cairn with a load of—"

His voice gurgled as an arrow streaked out from the nearby trees and lodged in his throat. Taol spat blood that splattered and streaked Flin's face. Then Taol pitched headlong off the cart, stone dead. His body fell under the wheels, making the carriage bump over the fleshy hump that had been Flin's companion.

"Attack! We're under attack," yelped Flin as he snatched the controls and tried to take over. The guards on the rooftop had already leapt to their feet, though nearly dislodged when the cart jostled.

Loud thumps echoed as arrows, aimed for the new driver, lodged into the side of the cart. Several hit armor and snapped under the impact, others caromed away, harmless.

Flin cracked the reins and urged the horses forward even as a fresh salvo of arrows flew toward him. One bit his flesh, piercing his chest and knocking him sidelong. With the reins still in his grip, his fall made the horses' rear back and stop.

Ahead of the traffic, a wave of fire and wind, cast forward by some spell-casting sidhe, flung the forward guards from their saddles. Any not killed in an initial encounter were quickly set upon by the mixed tuatha rushing from the trees.

Turning his head back, the impromptu driver saw that all the other guards had been killed by arrows or mystic forces. Returning his gaze, Flin watched as a diminutive black-clad figure approached. The creature was some other sort of tuatha, not one of the aes sidhe. *What other kinds of fey have magic like this?*

"I... I'm all that's left." Flin tried to right himself, hoping to frenzy the horses. If he could make them flee the attack and save whatever prize the king had sent them with, he might keep alive—something he liked even more than securing Oberon's favor at the moment.

Before he could crack the reins, a second arrow lodged in his belly and the magic user waved his hand and all the horses fell into a stupor. Two fell asleep, the other two simply laid down.

Flin blinked at the arrow and turned to watch the short creature direct a crew of thugs to rip the door off its hinges. Something entirely surreal washed over him as the pain of his wounds made him gentle his motions so the throbbing ache lessened.

"Wha... what is in there?" asked Flin. Barely moving his head, he shifted his eyes from one attacker to another. They were all wildfey, mostly long eared ellyllon sidhe, but at least one was shrouded, and Flin saw midnight black skin from the eye slit made for her eyes. *A trow, most likely... So this is a band of rogues?*

Grinning, one of the fey reached inside and pulled out several pieces of artwork and other royal accoutrements. One item was a simple stick protruding from a plain dirt-filled jar, but another was an ornate, lidded pot—something more akin to a vase, both engraved and gilded with intricate accents.

"Artwork?" Flin asked. Blood leaked from the corner of his lips. "You're killing me over a bunch of simple creature comforts?"

The small creature grinned as he approached, and Flin recognized him as a boggart. After the boggart tried to drag the driver to the soil and failed, he snapped his fingers, and two of the wild-fey elves tried to dislodge the arrow pinning Flin in place. They snapped the shaft at the rear and then tossed the driver off the platform.

"If you think your life has meaning beyond the castes the Summer Court forces you into, then you are mistaken. Worse, you are stupid." He reached for a dagger at his hip and snapped orders to his companions that they should take the cart. "Ride to the next waypoint and await further instructions."

Flin choked out a mouthful of pained words. "You... are you going to ki—"

Before the apprentice driver could finish his question, the boggart leapt down and plunged his dagger into Flin's heart. And then all went black forever.

"Good to see you, my Ronin," Xander Kent said brightly as Remy entered his employer's home office.

"Just Remy, please. Names and titles have never really worked out all that well for me."

The wealthy elf sat back in his plush chair and smiled. "Oh, please. Relish it. You are ina aonar... *a houseless duelist*. In fact, it's part of the reason why I hired you. I mean, aside from your raw talent."

The human furrowed his brow, not following his employer's meaning. Ina aonar was typically viewed as a lesser status: a warrior only a few would place faith in—the kind of faith that earns top coinage, anyway.

Kent explained. "Oftentimes, duelists will defer to the politics of their house and clan factions." He flashed Remy a grin. "If I was much beholding to all of that, I would have made a bid for status in Oberon's court decades ago. I'm more interested in building personal loyalty than any of the trappings of the upper caste. It's why I give you such freedom to follow those leads on your side projects as much as possible."

Remy nodded slowly. "And I thank you for that."

The business minded sidhe winked as he tilted his head. "It's how I know you will always side with me and my interests if any outside disputes come up. And they certainly might arise, even though I look like the shining bastion of light who I portray at first glance. But our hearts beat the same, you and I, we're outsiders for our industry, similar, even if we come from different realms."

Xander Kent was an entrepreneur from the city of Cathair Dé. Like many elves similar to him, he had many enemies, and that necessitated employing a licensed duelist.

In Arcadeax, much revolved around personal honor. Having one's reputation besmirched often resulted in a duel as the proper response. Any sidhe without a qualified second often found themselves losing more than their business clientele—it sometimes ended with a loss of life.

Prior to marrying Jaira, Remy had to fight for his life as he dueled for the simple right to earn his spot in society and gain a license to duel. Some of the population loathed the idea of a human rising above his station and carrying a weapon for battle, as if anyone could argue with the fact that Arcadeax itself had given him an ancient, mystic boon. Remy carried a dúshlán, a blade forged of pure vengeance that yearned for satisfaction. The Frith Duine could do little to argue with reality and the laws of magic.

"Speaking of those private ventures I've been funding, how has your research gone lately?" Kent asked.

Kent did not travel often, and he generally conducted his business from his own private estate. The elf was really only in danger whenever he was on the road. Remy acted as his bodyguard whenever Kent traveled, but nearly every place the businessman went was heavily fortified.

By and large, Kent allowed Remy to spend his time looking into local issues, almost like a private investigator might. Kent had insisted that chaos and civic decay were far greater threats to his business ventures than private assassins or dualist ribbon seekers ever could be, and that allowed Remy a significant amount of flexibility.

"I'm still looking into potential connections between students kidnapped from area sorcery universities and the disappearances of humans," Remy told him.

The elf, clearly not an adherent of racist philosophies, shook his head dourly. "The fact that authorities aren't even looking into the rampant kidnapping of your kind only shows the need for more to be done—and if the crown won't see to it, then by the Dagda, I will."

Remy walked to the wall, where he'd pinned information relevant to the case. A sketch he'd collected of Eldarian Cócaire remained posted at the margin. His sister, an elf named Odessa, had begged Remy's closest friend, Thoranmir, to find him. It turned out Eldarian was in far greater trouble than Remy ever gave him credit for.

Kent watched his duelist as Remy looked over what clues he'd judged significant to uncovering a larger mystery. Whatever the truth was behind the Cócaire family's troubles, it had swallowed up Thoranmir, and he'd pledged himself to unraveling its secrets... Secrets that eventually killed the well-intended elf.

Eldarian had died, practically in Anya's arms, and Remy had been nowhere near to stop it. He knew the death somehow connected to a group of apothik pushers that he and Thoranmir had stopped, but beyond that, he had yet to find a connection. For the life of him, Remy could not figure out why Eldarian had gotten mixed up with dangerous, addictive apothiks in the first place.

Because of his talent at magic, the he-elf had been enrolled for free at the maginarius—his stars had changed for the better, and all Remy's research indicated that Eldarian had not been an addict beforehand. Further, whomever oversaw the Dream Hollow had no influence on Eldarian's campus. The only thing Remy knew was that one night Eldarian had simply disappeared and not turned up again until he was found in The Haunts... the derelict part of the city where addicts went to whither until they died.

The common factor between the cases were the disappearances. Eldarian's case was not unique. Others had gone missing as well, though most had never been discovered. Those who had been found were already dead. Whoever, whatever, was taking people, it did not seem to discriminate between human and tuatha.

"I have no news yet," Remy reported. "I have a few leads I'd like to follow up on. What is your schedule for this week? I like to look in on the orphanage I sponsored some time ago. It's one of the few who treats human children with dignity and the headmaster might have more information that could help."

Kent waved a hand at a schedule posted nearby. He put his hand into a half-opened set of ledgers to mark his place, and his eyes seemed eager to get back to the business at hand. "I'll need you on an upcoming trip. But nothing out of the ordinary." Kent pointed to a couple of pieces on his itinerary that Remy should pay attention to. "Aside from these items, here, you can feel free to pursue those leads."

Remy bowed his head gracefully and then returned to his work, allowing Kent to do the same.

Fuerian Vastra strolled the grounds with his hands clasped behind his back. He stayed one step ahead of his visitor, a she-elf wearing a cloak trimmed in shimmering violet. She walked with confident authority.

"I'm still not entirely certain why you want to see this mine, High Maven Amarthanc," Fuerian said. His eyes lingered on the purple embroidery on the chest of the aes sidhe's tunic. They formed a kind of spiked, circular shape of interlocked stag's horns.

Like the other members of the aes sidhe, Amarthanc wore colored embroidery to denote her rank, class, and position. The color and number of tines designated both her order and authority.

Fuerian was keenly aware that hers was of the highest rank, placing Amarthanc on the maven council. Of course, the violet faction was the least respected of them and he was aware that she was the most junior member of the council.

"I am here to perform an audit, Mister Vastra."

Fuerian hid a wince. His title *should* have been *Lord Vastra*. He was supposed to have been wed by now, and Margrave Vastra was promised to abdicate his seat at the head of the family to him. Instead, Fuerian's hated cousin, Juriahl, gained control of the family's influence and politics.

Along with the title, Juriahl also inherited the Vastra's broken finances when Margrave abdicated. They'd long held contracts for lighting the city street lamps well into the evening. With the growing popularity of akasha, however, the need for oil lamps and a crew to light them had waned greatly.

Arcadeaxns took the akasha for granted. None really knew where the stuff even came from. At least it was not common knowledge, beyond details shared by some long-forgotten maven alchemist who discovered it eons ago. Fuerian had seen it manufactured at its source, and if residents of the realm knew what it took to create the oddly silk-like fluid that mystically powered mechanical devices, they might refuse to touch it. If the fey did not revolt with such knowledge, their stomachs certainly would.

"I heard this mine is operational once again," Amarthanc noted.

Fuerian nodded. "As you must be aware, Harhassus Morgansteen deeded this property to me when I was pledged to his daughter. I'll not return it, even if he wanted it."

Amarthanc's eyes twinkled as she glanced at him. Fuerian did not appreciate her amusement at the recollection. For most anyone else, the mine was a torturous liability.

"Oh, yes," she said. "That's right."

"I've not been left with much post separation from my fiance, but I'm devoted to casting my own stars," Fuerian said.

"Did the Morgansteens instruct you on the restrictions for a mine that's poisoned such as yours is?"

Fuerian narrowed his gaze. "I'm sorry, but no. That is the source of my confusion."

"You must know that mining iron is a capital offense. The Morgansteens placed the deed on a register of contaminated places when it became insolvent many years ago. It is too hazardous for fey workers."

"I'm aware of the penalties for harvesting iron. And I also know that there are many dangers for miners in general, even without iron," Fuerian said. "I've taken steps to circumvent harming any fey who might come into contact with the stuff."

A loud clamor arose from the mouth of the cave and two sidhe dragged a redcap out by the chains that bound him. Pale and grizzled, the powrie snarled and screamed like a small, frenzied animal as he jerked against his masters. Barely the size of a halfling, the imp's slouched hat was ruddy gray and tattered, and he kicked with his bare feet.

Fuerian raised an eyebrow as the taskmasters tried to bring the slave to heel. The powrie raged, shrieking insults and profanities in its native tongue. Fuerian only knew the curse words of that language, and the creature spouted them all.

"Do you have the proper paperwork for that slave?"

"Of course. I always keep an accurate registry of such things."

Amarthanc pursed her lips. "I'd like to see it. If your paperwork is not in order, any unseelie creatures in your possession will have to be destroyed."

The feral halfling suddenly screamed as one of the sidhe slave-drivers put the redcap out of their misery with a blade. Quickly, the thing bled out.

As the powrie went limp, Amarthanc shrugged. "Never mind. It's a moot point, I suppose. Should I assume you have other creatures on staff who are capable of dealing with hazardous substances?"

"You would be correct," Fuerian stated calmly.

"And you are certain that your operation has nothing to do with mining iron?" Amarthanc asked. She glanced inside one of the carts parked in the operations area. The maven held a hand over the top of it as if sensing for the telltale painful sensation a cart would likely have if it were transporting even trace amounts of the toxic metal.

She glanced sidelong at him. Fuerian shrugged, motioning for her to perform whatever tests she desired.

"I want there to be no confusion about whether I am mining the forbidden ore or not," Fuerian explained.

Amarthanc squinted momentarily. "Forgive the Radiant Tower's suspicion. No other mine to ever close has dared re-open, given the presence of such a dangerous, ferrous substance. What exactly are you mining here?"

Fuerian flashed her his broadest smile, which had melted the hearts and opened the knees of many local she-elves, as well as many more of Madam Holworth's gals at his favorite brothel.

The young maven, perhaps less than a decade older than Fuerian, responded as desired. Her cheeks darkened slightly and her irises took on a glint of sparkle.

"And that is why I will succeed where those other mine-owners have failed. I take calculated risks and work harder than any others," Fuerian told her. "I also understand the rules of the game."

He withdrew a pouch of coins. It jingled slightly as he gripped it and held it out, offering it to her.

Amarthanc tilted her head. "Are you trying to bribe me?"

"No." Fuerian chuckled. "I would not think you could be bought with so little—I am merely trying to ensure a long-term business relationship and I understand how the wheels of industry turn. I assume you will expect an annual tribute?"

The maven held his gaze for a long moment. "My job is to provide an inspection and ensure that your business is on the up and up."

Fuerian grinned. "I can assure you that it is, and I fully submit to your authority. What else can I show you?" He pushed a slightly flirty tone into his voice, half wondering if he could push the she-elf into a tryst.

She strolled closer toward where the mine entrance yawned open.

Amarthanc took barely a glance inside the mouth of the mine and spotted a dozen round faces looking back at her. Dirty, tear-stained cheeks of human children. Most of them were younger than the age of maturity.

She turned back and accepted the pouch of coins. Scribbling a signature upon a form which she'd brought with her from Suíochán Naséan, she handed over the document.

"Your mine has been authorized by King Oberon and the Summer Court. I'll see that your inspection paperwork gets pushed through."

"And the other thing?" Fuerian asked.

Amarthanc gave him a sort of half smirk. "My continued discretion is assured. I'll expect a matching purse every six months."

Fuerian bowed to match the maven's gesture and smirked at how she'd effectively doubled the tribute. *That's the kind of ambition I like—and if I could bed an aes sidhe and develop an arcane ally, then all the better.* "I shall make the arrangements," he said, and then the two parted company.

Chapter Two

Naked and with her breasts exposed to the moonlight, Jaira rode her husband into the throes of ecstasy. Both human and sidhe fell into each other, sweaty and exhausted.

They collapsed backward to the bed until the cold clamminess of the wettest parts of the blankets could barely be tolerated without laughter. Remy rolled out of the bunk and to the floor. Rising, he searched the shelf for a clean sheet.

Returning with that, he tried to pull the old one off the bed, dragging his lover with it. She merely giggled, pulling it around herself and being generally difficult.

"Gross," he joked, glancing at where his wife laid. "If you want to sit in that, be my guest."

She wrinkled her nose. "It's all biology, you know... Though I have several limits, I *would* draw the line at." She tossed the sheet aside and used its corner to dab off any stray dampness with a smirk.

"Oh, really?" he teased. "I've heard rumors about you, Miss Morgansteen."

"Oh, yeah?" Her tone was playful, and she snatched the fresh blanket and wrapped it around herself instead of putting it on the bed.

Remy put his hands on his hips. "I'm sure it's just a rumor, but the local folks seem to think you're some kind of sexual deviant, shacking up with a human like a freak with an unsavory but insatiable kink."

She arched her eyebrows and looked over her husband's naked form. "I reckon that must be true. But I guess that love is love, even if it means I must submit to my desires and squeeze my pet human's bulging biceps while he thrusts into me."

Remy laughed as the female half of the newlywed couple flopped backward onto the bed. "I guess I'm not that discriminating," she said.

He bent over and caressed her cheek. "See, I hear it's the other way around. The tuatha say that you're *very* discriminating."

She placed one hand on his arm, fingers touching Remy's tricep and her thumb stroking the bicep on the opposite side. Her other arm laced a hand through his hair and laid against his rounded, human ears. Then she pulled him close enough for a kiss.

After they finally broke apart, Jaira smiled at him. "I guess I hear different things in the market square than you do. And apparently I'm not the only she-elf who's taken a shine to the idea of a human lover."

Remy scoffed slightly. "Now, *that* is amusing."

Her eyes smoldered as she looked over her husband again. "You are a famous duelist. You're the only human to ever be granted a dueling license. Remember what I told you the last night of the competition?"

"The night I tried to break off our romance, and you refused?" She grinned. "Yes."

"You told me to make them, the public, love me."

"And it appears that many of them do." She flashed him a smug look. "I just happen to be the one able to lock you down and make you mine... but I'm not selfish. I know I must share you."

Remy practically spat. "Wait... Did you just offer to have a threesome?"

She tilted her head playfully. Remy expected she might have blushed, but she did not. However, her eyes twinkled.

"I mean, I'm willing to invite in another lover if it would please you. It is not uncommon with the fey, but I don't know human customs. It happens often amongst the méith if both spouses consent—it is the marriage vow that is important—the relationship more than the physical components. But I merely meant that you are famous. Famous and important. Many people will love you in their own way, and I'm not jealous of that. Perhaps the sidhe view sex differently than the sons and daughters of Adam."

Remy swallowed the lump in his throat. "You'd be surprised. I don't think there's that much of a difference between the fey and mankind." His mind jumped back to Madadh, leader of the Fianna.

Madadh had offered him a place within the nomadic group of humans, provided he remained with them. Part of that pact allowed him breeding privileges with the women of the tribe. All the females in Madadh's caravan made it clear that they were keen for him to accept their tribal leader's offer. Their desire was strong enough that a group of them seemed like they might drag Remy into their tent before he even had the opportunity to render an answer.

Remy kissed his wife again, reminding himself how happy he'd been with his choice. His encounter with Madadh had been difficult to forget... but not just because of the promised orgies and food. Remy was intrigued by Madadh. Something in the man's amber eyes seemed both *more* than human and yet *deeply* human at the same time. He believed the tribal leader truly had his people's best interests at heart and Remy hadnot known other leaders to do that.

"Let's revisit that again in the future. At least for now, and maybe for the next couple of years, let's keep it between us." He suddenly felt very self-conscious. "Unless, uh, *you* think we need to spice things up a bit?"

She laughed. "Just be prepared for a wild wedding anniversary one of these years. The fey are known for *deeply* indulging in all the pleasures life has to offer."

Remy smiled as they embraced. He teased her, "Okay... Then let's talk about it. I'm going to need to know names. Describe these she-elves who keep making gaga eyes at me in the marketplace."

"You mean, any sidhe besides Hazimon?"

Remy blinked at her dumbly and then stammered. "I, uh... I don't think I'm her type."

Jaira practically belly laughed. Hazimon was an ancient woman; none knew her true age. With olive green skin and weathered lines crossing her face like oak rings, she was a dryad. The green elves were tuatha, and looked every bit of sidhe without quite being sidhe, the varied elven species.

"Hazimon was once a grand beauty, you know," Jaira said. "All fey males desired her, and even the females." Jaira winked. "I've heard tales that *she,* above all other female elves, was invited to the méith orgies."

"Now, I can't tell if you're joking or not," Remy said. The old crone was one of the first people he'd met upon his arrival in Cathair Dé. He paid her for needed information even after the destitute dryad offered it freely.

"From what I've heard, she is no friend to the Queen," Remy said. "Though I suspect if anyone throws those sorts of parties, Lord Oberon is chief among them... And maybe that's part of why Titania lashed out at Hazimon in a jealous rage?"

Jaira raised an eyebrow. "So, you know the story?"

"I know Hazimon's side of it. We've chatted in the past. But, uh... not enough for me to be *intimate* with."

His wife laughed again. "I can respect your wishes, husband. I am not eager to speed our sex life up faster than it should go." She slapped his thigh. "I might break you."

He blinked.

Jaira laughed. "Although, your rhythm could use a little work."

Remy shook off his fugue. "Oh, uh, good."

"You know I love you, Remy? I've loved you since before I met you."

"That's not even possible," Remy said, knitting his brows and thinking back to the strange dreams that he'd had of late. In his past, he'd had dreams that seemed somehow prophetic.

Jaira looked off, far and away. "I think I saw you in a dream before I ever passed you in that ditch outside Vail Carvanna... Maybe it was just a fantasy. But I knew the moment I saw you that you would be the one to save me—the one who was destined for me."

Before either could continue, Remy's head snapped aside, his attention focused. He put a finger to his lips to shush her.

"I think I heard something outside," he whispered. "Stay here."

Something in his tone seemed to strike a chord in his wife. Her eyes widened with fear and she paled.

"Act natural," he whispered." And then Remy went into the main room of their small cottage and snuffed the candles.

Blanketed in darkness, the human crept outside and snuck around the side of the structure. He moved stealthily, rolling the sides of his feet and hugging the stone walls of his home to keep from being seen.

Still naked, Remy was keenly aware that his light skin might shine in the moonlight—especially given the earlier sweat he'd worked up.

Finally, he spotted a darkly clad figure half hiding in the shrubbery beyond the bedroom window. Remy could not see much, but he could tell by the figure that the intruder was sidhe.

After watching the prowler for a few moments longer, the intruder stood and began a departure. With his or her back turned to the cottage, Remy sprinted forward, no longer concerned with stealth.

Among the noisy footsteps in the night, the invader glanced back over their shoulder. Eyes went wide and then they sprinted, attempting to escape.

Remy charged. Unburdened by clothing or armor, and spurred forward by his protective instincts, leapt forward and tackled the elf who grunted with a masculine sound. Together, they rolled to a stop in the heather and undergrowth of a nearby grove.

Grabbing for the villain who struggled to get away, Remy tore away a section of black cloth at the he-elf's torso. Ripped free, the fabric fell and exposed the elf's face and chest. Remy did not recognize him, but he noted a large birthmark at the sidhe's chest; it peeked upward slightly across his throat and measured roughly one hand-span.

"Who are you? Why are you here?" Remy barked. He stood and towered over the elf.

"I... I am no one. Just an elf concerned for the corruption of our kind," he said, crawling backward on his hands and rump. "Especially that of our she-elves."

"So, you're one of *them*? One of the Frith Duine?" Remy growled.

The elf continued to scoot away. He did not answer the question, but he hissed in response.

"I see no duelist's pins or ribbons. Are you carrying a weapon? Did you come here to kill me?"

"I refuse to speak to any Ddiymadferth," spat the nameless one.

Remy lunged forward and subdued the elf. He checked the intruder for any sort of object that could have been used to harm him or his wife. The sidhe carried none.

Weighing his options, Remy understood the the optics of any reports that the only human duelist killed an unarmed fey in the middle of the night. Regardless of the circumstances, the yellow rags that passed for journalism would not care. Remy shook his head. "Get out of here before I change my mind."

The elf scrambled to his hands and knees and tried to hurry away.

Remy delivered a comparatively benign kick to the prowler's ass and tagged him directly in the taint. The elf yelped and hastened his pace.

"Don't let me catch you here, again, 'No one,'" he called after. And then he returned to his home.

A few moments later, he sank into bed alongside his wife. While he'd been outside, she'd taken the opportunity to make the bed.

"What was the problem?" she asked.

"Oh, nothing," he lied, so that she could sleep well. "Just a stray animal. It's gone now."

He sat on the edge of the bed for a few long moments. "You remember that I have to accompany Kent on a business meeting tomorrow morning? I might be in Saibhir Gaoithe for a few days."

"I remember. Anya was planning to stop by and keep me company at some point."

Remy stretched his lips thin for a moment. "Perhaps instead of her coming here, you should visit her. Or maybe your parents. I would be more comfortable if you stayed for the duration someplace, anyplace, else."

Their eyes met for a moment and he knew that she knew he'd lied about potential dangers lurking in the night. She nodded her slow agreement.

Remy kissed her and then blew out the bedside candle.

The note in Fuerian's hands was crumpled, simple, and written with a thin, hasty scrawl.

Get me out of here—don't be small-minded. You need me.

Fuerian crumpled the note and threw it aside. He knew where it had come from. Gareth Morass.

Pinching the bridge of his nose, Fuerian dismissed the messenger who'd delivered it. The he-elf did not move from his apartment doorway. Extending his hand, palm up, the sidhe cleared his throat.

"You've got to be kidding me," Fuerian growled. "You took a delivery job without guarantee of payment? There's nothing but risk when you work for cash on delivery."

He closed the door on the courier, barely catching the shocked look on the young sidhe's face as the door clicked shut. Several moments later, a loud thump cracked at the door where the courier had kicked it. Fuerian snatched the handle and flung it wide, intending to thrash the young elf for his insolence, but the lad was already running away, expecting retaliation.

Fuerian threw the door closed and paced a circuit in his apartment. The place was posh, filled with all the fancy accoutrements one would expect from an upper-class elf, one of those in the méith. However, it had been more lavish in the past.

He touched his neck. Fuerian used to wear a pendant there. It was a magical item that protected him from certain kinds of magic; it was also the symbol of power for House Vastra and had been engraved with the family crest.

When the Vastra family's wealth had begun to dwindle, so had Fuerian's stipend. He'd sold off a few pieces and began living a slightly more modest lifestyle. Moving back to the large family estate remained an option for him, but not one he was willing to entertain. Especially not after losing face to his cousin, Juriahl, who had engineered a way to steal his rightful place as head of the family prior to Margrave abdicating the leadership position.

Margrave had originally given Fuerian the pendant. It was an amulet that signified he was next in the line of succession. It also provided protection from magic influence.

Fuerian's lip curled when he thought of the day he'd had to hand the symbolic item over to his rival. Juriahl now wore the pendant as the sign of the patron's favor.

Juriahl and his young wife, Loitariel, had moved on site as they prepared to take over control of the family from Margrave once the patron stepped down. Margrave had made his plans known. As soon as Loitariel gave birth to a male heir, the elder Vastra planned to abstain from the Kings Cup, which meant that an elf of his age would slip away in his sleep some night without mystic means to keep him alive.

All méith were entitled to attend an annual feast with Lord Oberon. The Saol Nua celebration was what kept the elite elves long-lived. It was also why membership in the highest caste was so limited: there was only so much of the ambrosia to go around.

Legend had it that Oberon and his brother Wulflock, once the Lord of the Winter Court, each owned a magical artifact which produced the ambrosia: a food Oberon distributed once each year at the feast and in portions equal to his favor. The heads of the méith families then distributed the ambrosia amongst themselves. The stuff was old magic, food of the gods, and it was what kept any sidhe young.

There were many other myths about the stuff, including that King Wulflock's source of ambrosia had gone missing ages ago, or that the end of the world would begin if a dragon ate ambrosia. But Fuerian was still young and did not care so much about historical stuff, although he knew ambrosia was no clever fiction. He had eaten it before in small measure, and he knew it worked; Fuerian was barely thirty, and Oberon looked scarcely a decade older, despite being six times older than the elderly Margrave Vastra.

As interesting as ambrosia was, Fuerian had more peculiar consumables on his mind as he paced the length of the floor. He paused and stared at the crumpled note. Gareth had always been his patsy, and Fuerian knew the elf would do anything for him, including take a prison sentence. He'd proven that already.

The Morass family had lost favor with the Summer Court and been de-elevated from méith. They remained among the saibhir, the upper class part of seelie society, but only the méith got a portion of ambrosia from Coire Ansic, the legendary artifact. Even though falling from Oberon's favor did not result in execution, losing access to the ambrosia guaranteed *eventual* death.

Fuerian was no fool. He understood that Gareth saw his connection to the Vastra family as a way to eventually restore the Morass family's status.

Fuerian stroked his chin. Saibhir still lived well, and he ruminated on Nhywyllwch, his business partner. Nhywyllwch was saibhir, yet he seemed to have no intentions of ever increasing his status.

"What was it he had said when we met?" Fuerian wondered aloud. "That he was after power. *True* power."

The elf shrugged. "What good is power if it cannot last—or if its *owner* cannot last, that is?"

Fuerian had strong-armed his way into Nhywyllwch's enterprise because he knew the he-elf's true identity, and revealing *that* secret would certainly destroy him and end the elf's bid for power. Nhywyllwch worked with a figure that Fuerian could only assume was a maven. *A black maven*. Hymdreiddiech he had been called.

Nhywyllwch's Stór Rúnda was more than a business. They supplied the common people with akasha, a thin fluid with a magic charge. Commoners no longer needed to hire aes sidhe or any tuatha with arcane abilities—not when they could purchase mechanical contraptions powered by the akasha.

The stuff had been around for ages, tightly controlled by the Radiant Tower, by Suíochán Naséan and its council of mavens. Somewhere along the way, the secret to its production had escaped. And it was a horrific, terrible secret.

Nhywyllwch had built a business around distributing it and been wise enough to retain a fair amount of anonymity. Fuerian's interest was in dream hallow, an apothik byproduct of creating the akasha. Dream hallow was a drug, something addicts strung out in the dregs of every city from here to the Faewylds used to escape their troubles... until it eventually killed them. Fuerian and Gareth had taken over the trade of these apothiks; Nhywyllwch had simply given it to them.

Fuerian bit his lower lip. Nothing ever came free, and it seemed too large a piece of the pie simply for keeping silent. By agreeing to supply the dangerous reagent Hymdreiddiech needed to produce akasha and dream hollow, the savvy business-elf had also negotiated a sliver of the akasha trade and the first of the dividends were slated to arrive in his accounts soon and reverse his financial woes. The amount was significant.

Significant enough that, someday, that elf is going to call in a favor.

He glanced again at the wad of paper from the incarcerated Gareth. It seemed to call to Fuerian, demanding satisfaction. Fuerian snatched it up and argued with the niggling of his conscience.

The elf understood Nhywyllwch's plans, although he didn't know the sidhe's specific endgame. Fuerian understood the big picture, however. Apothiks were small thinking. Only addicts needed the dream hallow—but the whole of the unseelie could be made reliant on akasha, and *that* was the kind of power that even Oberon would have to yield to, if the game was played rightly.

Fuerian squeezed the paper in his fist and sighed. The apothik business was risky, and also illegal. "I need Gareth Morass," he grumbled, knowing he could call in a favor to get him released.

Prior to his arrest, Gareth ran the crews that sold, supplied, and moved the product to the buyers. He'd been as good at it as any could be, and if the venture was going to continue growing, the dangers associated with it would likewise increase and Fuerian need to insulate himself from those risks so he could advance himself within the careful game he played with Nhywyllwch and Hymdreiddiech.

There were also family matters. If he planned to retake his rightful place in the Vastran family, Fuerian needed a loyal elf willing to assume those risks and shield him from prying eyes so Fuerian could focus on whatever moves became most important.

Fuerian touched the empty nape of his neck again and scowled. He repeated, "I need Gareth."

Pausing, Fuerian thought for a moment. "Actually, I should leave him in there for another week at least. He's probably made some excellent underworld contacts while incarcerated. Those contacts could come in handy. Perhaps I should write to him and have him ensure that he develops such a network before I have him freed."

He uncrumpled the note. Smoothing it, he set it down upon his desk, and began making plans.

Hymdreiddiech followed the Spider Queen through the long tunnels of her inner sanctum at Arctig Maen, the fortress in the heart of Hulda Thorne, the Winter capital. He barely glanced aside. He'd been here so many times before, grown up here, skulking in the shadows. As a youth, he enhanced what he knew as a cast-off of the aes sidhe, hardened by the cold until he found... the *power*.

Rhagathena's pointed legs clacked upon the frosty stone of her corridors. They had moved ever downward, descending below the bedrock. The Winter Queen chittered as she went, prattling to herself, mostly complimenting her own forward thinking and schemes.

The black maven kept silent, walking and observing.

She was Queen of the Rime Throne, and yet, Rhagathena was not *his* queen, though he would never tell her that. To do so would guarantee a quick death, and Hymdreiddiech had so much to do before he succumbed to the grave.

"Do you like it?" she asked, splaying her arms on either side as they entered the chamber at the lowest level of her castle. "I built it just for him."

He raised a brow. This room was new, or at least its renovations were.

Hymdreiddiech scanned the Winter Queen. Her body was that of a giant spider, but where an arachnid's head would be, the hips of the gorgeous, nude she-elf turned upward much like a centaur's would. Breasts exposed and eyes deep as drowning pools, she was somehow both alluringly beautiful and horrifically terrifying. Rhagathena's sharp teeth reminded him that she was a deadly thing, as most females were.

She was not just the ruler of the Rime Throne and all the unseelie. The Lady of Arctig Maen was the Anansi, clan leader of the N'arache, the spider folk of the Spinefrost Ridge at the furthest east border of the realm. She weaved wicked webs so thick they might even catch the black maven if he was not careful. Hymdreiddiech paid no attention to the desiccant corpse lying in the corner of the room. It belonged to her most recent meal, no doubt.

Her majordomo, Chokorum, stood in the room and at the ready. Hymdreiddiech had no idea how long he'd been waiting for them, but he knew better than to pay the he-elf much heed. Chokorum was deadly in his own right, but the maven refused to give the majordomo recognition of that fact. His refusal to acknowledge the sidhe kept Chokorum in the shadows... And that was where Hymdreiddiech could best keep an eye on him.

"Isn't it marvelous?" Rhagathena asked.

Hymdreiddiech scanned the rows of tables containing alchemical reagents, spell craft artifacts and implements, and embroidery thread. One large workbench contained the collected body parts of an ancient cadaver that, if assembled, would have likely towered nine feet tall at the least.

He raised an eyebrow at the corptic parts and then nodded at the wall to his right. A curved, twelve-foot-tall archway, made of white stone opened there; shackles dangled, affixed at the top and bottom. Manacles made of brass, and each one inset with a large emerald, lay at the ready and nearest either side sat buckets of pure, white salt.

"Marvelous? It looks distrustful to me. Your allies in the outer dark would not appreciate this."

Rhagathena quirked a wicked smile. "And they shall never hear of it. I remind you, black maven, that you are unseelie. Besides," she deflected, "I am merely ensuring I take every precaution for the future."

Hymdreiddiech nodded, but slowly. He'd been intentionally biding his time with the queen, managing every stage of a larger stratagem that had unfolded over decades. He knew Rhagathena... had watched her throughout the years. If he knew her for any trait, it was her impatience... A dangerous trait when coupled with arrogance. Hymdreiddiech's lips stretched taught. *She has plenty of both.*

"What do we need next in order to move forward with this stage of the plan? I would very much like to see our patron revived before my next... ceremony," Rhagathena stated.

The black maven watched her from the corner of his eye. He knew what she meant. She intended to marry again... The last wedding of the Winter tuatha had not gone well. The marriage feast had ended in bloody carnage, the likes of which had never been seen in the royal courts before—and which had been instigated by a trusted ally turned traitor.

No doubt, the Queenslayer had tried to add a second monarchess's head to his total that day.

Ever since, Rhagathena had strengthened alliances throughout Winter, those that brought her the political and military might to help Rhagathena achieve her primary goal: defeating Oberon and throwing down the Summer Court. *Never mind that there are wolves at the gates and pressing in on every side.*

Hymdreiddiech was more interested in what some of those wolves could provide, anyway. With rumors of fomori building a southerly army, and other forces gaining strength, there were also literal wolves, though the fáelad did not concern him. He'd already set their factions against each other. Hymdreiddiech merely smiled at Rhagathena, revealing nothing to the queen, and not answering her question, which had seemed rhetorical to him, anyway.

"What news about my thieves? If I'm to be denied my measure from the Dagda's Pot over the years, then it is only fair I deny it to Oberon." She scowled, still looking somehow seductive as she did so, despite her spider-body and widespread rumors that she devoured any mates she took.

Hymdreiddiech's gaze pinched. "You cannot locate them with all the magic at your disposal?"

Rhagathena frowned. "I cannot."

"That is not a surprise. One of them is a Boggart who is both skilled and… *creative* when it comes to veils. Be happy that he is so talented." Hymdreiddiech knew the boggart was a spy Winter had placed among the wildfey. "Either he will convince his fellow thieves to deliver the goods to your hand at the promise of riches, or the Wild Queen will possess *both* of the Dagda's mystic pots. Regardless, you'll never see them until they arrive," Hymdreiddiech assured her.

"But they acquired the items days ago." Her voice rang with an impatient tone indicative of all the spoiled brats Hymdreiddiech had known.

"It will take them many weeks even to draw near the Selvages," Hymdreiddiech stated flatly. "You cannot rush magic beneath the veil. As long as they move slowly, nobody will be able to find them. If they move beyond the selvages, you will know they've played into your hand. If not—" He shrugged. The Selvages were technically part of the Faewyld lands.

Rhagathena pouted.

"You can have either victory, or you can have speed that ends with disappointment. You cannot have a fast victory—not given all the factors."

The queen glowered at him, leveling a gaze that would've withered most other creatures. Hymdreiddiech shrugged at it. He was right, and there were things about her plan—her *immediate* plans—that concerned him more. "You brought me down here to show me the vestiges of the demonsbreak and the fallen orcish leader?"

"No." Rhagathena's voice rumbled like smooth stones dragged through a babbling rapid. "This merely sets the stage for what I've entertained myself with these last many months."

Hymdreiddiech cocked an eyebrow. "And that is?"

The queen said, "My spies have assured me that *he* has resurfaced. The betrayer's location is known, and his defeat aligns with my other plans. Acquiring him takes priority for now... it is a grand game, a *test* for the next phase of my campaign."

"Your plan," Hymdreiddiech repeated it more plainly, "what is it?"

"Revenge upon the queen."

"You are aware that I am with child?" Loitariel asked her superior.

"So I was told by our agents," said Mithrilchon, the head Maven of the red circle, an order Loitariel belonged to as well.

The aged elf was her superior by both rank and age, being several hundred years older and, until recently, she had been one of two apprentices working directly under him. He looked down his nose at her, causing her to wilt inside. She managed to keep her face neutral and her posture resolute. Loitariel was now the lady of a powerful méith house and part of Seelie nobility, after all.

"Then I assume this is a social call?" she suggested.

The head maven shook his head imperceptibly while the servants of House Vastra scuttled about as they placed settings for them to take tea; Loitariel's guest had come unannounced. With Margrave's advanced years and reclusive tendencies, the old sidhe seldom entertained, and Loitariel wondered if the footmen and butlers needed a tea just to feel useful, more than anything else.

Loitariel cocked her head and gazed at her superior. Nobody in her new circle of influence knew that Loitariel was secretly a ranking maven, and that she had a long history with Mithrilchon; not even her husband was aware of her abilities. Juriahl was admittedly little more than a pawn in a larger game of houses and fey politics. Loitariel cared for him in the prerequisite manner—even if her emotions concerning the marriage were much that same as a farmer caring for a prized heifer. Juriahl was necessary to the industry, just so long as there remained a market for the milk.

The expression Loitariel flashed Mithrilchon communicated more than simple words could. It wasn't delivered by anything as fancy as mystic telepathy—it was a byproduct of proximity. The two had worked together for decades and had learned to read each other. "We shall take tea in the library," she informed the butler.

The aged sidhe butler stifled a gasp. Normally, social teas were taken in the drawing room, and Loitariel had learned exactly how stodgy Margrave's staff had been.

"It is a more private room," she explained to the servants. "And I'm certain that anything a maven wishes to impart will be topics needing the utmost discretion."

The butler did not quite blanch, but Loitariel knew he'd taken her point. She'd come, seemingly from nowhere, and married into a méith family, and gained nobility from nothing more than mist and words. Though Juriahl was not known for his stark intellect, nor his resilience in the face of temptresses, that she'd managed to lock him into a marriage mystified all those connected to the family.

Loitariel rubbed her growing belly where the Vastran future grew. She was certain the servants gossiped about her, but now that she carried the family heir in her womb, nothing else mattered.

After a few moments of fussing by the house staff, Loitariel led Mithrilchon into a more private part of the manor. She did not need to explain to her guest that this room was regularly swept for any means of mystic intrusion. Surveillance magic was a specialty of hers, an arcana similar to the spell the mavens had once placed upon Thoranmir Shelton to eavesdrop over great distances.

The Vastran staff performed their duty, served tea and small cakes with fruit, and then departed at Loitariel's insistence. She caught a surreptitious glance over one shoulder as the last of them looked back. *They'll gossip about this, indeed.*

Once it seemed certain any opportunity to eavesdrop was past, Mithrilchon asked, "So, you are doing well with your assignment?"

"You can report to the Radiant Tower that all is well in House Vastra. Margrave plans to abdicate as soon as the birth of an heir is certified. None suspect Suíochán Naséan has infiltrated a family and Court politics."

Mithrilchon nodded. "Good. We must keep it that way. For all our history, Lord Oberon has kept the mavens and the méith separate for reasons of his own. For us to intertwine these two demonstrates exactly how great our need has become."

Loitariel raised an eyebrow. "There is yet more to the intrigue? I thought we ended the threat of cataclysm when we upset the seer's visions of last year's duel?"

The older maven scowled as he shook his head. "Calithilon the White is uncertain if these new fears of apocalyptic doom are tied to the future-teller's last vision or if this is an entirely new one."

Loitariel pinched her gaze as she parsed his words. The gift of foresight was a tricky one. It was one of the magical gifts, but it functioned more like a curse; visions and potential outcomes came upon its host, but not all of them were true, and it took much skill to navigate which of the threads were absolutes as trails of prescience unraveled and rewound any given time when decisions, either actualized or imagined by the actors, made them. Knowledge seemed such a benign thing, yet in powerful hands it was so potentially damaging that Oberon had ordered the mavens to kill anyone with that ability millennia ago. Hunting the vatical was the original purpose of the Solais Cloaks, a seldom needed duty in modern age, but one the mavens could call on them to perform at any time.

Only the high-ranking mavens knew it, but Calithilon had secretly kept one alive and in the basement of the Radiant Tower. As the highest ranks of their number, only Calithilon had access to the seer, and he claimed to only use her insight to prevent prophetic, world-ending events that the mavens called Cataclysms, and to protect the crown and its interests. He hadn't much statements in the high tongue, however, and Loitariel did not trust the master of the Tower as much as she did Mithrilchon. Technically, their methodology was treasonous as seers' gifts were considered chronurgy, magic that altered time.

Recognizing that her mentor had only spoken of business Loitariel was already aware of, she thought over the many differing concerns the mavens managed and wondered where they overlapped, caused things that needed addressing. *The seer's visions of cataclysm. Oberon's fascination with akasha and desire to install systems in the capitol. The rise of rogue aes sidhe...* Certainly one of them was responsible for stealing secrets and creating an akasha industry that rivaled the maven's long-standing monopoly on it. And of course, there was the ever-present conflict between Summer and Winter.

"In my current position, how may I help my brothers and sisters in the Tower?" she asked.

Mithrilchon remained silent for a moment, and then Loitariel nearly balked as she realized his true aims for today's meeting. Loitariel knew all his tells and the way the creases near his eyes darkened when she'd said *brothers and sisters* gave him away.

The old maven cleared his throat and squeezed his hands before he began. "That is exactly the thing... You are still magic-user, Loitariel, and still a valuable asset and member of our fold."

"You are kicking me out of the Order? Am I no longer a maven? Are rendering me ina aonar?" When a duelist was rendered houseless, it meant he had no backing from any of his guild alliances; the ina aonar operated as a ronin amongst or against his or her peers. When it happened to a maven, it meant they were cut off from a tight brotherhood of arcanists and lost their access to news, the ability to continue studies and advanced spell craft, gain consultation and insight from their wisest members, or borrow powerful artifacts from their libraries.

Mithrilchon remained thin lipped. "No... But yes." He held up his hands to forestall any weeping before she could begin. "This was always the assignment. You knew that going in, even if it was never stated directly."

Loitariel remained stiff, tense, but she did not break. She did not abandon her composure or jump to wild conclusions. She and Mithrilchon had known each other for many years and, although she felt suddenly betrayed, he had not spoken falsely.

"When you married into the Vastra house, you joined a *new* family. I forestalled certain pieces of paperwork for as long as I could, which registers you as being wed into a méith house, but with Saol Nua approaching, your background will be scrutinized by Oberon's house staff." He frowned, but warmly. "Truly, you were the only one we could insert in this way given your... background."

Measuredly, Loitariel nodded. She'd been an orphan since childhood, and there were very few paper trails regarding her in the records guilds; the Tower kept separate records on any in their care and children demonstrating arcane talent were often left to the care of Suíochán Naséan's wardens until they were advanced enough to enter a maginarius for training.

She frowned with the twinge of regret. Loitariel had very little by way of family. Besides an uncle who'd disappeared ages ago, she only had her fellow mavens.

"You must pass examination at the festival. Only then can we be certain the throne will not discover who... what you are."

At Saol Nua, Oberon would distribute the ambrosia to the house lords at Saol Nua. The food of the eternal gods was highly regulated and only given to the most elite, those who had secured Oberon's favor. The Tower received a portion differently, and it was distributed by the White Maven.

Before she could speak, Mithrilchon placed a hand on her knee. "As far as I am concerned, you are still one of us. You are our insider, even if we had to mark you as an outcast on our official roster."

"So, I am not truly ina aonar?" She arched an eyebrow.

Mithrilchon opened his mouth to speak, but no sound came out. He shut it.

"I *am*, then."

"You are more than house-less, Loitariel. You are perhaps the single most important maven outside the eight High Mavens," Mithrilchon explained.

"You must not call me that, however. Maven?" Loitariel stated.

Mithrilchon set his jaw and then shook his head. "I know the truth, and at least two others. You are truly a maven."

Loitariel guessed at them. Calithilon would know, and probably Glirien the Blue; her order controlled the Agents of Gray, the vast spy network that supported Suíochán Naseán.

He practically confirmed her suspicions. "Also, Glirien asked that I tell you to expect a visitor in the future. Apparently, some

Agent of Gray intends to meet you. I have no additional knowledge of what that means."

She tilted her head. "Then the tower still has need of me—great need if you're working so hard to keep me in the fold. And now that I am in my position, you require my favor?" A smile played at the edge of her lips as she mentally stitched all the information together. Loitariel realized that the Tower would not burn its bridges with her because it *could* not. They needed her for inside information that not even their spies could access. Suíochán Naséan needed a sidhe on the inside, and whatever knowledge they lacked was probably connected to something Calithilon had learned from the seer.

"I want to know about this coming cataclysm," she demanded as the price for her compliance.

It came time for Mithrilchon's turn to grin. "Your new role as a lady of a powerful house suits you. You know I can't tell you that."

Loitariel nodded. "You need my help and cooperation. I want information so I can be most useful."

Mithrilchon groaned with a slight sigh and looked about the room. "I can tell you one thing. Regardless if this is a new vision or some new tangent related to the last, the coming cataclysm remains tied to a dragon."

She screwed up her face. "But there are no dragons in Arcadeax."

Her former mentor and superior pursed his lips and asked in a low voice, "Aren't there, though?"

Chapter Three

"Why the sullen face?" Xander Kent asked Remy. "It will be a long ride to Saibhir Gaoithe if you're acting so glum."

Remy merely grunted and stiffened his jaw. Saibhir Gaoithe was nearly a day's ride northwest of Cathair Dé, and they'd already made a good part of the trek.

Kent raised his eyebrows and did not press the point except to mention that if he'd have known Remy would be shit for conversation, he might have hired a minstrel to accompany them. "I could have had him make up a limerick or two about my grumpy duelist."

The comment drew a snort from Remy. It was a long ride, after all, too long to hold all his worries inside of him. Remy sighed and admitted to his employer, "I had an intruder last night. I'm sure he was part of the Frith Duine."

Kent had little to say. His sour look matched the one Remy had worn previously. "You are certain?"

"More or less. Pointy eared bastard who called me ddiymadferth, had a big birthmark on his chest, up to here." He motioned at his neck. "He accused me of corrupting female sidhe."

"Wait a moment? You say he had a big birthmark on his *chest*?" Kent asked. "Was he naked or something?"

"No. I mean, *I was*, but that's beside the point. I ripped his shirt off after catching him outside my window when I—"

"Hold up," Kent insisted, verging on laughter and grinning like a maniac. "*You* were naked... and you ripped some guy's clothes off?"

"Yeah, well... I was just trying to—"

"And he was afraid of you 'corrupting she-elves?" Kent looked like he might cry, he was having such a good time with his reasoning.

Remy grew red in the face.

"Are you sure he wasn't just a bugger? You know, I've heard a lot of folk with fetishized desire to catch a glimpse of the human duelist's girth, and, uh, prowess... He probably just wants that human cock as much as his wife does and can't bring himself to admit it!" Kent laughed again, and Remy was certain that every bit of what he said was true, except for the previous night's invader being only a simple voyeuristic pervert.

After a moment of silence in which Remy displayed his most dour expression, Kent's laughter sobered, and he finally quieted.

"I fear that my home is not safe, especially if the Frith Duine have learned where it is," Remy told Kent.

"You can always move into the other wing of the house that I've rented in the city," Kent told him. "You know the one. Anya lives in the east wing as part of her compensation. She's on retainer as my primary aithermancer, so there's no substantial cost to me since the other side of the duplex sits empty, anyway. There's more than enough space on the other side, and I know you get on with Anya."

Remy exhaled through his nose. Anya was like the sister Remy never had. At least, he didn't know if he had any family, given that his mind had been wiped all those decades ago in the faewylds.

She had grown especially close with him ever since her brother was murdered by Fuerian Vastra in the duels. About that same time, somebody had burned down her apartment building, leaving the aithermancer homeless in the interim and Kent's offer of employment had come with a litany of perks, such as lodging.

Remy entertained the idea for a long moment. Regardless of its benefits, something about losing any sliver of control over his life because of Frith Duine interference chafed him mightily.

Kent snapped his fingers a few times, gaining his duelist's attention, and Remy realized he'd drifted off in thought for several long minutes, weighing the pros and cons of such a move. "There you are. I thought maybe you'd fallen asleep. Is such a thing of interest to you? I can work it into your salary if you'd like, and the rent would be cheap. Because I keep Anya on retainer, paying for her home whether or not I need her, you'd actually be saving me money."

Remy nodded measurably, but only agreed to keep thinking on the matter. He had a few options, but he wasn't quite ready to give up his total independence until he was certain there was any actual danger.

"I've no intention of offering it to anyone else," Kent told him. "If you need it, just let me know."

"Thank you," Remy said, and they rode a little further in relative silence.

A year ago, Remy'd had a dream. His mind rushed back to his childhood and the woman who'd helped raise him in the unseelie, a she-elf with a secret gift that only a few knew about. Genesta helped him cope with horrific dreams, visions about when he'd been even younger... when he was training to become the fearsome Aderyn Corff: the Corpse Bird, slayer of fey queens, and so many other titles. It wasn't until recently that he'd had any kind of prophetic dreams like the ones he'd had in his youth.

Genesta had the gift of future sight—being a seer had led to her enslavement to the same orc warlord who had been Remy's master, and she'd been a kind of surrogate mother to him. *No... not any kind of mother, but a friend and mentor... My mother's name was Saorise.*

His mind reeled momentarily back to the snippet of information he learned during those fateful duels when he lost his best friend, but gained his wife. The only thing he knew about his life prior to arriving in Arcadeax was the name of his mother. He had a faded image of her that now only existed as a forgotten dream.

But he remembered the vision he'd had about Jaira. She'd birthed children by Remy and then the young family had been attacked by the Frith Duine who had killed them all.

More than anything, Remy yearned to meet those future children, but nothing scared him as much as losing his loved ones—even if they didn't yet exist. He locked onto the dream and let it motivate him to protect his family, despite wondering deep down if that family might ever arrive. Many parts of it had not yet occurred.

Perhaps it's all some kind of delusion—my deepest fears manifesting as a dream? Maybe it's a matter of timing? Once our family has begun, we could move to a safer place?

Kent cleared his throat, breaking Remy from his reverie and trying again to coax some conversation out of his traveling companion.

Remy shook himself back to attention and then met his employer's gaze. "Thank you. I shall... take your offer into consideration."

Hymdreiddiech followed Chokorum up the narrow staircase that led outside and to the courtyard gardens of Arctig Maen. The queen's majordomo motion for him to stay put at the rear and then Chokorum pushed his way through the gathered assembly and toward the front dais where a smaller, secondary throne had been erected in lieu of moving the Rime Throne. Moving it would've proved too great an endeavor.

Those assembled included a great mix of tuatha. While those in the Summer Court tended to be overwhelmingly sidhe, among the nobles of Winter those numbers reduced to roughly forty percent, though the average changed all the time as Rhagathena declared new edicts often based on the race of folks who had wronged her in some way or another, often villainizing entire species of folk for the transgressions of an individual.

The Black Maven noticed a large number of orcs present. Though the clans of the Demonsbreak had been largely eviscerated in Aderyn Corff's flight from the capitol many of their clan mates remained alive and they'd shored up at their numbers by drawing down kin from across the land, including nomadic tribes from the faewylds and from mountain dwellers in the Spinefrost.

Hymdreiddiech sniffed the air. It still smelled like sulfur at the fringes of his senses and he turned his eyes to a nearby pillar. Near the base, he spotted old carbon scoring and spat on it, then scuffed at the blackness with his foot.

Toward the front, some unnamed herald trumped a horn, silencing those gathered as a crier declared the titles of the n'arache and current queen of all unseelie. The formalities progressed at a predictable pace and pattern, and Hymdreiddiech mentally checked out. He had little energy for pomp and circumstance. His real interest in politics was regarding the dangers and intrigue of it, and mainly the sort that dropped bodies.

Finally, the politicians got to the heart of the ceremony. Rhagathena declared, "Today I elevate Rharzal Kathwesion, kin of the demonsbreak, to the highest warrior status of my Court."

Two orcs approached the throne where Rhagathena had been seated. One was easily recognizable by the distinct marking on his face. Hymdreiddiech had worked with Syrmerware Kathwesion before.

Syrmerware paused at the base of the dais, but his brother took two steps up to stand upon the first tier. Rharzal moved no further but knelt before the queen, three steps higher.

She bid him rise and offered him a sword emblazoned with the markings due to the status of a general in her army. The crowd murmured, and she raised the elven arms of her forward torso to silence it again.

"Furthermore," Rhagathena declared, "I have offered Rharzal a task that, if completed, will ensure my hand to him in marriage."

That quieted them. The crowd fell silent at the announcement.

Rharzal spoke both loud and clear as he turned to face the crowd. "The task I have been given, which assures my ascension to the throne, is to capture or kill Aderyn Corff, the Betrayer. The Queenslayer."

The moment of silence broke into raucous applause and cheering. Rharzal's face widened into a feral smile. Hymdreiddiech stared at the orc. To him, Rharzal looked like, well, any other orc. But Rharzal apparently had enough talents for fighting to climb the ranks once the vacuum opened at the top—courtesy of the Betrayer. Although the maven had never seen him in action, he knew orcs did not suffer ineffective warriors.

Chokorum had slipped away at some point during the announcements and reappeared near Hymdreiddiech's side. He whispered to the maven, "Ensure that these orcs get every opportunity to succeed. Rhagathena is also sending one of the twins so she can keep an eye on all things."

Hymdreiddiech glared at the majordomo, and did not attempt to hide his disdain. "I will not," he hissed. He took additional offense at the suggestion that one of her twin aes sidhe, a fey which would have a psychic link with their double, was required.

Raising his brow, the servant asked, "Are you a defector?"

Hymdreiddiech bared his teeth. "We are each bound by our oaths, *servant*. Do not forget that. The queen has entered a pact with me and with another party. I will not be pressured into further bargains without additional compensation."

"Syrmerware, Rharzal, and a few others have a mission which inserts them into the southern lands of the Seelie. The orcs lead a small team operating under legitimate interests and with the approval of Titania's border agents. The Winter Queen has a plan that works best with an aes sidhe present. The Salvatore has received a request for more of our lightstarved on the seelie side of the chasm. This plan actually aligns with your *other* plans, and so—"

"I am not your slave, Chokorum—not yours and not Rhagathena's. Hire your own spellcaster. I have other obligations and obey a time-line of my own," Hymdreiddiech growled.

The majordomo merely stared at him. "I said that—"

"I fucking heard you." Hymdreiddiech snarled. His gaze hardened, but he would not let some entitled unseelie prig push his boundaries. *She is not the one who I serve—she is just another pawn who sits on a fancy chair.* He softened his tone, but only slightly.

"If our paths cross in such a way that I might easily aid them, then I shall. But I am required... elsewhere in the near future."

Chokorum's face pinched with displeasure, but he nodded. "That willingness is all we ask."

Hymdreiddiech watched the sidhe lackey slither away and return to the queen's side. Deep down, Hymdreiddiech knew he'd been lying. *I have convenient alliances for now. But both the courts of Winter and Summer can burn for all I care, and I can scarcely wait to be done with them... Return to us soon, Lord Azrokar.*

Although Mithrilchon was not yet returned from official business, the wizarding circle of Suíochán Naséan met despite the red maven's absence. The remaining six leaders of their factions stood at their places, with Calithilon at the center. None of the High Mavens' apprentices were present.

Calithilon fixed them each with a serious look. The ranking mavens understood from it that whatever had caused his urgent summons was both dire and also damning enough that they couldn't risk the ears of their under-mavens.

Adlegrion, the Indigo, furrowed his brow. "Are you sure this business cannot wait for Mithrilchon?"

The White Maven shook his head subtly. Mithrilchon the Red was the highest ranking of all other members of the High Council.

Although mavens were not prohibited from owning property or building their own lives outside of the Radiant Tower, the nature of their guild was highly relational. The Tower was not specifically designated as a commune, but it did host a barracks for under-mavens and apartments for the ranking members. Members of their order ate together, studied at their on-site library, trained with each other, and many of them used the close proximity to sneak away and use the back rooms and alleys of the cloister to breed the next generation of aes sidhe, usually with none... or *few*... prying eyes.

"It cannot wait, and you shall see why in moments," Calithilon explained. Resting on the ground before the white maven was an engraved hourglass. Grains of sand trickled through, dropping from the top bulb and mounding up below. The amount of time it was measured to keep had been keyed to Calithilon's specific magical talent—a talent only held only by other aes sidhe who had read *The Veil of Ash* and other extremely rare texts that survived the great purge of forbidden texts. However, all Calithilon's peers were aware he possessed a kind of mystic hindsight because of his chronomancy.

Tinthel the Orange crossed her arms over her breasts. "All right, then, anything requiring a vote will still qualify for a quorum. Out with it, Calithilon."

Calithilon glanced back at his hourglass and estimated how much time he had to fill before using his chronomantic spell. "I will do more than tell you. However, first we ought to discuss an additional problem." He paused momentarily and swallowed the dryness in his throat. He gave a name to the concern. "The Shadow Maven."

The other members of his cabal returned his gaze with a serious expression. All except for Amarthanc, who remained relatively new to her post; she'd only taken her seat on the council a couple years ago. For her, most of the high-level information was new.

"We've known of the existence of a dark sorcerer known as the Black Maven, or the Shadow Maven, for some time now." Calithilon laid out the topic's context. "For nearly a decade, we have noted his or her movements, watched the fallout from their schemes. Mostly, it has been like observing the aftermath of a storm rather than witnessing the storm itself. Regardless, it seems likely that this spellcaster is both aes sidhe and an unseelie agent."

Amarthanc tilted her head. "Is this somehow related to the Vastran mine you sent me to visit?"

Calithilon nodded. "Did you ascertain anything during your inspection?"

The maven bowed her head and then gave her findings. "Fuerian Vastra's mine is not collecting iron. He was not keen to give guided, personal inspection, which seems perfectly reasonable considering the toxicity of the place."

"What is he mining then, if not ferrous poison?"

"I noted a redcap and a motley collection of human slaves, including children," Amarthanc noted.

Calithilon said, "Then it is likely as suspected, and Mithrilchon was wise to insert one of our own into the Vastra family where she can monitor things."

The next-most unseasoned of them quirked an eyebrow. "And this is connected somehow to the Shadow Maven?"

Gorvon the Yellow turned to Amarthanc. "The Violet mavens do not deal with the akasha trade, but it is useful for you to know its inner workings." Both he and Amarthanc turned their eyes to Calithilon.

The White Maven bobbed his head and then explained. "The akasha that powers most magitech is owned by Suíochán Naséan. We alone know it secrets and how it is created." He paused to grimace. "At least... we were."

Amarthanc nodded. She clearly followed along.

"The stuff is created by a very... uncomfortable and unconventional means. We began creating the akasha generations ago in small-scale and had used it to ease the life of the residents of Faery Cairn once we had perfected the process here at the Tower. From there we began granting access to our ready supply to the citizenry nearest our capital. It endeared many to Oberon and his aes sidhe."

He silently worked his jaw fora moment. Oberon was not a maven, but he *was* a powerful aes sidhe... and even he had no idea how the stuff was made.

"Many cities far away from us now have akashic drip networks," Amarthanc said.

Calithilon set his face into a grimace. "Most of those are ventures planned by the Radiant Tower, with half the revenue going to the crown. But not *all of them*."

The way Calithilon said the last line made Amarthanc knit her brows. She ventured a guess. "So, the secret to creating akasha has not remained as hidden as hoped?"

"Precisely. And one of the reagents necessary for its manufacture is a fungus that grows only upon iron: foil milferra. Not only does the milferra grow in Fuerian's mine, but he has been working with a person who started his own akashic center to rival our monopoly. Currently, they have contracts supplying akasha to seven cities. We've been keeping an eye on the company, but have yet to learn where they are actually making this stuff. Anyone capable of avoiding the eyes of a maven, or our Agents of Gray, indicates some level of mystic involvement."

"You suspect this Shadow Maven is involved somehow?"

Calithilon nodded slowly and then glanced back at his timepiece. "I do. It is largely why I authorized Mithrilchon's plan to insert one of his past apprentices into a prominent house of a problematic family."

None spoke a word at the White Maven's admission of the Order's casual treason. Every High Maven understood that tiny chronurgic spells were allowed with discretion, provided they looked *backward in time*, seers looked *forward*, however, but their ability brought only knowledge, which is where Mavens drew the line on legality, even if the throne considered the ability to act on that knowledge was something too dangerous to remain at large.

"However, for now we can do nothing but watch and wait, hoping that we soon learn the source of this rival akasha source. We must assume that Fuerian's interests are intertwined with this dark maven and hope we can track one of his deliveries of foil milferra back to our enemy," Calithilon concluded. "Once we have this shadow maven, we can learn the source of his or her power—a power that is not of Arcadeax."

He drifted off momentarily, mumbling several thoughts aloud. "It has the markings of infernal influences, even if the black gateway to Hell remains shut against its power. This Black agent somehow uses power not possible to channel."

Calithilon shook his head to clear his mind. His eyes flitted briefly to the timer. "Which brings us to the topic of the great Cataclysm. I must show you all my reason for assembling you today. Follow."

The White Maven did not need to issue more than a one word command and his tribe obeyed. Calithilon retrieved his hourglass and headed for the stairs.

The Maven Council descended into the bowels of the Radiant Tower. Down they went, stomping their footsteps upon ever dampening walls hewn from stone. The temperature shifted as they delved deeper than the bedrock.

Finally, the stairs beyond open into a large room. There, at the center, sat a she-elf. *The seer.*

No one else, not even members of the High Council, were allowed to visit this sidhe. Possessing a seer was an ultimate act of treason, and her presence had been hidden even from Oberon.

The room was decorated with comfortable furniture and appointments. Books and other entertainment had been provided for her, including a few akashically powered magitech items that lay nearby.

Seated upon her bed, and rocking gently, her eyes were vacant, white and unseeing. She did not stir at the arrival of guests.

Calithilon frowned when he looked at her, but he set his jaw. The girl was pretty, and young, even for an elf of such power. The White Maven had brought her a portion of ambrosia from Oberon's table after every measure provided. She was too important of an asset to let her grow old and whither.

He bit his lip as he scanned her form. Long had Calithilon wished he could do more than merely meet with this girl and learn from her visions of the future. Her powers intrigued him, almost as much as her lithe form and nubile figure did. Given that he was the only one with access to her, every time she rebuffed him and denied his advances, it stung all the more. However, he was also the highest ranked maven of the Summer Court, and oftentimes, Calithilon simply took what he wanted.

Estimating he was passed the more lecherous parts of what had transpired earlier, the maven summoned his power and latched onto the magic coursing in his veins.

Lines of light shone out from him, washing over everything in this chamber. It flowed around his peers much like a river's current. Gold, ethereal images spawned all around, re-creating the events of earlier today with arcane luminescence.

Calithilon's ability let him revisit the past, however, he could only go back a couple of hours at most. Time moved around him, re-creating the previous events with astral ability. History could not be diverted, only witnessed, and the ability had provided the White Maven many clues to past events, including details of assassination attempts and many other high crimes.

As the images moved around them, bursting into visibility to all of his peers, a shimmering re-creation of Calithilon blossomed into view, seated next to the seer. Astral Calithilon removed his hand from the girl's knee and shook his head with a glower.

Calithilon knew the scene; she had refused him again. He had prepared to force her compliance when the girl shook and uttered a new vision. The signs were clear to him; he had witnessed the gift of sight overtake her on previous occasions.

The White Maven, the physical and present version, motioned for his companions to watch.

She screamed. The seer shook back and forth as she'd wailed. "The dragons are coming... The dragons are coming... The dragons are coming..."

True to the events earlier that day, Calithilon had snatched her by the shoulders and shook her, demanding answers, wanting to know more details about what she'd seen.

The terrified looking seer met her captor's gaze and then looked as if she might laugh—as if she found it funny when she told him, "The dragons will renew the cataclysm. You cannot stop them."

Before Calithilon could process what he had heard, she rattled off a string of words in the olde tongue, an ancient spell of fetiche power, and then her eyes clouded, blinded with a curse she'd placed on herself, condemning herself to silence. To blind catatonia.

All eyes turned to Calithilon. "What does it mean?" asked Fimion the Green.

"More importantly," asked an awestruck Amarthanc, "how does she know such a powerful spell?"

Calithilon set his jaw and told them. "She should not know that spell or any others. She was collected when she was very young, taken from her mother, who also had foretelling abilities but had escaped us... Well, she was kidnapped, to be precise. This girl did not have any magic training."

He crossed his arms and turned to stare at the young elf seated on her bed. *This girl has escaped, too, albeit in a different manner.*

"She can neither see nor hear us?" Amarthanc asked.

Calithilon nodded slowly. He knew what they were all thinking. She must've used her future knowledge to learn the spell—she'd learned this curse from some person in one of her horrific visions of the future and then cast it upon herself... possibly to guarantee the Cataclysm.

The girl had made herself completely obsolete and of no further use to the mavens. As the group of spell casters stared at the impotent thing on her bed, none dared speak about the one new thing her vision had told them.

There was no longer a dragon bringing the Cataclysm... Now, there were multiple.

Arawyn Ellyllon hung his head as his peers mocked him. His ears drooped slightly beneath his dreadlocks and their derision; a wildfey, they were slender and longer pointed than the more common sidhe. Arawyn twisted his wrists, but they remained firmly tied.

"You will never be aes sidhe," the first cajoled, shoving the youth through the undergrowth. The he-elf glanced sidelong at the pretty female who accompanied him. "What do you think, Mikara?"

"You're right, Andreyai—nobody will even miss one dirty tylwyth teg," she hissed. "Keep walking." She prodded him forward.

Arawyn continued walking, certain he would not survive this encounter. He grumbled a few words under his breath as the bullies forced him onward and deeper into the trees. They were all roughly the same age, three to five years past the first decade of life. They were also students at Ollscoil Maginarius, the sorcerous university a short distance from Cathair Dé.

Andreyai grabbed Arawyn by the tunic and yanked him backward, beating him about the face with his hand. "What did you say to me, israddol?" He used the insult that the sidhe reserved for inferior species of elves, especially the tylwyth teg.

Righteous indignation welled up deep within Arawyn. He used his bound hands to push against his oppressor. "I said I am not israddol and I am not *just* tylwyth teg. I am an ellyllon."

Mikara practically giggled at the fiery display. "They're all the same."

Arawyn glanced sidelong at her. His eyes smoldered. "They are *not*. And the wildfey are not all the same. There are five kinds of tuatha in the tylwyth teg and only two of us are elves. I am ellyllon, and I am more than just a tylwyth teg. That's a vague term."

Andreyai's face pinched as he tried to comprehend. "That doesn't make any sense, you stupid israddol. Your last name can't be your species—that would be like that human duelist who won last year's competition being named Remy Human." He spat a raspberry and laughed, which signaled for Mikara to laugh, too.

"Yeah, but you know what he *is?*" teased Mikara. "He's an orphan. Maybe we should call him Arawyn Orphan. Now, keep walking."

Arawyn's enemies pushing forward again and deeper into the woods outside the maginarius where they'd been walking for some time already. He'd been enrolled after someone at the orphanage recognized he had magical aptitude. Unlike the institutes of higher learning that made up the more secular colleges, many maginarium, including Ollscoil, accepted students of any age for arcane training, provided they were old enough to take care of themselves.

"We won't call him anything at all after tonight," Andreyai chortled.

Arawyn swallowed the lump in his throat. "What—what are you going to do to me? Leave me in the woods?"

"Something like that."

Arawyn could hear the malice in Mikara's voice.

"And you'll be dead," laughed Andreyai. "Were going to tell everyone that you tried to kidnap and rape Mikara—I mean, what would your kids even be like, israddol? Would they even be fey, or would they technically be a changeling?"

It was common knowledge that the ellyllon were a subtype of sidhe and very capable of interbreeding with the other sidhe and with humans. Human and fey offspring resulted in half-elves known as changelings, but neither human nor sidhe could breed with other tuatha, saving for rare exceptions. Ellyllon were fully elven, they had simple differences in culture, the ferality of wildfey being one of them.

"Everyone knows you want me," Mikara said, "and everyone is disgusted by the thought."

So, that's it, then? I gave a she-elf a compliment, and it spirals into a plot for my murder?

He considered using the magic he'd been taught to escape, but he did not feel it very likely. Although Arawyn knew he was more powerful than either of the two, both had more years of training at the maginarius. Arawyn could do simple tricks, like potentially unravel the rope binding his hands, or maybe cast a veil and make himself invisible. While both were possible, it would be difficult fending off both of them, and that fact meant concentrating would also be reduced. Without the ability to focus, he could do no magic, and staring in the face of death was a hell of a distraction.

Behind him, the students continued prattling as they prodded him forward. Mostly, they hurled insults and talked about what they were going to do to him before killing him and abandoning the body. *Probably meant to dishearten me and make it more difficult to try any mystic means of escape.*

Arawyn's long ears twitched at a strange sound in the trees. "Wait? Did you guys hear that?"

Mikara interrupted Andreyai as he talked through his plans to claim that he killed Arawyn while defending the she-elf and emerge as the hero of their story. "Stop trying to get us to take our eyes off you. Even if we did, you wouldn't get away."

"No, really. I heard something," Arawyn said, eyes looking past his two murderous classmates.

Both of them laughed dismissively.

Fear took root in Arawyn's eyes as the ellyllon spotted the danger in the trees and dawning recognition blossomed on their faces like tiny seeds of terror. They whirled just in time to spot the enormous beast sprint out from the undergrowth.

Taller than Andreyai by a huge margin, and shaggy with fur, a massive, fanged animal dashed toward them. Snarling, he brandished claws and slashed him across the chest, ripping him wide open.

More sounds crashed through the brush. Arawyn seized the opportunity. The jolt of fear and adrenaline inspired the moment of clarity he needed to cast a spell. In a burst of air, his bonds snapped and fell to the ground while he simultaneously put up a veil of invisibility.

Masked from sight, he dashed to a nearby tree and scrambled up it while Mikara screamed. A second creature emerged on the first one's haunches. Like the other, it resembled a massive wolf, though it walked on two legs like a man. This one was taller than the first, likely unable to fit through a door without stooping, and it moved with murderous precision.

As the first beast savaged Andreyai with tooth and claw, the next one sank its talons into Mikara and tore her throat out with ease. The aes sidhe hopefuls crumpled into a heap of gore as three more of the lupine creatures emerged.

"One got away, Oddur," the shortest one reported.

"I saw him," growled the leader. "But I lost him when you two got in the way."

As the five creatures stalking through the woods and searching for him, Arawyn felt certain they would spot him perched near the top of an evergreen. He held his breath and remained still, continuing to focus on his veil and remain invisible.

"I *smell* him. He must be here, somewhere," insisted the scout.

All the forest noises had stopped. Insects refused to buzz, bird songs ceased. Nature itself seemed to recognize the presence of predators. Monsters. Nothing dared chirp or peep for fear of revealing itself and begging for destruction.

After a few more minutes of searching, the intruders did not find the elf, and they growled with increasing frustration.

They spoke to each other in the unseelie tongue, likely imagining that any young tuatha from this part of the world would not understand them. But Arawyn was not from here, not originally, and wildfey raised their children to know the three major languages. Arawyn had not been an orphan his entire life, and he understood them plainly.

"We are so close to our goal," insisted the leader. "If you two bungled our mission because you couldn't keep your bloodlust in check, I'll put silver to your flesh." He drew a dagger from the loose belt that weaved through his shaggy coat. The blade shimmered with an alchemical quality, like lantern oil on water, and Arawyn recognized it as a silvered blade.

The taller of the attackers made a kind of whimpering noise.

"Forgiveness, Oddur. The aes sidhe will never know what hit them," assured the scout. "I'm certain there's a connection to the kidnapped humans and the aes sidhe—probably a connection to the disappearing magi as well."

Tall Wolf nodded. "Not that we care much for them, but killing aes sidhe now means fewer to contend with later."

Small Wolf insisted, "I want to burn them all to the ground."

I've got to get back to Ollscoil! Not everyone there was like Mikara and Andreyai—and even if they were, they don't deserve to die.

"And not just the spell casters," growled Oddur. "All the fey."

Silence reigned a few long moments as the leader of the wolves sniffed the air again for final measure. "You are sure he was one of them, another student magi?" Oddur glanced at Small Wolf. "You insisted you could kill them before they knew we were here."

Small Wolf wilted at his leader's admonishment.

"Shall we use the dallineb weed?" asked one who hadn't spoken yet.

"We could smoke it out," agreed another.

The leader shook his head. "No. It was just a child... And he wasn't even aes sidhe. The whelp was a wildfey—looked like those initiates were toying with him for sport. It's not worth wasting any of the incense to find him. Besides, it's more likely it doesn't even have any magic, and you fools just can't find his hiding spot."

Sniffing the air again, the others took one final look around before shrugging.

The leader stabbed a claw at the smallest of the creatures. "You stay here and watch. We must rendezvous with our clan mates before we lose any more time. If the whelp emerges from hiding, kill him. Otherwise, consider your prey escaped."

Nodding, the scout asked, "For how long?"

Oddur's face pointed toward where the maginarius lay beyond the cover of the woods. "When you hear the signal, you may end the watch and join the rest of the pack."

The creatures departed as silently as a wafting mist.

Arawyn remained in his tree, silent as a mouse beneath the shadow of an owl. Late morning turned to afternoon, and then to evening. His watcher patrolled the area once each hour, sniffing the air and searching for any sign of the elf, but Arawyn renewed his veil with each search. Still, he wasn't certain he could maintain his focus long enough to last through the night. Without food or water, he felt fatigue more intensely than normal.

Even thinking about the weariness enveloping him caused it to intensify and his veil nearly slipped. Before it could dispel altogether, the silence of the forest broke. A wolf's howl split the quiet and Arawyn's guard snorted once and then sprinted through the trees, headed toward the maginarius.

Waiting several minutes to make sure this wasn't some kind of trap, Arawyn finally climbed down the evergreen with weary, shaking hands. Then, curling up in a ball, he cried. He hadn't cried since his parents died in the faewylds—but hot tears streamed down his face. And then, mentally and physically exhausted, he slipped into an uneasy sleep at the base of the tree where he'd hidden.

Chapter Four

The city of Saibhir Gaoithe's buildings towered overhead, surrounding Remy. It was much the same as Cathair Dé. It boasted a great variety of different sized buildings, each custom tailored to what they housed. There were abandoned districts relegated as slums, bastions reserved for religious observance, and many areas for shopping and commerce, banking, and whole tracts where industry ruled over anything else.

If Remy noticed anything that differed significantly from his home city, it was that the thin tubes and lines which carried the akasha were newer. The burnished metal which delivered the mystic fluid had not yet greened at joint welds or faded with weather and oxidation.

Hearing a door close behind him, the duelist turned to spot his employer exit the building and descend the stairs toward him. Remy did not mind being asked to wait outside while Xander Kent performed his business within. Although many employers insisted on having their duelist guard them throughout such normal things as business meetings, Kent had a more low-key personality than Fuerian possessed.

Remy had rarely encountered Fuerian without the guard's presence nearby. A monstrous creature had killed Fuerian's long time duelist, Naz Charnazar, sent to attack the Vastran heir.

Luckily for Remy, Kent did not have Fuerian's gallery of enemies. By and large, his employer was well-liked, gave to charities, and was a pleasant fellow. Not being a top-shelf tuathan twat counted for a lot when it came to public perception.

The duelist made eye contact with Kent and nodded toward the horses which Remy had been watching over; nothing might slow their return trip home like stolen mounts. "Your business has concluded successfully?"

Nudging him with an elbow as he caught up, Kent grinned ear-to-ear. "Very successful," the elf said.

Rather than crawling atop his horse, Kent turned a slow circle. They were near the city's central square which was where the bulk of the marketplace commerce occurred. Like most cities under the rule of the Summer Court, this was the best place to observe commoners. Every urban sprawl had seedy places, where back-alley deals occurred and where local destinies played out between blackmail and blade. They also had monuments of stone and glass where trade moguls and elites engaged in the same craft, only with more polish. But the truest place to get the heartbeat of a city was in the local market.

Kent was not watching the people, however. His eyes flicked from conduit to pipeline and the raised trestles that held the akashic delivery infrastructure overhead and out of the way of

Saibhir Gaoithe's citizenry, keeping the network of pipes and wires unobtrusive and practically invisible.

"Something got your eye?" Remy asked.

Kent grinned. He pointed to the piping that remained just out of the way. "That. That was my business. The whole maze of conduit is now mine."

Remy raised an eyebrow. "Pardon?" He didn't quite understand what his boss was telling him. "It looks new."

"That's because it is. Suíochán Naséan recently paid to install this extensive infrastructure throughout all of Saibhir Gaoithe and at great cost, but they've been very slow in delivering the akasha, prompting the civil engineers to look for alternatives." Wicked gleam flashed in Kent's eyes. "The Radiant Tower built all that... and I just stole it."

Remy's lips quirked. "I'm not sure how you can steal all that."

The rich business person chuckled and waved a hand to it all. "I own a rival company which distributes raw akasha. Just a few minutes ago I inked a deal with the government officials of Saibhir Gaoithe, giving them such a price break on the stuff that they've agreed to make me their exclusive distributor for the next ten years."

His face must have conveyed his confusion since Kent explained. "One of my chief costs is building the infrastructure needed to pipe the stuff directly to every end user."

Remy nodded, finally understanding. As far as he knew, there were no rules against such a move... at least, not yet. *Like dueling, most is fair game when it comes to business.*

"Well, then," the human nodded toward the amounts. "Shall we?" He was eager to return home and ensure Jaira was safe. She'd agreed to stay with Anya until his return. It seemed too obvious that she might stay with her parents, Harhassus and Eilastra Morgansteen, while he was away. If there truly was any danger, it would look for Jaira there, first, rather than at an unlisted residence owned by Xander Kent.

The elf clambered into the stirrups and urged his horse through the crowd.

Remy kept a wide berth of the tall posts near the center of the marketplace. He'd already scouted the area while waiting on the steps for his boss; there was no mistaking the engraved symbols upon those posts. They marked the boundary for the dueling area. Any licensed duelist could not refuse a challenge while inside that zone, and he'd already spotted a half dozen sidhe wearing the mandatory pins that marked them as official duelists. Remy's own gleamed at his lapel.

Each pin designated which of the houses and clans the fighters belong to. Remy glanced down to his own. It had no insignia denoting an affiliation. He was ina aonar, houseless. Beneath the badge, a few ribbons hung in place as trophies.

Of those duelists he'd spotted, many of them had similar prizes pinned in place. *Damned ribbon seekers.*

Many younger fighters tried to earn honor flags by camping out near the boundaries of the zones in which combatants could not refuse a challenge. For each victory, they got to wear their trophies for the following year and, for many duelists without a regular gig, the more trophies one had, the higher price they could command for their services.

If Kent had any weakness, as far as Remy knew, it was his love of the duels, which often occurred as sport among higher-ranked warriors. The human thought it less than a weakness, though. It was more of a fascination. After all, had it been otherwise, Remy would not have found himself gainfully employed by one of the more upstanding Summer sidhe.

Remy had little interest in random duels with cocky fighters. There was too much risk involved with the public dueling scene, even if it offered an occasional thrill for the locals. He had seen fights go catastrophically, lethally wrong.

Instead of following his lead, Kent veered toward the public dueling area.

"Where are you going?" Remy called after him.

Kent, still flushed from the excitement of a major win for his company, nodded toward the nearest guidepost that created a boundary for the duels. "I feel like stirring up some local trouble." He winked at Remy.

Remy sighed and closed the gap. "You're jeopardizing your security here."

The elf scoffed and waved him off. "What fun is it being the boss if I can't turn situations to my own amusement, sometimes?" Kent scanned the area, eyes lingering on each of the ribbon seekers camped out nearby. "Take one of these elves on. Remind the world of who you are."

Remy scowled. He was well known as the only human duelist. He was perhaps the most famous human in the Seelie Kingdom. Dueling followed a strict set of rules that revolved around drawing first blood with the possibility of escalating egregious insults to a fight to the death.

What the world at large did *not* know, was that Remy had grown up trained to be the feared unseelie assassin Aderyn Corff—the Corpse Bird. *Queenslayer.* He was an excellent fighter, however he'd been taught to do more than merely fight. Remy was trained to kill, and whenever his employer put Remy's honor on the line, it put him in a position that forced him to potentially kill again. It was the one thing Remy was good at, but that fact was what made him flee the unseelie in the first place, and he'd burnt every bridge on his way out the rival kingdom.

Kent waved off any trepidation on Remy's behalf. "Don't worry so much. Just one quick duel and then we'll be on our way back home."

The human sighed, but dismounted and angled toward the edge of the bounds. He glanced from fighter to fighter, assessing their stance and their ribbons.

One of the sidhe held Remy's gaze. He had a hawkish face and angular ears. Three yellow ribbons hung behind the elf's badge; the yellow ribbons denoted a public duels won. Two of them had a red stripe, and the third had a black one: a pair of wins earned by drawing first blood, and one victory had resulted in an opponent's death.

All of Remy's ribbons were purple, the color that marked a successful defense against a private contract. He was not particularly keen on wearing ribbons like some peacock, but Kent preferred him to, even if actually getting his ribbons was a more arduous task for Remy. As ina aonar, he sometimes had to petition the red mavens directly to work on his behalf. Typically, the head of any duelist's guild house would get them from the house of a defeated opponent; without a house master, it proved sometimes arduous to get satisfaction.

The human's gaze did not waver, and he cocked his head at the nearby fighter. "All right, then. Your intentions are known." He strode confidently across the invisible line that marked the point of no return.

It was no secret that many ribbon seekers hoped to make a name for themselves by being the first to beat the human duelist in combat. Remy had even heard that some guild houses had petitioned the mavens to create a new ribbon color specifically for beating Remy Keaton. There was no provision for it in the rules, however, but it was being discussed among Oberon's court.

Remy stood three full steps inside the area. Vendors and shoppers began to clear away. They seemed more enthusiastic than scared. Duels rarely resulted in additional casualties, just so long as nobody interfered with the entertainment of a match... But *usually* was not the same as never.

The cocky sidhe drew his sword as he stalked directly for Remy. As soon as he crossed the line, he issued a loud verbal challenge with a reminder that it could not be refused.

Remy shouted, "Parley? An unarmed moment to discuss the fight?"

The elf did not move, but he tilted his head with interest.

Remy stuck his sword tip down into the dirt and then took two steps to his right. His opponent, understanding the measure, did likewise, and then Remy withdrew his sheathed dúshlán blade, a mystic dagger bound to him by arcadeaxn magic. He motioned to get Kent's attention and then tossed it to the man's waiting hands.

Completely unarmed, the human and elf walked toward each other. Remy could see hatred burning in his opponent's eyes and wondered if the man was sympathetic to the Frith Duine. He knew that many of those folk who desired Remy's downfall did so out of racial hatred.

As they came together, the elf howled to the crowd, "It looks like the human would rather talk his way out of a challenge than fight?"

His cajoling elicited both laughter and catcalls. A few in the gathering audience shouted, *"Ddiymadferth."*

Remy said nothing. He kept his hands at his side and waited for the sidhe fighter to get close enough that his conversation with the elf would not be overheard. The smug duelist finally came to a stop nearby and shut his mouth long enough for Remy to speak.

"Before we fight, you should know something about me."

The elf's brows knit.

"There are rumors that tie me to the famous Winter assassin. Many duelists believe that I am, in fact, the famous Aderyn Corff, private killer given to Rhagathena, the unseelie Spider Queen. You have heard this?"

Crossing his arms over his chest, the elf scoffed. "I hear much idle talk. Mere rumors. You've capitalized on them quite handily, ddiymadferth. And now, it's my turn to use that legend to further *my* career." He flicked the trio of ribbons behind his badge. "You see these? I have a one hundred percent win rate, officially, anyway."

Remy's voice dropped to a whisper. "You should know something about the speculation: it is not mere legend. I *am* the Corpse Bird, and I need you to understand something before we fight. Dueling rules decides victory at first blood but permit a fighter to demand satisfaction. I know you understand this because you have a black line through one of yours."

The human then nodded toward Kent. "That is my boss over there. He's here to watch, and if you draw first blood with my honor on the line, do you really think I would fail to escalate the conflict? Doing so would harm *his* prestige... I merely want you to know the stakes."

Eyes bugging out slightly, the elf realized what Remy was telling him. *This duel only ends in death, unless the elf yields to first blood.*

"My talents have always been more at *ending* a fight. Permanently. I did not start this one, but it only ends with your loss or your death." Remy kept his gaze cool.

He recognized the blood draining from his opponents cheeks as the elf blanched. And then Remy snatched the duelist by the shoulders and crashed his forehead into the elf's nose, smashing bone and rupturing blood vessels.

The elf fell to his butt, face leaking blood down past his chin and spilling onto the dirt below.

Remy shouted, "I have drawn first blood. Do you wish to contest?"

The wounded fighter sat on his rump and nursed his mangled nose. A look of betrayal burned on his cheeks and Remy could practically hear the elf's unspoken thoughts: *ddiymadferth*.

Remy yelled again, seeking a verbal signal. "Do you contest, sir?"

With a voice more nasal and choked than it had been a moment ago, the elf responded, "I yield the contest."

The human nodded and then stopped back to retrieve his sword. He glared at the other ribbon seekers, warning them off with a glance. Once he'd grabbed his weapon, he returned and extended a hand to his wounded opponent, helping lift the elf back to his feet. When they were close, he spoke quietly to the duelist. "Tell your friends in the other dueling houses what will happen if they come for me. I mean it."

Remy snatched the duelist's pin, ribbons and all. He took one glance at the crest upon the pin and which house his opponent had belonged to. "You can retrieve this tomorrow from your guild house office. I shall give it to them as proof of my victory."

The elf nodded, despite his scowl.

"I am sick of everyone thinking they can take the human down a notch or target me for sport. Tell them. Tell the others that I'm not prey to be trifled with."

And then Remy turned his back on his defeated enemy and walked back to where Kent sat upon horseback, beaming with amusement.

"I suppose we'll need to stop by a guild house before we leave town?" Kent asked.

Remy gestured his agreement and spurred his mount forward. He was eager to return home.

***

Fuerian crumpled another letter in his fist. "Infernal suffering," he growled. "I suppose it's my fault for making rash oaths."

I should consult the warden of the prison and insist he limit the amount of paper prisoners have access to before I have the whole damned cellblock writing to me.

He shook his head and exhaled through his nose, expelling the tension. "I suspect Gareth and Trishana may have encountered each other while incarcerated. That might explain why they've both written to me so recently."

Gareth could call upon Fuerian for aid given his long-standing relationship with the elf. Trishana Firmind was different. She was more of a business acquaintance who had been his aithermancer for several years, participating in different schemes that helped advance Fuerian's aims. But he owed her a favor in very explicit terms. She had demanded payment in this form after a big job she did for him in the past, and it seemed she had finally called in that chip.

Fuerian spat a few more curses and then gathered his cloak and a sack of coins before hanging his sword from his belt. Shaking his head, he headed out from his apartment and into the streets. "I suppose I shall have no peace until I pay what is owed," he grumbled to himself.

The city sprawled all around him, gleaming and clean in this part of town. Given that an elf of his stature could not live in a lesser district, the stables were a short distance away. Prompt access to a person's mount was convenient, but not at the expense of streets mired with shit and the risk of tainting the bottom hems of pants, dresses, and cloaks. His personal horse was kept a quick walk down the lane.

Before he'd gotten very far, someone grabbed Fuerian near the mouth of an alley and yanked him within, seizing him with an unbreakable grip. Before he could draw his weapon, a voice hissed, "Stop struggling."

Fuerian recognize the voice. It was gravelly and dark, filled with all manner of corruption. In moments, his eyes adjusted to the dim light, and he gazed upon the creature he'd called a shadow maven.

Hymdreiddiech was an albino sidhe, and he wore a scarf from the nose down which concealed much of his face below those hideous red eyes. They peered out from below a hood that contained his pale hair. "Your last shipment was light. I require more ore from your mine."

Irony crept through Fuerian's mind. *Why in the fey have all the devils I've made deals with decide to call in their banners at the same time?*

"I have sent what I can. The Radiant Tower has been sniffing around very closely to ensure none of that illegal metal leaves my property," he said.

Fuerian gritted his teeth and flared his nostrils. He *had* made a deal with the devil, allowing at least *some* of the iron from Harhassus's old mine to be removed and turned over to the shadow maven. Whatever the creature wanted with it, he did not know, and Fuerian hoped to never find out. His interest in the mine was to collect the foil milferra, and so long as he helped provide the dark creature with enough of the toxic iron to satisfy him, Hymdreiddiech had promised to sponsor Fuerian for both greater involvement in Nhywyllwch's schemes and to back Fuerian when he moved to insist on a greater cut of the profits in the future.

A trade of worthless metal for an extra ten percent in the akasha trade futures seemed like a good barter at the time. Now, Fuerian was not so sure.

"The mavens are of no concern," Hymdreiddiech promised. "And even if they were, you and I have an agreement, one that not even our third partner, Nhywyllwch, knows about. You owe me more iron."

"And you owe me more workers," Fuerian snarled. "I'll not send my own companions into *that* mine. Where are all of these unseelie light-starved you promised me when we made this deal?"

As the mine had first become operational, Fuerian knew he would need to staff the place with creatures capable of handling, or at least being around, iron ore. The shadow maven promised he could provide a motley collection of human and redcap workers. Most of what he'd turned over were children or prisoner-slaves so feisty that they were more hassle than they were worth. Human kids could easily pick the fungus that Nhywyllwch needed as a reagent, but they couldn't wield pickaxes and giving those tools to former resistance fighters was a coup waiting to happen.

"Humans are difficult to capture in the wild, especially lately with that ddiymadferth Remy Keaton inspiring hope in them," said Hymdreiddiech.

"Still not my problem." Fuerian stepped back to put a little space between them. He did not like the shadow maven cornering him like this, especially not in a narrow area with tall walls that would make swordplay difficult. It made the aes sidhe's spell craft a far superior tool if their disagreement devolved into its baser forms.

The black maven's eyes narrowed and his presence loomed larger. The tops of the buildings seemed to curl in around him and threatened Fuerian with overwhelming madness. It was all he could do to keep control of his bladder as his hands trembled and his feet froze to the cobblestones below.

Somewhere deep in the recesses of his mind, Fuerian knew that the maven was using magic upon him, intimidating him to his very core. Whatever this spell was, the maddening terror was barely a fraction of what Hymdreiddiech had inflicted upon those poor aes sidhe hostages the albino exploited and squeezed for their magic.

That was the true, dark secret of the raw akasha; it was arcana wrenched free of terrified victims and distilled.

"You *will* provide me with more iron." His voice rumbled.

Fuerian nodded, trying not to tip over as his head rocked back and forth. "I-I will." He said it, but his inner grit still managed a slight grip on his will and the words rang with a resentful tone.

"Good." Hymdreiddiech's gaze moved down to Fuerian's pocket, as if the dark aes sidhe knew what it held. And then he released the spell, and the world crashed back into some semblance of normal reality. "I will send you what light-starved I can sneak across the Solstox Bridges. Anticipate the arrival of the slavetaker. He has already been dispatched."

Fuerian gulped. He'd heard of the notorious orc who trafficked in stolen children and other tuatha that could be pressed into eternal service. His specialty had always been in hunting and selling ddiymadferth.

And then, Hymdreiddiech was gone.

Fuerian tried to calm his trembling hands. The effort was futile, and he reached into his pocket withdrawing a charm—the amulet he'd promised to return to the leader of the Vastra House. The one he'd surrendered to Juriahl at his family's insistence had been a replica.

As he stared back out the mouth of the alleyway, Fuerian's heart sank. He'd had people try to exercise magic over him in the past and the thing's spell resistance had always protected him. He would not part with it under any circumstance—except the thing hadn't worked this time.

How in the fey was Hymdreiddiech able to do that? Either his magic is stronger than Calithilon the White's, or else his magic is not from Arcadeax!

With a grimace, he slung it around his neck for fear that its effect was less potent if not touching his flesh. He'd never heard of such a requirement for artifacts before, but the weight of it against his collar bone brought Fuerian comfort.

He bit his lower lip, and then hurried for his horse, clutching the sack of coins he knew he could use to secure the release of Trishana Firmind and Gareth Morass. The warden was known to the Vastra family and Fuerian knew the price of two low-profile prisoners. He could afford to purchase a paroled release.

With whatever Hymdreiddiech had brewing beneath the surface, Fuerian knew that he needed more allies who he could trust.

Arawyn approached the maginarius from upwind; dread filled his gut. Those feral beasts had finely attuned senses. As he wondered if they'd be able to smell him coming, he nearly tripped over a mounted bundle of smoldering material. The punk was bound to a stick and propped up, left to burn, but it had long since gone out.

Arawyn recognized it. The stuff was called dallineb weed. He'd read about it in the libraries of the maginarius. The relatively uncommon incense had a pungent scent and temporarily removed the ability of aes sidhe to connect with their arcane abilities.

He found several other bundles in a line nearby where the breeze would catch the withered sticks' fumes and carry them across the region. *That one wolf threatened to use them on me to dispel my veil.*

Ollscoil lay directly ahead of the wildfey. The maginarius owned a sprawling patch of ground. Its campus consisted of several buildings, mostly made from stone and mortar, with neatly manicured lawns and walkways connecting one structure to the next. The college did its best to maintain an appealing nature and an air of noble regality which would appeal to its donors and sponsors.

Arawyn crept through a passage in the stone fence that marked the boundaries and sniffed. Wildfey were more attuned to the dangers of the uncivilized world than other sidhe. He could smell the metallic aroma of blood as plainly as day.

The walk back had been slower than expected. He'd stopped regularly in order to listen for more of those creatures. The wolven things still prowled nearby, making occasional noises, but Arawyn managed to arrive unmolested. He spotted one of the monsters through a window, but then lost track of it—they'd gained entry to the building.

Something burned deep within Arawyn. Ollscoil Maginarius had become his home. He had none other. Even if his being ellyllon meant he'd been regularly abused and dismissed, this place was all he'd known these past few years. Arawyn had no place else to go. He reached deep into himself, tested his connection to the magic of Arcadeax and hoped it wasn't dampened by any residual odor of the dallineb weed. He already felt sluggish being so fatigued after the long day he'd had.

Arawyn smelled the aroma as it wafted past. It reminded him of crushed phallaceae, stinkhorn. Regardless, he found a store of magic and harnessed it while wrinkling his nose against the piquant film hanging in the air like an oily soot.

Renewing his veil of invisibility, Arawyn stalked through the yard. He did not explore for long before discovering his first body. An older elf who he'd known to be a forthcoming graduate lay dead. Claws had shredded her torso, and the mage had bled out upon the grass.

Ahead, he found three other corpses in similar repose.

Someone screamed in the distance.

Not knowing what he could do, or how he could help, or if helping was even possible, Arawyn hurried toward the main building.

A central hall dominated the landscape. Shaped distinctly, a large bell-tower jutted off of one side; it was an iconic building and when people thought of Ollscoil, this structure came to mind. Within its walls were classrooms, offices, research labs, and all other manners of places necessary to the operation of a maginarius.

Arawyn slipped within a wrecked door that hung ajar. Someone had smeared blood on one wall and deep scratches grooved on another. Debris and wreckage from the creatures' attacks lay strewn upon the ground. As stealthily as possible, Arawyn moved through the corridors.

Another scream echoed and Arawyn's nerve broke. It was all he could do to keep a hold of his spell and he spun on one heel and fled, aware that the sound of his footsteps would help these predators locate him, even while invisible.

Fey, they'd been able to sniff me out in the woods like Cù-sith tracking prey across the moors.

Another scream. Closer this time, and louder than Arawyn's footfalls which sounded like hammers in the wildfey's long ears. Panic rose in his chest and he grabbed the door handle to the nearest room.

Locked!

Growls reverberated nearby causing hair on the back of Arawyn's neck to stand on edge and chill his blood. The young aes sidhe dropped his veil so he could focus on a different spell. He used a minor trick and tripped the tumblers inside the barrier, accessing the closed chamber and shutting the door behind him. Arawyn winced as the sound of the lock clicked. It seemed as loud as charging hooves.

Surprised eyes greeted him incredulously.

"W-who are you?" asked the professor who stood there. Arawyn was unfamiliar with him.

The campus was a big place, and Arawyn was still a very young recruit to the aes sidhe. He took one glance around the room while stating his name and recognized it as some sort of research lab. The air was better here, untainted by the dallineb. It had no windows and there had been no signage on the door. Dark black slabs of metal rested upon workbenches with beakers and phials of unknown liquids placed between them.

Is this place supposed to be a secret? Some kind of laboratory?

Hopes of any conversation were cut short when something pounded on the door.

"Quickly, lad," the older elf insisted. "Raise a veil. They can't attack what they can't see."

Arawyn shook his head. "But they can. These creatures are monsters. Animals."

A howl split the air and the older aes sidhe blanched. He glanced from the long-eared boy to the door and his breathing quickened.

"You know what they are?" Arawyn asked.

The researcher nodded.

"What can we do? They're slaughtering everybody!"

Brimming with hopelessness, the older elf whispered, "There is no fighting them, not without more of us... The only choice we have is to run—but they'll be fast—we'll run. We should go on my word."

Arawyn felt the elf's eyes narrow as they gazed upon him. He felt certain of the sidhe's intentions. *He's going to trip me as soon as the creatures close in, leaving me as a distraction so he can get away.*

He'd seen that happen before, in the faewylds. Arawyn understood fear and there was nothing more terrifying than facing an imminent death.

Before giving the other elf a chance to argue, Arawyn hurried and slipped into a nearby cabinet. "I'll take my chances from here, instead."

And then the door burst inward, splintering to shards. It torn free from hinge and mooring. Yelping, the elf caught in the middle of the carnage recoiled.

Dagda, help me!

Arawyn raised a different spell from his hiding place. The younger spellcaster had learned from his past encounter.

Using magic, he cleared the air from around him, cleansing it of his personal odor. Then, he held the enchantment and hoped the creatures wouldn't look too closely.

As three of the monstrous, lupine creatures flung themselves through the door, the aes sidhe blasted the first with the spell, summoning a bolt of pure force, flinging it across the room. It had little effect except to relocate the brute. The second one he torched with an evocation of fire which sent the thing into a frenzy.

Burning and screeching, it reeled and flailed until it fell and rolled, in its efforts to put out the flames.

Smashing one fist into the magi as the next creature moved, the final lycan grabbed the aes sidhe's arm, snapping it and breaking his concentration, killing the spell.

Arawyn recognized this one. *Oddur, they had called him.*

The wounded elf's eyes widened with recognition. "W-what are the Fianna doing here?"

"The Fian Bairn, actually. We are exacting revenge for crimes against humanity," Oddur growled as he looked around the room with narrowed, golden eyes. He took the elf by the throat, effortlessly shaking him like a rag-doll, but not so hard as to kill him. That wolfish gaze rested upon the black slabs.

"You have iron here. Why?" Oddur demanded, squeezing the aes sidhe's throat slightly.

The sidhe would not answer.

Oddur growled again, "Why?"

Adamant in his refusal, the fey tightened his jaw, and then Oddur released him. Arawyn realized why.

The attacker who'd been burned rose to his feet and growled menacingly. Skin had blistered and formed boils between the remaining patches of fur.

Arawyn recognized him as Small Wolf, the monster who'd stayed behind in the woods in order to find and kill him. Hate burned in the creature's eyes.

Scorched, Small Wolf snatched his enemy and dragged him to the plates of iron. "Let's see how you like it," Small Wolf growled as he shoved the sidhe's face onto the ferrous slab and pressed down.

The elf screamed with mind-bending anguish. Small Wolf refused to relent and only pushed harder, rolling the creature's face across the black metal, making sure he spread the pain around.

Oddur asked again, "Why do you have iron here?"

"Tests!" the victim shouted. "My client wants me to cultivate a reagent upon it! He wants me to grow foil milferra!"

The leader of the wolves tapped one bloody claw against his chin. "Why? What value is there in some fungus, even a rare one?"

Small Wolf kept the pressure up, placing any unexposed skin against the stuff.

"I don't know! It's worthless—please... Stop!"

They did not.

"Where did all this iron come from, then?" Oddur asked as if they'd engaged in polite conversation.

"These test slabs are certified by the Summer Court and have been here for a decade—the mavens know they exist."

Oddur snarled and rushed forward. He used a claw to cut the elf's tunic free and flipped him over, smashing his body onto the large brick of iron, pressing the whole of his back onto it until fey skin sizzled. "That was not the question that I asked."

"The old Morgansteen mine," his victim screeched. "The Vastras own it now!"

Oddur's lips curled, exposing fangs. "What else do you suppose I will find in this Vastran mine?"

Then he flipped the elf over, and held him belly-down onto the metal, tormenting him until the pain overwhelmed the sidhe and he fell unconscious. The trio of them chuckled and Small Wolf tore the elf's throat out in one quick motion, dropping him to the floor where he bled to death. It was, perhaps, a mercy.

"We know something new," Oddur remarked to his peers. "A mine which has transferred ownership is filled with iron. It should not be difficult to find… and where there is a vein iron, you know what we will find?"

Small Wolf replied, "Lightstarved."

The trio nodded, and then Oddur and his companion departed. Small Wolf followed, but paused. He sniffed at the air again and looked directly at the cabinet where Arawyn hid, watching the scene from a crack between the doors.

The fey youth's heart raced, and he clung to the obfuscation spell with all his resolve.

Small Wolf snuffed one big, final breath and then shook his head.

Oddur's voice barked in the hallway and Arawyn heard him plain as day as he responded to someone else who gave a report.

"What do you mean, 'you killed some Fian Faolchú?' The other Fianna are not to be harmed. I was clear about this."

Another, unfamiliar voice insisted, "We don't have time to argue, Oddur. They attacked *us*, trying to defend this place and the tuatha weaklings it hides. Besides, we've just received word that our unseelie kin are being smuggled through the region."

The voices faded away as Arawyn concentrated on the spell. He was no longer able to pay attention to the distant conversation *and* hold the air cleansing. Finally, Small Wolf turned to catch up and headed out of the room's only exit, muttering about how he could hardly wait to see this place go up in flames.

The return voyage from Saibhir Gaoithe went quicker than expected. Remy's desire was to get home quickly. That, coupled with Kent's chipper attitude after seeing his duelist beat the pants off a ribbon seeker, meant they made surprisingly good time.

It was after midnight and the distant lights of Cathair Dé burned just beyond the nearest rise. As the road bent around a forested region, Remy smelled smoke.

He stopped paying attention to Kent's gibbering and held up a hand to stay him. The elf promptly shut up and moved closer to the duelist who'd gone quiet. They kept moving, albeit at a slower gait and the horses had moved to the side of the road where their hooves would not clop so loudly.

"Is there danger?" Kent asked quietly.

Remy's lips stretched thin, but he shook his head. "I do not think so. But I smell smoke." After another length of traveled on the grass alongside the tarmac, Remy felt certain that the odor came from within the trees.

The duelist pointed. "Do you know what is in that direction?"

Kent frowned. "Ollscoil Maginarius. It's a training institute for aes sidhe."

Remy sniffed at the air again. "I think it's on fire."

The sidhe scowled as they rode in the moonlight and passed a signpost that labeled the small wend in the rode as the path to the maginarius.

With his heart sinking, Remy remembered Eldarian, the aes sidhe trainee who Thoranmir had searched for, and ultimately located. The poor elf hadn't been found in time for a rescue, but his death had provided some insight, at least, into the strange disappearances in this region. *Disappearances which have yet to be explained.*

Remy stared on the trail which curved beyond his sight. Foliage formed a canopy over the top which would have blocked his vision even if it had been full daylight.

"I would like to investigate this, sir?" the human asked.

Kent frowned. "I think it may be a good idea, however, if there is trouble afoot, I'd much prefer not to be caught out in the open and without the companionship of my duelist. See me to my estate first, and then do what you will."

Remy nodded curtly, then he spurred his horse. They hurried at a quickened pace and aimed directly for Xander Kent's home. As the distance from Ollscoil increased, the air cleared of smoke. Remy mentally laid out his plans. As soon as Kent was put safely into his home where he could easily defend himself by his own measures, he would ensure that Jaira was safe with Anya. Hopefully, he would not wake her when he checked in. After that... he felt it was his duty to investigate.

From what he learned from Odessa, the she-elf Thoranmir had fallen in love with, Eldarian had studied at this exact institute. Perhaps he'd find something relevant to that? He could not be certain. But he felt sure that, whatever incident had occurred, it needed someone looking into it.

Chapter Five

Fuerian stood outside the main gates of the prison. The sun had not fully come up and the misty morning air bit his exposed flesh with remnants of its pre-dawn cool.

Next to him stood the warden of the facility. He looked weary, but surveyed his domain with keen, watchful eyes.

Fuerian followed the elf's gaze and spotted guards in the towers and along the top of the bastions. There were no parapets here. This was not some defensive castle that needed archery positions to hide behind. *These* walls kept things within, rather than out. In the event of unruly inmates in the yard, guards could loose their bows with impunity.

A loud clanking noise shook Fuerian from his thoughts and he turned his eyes inside the facility. The warden turned, as well.

Set in the wall were a pair of massive cupronickel gates and the shafts of vertical bars. Visible through them was the path through the main court; flagstones ended at the heavy wooden doors of the bastille.

Those doors opened with groans indicative of their weight and a guard emerged, escorting a female elf. She was very thin and dirty, with bedraggled red hair and unmistakable cold, blue eyes. They arrived shortly after at the main gate, and the warden cleared his throat.

Fuerian scowled but turned over a pouch of coin.

Peeking within, the warden frowned and made an openhanded gesture into which Fuerian added a second purse. He removed a key ring and jangled it loudly for effect before unlocking the gates.

"You have been hereby pardoned, Mizz Firmind. You would do well to remain beyond of my jurisdiction in the future." The warden shot her a pointed glare before departing.

The prison guard closed the door behind the released prisoner and then returned to his post.

Neither Trishana nor Fucrian uttered a word until they had walked beyond earshot of the penitentiary. Fuerian finally broke the silence. "The warden charged me four hundred silvers for you... Double what he had previously agreed to."

She shrugged sheepishly. "Yeah. He's got a personal grudge against me."

Fuerian raised an eyebrow.

Trishana laughed mirthlessly. "I once cheated him out of a large sum of money in a game of chance. Not five gold nobles' worth, but what price can a he-elf put on his pride?"

"And he didn't come for you sooner?"

"I had some dirt on him, evidence of an affair that I'd stashed in the aither in case I needed some leverage," the aithermancer told Fuerian. "His divorce was finalized shortly before they locked me up."

Fuerian shook his head and chuckled. "Ah... So, this favor you backed me into was *premeditated*?"

She tilted her head. "You never know when you will need a favor."

He nodded at the truism, but his eye gleamed with amusement, even if it came with a steep price.

"You got Gareth out already?" she asked. "I made assumptions when the guards arrived yesterday."

"I did. It took me a little longer to gather the sum the warden demanded for you." Fuerian squinted as he looked at her in the early dawn. "He mentioned that there were no humans in this prison, even though I'm aware there have been arrests. The Frith Duine have been very active lately, and I'm certain humans have been incarcerated, even if most of their charges have been falsified."

Trishana could only offer a flippant look. "Every now and then, one would come in. They'd only stay for a day or two before being retrieved and sentenced to the Royal prison under the *Radiant Tower's* jurisdiction."

Fuerian swallowed and nodded gravely.

The aithermancer arched a brow. "Do you need human slaves for something?"

Fuerian had known Trishana for many years, but he did not want to share everything. She was his asset, not his friend.

"Just curious," was all he said, and then they arrived at the carriage and he escorted her back to Cathair Dé.

Jaira awoke to the feeling of soft lips pressed against hers. She stirred slightly within the covers, recognized the smell of her husband, and embraced him without ever opening her eyes. Jaira dragged him into the guest bed of Anya's apartment with a soft moan and leaned into him.

His posture felt tenser than normal, and Jaira groggily opened her eyes, sensing he didn't intend to stay. In the dim glow of moonlight, she identified the serious look on his face.

"What is it, my love?" she asked.

"I can't stay. There's something I must go investigate."

Jaira frowned with concern. "Is everything all right? What time is it?"

Remy's face remained blank. "It's early. There's nothing to worry about."

"Is it Kent?"

"No. He's fine. I got him safely home from Saibhir Gaoithe. But I spotted something amiss on the trail to Ollscoil Maginarius."

Jaira said, sitting fully up in bed now, "You think it has something to do with that mage Thoranmir was searching for? The one who died?" Every word she spoke stuck in her throat. She knew that even mentioning his friend tore Remy up inside.

Remy had confided in her one night how he wondered if his best friend may still be alive if he hadn't obsessed so thoroughly over Jaira. While he had confessed his innermost secrets to her, she had not done the same—she *could not.* None could know that Jaira was a seer. *And worse, Remy can never know that I knew Thoranmir would die that day... that only his sacrifice meant that I would live.*

If anyone ever discovered that she possessed clairvoyant gifts, nothing would stop Suíochán Naséan from pursuing her. Not even her husband could stop their Solais Cloaks and the Agents of Gray—no matter how talented Remy was for violence.

If the Radiant Tower could not catch her, they'd tell Oberon and he would send his entire army after her. Seers were good at using their talents to circumvent capture, but not every net could be escaped from. Jaira had lived all her life as a secret-keeper, and she was *very* good at it. Nobody had discovered her, yet.

Well, *almost.*

Anya had figured it out. Thoranmir's sister, the legless aithermancer, had put the details together. Somehow, she'd seen right through her. Perhaps it was because of her special skills, or maybe Jaira had simply let her guard down around the she-elf. Regardless, it had knit Anya and Jaira together in a sisterhood of secrets bonded closer than even Remy and Thoranmir had been.

Since the recent scare at their cottage, Remy had been on edge. He had insisted that she stay at Anya's while he went with Kent on business.

Jaira knew what it was like to be on edge.

"I should be back by midday at the latest," Remy told her, kissing her forehead. He laid her back on the bed and pulled the covers over her. He "I must go," said, leaving no room for argument.

Still not fully awake, she watched him depart. He'd already been gone for a few days and she wanted to protest. But her husband was away before any argument could be made. By the time she heard the door locks click shut on the apartment, she'd finally arrived at a state of full wakefulness.

Try as she might, Jaira could not return to sleep and so she got out of bed. Wandering the place in the early morning hours, before the sun had even arisen, she stumbled into the watchful gaze of Anya.

"Can't sleep either?" Anya asked.

Jaira sighed. "No. Should I make us some tea?"

"That would be fine," Anya said.

As Jaira busied herself by filling the pot with water, she sensed her friend's watchful eyes upon her. "What?" she finally asked. Jaira turned and met Anya's gaze as she flipped the switch on the akasha powered heating element.

Anya's eyebrows rose. "I *know*."

Jaira's lips quirked upward in a smirk. "What do you think you know?"

"I know your secret."

"You know *all* my secrets, Anya. You're the only person who knows things I've hid, even from my husband."

The dark-skinned aithermancer grinned triumphantly. "You think I don't know *this one*, though. But I do... I just don't know why you've kept it from Remy."

Jaira cocked her head. She said nothing, however.

And then Anya told Jaira her *other* secret—the *other* thing she hid from every living person, be they human or fey.

Jaira's jaw dropped. *Somehow*—somehow, Anya had figured her out.

The teapot whistled in the background and Jaira stammered, "Please, don't tell Remy."

Juriahl meandered the hallways of the Vastra estate. Much like everything else about his clan, his familial home's walls, floor, and accoutrements were cold and hard. Only furniture in the poshest public rooms had padding; they were mostly made from burnished wood, worn down and darkened by the stains of age and many generations' worth of hands and feet.

Irony struck the elf as he looked around. His family had made its initial fortune off contracts to light the city lamps at Cathair Dé and had added many other cities to their client list. Their holdings have grown through the years and built generational wealth with various small investments. *Ironic...* unlike the hard, cold surroundings of the estate, what had propelled the Vastras' rise to the méith class had been the soft warmth of light.

Juriahl shrugged at the notion and then discarded it. The Vastras were not known as a nostalgic family. They were made of firmer stuff, cutthroats of industry. When Juriahl had seen a chink in his rival's armor, he went in for the kill and deposed his cousin, Fuerian Vastra, as Margrave's successor.

The elf grimaced slightly as he continued stalking the corridors, hoping to catch any snippets of conversation from the house staff as to Margrave's condition. An amulet slung around Juriah's neck swayed with his movements and brought a grin to his face. The look of disgust on his cousin's face, when Fuerian had been ordered to turn it over, had been priceless.

Juriahl wished he could afford many more priceless objects—flair fitting for one of his standing. Only once he'd taken Fuerian's position did he realize the state things. Decade's worth of bad ventures and poor investments had left the family in a worsening financial condition, something Margrave had not let on to the rest of them. He was now one of only three sidhe to know the full extent of it—Margrave, *Juriahl, and Fuerian*.

Juriahl paced back and forth a few times in one of the hallways nearest his great-uncle's quarters. Margrave was nearly four-hundred years old, and his health was failing.

Turning his eyes to the paintings hung at the walls, Juriahl noted a much younger, vibrant looking sidhe. Margrave was the epitome of health in that image which had been commissioned nearly fifty years ago based on the date scrawled near the artist's signature.

He's gone soft since then... Given himself smaller and smaller shares of ambrosia every year from Oberon's table. If he forgoes his portion at this year's feast of Saol Nua as promised, he will not survive the year. Juriahl pursed his lips as he stared at the painting, wondering what famous artist he might hire to capture his likeness.

It would hang alongside Margrave's in perpetuity. *Good. He's had his time in the sun, and it's time for fresh blood.*

With a set jaw and a sudden pang of guilt, Juriahl exhaled through his nostrils. As excited as he was to finally take the reins of the family business, he hoped that his uncle could, deep down, at least get to see the child born to him and his young wife, Loitariel.

A smile played at the edges of his lips. Loitariel had turned out to be a boon. So far as Juriahl could tell, she had no history, no rank, nothing that would tie her to any other high-ranking family, or even one of the solid middle class, that helped rule out any kind of plant with ulterior motives. She'd been something of an orphan as best as he could tell, or as any of his private investigators could assert. Neither did she even have a presence in the aither, as was popular with so many of the younger fey.

Regardless, Loitariel proved an extremely quick study and Juriahl assumed she may have been caught up in some shady business in the past. Something might have made her jettison her previous life in its entirety—but none of that bothered him. Whatever risks she brought with her when he'd let her attach herself to him outweighed the rewards. Besides, once she tasted the ambrosia and all the other greater things that came along with a life of Méith status, there was no way she would ever sacrifice it. Juriahl owned Loitariel, lock, stock, and barrel. He was certain of it.

After a few more minutes of wishful thinking and envisioning himself receiving sudden news from a servant that Margrave had passed in his sleep, Juriahl turned and headed for his wing of the house. Juriahl's footsteps echoed in the hallway, a stark reminder of the barrenness of the empty corridors.

A long forgotten memory resurfaced. Juriahl remembered running through these passageways as a child. He was several decades older than Fuerian, and Juriahl's recollection of those early childhood years in this place had changed by the time Juriahl was twenty, but in his memory, the halls were lined with soft velvet furniture, end tables, and pieces of art.

When he'd been a whelp, the Vastras were not connected by business above all else. They'd also been a true family, bound by relationship and mutual ties that went far beyond business concerns. As best as Juriahl could tell, most of that had changed because of their méith status. Over time, they'd grown increasingly political... Each family branch argued over the smallest fractions of ambrosia, the thing that would give them increased longevity and health.

Juriahl thought about the fact he would soon be a father; it evoked several emotions deep in his gut. *Maybe that's why Margrave has been taking a smaller and smaller cut every year?* He shrugged. *Maybe the old ways were better... Maybe under my guidance, they could return?*

Margrave was the first family patron to have access to the stuff, and nobody quite knew what specific deed he'd performed for Oberon to secure their seat at the table so long ago.

He looked around. Many doors to many rooms lined the halls in this part of the estate. The main family heads had apartments here. In his childhood, Juriahl remembered many of them staying regularly. Given the backbiting in the politicking, those quarters were rarely ever used now except to sometimes entertain illicit meet ups that family members were oath-bound to never speak of.

Juriahl's steps seem to echo even louder here, reminding him of the great emptiness that had overtaken the family.

Then a door swung open.

Juriahl recoiled in surprise. "Wh-who are you?"

A hooded figure wearing a cloak stood on the threshold of a distant cousin's apartment. Only a pale, angular chin was visible. The creature flung himself toward Juriahl with unnatural speed and the thing's cold hands snapped around Juriahl's throat like a vice.

Juriahl choked and tried to cry out, but his mouth barely released anything more than a wet, pained gurgle.

"My name is Hymdreiddiech and I am here on your cousin's behalf," growled the intruder.

Juriahl's eyes bulged. *That bastard Fuerian has hired an assassin! I should have guessed he might try something like this—though I thought he'd have had the guts to attack me himself.*

And then his assailant released him momentarily.

Juriahl coughed with a ragged, wet gasp. "Whatever Fuerian is paying you, I can double it if you'll go back and murder him slow."

The black clad intruder stiffened and cocked his head as if entertaining the notion. "You would like me to do great harm to your cousin? I admit that I would do so gladly. I find him... a potential nuisance."

Relief washed through Juriahl, and he nodded vigorously. "Name your price. I will pay you half now and the remainder once the job is accomplished." Hate dripped in Juriahl's voice.

Moments ago, he had felt waves of nostalgia and benevolence. However, there was no such room for Fuerian in Juriahl's new world, and he would be glad to eliminate his cousin.

"Fuerian Vastra is a part of a larger game—a game which does not touch you," the intruder said, as if working through his thoughts aloud. "I plan to see his part in it ended, or at least vastly reduced. He is a wildcard. Unpredictable and difficult to control."

Juriahl nodded, feeling as if he'd built the slightest rapport with the assassin who had accessed his home. "Then do what you must in order to take him off the board. I will make it worth your time."

The killer's head bobbed from within the hood.

"I can't help but note that you haven't yet named a price," Juriahl said. "What is it?"

"I would do this thing for free."

A smile stretched warmly across Juriahl's face. *Finally, my pretentious cousin will get what he deserves and I'll never have to worry about his schemes again.*

And then Juriahl's grin vanished when the intruder snatched the chain holding the amulet around his neck and tightened it like a garrote. As he choked, the killer pivoted around to Juriahl's rear and pulled hard. He could feel the filigree metal biting into the flesh of his throat; it would leave a scarlet line, no doubt.

"Your death will take your cousin down by several notches," Hymdreiddiech promised. "As soon as I snuff the life from you,

I will destroy this piece of jewelry... which is fake, by the way. Fuerian still possesses the real one. If there is an investigation, it will be found in his possession and he'll spend the rest of his life behind bars."

Juriahl thrashed and struggled, clutching at the cord that promised his death. The effort was useless. His cheeks flushed red, and then purple, and then shifted even darker shades as he felt blood vessels bursting in his head and face. Still, he felt a sort of subtle satisfaction knowing that Fuerian would not benefit from his murder.

And then his vision faded, and he felt his life come to a close, as if drifting off to sleep. A horrible, nightmarish slumber from which he would never return.

Juriahl choked a final gasp, felt his larynx snap under the crushing pressure, and then his whole body fell limp. Forever.

The corpse on the floor had been cracked open like a fresh lime, rind mangled with juice spilled everywhere. Remy wrinkled his nose at the faint fungal odor as he crept silently through the door of the maginarius.

He narrowed his eyes at the cadaver. There had been flames last night, indicating some sort of recent attack. That data did not seem important to the body currently bathed in the burgeoning lights of dawn. Nothing again ever would.

Remy was no stranger to death. He knew that it generally took at least three days for a body to bloat and then deflate, expelling the noxious odors of decomposition, and that was the minimum. By the weekend, this place would smell as noxious as an old privy in dire need of lye.

Propping a rock in the pathway of the door so that he'd have enough light to operate by, Remy turned the body over and discovered that her abdomen had been shredded. She was human, and something had torn her open with a vicious gut-wound. "What a terrible way to go," Remy mumbled. Gut wounds were horrifically painful. *At least she'd died here rather than languishing for weeks as infection and stomach rot set in.* Now exposed, the odor of turning stomach bile made his eyes water.

Turning aside for a lungful of better air, he detected another aroma. The faint residue of fungal stinkweed was also present, but only traces of it. The cloying scent felt like gunk at the back of his tongue, but had little to do with the murder.

The body, a human female, was pretty, blonde, and looked strikingly familiar. He stared at her for a few moments before realizing where he'd seen her before. "She was one of Madadh's."

A few other human corpses lay strewn nearby. Blood splattered the areas where they lay. Beyond them, all the remaining corpses belonged to tuatha, most of them being sidhe. Judging by their garb, these were *aes sidhe*... spellcasters. Remy knew that Ollscoil Maginarius was a kind of preparatory school for potential mavens.

He turned his eyes back to the dead blonde. There was no way Remy would ever forget the face of the female lying dead on the floor.

She and a handful of other beautiful women had thrown themselves at Remy, offering to do whatever he wanted as long as he stayed with the company of humans, the Fianna. They'd wanted him to sire offspring with them—strong, healthy human babies for the community. Although Remy had declined, it was certainly something he'd remember forever.

Frowning, Remy stood and left her behind. He moved from body to body, checking each of them for a pulse. Remy did not find a single one. Whatever had inflicted such carnage had systematically and thoroughly killed every person, both human and fey, within the atrium foyer of Ollscoil Maginarius.

Remaining as stealthy as possible, he moved up the stairs and then through the campus, checking it room by room. In most of them, he discovered more bloodshed. Some beast had killed without compunction, hacking some of the bodies apart limb by limb.

Remy's mind reeled back to his time as Aderyn Corff, when the orcish warlord Rhylfelour set him upon eliminating a list of names provided by Rhagathena, the Spider Queen of the Rime Throne. Not even the unseelie had murdered with such apparent glee. He shuddered at the memories of what he'd done to escape the bonds of the Winter Court. *Only humans kill with such reckless abandon an obvious pleasure.*

He scowled, further examining the evidence. None of it quite made sense to him. So much gore... So much wanton destruction; it looked like a glory killing.

Remy ventured further through the corridors, noting where sprays of blood indicated a victim. Streaks of red marred the tiles where victims had been dragged into adjacent rooms and finished off with grisly scenes that greeted the duelist investigator.

"What kind of monster does this?" he whispered.

Finally, Remy pushed through a door to a large antechamber. It groaned as he opened it, complaining as if the entrance had been opened millions of times before, but never so slowly. Within, he discovered a display of such brutal, animalistic butchery that he nearly lost his stomach.

The room was an obvious lecture hall for students of the magi school. Desks lay overturned and smashed into pieces. While the furniture was barely identifiable, the flesh and bone of the victims were even less so. Crimson smears painted the walls, still red enough that they were a better indicator of the victims' time of death than the human bodies at the entrance. The uncongealed splatters had not yet shifted brown and still burned with vibrant cerise notes.

At the center of the hall, Remy found a mature he-elf. He'd been nailed to the floor, but flayed alive with his innards pulled out and stretched as if a victim of some monstrous dissection. His pointy ears had been ripped from his head and lay discarded nearby.

The poor creature's hands remained intact, and his fingers had clawed at the wooden floor to which a single nail had affixed each appendage. *He was alive when they did this.* Remy had no doubt that this elf had suffered greatly.

"He looks like the headmaster, or whatever they call the principal at a magi college," Remy noted, studying the aes sidhe's robes and the sigils of rank embroidered there. The elf looked vaguely familiar. Then again, with so much blood and carnage, all the faces had begun to blur together. *So many faces.*

A floorboard creaked behind him and the human stood, whirling to prepare for whatever he might find.

Too-late! A quartet of elves gang tackled him. They shouted as they beat him with clubs.

"Ddiymadferth scum!"

"We knew it was you all along, bastard of Adam!" screamed another.

Remy tucked and held his hands and forearms over his face to block any blows from doing irreparable damage. He kicked out of the scrum, knocking one of the aggressors back while shoving another to the side. Snatching one of them by the tunic, he slammed the elf to the floor, cracking his nose with a spray of blood as he rolled away and came up at his feet, brandishing his mystic dúshlán knife and taking a defensive posture.

The human duelist glanced down momentarily without moving his head and noted that the blade did not glow. He snarled, "Who are you?"

Another creak of floorboards signaled the arrival of another person. Remy recognized the face before he spotted the badge the elf wore—that *all of them* wore.

"Stand down! Stand down," the elf said. "I recognize this man... He's not the culprit we're after."

Something about the he-elf's commanding tone and presence made the other four take a less aggressive posture, even if grudgingly so.

"Captain Ochara, what happened here?" Remy greeted, wondering aloud at the same time.

The elf nodded curtly. He had been the elf detective to help put away Gareth Morass and, even though he'd not been required to, investigated further and discovered ties between Morass and the aithermancer Trishana Firmind. Ochara had put Fuerian's chief allies behind bars after an unbiased investigation. Ochara had earned Remy's trust because of that.

"It's me," Captain Ochara confirmed in the dim light. "You're Remy Keaton, right? The human duelist?"

Remy nodded.

"What in the fey happened here?"

"Morrígan's three faces... I have no idea," Remy cursed as he confessed. "I was escorting my ward back home last night and noticed signs that something was amiss at Ollscoil. I came back as soon as I got my employer safely home."

Ochara made a grumbling noise to indicate he accepted that answer as true, even if two of the constables under his supervision sniffed at the human's response.

Remy noted they had both made racist remarks about him during their initial clash.

The captain seemed to note the dissidence and pulled Remy aside, putting some space between him and the scowling constables. "You really don't have any idea what happened here"

Remy shook his head. "I only just arrived."

"Same here." Ochara frowned. "We had a few reports that something seemed amiss here last night. We waited until first light to investigate. Honestly, if the aes sidhe were ill-equipped to handle a problem, it's certainly not something a group of Cathair Dé's peacekeepers would be able to address."

Remy kept his mouth shut, but the way Ochara kept sweeping his eyes up and down him prompted a question. "You... do you think humans had something to do with this?"

The captain kept his voice low. "The Frith Duine has a lot of sway in these parts. They've lodged many complaints against human aggressors as of late. And nobody can deny there are several dead humans down by the doors." He squinted at the renowned duelist. "Only part I can't figure out is how a bunch of children of Adam would able to overwhelm this whole facility. I mean, many of these were highly trained aes sidhe. You ever know a mortal threat capable of killing several elven magi—some of them even being mavens?"

Remy tightened his jaw. His thoughts rushed back to the time he'd killed an elf spellcaster in the Faewylds. It had been single combat and Remy had beaten him handily. *Arcane abilities do not make one invincible.*

Ochara watched him for a response.

Remy could only nod. "It is possible for martial warriors to kill the aes sidhe. And I know this for a fact," he said without admitting to any personal liability. Deep down, he wanted justice for the victims of this slaughter. Even more, he wanted to know what had happened here... Why were humans involved?

At least I know who I can ask about it.

The elven constable merely nodded, acknowledging Remy's answer in the spirit that it was given. It made Remy like the elf more.

"Any ideas?" Ochara asked. "Feel free to speculate."

Remy shook his head slowly. "None that come to mind immediately."

Ochara sighed. "Any chance you'd be willing to consult on this case? Given our suspicions of human involvement, it seems like you'd have a vested interest in figuring this whole thing out."

"You don't think I'd try to spin it in order to absolve my species?" Remy asked.

Ochara frowned. "You've not given me any indication you might lie to me so far. Is it something I should be worried about?"

Remy sighed, shoulders slumping. "No."

"Good. Let's keep it that way." Ochara turned to his other investigators. "The duelist is helping us on this case. Give him full run of the grounds and don't interfere. He'll share whatever insights he might have with us later." He pointed at the two elves, who seemed unenthusiastic about Ochara's latest command. "Go and tell the other teams about my orders. Make sure nobody hassles the human."

When they didn't move to fulfill his orders as quickly as he'd hoped, he snapped at them, "Go!"

The detectives leapt into action and hurried out of the room while the others examined the macabre scene surrounding them.

Captain Ochara stepped closer to Remy but kept his voice low. "Perhaps you are unaware, and this information might lend you further insight, but someone... *something* has been abducting low level aes sidhe around the area. Whoever... *whatever* desecrated this place might certainly be the same thing."

Ochara paused as Remy gulped audibly. The human was aware that something had been kidnapping both aes sidhe and also humans—Thoranmir had stumbled onto those exact findings. Remy just had no idea what might be causing it.

The investigator stared at the disemboweled, tortured headmaster. "By the Dagda, I just wish I knew what could do such a thing to an aes sidhe—mainly so I can make sure to avoid it."

Chapter Six

Loitariel heard screams in the hallway and she leapt into action. Her bare feet padded along the cold stone of the mansion's corridors and she linked both hands beneath her swollen belly as she hurried.

She and her husband had been waiting for old Margrave to die, though she did not anticipate it occurring for at least a year, though Juriahl was ever hopeful of a much shorter timeline. Worry rose up to Loitariel's throat. *The shouts were much too close to have come from the old elf's quarters.*

It took only a few moments to find the source of the commotion. Two maids stood on either side of Juriahl. One sobbed uncontrollably, and the other looked around, panic pinching her face.

Loitariel hurried into their midst and examined the body. Juriahl seemed to have been dead for several hours, only now being discovered in the morning rounds of the house staff.

The weeping maid, who Loitariel knew had been in Juriahl's personal service for many years, stood frozen with shock. The only evidence that she was not a statue was the occasional wails she emitted.

Juriahl's throat burned scarlet, indicating an obvious murder. The more worried of the two maids paced a short loop. Loitariel sensed her fear: terror that whoever killed Juriahl might still linger nearby, deciding who the next victim should be.

Just as the panicked she-elf bolted, Loitariel shouted a powerful word, imbued with Arcadeaxn magic. [Stop,] she commanded in the olde tongue, the language of magic. [Silence,] Loitariel bound her tongue.

Both of the she-elves froze. Neither made any further sounds under the thrall of Loitariel's spell.

I am glad that worked, Loitariel mused. Magic that affected minds or willpower of another was tricky stuff. Many fey could resist such charms, but maid-staff were not well known for possessing firm resolve. *A fact that bothers me all the more, knowing the circles I run in.*

The former maven used the fresh calm to further examine the corpse. She bent to peel back the ruffle of cloth at Juriahls neck below where the scarlet line marked where the garrote had taken his life. As anticipated, she found his windpipe had been crushed. Loitariel noted that Margrave's amulet was nowhere on the body. That fact made her crook her jaw, but it was a concern for later.

Fretting slightly, Loitariel walked both lengths of the hallway to ensure that no other witnesses wandered nearby. Spying a doorway to one of the Vastran apartments, she used her command of the two maids and had them drag the body within to hide it for the time being.

Loitariel knew that her position was not yet solid within House Vastra, and it would not be until the child was born. *Nothing is certain nor safe... If someone has killed Juriahl in order to force a different chain of leadership, then I could be easily deposed should Juriahl's death be made public.*

Her hands splayed across her abdomen and she felt the child stir within. Loitariel arrived at her decision quickly. There were many magical means available for her to make the corpse disappear permanently, and Loitariel planned to come back later and do so once her focus had improved.

She turned to the maids, both still under her enchantment. [Return to your duties. You will remember nothing that has occurred within these last fifteen minutes. Your only recollection will be preparing for work, performing your daily, mundane duties, and nothing more.]

"Yes, Lady Vastra," both she-elves said in rote unison.

And then, with automaton-like movements, both maids exited the room. Once she was alone, Loitariel nearly collapsed from the adrenaline rush of a disaster averted.

It is not an averted disaster; she realized. *Just a mitigated one.*

The future heir of House Vastra pushed outward from within her womb, using some limb or another to make Loitariel's skin stretch and bulge slightly. And then Loitariel formed her plans.

Morning had barely arrived as Fuerian led Gareth out of the city. The portly elf beamed, obviously pleased to be out of prison. That he was in Fuerian's company as he drove a fancy hovercar was a bonus.

"Calm yourself," Fuerian said wryly, "or I'll have to hire a replacement for my murdered guardian."

Both fell silent at the reference to Naz Charnazar who'd died a year prior. The akasha-powered vehicle moved silently upon a cushion of air, as if it slid upon nothing at all. Portable magitech was powered by batteries that had been charged with the powerful energy source; the larger mechanics, such as the hovercar, consumed a great amount of akasha, marking it as a symbol of great wealth.

But I can stow this on-site at my apartment's largest storage locker, rather than needing to trudge off to get my horse. Actually, *I probably* should *replace Naz.*

Gareth finally broke the stillness. "I'm just happy that you brought me into the fold on this, Fuerian. You need friends more than you could know."

Fuerian glanced at him. "That may be true," was all Fuerian would say.

He'd left Trishana sleeping at his apartment. She'd taken Fuerian's lavish bed and not allowed him any complaint, locking the door behind her, and claiming she'd take a week's worth of rest before she planned to emerge.

They traded glances. Both seemed to silently acknowledge the fact that the business they found themselves caught up in, both the production and distribution of dream hallow as well as raw akasha, was dangerous, and fraught with powerful players who knew the game better than they did.

Fuerian looked at his friend of so many years. After his time incarcerated, Gareth was still chubby, but only just barely. He had the sort of girth, now, that only the most elite elves had: those who'd trained their bodies to pack on the muscle mass that seemed to come easier for the sons of Adam. Gareth looked like he could overpower many adversaries, sidhe ones, anyway, with brute force. However, Fuerian knew his skill with the blade could far outperform whatever raw strength the newly muscular elf could produce.

Gareth had, however, proven his loyalty. He could have bartered for his freedom with the lawyers. Gareth wasn't stupid, but he was clearly *not* the mastermind of the criminal operation. Instead of flipping, he'd held his tongue and taken the full sentence—certain that his friend would rescue him with the judicious application of coin.

The Vastran elf merely grinned at his larger friend and his hands clutched the controls of the magitech vehicle while he pushed the throttle higher. Fuerian winked at Gareth, eliciting a look of pure joy on Gareth's face.

"It's you and me, Fuerian," Gareth insisted. "Together until the end."

Fuerian nodded slowly, hoping he hadn't miscalculated and made a long-term mistake. *If nothing else, I can always set him up to take the fall for some future scheme if I need to get rid of him.*

"So, where are you taking me? What lies beyond the outskirts?" Gareth asked.

Given the added speed, the cart hummed with a slight shudder as Fuerian steered it. *Maybe it's best not to invest too much into magitech transports until they improve.*

He glanced backward to reassure himself that he had additional akashic charges deposited in the storage area which doubled as extra seating. This craft had been used once before when some mysterious force had sent a sluagh to kidnap Jaira Morgensteen; Fuerian had been still betrothed to her at that time. Whomever had been in control of the undead thing—which took the form an elf Fuerian had killed in a previous duel—had never been discovered.

Remy Keatonhad caught up to them when the machine ran out of akashic power and rescued the girl. Fuerian made a mental note to always keep a fresh cell to ensure he wouldn't be left stranded like Remy and Jaira had been on that fateful night.

"We shall arrive shortly," Fuerian promised. "Let's not ruin the surprise."

Gareth sat on the edge of his seat, eager for the big reveal.

Something niggled at Fuerian's conscience. A sourness rasped deep down when Fuerian thought all the time Gareth had lost. He'd suffered in prison for a year on Fuerian's behalf. *Is this what guilt feels like?* "Fine. I'll tell you."

Fuerian reminded the elf about how the akasha was produced. The horrific ordeal that Hymdreiddiech put kidnapped mages through, a torturous ceremony. It included feeding the victims a dose of foil milferra, causing convulsions, sweat, and vomiting. It also resulted in both akasha and the drug known as dream hallow. Gareth had been there, along with Naz, when Fuerian first observed the process.

"Yeah, what about it?" Gareth asked.

Fuerian flashed him a grin. "How valuable do you suppose foil milferra could be in the grand scheme of things?"

A light grew behind Gareth's eyes. "Doesn't that stuff only grow on ferrous ore?"

Fuerian nodded. "Who do you think now owns the region's largest iron mine... Not that we can mine the metal, mind you." Fuerian grinned. It was a statement, not a question.

"You son of a bitch." Gareth smiled broadly.

"I thought you might like to see what I've been up to in the year since they hauled you off... You know, so you could see I hadn't really abandoned you to the horrors of the bastille. I was busy here, and hoping you'd build the kind of connections necessary to move the dream hallow before I came to your aide," he lied.

Gareth barely paid him any heed and watched the shifting road ahead of them as the mine took shape in the distance.

"That's odd," Fuerian noted as they arrived. He put the vehicle into its shut-down sequence. It slowly squashed the cushion of air beneath the under-carriage until it rested upon the ground.

"This place is supposed to be running around the clock," Fuerian said, mostly to himself. He'd become accustomed over the last year to keeping only his own company.

The mine was quiet, however. No sounds of industry, nor of life.

Fuerian scowled and then checked the power meters of the hovercar. He pulled a lever to eject a depleted cell and replaced it with one of the freshly charged akashic batteries.

Gareth tilted his head and waited for an explanation.

The mine sat silent in the morning rays of sunlight.

Both sidhe strayed from the mobile contraption and crept more closely into the staging area outside the mouth of the cave which served as the mineshaft's entrance.

Someone had chained a redcap outside, confined by a set of bonds that anchored him to a massive stone. Their approach stirred the groggy powrie, as if from slumber.

"You," commanded Gareth. "What happened here?"

The redcap yawned in the middle of the elf's question, making him repeat it.

"I saw everything," he admitted, resting his eyes upon Fuerian.

"Why are you chained to this rock?" Fuerian asked. From the corner of his eye, he noted a symbol painted with pitch upon the boulder.

The powrie shrugged, making his chains jangle. "The foreman didn't like my attitude."

Fuerian frowned, but nodded. His crime must not have been too severe. He'd already seen what his taskmasters did when they thought a slave had outlived his or her usefulness. "Out with it, then. What happened? Why has my mine gone dark?"

"Your new lightstarved arrived yesterday, scary fellows. They'd been so beaten by their unseelie masters that no hope remained in their eyes. Only just been integrated into the workforce when a pack of monsters arrived and set them all free."

"Free?" Fuerian asked. "How so?"

"*Free*," repeated the redcap, pointing to a pile of chains lying near the cave's entrance.

A brow arched on Fuerian's face. "Only the foreman had the keys to those manacles. He knows his life is forfeit if he released them."

The powrie laughed with a raspy voice. He merely pointed to a nearby ravine where Fuerian's workers tossed refuse.

Gareth hurried over and glanced into the pit. He turned back, ashen-faced, and looked as if he might vomit. Meeting Fuerian's eyes, he nodded uncomfortably.

"How many? How many fey did we lose?"

Gareth looked back only briefly. "I dunno how many you employed, but all of 'em by my best guess. Not much left over, either... Might as well have put them through a meat grinder."

Fuerian worked his jaw as Gareth returned. "I'll have to find more slaves to supplement the workforce. We have... contracts," he said, not wanting to share the depth of involvement by the dark maven with Gareth. His nostrils flared, "*And* I supposed I'll need to hire security.

He turned back to the chained powrie. "You called them monsters? I can't help but notice they released the humans and made it a point to slaughter the sidhe—but left *you*."

"They may have come to free slaves, but they only wanted humans in their ranks," said the redcap. "And I think they left me here, so you'd know who took your slaves."

"Name them."

"Bunch of humans who called themselves the Fianna."

"But you called them monsters," Fuerian said. "I have heard of these Fianna. They are humans. Ddiymadferth."

The redcap cast him a shrewd look. "My current point of view? Elves are monsters, too."

Fuerian paced a few steps, shaking his head. "This could certainly impact timelines for my plans. We need every last worker we can get in order to work the mine. Workers capable of enduring exposure to iron are best," he told his companion.

Gareth nodded slowly. "I may have made a few new underworld contacts while incarcerated. At least one guy I made friends with knows some under dwellers who might come in handy. Miners."

Pinching his brow, Fuerian noted, "Coroniaids cannot touch the cursed metal, either."

"Deeper fey," Gareth said.

"Trow?"

Gareth shook his head. "*Deeper.*"

"The dvergr," Fuerian guessed.

Gareth nodded. "But they do not work cheap and it may prove cheaper to purchase all new human slaves."

Fuerian shrugged indifferently. He stood in front of the giant rock and the sigil painted upon it, abandoned in the wake of the Fianna's raid. It was the symbol of the Frith Duine, but with a large X through it.

The redcap chuckled below his breath as he watched the mine owner's displeasure.

Quick as a flash, Fuerian's blade slashed outward from its sheath, slicing through torso and neck with a spray of carotid blood. The unseelie tuatha tipped over, shock locked onto his face.

"More slaves it is," Fuerian growled, without even looking at the creature he'd just murdered. "Fucking ddiymadferth."

Along with Captain Ochara, Remy finished touring the neighboring hallways of the maginarius. Everywhere they turned they found macabre scenes of grisly red. Finally, they grew close enough to the entryway that Remy found a half dozen sidhe detectives from Ochara's office.

Investigators drew sketches and wrote detailed notes. At least one of them had a magitech recorder, powered by an akashic charge and tethered to a wall-mounted aitherport so that detailed images of the attack could be recorded with perfect recall and stored in the aithersphere for the duration of their investigation.

The human frowned. He was not a fan of the aither after a bad experience long ago. The astral realm was a plane of thought and will, but aitherspace was more than mere data and will; it was possible to become disconnected from one's body while in it, and *that* led to certain death. *Untethering, Anya had called it.*

Remy looked away from the bustling scene and back to the captain.

Ochara held his gaze. "You really do want to know what's going on here, duelist?"

Remy nodded gravely.

"Perhaps you can pull on different insights. We will be busy in this section chronicling the attack one quadrant at a time." Ochara looked away. His eyes followed the two sidhe who'd given Remy grief earlier.

The captain had not said it aloud, but Remy understood what he meant. *Some of these sidhe I am with are Frith Duine sympathizers... Perhaps even members, and they'll pin this murder on the Children of Adam if they can. If you want to find out what really happened, do it now, while we're busy.*

Remy and the constable's eyes met momentarily. The human knew in an instant that Ochara wanted nothing to do with the Frith Duine.

"Thank you, Captain," he said. "I'll be sure not to disturb anything I find and report directly to you should I discover anything noteworthy."

Ochara bobbed his head stiffly, dismissed the human, and then turned back to manage the systematic chaos of a forensic investigation. Remy slipped away without further word.

He ventured deeper into the campus of Ollscoil Maginarius. Remy'd already seen the carnage at the front end. He wanted to see what it looked like further within.

As Remy penetrated the central areas of the main hall, he found the scenes much unchanged. Offices and classrooms had each been hit hard and fast by a creature, or more likely creatures, of ferocious power. Remy's mind flitted through different types of monsters, cataloging them and entertaining or discarding them based on the knowledge at hand.

A single monster of great power might be able to do such damage. He remembered the troll beneath the bridge which had helped him destroy the shade that had taken Jaira. The seed of dread stirred slightly in his gut; Remy never discovered who or what had been controlling the sluagh.

He decided the murders had to have been multiple creatures. A troll the size of Skreekuzz would not have been able to move through these halls. In order to have eliminated so many of the aes sidhe in one fell swoop, the attack had to be fast. *And they would have to have some kind of magic resistance or countermeasure.*

Remy knew that *he* possessed some kind of spell resistance he'd always chalked up to the presence of the dúshlán that he carried. Fetiches often carried an anti-magic component. His had once deflected direct, powerful spells before. *Another mystery for another time,* he reminded himself. Given how his memories had been erased when in the faewylds when he was a child, there was plenty about his past that he did not know—and likely never would.

Remy rarely dwelled on odd circumstantial happenings surrounding his life.

Pausing at a wide spray of blood, Remy crouched and examined it. Droplets were thin and scattered broadly rather than falling in thick, spurted globules. Cast as a wet field across the polished stone floor, the splash of red had recorded footsteps from the attackers. Remy had to assume it was the attackers since most victims appeared to have died before they could take more than a few steps.

The footsteps were slightly larger than any man's, and smaller than a troll's. Narrowing his eyes, the duelist tilted his head as he memorized the shape in the blood. It appeared both human and animal at the same time.

Curiouser and curiouser. He explored the halls deeper yet. Half of the akashic light emitters had been smashed, bathing the building's interior in intermittent darkness.

Another thing that tugged at Remy's comfort meter was how many of the spellcasters were killed. *Thoranmir and I had been looking into the disappearances of aes sidhe. It doesn't make sense for the same forces who have kidnapped so many to suddenly start killing them. This must be something different.* He paused and entertained the thought of an internal schism within Suíochán Naséan. *An arcane civil war? The Solais Cloaks could have pulled off an attack like this... But they wouldn't have left the place like this, would they?*

Remy frowned and cast that notion out. Not only did the Radiant Tower have a strict hierarchical system that would discourage such a thing, but that kind of split could only lead to apocalyptic chaos, and there was nothing anyone could do about it. *High-pow-*

ered arcanists slugging it out behind the scenes could literally burn down Arcadeax and invite in the outsiders lurking at the gates.

He shuddered at the premise. It had been the primary plot of the Great War between the Winter and Summer courts. If the mad Spider Queen Rhagathena wanted to ignite a new war and crack the gates, as some had wanted Wulflock to do thousands of years ago, there was little anyone could do to stop her... Besides taking up the mantle of Aderyn Corff and killing another fey queen.

It would not be the first time I've had to do so.

Remy scowled and ventured further. He was just one man, and taking down the whole of the Unseelie Kingdom was beyond his ability. *Best to focus my investigations on where I can have an impact and take it from there.*

Doors powered on the left and on the right. Signs labeled each and every one: *Janitorial Closet, Evocation Track 301, Office of the Dean of Abjuration.*

Then Remy found a door with no placard upon it whatsoever. He narrowed his eyes at the barrier. *Curiouser, indeed.*

Remy pushed his way through the door to discover a nearly sterile laboratory. Its pristine condition was marred only by a single sidhe corpse lying atop a long bench with an iron plate resting upon it. Blood had leaked to the floor and pooled there from some grievous wound the attackers had given the victim.

Intrigued, Remy shifted the body off of the dark, forbidden metal. The sidhe was shirtless and his shredded garment lay nearby. When the body fell to the ground, it hit with a heavy thud that splattered congealed blood onto the floor, Remy saw the elf's back.

The skin that had been in contact with the ferrous slab so long it blackened and bubbled, festering worse than any plague Remy knew.

"It's a mercy they killed him," Remy said. And then he whirled when he heard a shuffle at the back of the room. His hand found his dagger in an instant, even though Remy didn't remember drawing the dúshlán.

Creeping toward the set of cabinets, Remy steeled himself, took a hold of the handles, and flung the doors open.

A young fey child screamed and held his hands up defensively.

"Please! Please, don't kill me!"

Remy stayed his blade and watched the elf boy for a few moments.

The young elf had thin arms and legs and a gaunt face. Remy would have thought the boy to be in his early teen years, and perhaps he was starved? *No, he's a tylwyth teg,* Remy realized once he spotted the longer, pointier ears. They protruded at a flatter angle, rather than the upturned, shorter points of the ellyllon's sidhe cousins. The ellyllon were generally of a slighter build, although they were often times taller than regular sidhe. The boy looked very tired.

"What is your name, boy?"

"A-Arawyn. I... I was a student here. And then... And then..." Terror overtook Arawyn's face as he trailed off.

Remy lowered the knife and extended a hand to help the young tuatha out from the cabinet. Arawyn moved stiffly as if his legs had long since gone to sleep while he'd been hiding.

"Arawyn, did you see what happened here?" Remy asked.

The young caster set his jaw, as if trying to decide if he could trust this human or not.

"I'm not here to hurt you," Remy promised, sheathing his dúshlán. "If I wanted to, I could, and I would have done it already."

Some of the panic bled out from Arawyn's expression and he slumped. He didn't look like he had enough energy to resist if he'd have wanted to.

Remy repeated the question. "Do you know what happened here?"

Arawyn nodded, though he refused to meet his rescuer's gaze.

"You saw it?"

Another nod.

Thinking back to what Ochara had implied and how some of the constables had connections with the Frith Duine, Remy bit his lip and made a difficult decision. *I cannot turn this boy over until I know everything he knows. Until then, I must protect him... For the sake of my kind, I must keep him safe.*

Remy crouched to the teenager's level and placed a hand on both of his shoulders. "Arawyn, I need you to trust me. I have to get you out of here in order to keep you safe. I have to know about whatever monsters caused this, but you can tell me about that later. They are gone, but there are other bad guys here, now. Will you trust me enough to lead you out of here and into the city? Can you do that?"

"I got nowhere else to go," Arawyn admitted. "And everyone else I know is dead."

Remy's lips stretched thin with an expression of compassion. There was no way to help that at the moment, but he could, at least, save Arawyn.

"Come with me. I've got a safe place in Cathair Dé," he said, and then he led the aes sidhe postulate out the back of the maginarius before anyone could be wise to them.

Chapter Seven

The morning sun had already crept into the sky as Remy stole across the campus with Arawyn hurrying behind him. The route kept as much of their visibility obscured as possible from the main area where Ochara's investigators did their work, and Remy kept as many other structures blocking the lines of sight as he could.

Bodies littered the lawn near the rear of the maginarius as much as they had the interior of the buildings. Remy ushered Arawyn into the stables and was grateful to find that none of the animals had been killed. Only the sidhe.

He sighed with relief, knowing that he'd taken a long shot. "Arawyn, can you ride?"

"I know how."

"You look exhausted, though. Are you capable?" Remy asked.

The ellyllon nodded enthusiastically, as if he were eager to get away from so much death.

Remy threw a saddle on the nearest mount and buckled it for the younger rider. "Go out the back and ride around toward the front. Stay out of sight if you can, and if you can't, act casual, as if you're just passing through on a convenient route. I'll meet you just past the gates; my horse is over there."

Arawyn nodded and then climbed into the stirrups.

Remy hurried away from the structure that housed a dozen or more animals and cut through the yard. He passed the investigators quickly. Ochara tilted his head quizzically, but the duelist merely shook his head, indicating nothing more lay beyond the main foyer but additional death and destruction.

The detective's face collapsed into a grimace, but he nodded and returned to his work, letting Remy depart. Soon after, the human cleared the entrance and found his horse where he'd left it and got into the saddle.

He felt bad about lying to Ochara, even if by inference, but he didn't want to delay even momentarily with the boy out of his sight. With a steady gait, the horse clopped past the main gates of Ollscoil Maginarius. Only seconds later, Arawyn emerged from the nearby foliage.

The younger rider fell into cadence alongside Remy and they traveled side by side. With the brilliance of the morning sunshine now beating down upon them, something in Arawyn's countenance brightened, though Remy figured it had more to do with the distance they put between them and the site of so much carnage.

Once they'd gone a good distance, Remy noted, "You are wildfey; all of 'em that I've ever encountered are good at hiding. And I've known many of the ellyllon."

Arawyn's eyes narrowed. "You've known many of us? How so?"

"It's a long story. I'm not sure that we have time for it."

The sidhe youth squinted at him, tightening his hands on the reins is if tempted to crack them and send his horse into a gallop. "How do I know I can trust you?"

"You mean other than the fact that I didn't kill you when I found you?"

Arawyn nodded slowly, his eyes still filled with distrust. "There are many reasons to keep someone alive. Some of them are worse than death."

Remy grimaced. His thoughts turned to that elf he'd found lying upon a slab of cold iron. He sighed with reluctant admittance. "Okay. Let's see if I can shortcut through the bulk of my story until later." The duelist's horse slowed as Remy tensed.

"My tale is not exactly a secret, although it's not widely known that it belongs to me. It's mostly just rumor, still. I mean... The things I went through to escape the unseelie are still being discovered by Rhagathena and by Queen Maeve."

Arawyn's eyes widened. "You know about the queen? Mab was murdered by unseelie assassins several years ago."

Remy nodded. "So, you know about Aderyn Corff?"

"The Death Bird," Arawyn told him. "Everyone knows about him, at least in the faewylds. He killed Queen Mab. Rhagathena sent him on a mission of murder and he struck her down in front of the entire Wild Court. Aderyn Corff is famous."

Remy choked on a laugh. "Yeah. He did that, I guess... It depends on how you look at it, kid."

Arawyn shot him in the askew look. "He's famous. A fiend in the night, trained to kill on orders from the Rime Throne. Parents tell their children stories of him to make them behave... but *I know he is real*. I was there in Capitus Ianthe when Mab fell. That was before... before my parents died and I wound up here."

"*Morrigan's three faces*... How old were you? That was years ago."

"I was very young, but I remember snippets of the night. Especially Mab's atomie drawn carriage," Arawyn said, looking over Remy skeptically. "You... you were there?"

Remy shrugged, but followed it with a slow nod. "I kinda had to be. I was the big bad boogeyman. Your memory might be fuzzy on many details, but killing a fey queen is no small task, and I can't forget it if I wanted. Mab herself had a significant hand in arranging the whole ordeal."

"You are Aderyn Corff." Arawyn did not say it is a question.

"I am... *was*," Remy admitted. "There are very few who know that for certainty, but it is true. Surely Rhagathena has heard rumors I still live, but if she knew it for a fact, she would send as many assassins after me as she could afford. I wronged her greatly when I made my escape."

"You broke an oath?"

Remy's lips stretched thin as he grimaced. "It was more than that. I slaughtered the entire council of the Demonsbreak warlords, the ruling caste of orcish champions... And then I destroyed her invasion force near the Solstox Canyons."

Arawyn's eyebrows rose so high that Remy thought they might leap off his face. "You are responsible for raising The Iron Wall?"

"The Iron Wall?"

"For seeding the bridge with ferrous shards so that travel is difficult."

Remy shrugged. "The name is news to me, but fitting. Yeah. I did that." He looked far off and away, thinking back to what it had cost him—what else, *who else*, was lost in the final explosion.

Arawyn spoke, shaking him from his reverie. "Okay."

The human cocked his head. "Okay, what?"

"Okay. I'll trust you."

Before Remy could ask him further questions, Arawyn told him everything about the attack: how his classmates had tried to kill him, how the wolves had slaughtered everyone at the maginarius, that their leader was someone named Oddur, and that they called themselves the Fianna. They'd come so hard and fast that none could fight back.

"Were they immune to magic?" Remy asked him.

"No," Arawyn told him. "But they had some kind of incense that they burned. They started many of the bundles upwind and the fumes made it difficult for aes sidhe to cast spells."

Remy's brows furrowed with thought. "What did it smell like?"

"Stinkhorn," Arawyn said. "Do you know what that is? It's a nasty kind of mushroom that looks like a stiff and slimy cock but smells more like unseelie assholes."

Despite the darkness of the situation, the kid's candor nearly made Remy laugh. Arawyn reminded Remy of Thoranmir in that way. "Yes. I know it." Remy's throat stuck with momentary dryness.

"It's called dallineb weed," Arawyn said. "I had a lot of free time to read and only knew about it because it was in one of the mavens' libraries at the Maginarius."

Remy filed that information away in case he might ever need it. He confirmed, "You are certain it was the Fianna?"

Arawyn shrugged. "I can't say for certain. I just know what they were called by that elf they tortured with iron."

"Did you hear the name Madadh mentioned at all? Think hard; it's important."

After a few moments, Arawyn shook his head. "No. The only name I ever heard said was Oddur's, and he was clearly in charge. Actually, now that I think about it, there were some other things they said. Something about a mine owned by the Vastra family, and it seemed like someone else had come and tried to stop the attackers. The Fian Faolchú, they called them. They were also Fianna, but I don't know what any of that means."

Remy tightened his jaw. "I don't know for certain, but I have an inkling. It's kinda how you are a Tylwyth Teg, but also an ellyllon. All Ellyllon are Tylwyth Teg, but not all Tylwyth Teg are ellyllon. Make sense?" He did not drag out the analogy further; the ellyllon were also sidhe, but not all Tylwyth Teg were, and Remy didn't know much about the Fianna but inferred there were factions among them.

Arawyn nodded.

"Good. Now keep your head down as we get closer to the city. I've got to find someplace safe to keep you."

"Are you going to find these Fianna and demand justice?" Arawyn asked. An expression on his face subtly implied that it would be a terrible idea for him, even if he was the notorious and capable Aderyn Corff.

Remy sighed. "I might have to, but I have friends among them, I think... I hope." He looked at the young aes sidhe. "They didn't, uh, happen to mention anything that gave you any indication where they might be at present?"

Arawyn shook his head.

"Shit. That means I'll have to search them out."

As the city took shape in front of them, Remy told him, "No mention of humans or werewolves from here on out. Your life may depend on it."

The boy signaled his agreement with a gesture, and they quickened their pace.

"Before anything else, let me ask one final thing," Remy said. "Have you heard any other rumors about disappearing aes sidhe or humans?"

After a moment of thought, a light seemed to ignite within the youth's eyes. "They said something about that when they were in the woods, trying to kill me. It sounded as if these Fianna wanted revenge for kidnapping humans. They did not say much, except that they were aware it was happening. However, I'd heard rumors about it at the maginarius when I first arrived. I don't know how true they were, but staff told students to use all due caution, especially if leaving the dormitory during in evening hours. It was never important to me, though. It was really only a concern for the older students who sometimes traveled into Cathair Dé to experience its night life."

Remy blasted a hot lungful of air through his nose and nodded. They arrived at the outskirts of Cathair Dé. "All right. No more word on the serious topics for now."

"And you will take me someplace safe?"

The human made a sour expression. Unwilling to make such a big ask of Anya, and with his current home decidedly unsafe, Remy had one other place he could ask. He nodded. "I am certain it's safe there. And I'm sure you'll be well hidden where I'm taking you, but it's not going to be pleasant for me to ask."

Wrapped up in an impossibly soft robe, Trishana Firmind flopped backwards and onto the hotel's downy bed, which practically enveloped her as she landed. She'd insisted that Fuerian rent her a private space until she set up shop and got a place of her own. Stealing his bed the previous night was a calculated ploy to get his agreement on renting her a room.

She knew Fuerian well and knew how to play exactly within the boundaries of what chivalry he had. That meant she knew exactly how to play him. Perhaps, she'd borrow Fuerian's spare room, later, or bunk with Gareth until she was able to call in a few other favors and get back on her feet.

Fuerian's apartment was more than adequate to put her up. However, Trishana desperately wanted her privacy. She'd spent the last year surrounded by other incarcerated fey. More than anything else, she just wanted the ability to piss in private, away from greedy eyes searching her for weakness. Bladder evacuated, she planned to succumb to the bliss of the hotel's creature comforts.

She'd just taken a hot bath and felt clean for the first time in over ten months. The hotel was fancy enough that it had an akasha drip that heated their tubs. It's why Trishana chose this particular establishment.

Presently, her washed hair lay splayed across the top sheet. Trishana didn't care that the bed was getting damp. She'd slept in such worse conditions that thoughts of a wet spot barely registered.

With a loud sigh, she stretched out and turned herself over, enjoying every soft tuft and plush rumble of the fabric.

A knock at the door made her kick her legs over the edge of the bed and hurried to answer it, bare feet padding on the ground and leaving wet prints. Trishana had ordered room service earlier and opened the door to find everything delivered as expected.

An attendant stood outside the door with a rolling cart that contained the items she'd requested. Beads of sweat upon the tray's cover promised the meal below was still hot. On the shelf below it, Trishana spotted an aitherdeck and other peripherals that she'd asked for which would let her into the aithersphere.

Bending low, she checked them over and found them satisfactory. Trishana grabbed the cart and pulled it into her room and refused to glance back at the hospitality staff, who remained outside the door with his hand extended. She closed the entrance on him. Trishana didn't feel bad about it, although she didn't have any coins, anyway. Everything on this bill was being sent straight to Fuerian.

Her eyes scanned the walls as she searched for the aitherport to jack into. Many different people, some of them wealthy and powerful, owed the aithermancer favors. Once she called them in, she could reestablish her life and go back into business. But first she needed to confirm she still had access to her security policy: a cache of dirt she'd gathered on those various contacts. That data had been stored safely in her protected corner of the aithersphere and as long as it was still there, she'd be able to start a blackmail scheme that would put her back on top.

Trishana's stomach growled, and she parked the cart next to the desk-mounted port and then turned to lift the lid from her tray. A tall, hooded figure stood at the opposite end, causing her to jump with surprise.

She screamed, but no sound came out. Trishana felt the vibrations in her throat and opened mouth. She realized the intruder was using magic to deaden all sound.

Recoiling, Trishana backed up a step and found herself pinned against the wall.

The hooded figure brandished a black cloth sack and a rope. And then he rushed at her, hooding her head and blinding her.

Midday had come and gone by the time Remy had deposited Arawyn in the care of two trustworthy individuals. He then navigated his way through the major streets of Cathair Dé and arrived near the central marketplace square where many vendors sold their wares, and where the open dueling area was.

Remy had no desire for further bloodshed this day, but he'd strayed into the area in search of a tuatha he thought might have some insight for him. Finally, he spotted the old woman with long ears and mottled skin covered with patches of mottled olive green.

Hazimon was exactly as Remy remembered her. She appeared to be a homeless, elderly she-elf, though Remy knew her to be a dryad, in fact. Nearest a dark alleyway, she sat at the edge of a tattered blanket upon which she'd set out her wares.

Most of her trinkets were valueless things she'd made or acquired; she possessed little of value but refused to take charity. Remy believed she had to have been an incredibly proud person in her prior life.

Her eyes brightened as Remy approached and crouched near the edge of her carpet. He picked up a couple of the trinkets and eyed them appreciatively. Pocketing them, he tossed several coins onto the blanket, grossly overpaying for them.

"Sir, that's far too much," Hazimon insisted.

He shrugged. "You can make it up to me by providing information I need, then."

She squinted at him as if reluctant to make a deal. "And what if I don't have answers for you, or if you don't like my answers?"

"Then your part is complete. Just because I don't like the information or if the answer is that 'you do not know,' you will have provided exactly what I asked for. It is an answer, all the same, provided it is truthful," Remy said.

An amused light played in her eyes.

These fey and their love of transactions.

[I shall speak the truth if I know it,] Hazimon promised in the old tongue.

Remy noted appreciatively. "I am looking for someone."

"Again?" Hazimon teased. "This seems to be a recurring problem for you, Remy Keaton. Who have you lost now?"

He smiled, though it did not reach all the way up to his eyes. He'd first met the old dryad on his first foray into the city with Thoranmir in search of Eldarian. "Let us hope this is the last time, then."

"Pardon my interruption. Please, continue," she said.

"Some time ago, there was a group of humans off the road past town. I know they travel and often pass this way. I have reason to believe they've been in the area recently in which to pay my friend a visit. He is a member of the Fianna. Do you know them?"

Hazimon nodded solemnly. "I know *of them*."

"Do you have any idea where they might be?"

"I've heard rumors," Hazimon said. "I do not travel very far nor very often. Not any longer... not since..." She trailed off and frowned.

Remy knew what she meant. Unlike other tuathan elf species, the dryads were both easy to kill and almost immortal. Every dryad's life force was tied to a specific tree somewhere. Allegedly, Queen Titania had, as either punishment or out of jealousy, cut down Hazimon's tree, but then refused to let it die, keeping a section of root alive out of spite, drying her up and withering her beauty and youth and forcing the old she-elf to languish in the gutters.

The duelist scowled and shook his head. He had more than his fill of angry, jealous fey queens. Remy caught her eye, and she continued.

"I cannot promise you the information is accurate, but I can provide directions for you to follow."

Remy asked, "What's the source of your information?"

"Just idle chatter I picked up. Speak the infernal name, and he shall appear." She sighed, citing an old adage. Her eyes locked suddenly onto a wagon that pulled into the square near the edge of the dueling boundary-posts. A group of elves rode upon the flat bed and shouted as loudly as village criers.

"The Frith Duine," Remy growled, identifying them at a glance.

Some of the members of the anti-human hate group had meandered away and into different parts of the crowd as their leader shouted his rhetoric. "Say it with me. 'No more humans! No more humans!'" The sidhe who'd spread out as shills started chanting along with the speaker. Elves whose clusters they'd infiltrated started copying them, not wanting to appear contrary.

As the shouting dwindled to a dull roar, the crier shared a story, practically yelling so he could be heard. He shared a tale about an upstanding, middle-class he-elf whose wife had become obsessed with a human who was more than willing to commit acts of sexual deviance with her against the husband's wishes.

"I am no prude," said the Frith Duine speaker, "and I even understand the attraction. Nobody can deny that the sons of Adam are often broader of chest and have thicker biceps. Ladies, we men can relate. We all love tits. Well, most of us, anyway," he remarked, drawing self-incriminating laughter from several of the sidhe near the fringes. "And the daughters of Eve tend to grow busts larger than seasonal melons!"

More laughter, though the speaker's face took a sudden flinty edge. "But do these *creatures* think it acceptable to cuckold their betters?" Many of the he-elves shouted and hissed. "If it can happen to an oibrithe," he named the middle caste, the largest segment of the city's population, "then it can happen to any of us."

His eyes scanned the crowd as it gathered in around him. "I'll not sit as judge over whatever sort of carnality you each enjoy. To each your own. Fuck whomever you want as often and in as large of a group as you think best, but this oibrithe whose story I share did not consent to sharing his wife with an… *an animal*. And that was why I set him free for killing the human."

Standing next to the dryad in her alley, Remy swallowed the lump in his throat. "I think I recognize him."

Hazimon nodded dourly. "That is Elethiel Ciníoch, the local magistrate." She scowled, flaring her nostrils. "He's been very popular with some of the saibhir. He's now making much headway with the oibrithe and it is rumored he will make a bid for the governor's seat of Cathair Dé on the next election cycle." She frowned. "That could spell bad news for your people," the dryad said. "Although you'd probably be fine given your station as a celebrity duelist."

But Remy was barely listening to her. "I *do* recognize him." And then Remy's eyes locked on the low-cut neck of the elf's tunic. He spotted a large birthmark peeking up Elethiel's neck.

Behind the dryad, the Frith Duine kept shouting. "I could not sentence a fellow sidhe for enacting justice upon a lesser creature—for snuffing out one of these... these *ddiymadferth*. It was that experience that led me to becoming one of the first members of the Frith Duine. I encourage anyone wishing to preserve the integrity of our species and our culture to do the same!"

"It may be best for me to get out of here unseen," Remy told Hazimon.

She nodded toward the alley, which Remy knew would allow him to slip away quietly. "The Fianna are out past Baile Dorcha. Do you know that village?"

Remy grimaced but nodded. He'd been there before. "I heard it's been repopulated after... the deaths."

"I have heard as much." The dryad gave him instructions from Baile Dorcha to the last known location of the Fianna.

"Best of luck, human," she called after Remy as he made a quiet exit.

Chapter Eight

Remy's horse ambled at a slow gait. He'd followed Hazimon's instructions and made sure to take his time looking for signs of the Fianna's camp.

When they'd first met, Remy had stumbled upon them almost accidentally. Half-starved in the wake of a "lesson" that Fuerian and his thugs had taught him, he'd awoken a long distance from home and starving after floating downriver.

With his mind straying to the memory, Remy hoped that Jaira and Anya were safe. He'd checked in on them after returning from the market and his meeting with Hazimon. Neither had been home at the time, and he'd barely had words with his sleepy wife in the pre-dawn hours. Neither of the she-elves knew what he'd discovered at Ollscoil Maginarius, and he'd barely had a moment to himself since he and Kent left for Saibhir Gaoithe many days ago.

Come to think of it, even the night beforehand was fraught with incidents—Elethiel Cinioch had been spying on me for those Frith Duine bastards... I think I need a nap.

Remy smelled meat roasting over flames and licked his lips. The aroma was faint, but unmistakable, and he followed his nose in the direction of food. He'd barely left the road when a spotter shouted from the trees.

"That's close enough, Adam!"

Remy held up his hands but dismounted. He called, "Pretty good eyesight from such a distance to spot my ears." He searched the tree line until he spotted a camouflaged human male holding a bow with an arrow nocked. "I am a friend of the Fianna. Madadh knows me."

The scout narrowed his gaze at Remy. "Of which faction?"

Remy scoured his memory. Finally, he said, "*Not* Fian Bairn."

"Fian Faolchú or Fèidh?"

Grimacing, Remy shrugged. "Listen, I don't have any clue. But I'll gladly wait here until Madadh arrives if you'll go fetch him."

The scout glared down his nose at Remy and growled. "Fine. But don't come one step further. I am not the only scout hidden here and each of the others has a bow trained on you."

Remy's eyebrows rose as the human scrambled down the tree and darted deeper into the forest. *Either he's an excellent liar, or those other scouts are very well hidden.* He paused a moment and recognized that both thoughts could be true.

A few minutes later, Madadh arrived, along with the scout. The sentry shrank back as Madadh hurried out to greet his friend with a broad, warm grin on his face.

Madadh was half a head shorter than Remy and sported curly, dark hair and an equally wild beard. "I told you when last we parted that I felt certain we'd meet again." He rose to his toes as he embraced the duelist in a grappling hug. And then, shifting on his feet, he turned to wave off the scouts who had been posted nearby.

"Stiffer security than you had at our last encounter," Remy noted. Rustling leaves in the trees marked the locations of the remaining shooters; as they relaxed, they finally became visible.

"We've, uh, had some recent excitement. It has forced us to keep our guard up," Madadh said. "Please... join me for dinner, won't you?"

Remy sniffed at the air and nodded. "I wouldn't miss it."

Anya steered her akashically powered wheelchair toward the main storefront of a business in the more affluent part of Cathair Dé. The signage across the front read *Ionad Imports and Exports*.

She took a deep breath as she read the title. "This is for you, Thoranmir," she said quietly. With a puff of vapor, a whine emitted from her wheeled seat and Anya headed for the door.

Ever since her brother's death, she had done her best to champion the causes that Thoranmir had believed important. The crippled elf had even gone so far as to complete an oath he'd made with a gang of street ruffians, even if the power of an oath in the olde tongue did not bind her to it after Thoranmir's death.

Of course, Anya had coordinated with Captain Ochara and used the encounter as a way to help the constables gather the last scraps of evidence needed in order to arrest the entire group of dreamhollow pushers. Thoranmir had been very keen to get the drugs off of the street—and Anya agreed with him on that. She had been in the aither, trying to hold poor Eldarian Cócaire's fragile psyche together, when she saw the effects the stuff had on the spirit of its users. The encounter had not gone well, and the strung out sidhe's very soul disintegrated in her grasp.

That Ochara's investigation had also pinched Trishana Firmind, Anya's primary competitor and social rival, had been a happy accident. *Nothing happy about the whole thing,* she decided. No matter what good had come out of the incidents surrounding the duel, she'd still lost her brother, and Arcadeax was worse off for it.

In Thoranmir's honor she'd sent a regular stipend to support Odessa, Eldarian's sister, who Thoranmir had been attempting to woo. It wasn't much, but she felt sure it helped. Odessa lived in Vail Carvanna, and Anya preferred it that way. Seeing her regularly would be a constant reminder of what Anya had lost.

Also in her brother's honor, she looked into the mystery of the disappearing children and the aes sidhe. The fact that humans had been going missing had already been known to her, but she'd learned a great deal more about the kidnapping of magically gifted fey in their search for Eldarian. He was the only one to have been found alive, to Anya's knowledge—though he'd died before more could be learned.

Anya was one of the top five most gifted aithermancers in the region and that meant there was little that could stop her from finding information stored in that plane. Information was scarce in the sphere, but that was a far cry from nonexistent. Her research had led her to believe that Ionad had dealt in trafficking humans, and that was as good a lead as any if searching for missing humans.

A bell jingled on the threshold as she struggled with the door. An attendant on the showroom floor hurried over and helped her manage the barrier, welcoming her in.

Anya had worn her finest clothes for this particular event. These had been purchased new since her previous wardrobe had been destroyed in the fire on the morning of the fateful duel.

The clothes seemed to have the desired effect. A fine blouse shrouded with a jacket of crushed velvet and gilded seems made her fit in with the posh crowd that made up this business's regulars. She'd rolled up her slacks and pinned them near the stumps of her legs with fine brooches.

"Greetings, my lady. Welcome to Ionad Import and Export. Are you looking for something in particular, or are you just here to browse our showroom? We have many exotic pieces of art and rare items, both modern and from antiquity."

"I... uh... I am looking for something in particular," Anya told the she-elf helping her.

"Might I know what that is? I should be able to help you, and if I don't have what you desire in stock or in our storage area, I may be able to procure it. How should I address you?"

Supplying an alias, Anya nodded and glanced around the showroom suspiciously. She steered past the partition wall that acted as a small gallery of valuable items so that she could ensure no others were present who could eavesdrop.

Finally, the legless elf turned to the attendant. "I was told that customers could purchase certain items through your services."

"We have acted as an agent for many different buyers and have a whole variety of items." The agent lowered her voice. "I'm not sure what you have heard, but I can guarantee discretion above all else."

"I would like to buy a human slave," Anya stated plainly, but quietly.

The attendant flashed her with a furtive look. "You know that such a thing is illegal. Slavery was outlawed three hundred years ago and only those non-sidhe who were slaves at that time remain in service. I'm not sure where you might have heard that we—"

Anya cut her off. "I meant no malice or disrespect toward my request or with my desire." She motioned toward the stumps where her legs should have been. "This comes more from medical necessity than from someone who's simply lazy and desires a life of ease."

The salesperson said nothing more, but she tilted her head. Anya took that as a sign of sympathy.

"You are looking for a caretaker that you could own... like a trained pet?"

Anya nodded slowly, careful not to show any emotion on her face lest her disgust slip in.

"I have heard of these arrangements before, though I'm afraid we can't help you without some kind of a referral. Can you supply me with one?"

Anya checked her timepiece, and then nodded. "My dear friend, Mrs. Pompero, said that she could supply you with one. She told me this morning she would send a message to you today via the aither."

The aithermancer had done her diligence and her research of the place. She'd followed a trail of rumors in the aithersphere that indicated Mrs. Pompero, a wealthy sidhe from the saibhir caste, was a customer who had purchased a human from Ionad. By all indications, it was no mere rumor.

Saibhir fey were mere degrees from being méith. They had all they could want except for the favor of Oberon and Titania—which meant they remained mortal, aging more slowly than the sons and daughters of Adam, but with a keen knowledge of some future expiration. The prevailing méith envy led to many saibhir, like Mrs. Pompero, to use the sphere to build up a larger than méith persona in the aither as a way to compensate, earning figurative accolades and a pseudo-life in the sphere.

Anya had timed a message to have delivered from Mrs. Pompero's account, which Anya had breached in the last few days. Everything about the message, except for its contents and the fake name Anya had made up for the endorsement, would pass a sniff test. She was not overly worried about Ionad looking too deeply. They were a business and therefore interested in profit.

The attendant slipped away to access an aither device, leaving Anya to contemplate Ionad's dealings.

While owning humans was not illegal, purchasing them was outlawed three centuries prior. Because those slaves' legal status had been grandfathered in, nobody looked too closely at the laws and there were *many* loopholes in the rules of the Summer Court. On paper, humans apparently lived forever and document pushers doctored deeds with regularity, assigning new, younger replacements to slave certificates which became, effectively, licenses to own otherwise-illegal servants. The worst punishment ever doled out for breaking the rules was a simple fine; a steep financial penalty paid to the throne, but nothing that came with incarceration.

Most humans were free in the Seelie kingdom, although their numbers were not overly large; few members of mankind in the Unseelie were free, but they were popular in none of the realms.

"Ah, yes. I found Mrs. Pompero's message," said the worker as she returned. She looked around the gallery, double checking Anya's conclusion that there were no other folk about who could eavesdrop. She removed a piece of magitech from below the front counter and activated it.

The thing, mostly tubes and an interlocked, rotating cylinder, glowed with a slight aura as it worked. Anya recognized it as an interdiction vault, a machine that expelled any presences that might be eavesdropping via astral means—many aithermancers of merely average skill could access parts of the aithersphere that fixed to physical locations in Arcadeax. The aither was as endless as a dream, but it also contained the entirety of all places, as well... except when someone used an interdictor to prohibit access to it.

After securing the establishment, she asked, "How soon would you like to make this purchase? I will need a few details in order to get one from my supplier."

"What is the soonest timeline possible?"

The worker bit her lower lip as if afraid of losing a sale. "I should think two or three weeks."

Her supplier must be from the Unseelie. Anya hid her frown. *That means this is a dead end for the local abductions. Unless...*

"Our ownership team has a special friendship with Titania. It allows us certain access to trade across the rift and bypass customs. The queen really has a distaste for ddiymadferth," she explained. "Are you looking for any age range or gender in particular?"

Anya shrugged. "I really don't know much about them. What can you tell me?"

The salesperson said, "In your case, I would recommend an older child. Prepubescent, but on the verge of adolescence. You want one capable of doing the work you require of them, but also young enough that he or she can be trained. I suggest not sparing the rod. Remember, these creatures are not tuatha. One must not spoil them lest you make them untamed."

"I'm not really even sure what they eat? Are they expensive to maintain?"

She grinned. "Children tend to eat less. That's an additional bonus, for sure. I feed my houseboy table scraps. In general, they'll eat the same as what you might feed any pet. But we ought to discuss price; a deposit would be required for us to begin."

Anya offered her a false frown. "I am not a grossly wealthy oibrithe, despite my friendship with Mrs. Pompero, but I feel this purchase is a necessity as I age."

The she-elf nodded. It was not uncommon for fey of different castes to fraternize with each other, provided they were within one rank. Many well-to-do oibrithe were friends with saibhir, but it was rare for an oibrithe to be in a méith's regular social circle.

"Because of all the benefits previously mentioned, ddiymadferth children are typically in greater demand. A typical adult costs a noble, and a capable child sells for a mark. There is some wiggle room on the elderly or the very young."

Both denominations were units of gold, with the mark being slightly larger and equal to one hundred silvers. Most arcadeaxns considered an average income for an oibrithe set at one noble per month.

Anya wondered aloud, "What use would anyone have for them at either end of the spectrum?"

"Mostly it is... unsavory," the she-elf said.

Anya sucked in a breath to keep her anger in check. "Would it be possible for me to use your aitherport?" she asked. "I should double check my accounts before I bother taking up additional time from you."

The elf female motioned with a hand and ushered her near. She pulled free a cord for additional length and handed Anya the deck and interface peripherals. So long as Anya was wired directly from within the interdiction vault, she could bypass it as easily as someone with a key to a door.

Anya fumbled with the equipment, pretending she was only passingly familiar with the most basic of the components. "Apologies. I'm not very good with technology... with one obvious exception." She motioned to her akashic mobility chair.

The worker smiled politely; no warmth reached her eyes, and she glanced away. Anya's mention of her disability had the exact intended effect: it put the worker off-guard and focused anywhere but on her.

"I shall just be a few minutes," Anya said apologetically. "It's always a struggle for me to use the sphere." She pulled the hood onto her head and rested the eyepiece on the bridge of her nose.

Anya did not need the visual input device to parse the aither, though any novice certainly would. Her skills were far beyond those of most aithermancers except for those with mystic abilities who were capable of entering the plane without a technological port—that meant either arcane abilities or pharmacological assistance, and neither tended to spherewalk for functional purposes, but rather for religious ones or as a pleasure seeker.

As soon as Anya had jacked in, she flew across the planar space with god-like precision. Ionad's stronghold looked like a castle, and Anya recognized the design. *One of Trishana Firmind's builds.* Without bothering to verify, she knew where to find all the place's weaknesses and exploits.

She disabled security protocols with ease. Faster than a blink of the eye, she gained full access to Ionad's records, history, and transactions. Accessing loads of personal data stored in their aither-based stronghold, Anya felt the exhilaration of the mental exercise.

After she'd lost her legs in a horrific accident as a teen, she discovered her aptitude for spherewalking, for parsing the aither; she'd always believed that her mind had shifted, redeveloping new skills that would have otherwise been necessary to run physical limbs that were no longer there. She did not know if she would consciously choose her skills over having legs, but she was grateful for her abilities. It was a moot question, anyway, and not worth dwelling on, in her estimation.

Anya scanned lists and customers and their invoices. Lines of numbers scrolled past her as she compared business deals to profit and loss. Ionad Import and Exports' books were open to her.

She found one recent entry for Fuerian Vastra. The subheading read *Old Morgensteen Mine* and the invoice line listed *ddiymadferth*, sixty times, followed by *powrie*, three times. The cost and revenue of each ddiymadferth was listed as eighty silver, which everyone knew was the value of a gold noble, and Ionad's ledger claimed a profit of thirty-eight silver, three shillings, seven pfennigs, and three eights. Powries were much less valuable.

Scowling, the aithermancer had at least learned one thing today: that Fuerian had purchased several humans to work his mine. She was just about to leave the sphere when she spied another name she recognized. Much further down in the books she noticed Xander Kent. *Her employer.*

Anya looked closer. There was no company name listed, and no label to the invoice. Only a financial note and a date more than a year prior. She could not tell what sort of transaction had occurred, or if any had. The note read *thirty-eight silver, three shillings, seven pfennigs, and three eights.*

Squinting at it, she furrowed her brow, knowing that her actions in the sphere would not be shared by her body; Anya was too talented an aithermancer for that. But she could feel the elf import worker shuffling about nearby in the physical world.

Anya risked only a moment longer and peered more closely at the possible transaction. There was nothing more, and a quick scan of the ledgers had no other mention of Xander Kent or any companies of his that Anya was familiar with.

She pulled out, acting slightly dazed as she did so, and met the she-elf's expectant gaze.

"Well? What were we thinking? Shall I process an order for you?"

Anya frowned at her and pretended to be flustered. "Apologies. Hopefully, I might return in a month or two. My financial standing is not quite what I remember it being." She shrugged. "I have a joint account and my heir appears to be outspending his stipend. Allow me two months to rectify that, and I shall return," she lied.

The sidhe bowed and then opened the door for her.

Anya steered her chair through it and out into the streets, leaving the business behind and feeling dirtier for having been within it.

Remy followed Madadh through the woods and emerged at their encampment. Carriages with canvas affixed to hooks helped create rudimentary tents where they were tied off to trees; collapsible lean-tos were erected, and both horse and oxen milled near terret and tongue. Madadh's camp looked as if it could be packed up and moved on a moment's notice. Remy found it much as he'd seen before, except that the joy of the place seemed absent.

The last time he'd been among the Fianna, they'd been a happy group of nomads enjoying life in the company of each other, thriving despite arcadeaxn oppression. No longer did they seem a group of wild, plucky nomads. Their eyes had darkened, and the tables had more than mere food—sword, bow, or halberds leaned near each bowl of stew. Axes leaned against chair and stump—but not the kind used for woodcraft. Those were battle-axes.

As Remy turned to look back at Madadh, Remy noted many faces. Some of them he recognized. Some of those had wounds added to them. Scars puckered with fresh pink and stitches held flesh together from recent injuries.

That explains the dour expression so many of them wear.

"Madadh, what happened here?"

Madadh took a seat adjacent to Remy and slid a bowl to him. Both were filled with stew. "The Fianna are at war."

Remy tilted his head and shot his friend a shocked expression. "At war? With whom?"

"With itself." He caught Remy's bewildered expression. "The Fianna have different factions within our number. My pack is the Fian Faolchú. There is another pack in the faewyld called the Fian

Fèidh, but we seldom have contact with them outside of formalities." He sighed and then spoke as if weary. "Fian Faolchú has been the leader of the Fianna for many generations, but Oddur, a man who leads the Fian Bairn, has called for schism."

Madadh held Remy's gaze with cold eyes. "He attacked us when we... *intervened* in his recent, local activities."

Remy nodded. "I saw her."

The Fianna leader angled his head and furrowed a brow.

"The blonde. I remember her because she'd thrown herself at me the last time I visited."

Madadh nodded. "I remember... And I wish you had taken our offer, though I understand you are now married and have taken a different path. But had you been with us at the maginarius, perhaps the magi would have survived."

Remy's brows rose. "You went there to save the aes sidhe?"

"More or less," Madadh admitted. "We have no love of the aes sidhe. In fact, we suspect Suíochán Naséan is involved in the disappearances of so many local human children, at least to some degree."

"Have you recovered any of them?" Remy asked.

Madadh nodded solemnly. "We have. Those ones have endured great tribulations. I fear our inducting them fully into our number..." He trailed off as if stopping himself from sharing too many details. Remy knew the man was cagey about their tribe's details. Madadh had told him last time, then if he shared certain information, Remy would never be allowed to leave. "Those recovered are... damaged... bent toward hatred in their minds. The Fianna are meant to follow a secret path—it would be unwise to set a broken person upon."

Remy nodded knowingly. "Let me contribute to their support as I have done before." He held up a hand as if to forestall any argument. "Providing for their care is a burden we must all share, and I have both the heart and the means to help."

He dug into his pocket and searched for a handful of coins to donate to Madadh's cause. As he fished out a fist full of money, a silver band of metal came out with it and tumbled to the ground. Remy took Jaira's earing with him everywhere. It was a constant reminder of her, and how he'd won the she-elf over. *Actually, it was she who won* me, he mused—she'd intentionally lured him with the lost earring.

The tumbling jewelry came to a stop near Madadh's feet and he bent to retrieve it. Picking it up, he paused mid-motion and winced, releasing it and recoiling with a pained hiss as if it had been hot.

Glinting silver in the light, it fell into the grass near Remy.

Remy recognized it for what it was. "You're... you're not human. Not truly?" He stated it as much aloud on impulse. His gaze narrowed as he looked over his friend.

"I'm rather surprised it took you this long to figure it out." Madadh sighed and gave him a tiny shrug. "Though it may be more apt to call us *more than human* than just as merely human."

Remy studied Madadh a moment longer and then glanced at the other Fianna nearest them. "What are you, then?"

"We are... gifted. Touched by the moon." Madadh gave him a serious look. "We are the fáelad. The wolf folk."

"You're, uh, not going to force me to stay and join you for telling me, are you?" Remy revisited the terms of knowing such things.

Madadh shook his head. "You are asking very specific of questions. You would've learned the truth of it before long. I thought it best to speed the process up in hopes that you may be able to help us." A placid expression formed on his face. "We shall consider you a *friend of the fáelad*."

Remy nodded slowly. "This Oddur person... is his pack also a group of fáelad?"

"Yes. And I fear they have acquired a taste for blood."

The duelist grimaced. "Do you know why the Fian Bairn is set upon violence?"

"Oddur and his pack have long wanted war with the fey. It seems he's found the proper excuses for it and told many of us that the fey courts have begun sacrificing children again in order to satisfy the hell tithe. The blood of our offspring has being used to keep the devils at bay," said Madadh.

Remy shook his head slowly. "That's a lie. You know that, right?"

"I suspect you're right," Madadh told him. "But do you have proof?"

"Not exactly," Remy said. "But I know Rhagathena—I worked under her in my younger life. The unseelie spider-queen *wants* the black gates to the infernal realm opened. She's psychotic. There's no way she's made sacrifices to keep the hell tithe paid and keep the gates shut. Besides, neither Winter nor Summer has paid the tithe's blood requirement since the Great War."

"Such is the rumor," Madadh said.

Remy walked through the logic of many widely known rules of magic. "Which means that King Oberon has been exhausting a great deal of his arcane power every year to ensure that the Infernal Black Gate remains closed, since he does it without the support of the Rime Throne." He scowled. "His brother, King Wulflock, had been in agreement with him on that matter, at least."

Madadh sipped the stew while he watched his friend talk. He finally asked, "You are sure of this?"

"Positive."

"Good. So am I," Madadh told him. "I actually know where many of the stolen children have gone."

Remy arched one brow.

"They are in the area, in fact. Many children are taken as slave labor and pressed into service; we know a group was sold to a local mine. Because they're human, they can touch the iron within it." Madadh fixed the duelist with a serious expression. "Will you help us reclaim them?"

"I... That depends. What sort of opposition will we encounter?"

Madadh splayed his hands. "Much. The sidhe rarely give up what they believe is theres. We also anticipate that Oddur will make a play for them once he learns of their presence." He bit his lower lip. "I am sending scouts to investigate the rumors first. We shall launch an attack in a few days."

Remy squinted at the man. "It seems to me that you and Oddur are aligned on that, at least. We all want the children saved, don't we? Who cares who rescues them?"

Madadh set his jaw. "If the children go to Fian Bairn, they will be made into ferocious monsters and turned back upon the sidhe to seek retribution."

The fáelad leader sighed wearily. "There is a delicate balance between us and the fey. Should we fall under the watchful gaze of Oberon, he may decide we pose too great a threat and send his armies upon us, eradicating our existence—and not discerning between other humans and those who are... like us."

With eyebrows knitting, Remy watched Madadh stand and begin to shift forms. Normally shorter than Remy, Madadh stretched with pops like cracking joints as his arm grew, elongated. It looked painful, but within moments, his arm transformed into that of a hulking, lupine monster. Muscles rippled and dark fur bristled; claws gleamed sharply upon fingertips. He'd limited the change to the one arm, but it had grown significantly longer than Remy's.

When Madadh spoke, his voice came out as a low grumble, as if it pained him to transform only fully and demanded concentrated effort to hold off fully assuming one form or the other. "The worst part is, Oddur has gotten his claws onto weapons made of silver. Blades that harm his own kin, much how iron wounds the sidhe."

Remy clenched his jaw and stared up at his friend. "I... I will help you if I can," he promised. "Where is this mine?"

"On the outskirts of Cathair Dé. It is owned by Fuerian Vastra."

Anger flashed through Remy's eyes like lightning. "Well, you should have led with that fact."

Jaira sat on a pillowy seat in the drawing room of her parents' home. She had not been by often to visit ever since the wedding. She looked around as she sat across from her mother. "Is father home?"

Lady Eilastra shook her head. "Your father is here, but he is otherwise preoccupied."

Jaira nodded slowly and looked the Morgansteen's new maid over. The younger she-elf smiled at her with a twinkle in her eye and Jaira recognized the gardener's daughter, a woman about her age who'd help arrange Jaira and Remy's earliest encounters. The sidhe did not have many prospects in life and a position as a maid in a méith house was a serious step upward for her.

"Thank you, Liara. That is all," Eilastra said as the maid placed a tea service on a tray between the mother and daughter.

Liara curtsied and then departed.

Jaira watched her go. "She seems very good at her job."

Eilastra offered a noncommittal shrug. "She's good at serving tea and a few other things, but she's still learning. This is all very new to her. Your father sponsored her training, and she's a quick study."

"That is good," Jaira said, her expression melancholy at the mention of her father, despite his efforts at charity. Harhassus

Morgensteen had been dead set against her marriage to Remy, though he had not quite delivered an ultimatum. If he'd threatened to disown his only daughter for going through with the wedding, he'd have been sorely disappointed. *Thank the Dagda for small miracles.*

Jaira and her mother made small talk for several minutes while they sipped their first cup of tea. Neither addressed the fact that Jaira had barely spoken to them since the marriage. Such a thing was not uncommon with newlyweds, anyway, Jaira had figured.

When their visit failed to progress beyond conversational pleasantries, Eilastra tilted her head and looked over her only child with piercing eyes. "Liara's tea notwithstanding, what truly brings you here today?"

Jaira bit her lower lip for a few moments and then sighed. "Am I so easy to read?"

Eilastra smiled wryly. "Not particularly. But I am your mother; I've learned how to read you over the years."

After a few moments spent composing her thoughts and emotions, she turned her eyes up to her mother's. "I need your advice. For years now, I have rejected your efforts at getting me to play a larger role at court." She made a hand motion to calm her mother, whose expression turned suddenly wary at the notion of the ddiymadferth-lover trying to gain attention in Oberon's court. "I know what you're going to say."

"Oh, I don't think you do," Eilastra said, with words that felt deliberate, yet restrained.

The daughter continued, "What you want to say, what you really *should* say, is 'I told you so.'"

Jaira met her mother's gaze. "After thinking about it long and hard, I don't think I have any other choice. I must find a way to gain Queen to Titania's favor before word reaches her."

"Word of what, exactly?"

Their eyes met and Jaira's did not waver. "Mother, I am with child."

Chapter Nine

Gareth stood at the forefront of a group of brigands he'd hired with Fuerian's money. Fuerian had given him an operations budget and put the ex-convict in charge of the mine as the new manager. Half the ruffians were former accomplices who'd escaped sentencing, arrest, or both during Ochara's roundup of the dream hallow gang. The rest of his staff were made up of either old friends who Gareth knew he could trust, or new contacts that he'd made while stuck in the bastille.

He and his group each wore short swords at their hips and also carried baton-style clubs for keeping their workers in line. Of course, when Gareth had taken over, there *were no* workers left to harvest the foil milferra.

Today was the day he succeeded where the previous foreman had failed.

Emerging from the trees on the outskirts of the Vastra mine approached a rider upon a shire horse, one of the largest breeds that could be tamed. The green-skinned creature in the saddle curled a lip to expose yellowed teeth, and he wore a broad hat.

Hooked to the orc's saddle gear was a web of straps and chains. The massive shire horse dragged the crowd of slaves behind it, manacled to several adjacent lines. They couldn't struggle against the binders with the power of that much force.

Like many of the non-sidhe tuatha, orcs had a distinct tie to one part of Arcadeax; they were unseelie. This one bared his teeth at the captives behind him while glancing over his shoulder. "Welcome to hell." He growled. "You've all arrived at your new home."

Gareth and his company moved to intercept the slave dealer. He did not like working with orcs, or any other of the winter fey for that matter, but these had been already been sent to shore up the weaker-than expected workforce. Hymdreiddiech had seen to it after he and Fuerian had their disagreement. Gareth had still been in prison, but Fuerian had given him as much information as necessary for him to get his output goals met.

And a good thing, too—even if that shadowy aes sidhe gives me the creeps. The mine has been silent for days now, with no one to collect the fungal reagent... Even with these new workers, we'll have to work them hard to catch up and make the quotas.

"What are you looking at?" the orc barked from his seat atop the high saddle.

Gareth turned to address the creature and found him berating one of the sidhe members of his gang. The elf wilted, trying to downplay the incident.

"N-nothing."

The orc snarled, but none of his other utterances were in languages that Gareth knew. Below the unseelie fey's wide-brimmed hat, Gareth spotted what must've been a sore spot for the orc... quite literally.

A boot-sole shaped burn marked much of the creature's face with a nasty wound. Gareth did his best not to stare at it. *Only one thing could have caused such a severe and detailed injury: iron. By the looks of it, this orc had been kicked in the face by an iron boot.*

Only one species in all of Arcadeax was known for their iron boots. Powries... redcaps. They were nasty goblinoids that looked like feral human children and had a thirst for both blood and mischief. Gareth knew they were incredibly difficult to tame and even more difficult to manage. However, they *could* touch ferrous metals.

Gareth spotted one of the tiny creatures near the back of the pack of humans. His short stature made him stand out, and the elf recognized the thing right away as one of them. Its iron shoes had been removed, and the powrie had been forced to walk all the way from the Winter Kingdom while barefoot. The powrie's feet were bloody and injured; old scrapes had scabbed over on its legs, belly, and arms where it had fallen and been dragged over the last few days.

A cold-hearted glint in the orc's eyes revealed exactly how much compassion the slave taker had for his cargo. *None.*

Gareth's gaze spotted two other orcs and three winter sidhe, all males, rounding out the slavers' caravan. The others hung near the rear, acting as spotters and prodders in case any of slaves in the chain gang needed encouragement to pick up their pace. Something about the way one elf carried himself made Gareth assume he was aes sidhe.

"My name is Syrmerware Kathwesion," the mounted orc announced. "You may have heard of me. Who is in charge here?"

Raising a hand in stepping toward the slave taker, Gareth welcomed him. "I am the foreman and authorized to act on Fuerian's behalf."

"Good. I would like to complete this transaction as quickly as possible and then get back to my side of the canyons," Syrmerware Kathwesion said.

Gareth squinted at the orc. His survival in the prison had forced him to develop a good bullshit detector and something in the orc's timbre made him think Syrmerware was lying... or maybe it was the response to those words by his crew. *I don't really care, as long as I get possession of the cargo and send them away.*

"An intermediary arranged this delivery, so I shall want to inspect the workers," Gareth told him.

Syrmerware Kathwesion glanced around the area; a scowl plastered to his face. "Whenever I find myself in the Seelie..." He paused to inhale a deep sniff through his nose and then grimaced as though he'd tasted something foul. "I always find it... lacking."

Gareth ignored the insult. He was more than ready to be rid of the orc, even if he was grateful for the labor force. "Let me see what we have to work with and then our business shall be concluded."

Five lines of eight workers were tethered to each chain. All were human except for the lone powrie at the rear. Each of the ddiymadferths were mature; most looked either past their prime or were emaciated. That many years of hard labor tended to make them compliant. Their skin looked much too pale to be natural, as if they'd spent years below ground or cloistered away as they toiled for their previous master's whims. Most of them wore a nasty scar on their face; the flesh was ridged and white where they had been branded by the slaver in years past—a mark of their capture in the wild. The redcap's brand was still ringed with fresh pinkness, however. *He must be a new acquisition.*

"These do not look particularly virile," Gareth noted.

"The condition they were ordered to be in was merely stated as 'alive,'" said the orc. "These lightstarved are alive *and* broken so as to be compliant."

Gareth pursed his lips and nodded slowly. *Older ddiymadferth are able to work longer and require less coddling,* he convinced himself. *And are probably least likely to revolt.* "Fine, fine. If it means will have fewer issues with insubordination, then I suppose it is a trade-off worth making."

Syrmerware Kathwesion chuffed with grating laughter. "You don't know the half of it, elf."

Gareth tilted his head as the orc explained his reasoning.

Tilting his hat further back upon his head, Gareth spotted the full extent of Syrmerware Kathwesion's festering flesh. It had indeed been an iron marking.

"One of the more rebellious prisoners I've ever taken blistered my face permanently when he escaped with a damned powrie." As Syrmerware Kathwesion turned to glower at the red cap down the line of chains, he growled a name. "Remy Keaton... I owe that ddiymadferth a brand." He pointed to the redcap. "And you will want to watch *that one* as well. Powrie are difficult to teach—they usually die before they understand a slave's only lesson: don't fuck with your masters."

The orc massaged the skin right next to his foot-shaped injury and then retrieved a cloth bag from the furthest saddle bag at the rear and tossed a sack to the dirt. It clanged, giving away its contents: a pair of iron shoes. "If he gives you any trouble, I recommend you kill him right away."

Gareth did his best not to let emotion or recognition reach his face when the orc mentioned the human duelist. He *hated* Remy Keaton, the ddiymadferth responsible for getting him locked up. At least it was true the way Gareth understood it. He didn't owe the Winter fey a damned thing.

Syrmerware Kathwesion waved a hand at the rest of the humans. Their shoulders slumped and their spirits were clearly beaten. None even lifted their eyes to Gareth and his gang of enforcers as they came for them.

[I, Syrmerware Kathwesion, have faithfully delivered on a contract agreed upon with the strictest of confidence and prudence, obeying all provisions of my commission,] the orc spoke as if reciting a memorized piece written in the olde tongue. It would not have mattered if it was. Even rote recital in that language had power—it was the language of magic.

The elf bobbed his head and spoke in the old tongue as well. [I, Gareth Morass, accept the results of this transaction and consider it complete on behalf of my employer, Fuerian Vastra.]

Syrmerware Kathwesion nodded deeply once, and then inserted a large key into the lock mechanism at the rear of his saddle. The bolt fell away, and the chains dropped to the ground, only barely startling the massive horse who supported the orc's bulky frame.

After tossing the key to Gareth, Syrmerware Kathwesion took up his reins and turned his horse while signaling to his companions. Moments later, the delivery crew filtered into the woods on a course for their home somewhere across the Solstox Canyons.

Or maybe they're going elsewhere... but that's not my problem. Gareth nodded to his enforcers, and they hurried to push their new acquisitions down toward the mines while shouting orders.

"I hope you're all ready for some work after your little stroll," one yelled, clubbing one of the lightstarved across the rear of one leg, causing it to buckle. The slave barely yelped any complaint. He merely righted himself and continued onward, too beaten down for complaint.

Gareth snorted with mild amusement. "We might make our quotas, after all."

Jaira waited for the shock to pass from her mother's face. She recognized a momentary look of disappointed resignation, but Eilastra's expression quickly shifted to enthusiasm.

Eilastra hid her emotions well, but Jaira knew when she was faking it. After all, they shared mostly the same tells. Jaira knew her parents desired something different for her and so she did not hold her mother's feelings against her.

Jaira felt her mother's eyes searching her, feeling out whether her daughter was excited for this turn as well. If her daughter felt dread over her condition, a conversation about apothiks that could terminate the unborn could be had.

As Jaira's hand brushed against her as-of-yet unswollen abdomen, she let her eyes sparkle, signaling her joy.

Before she and Remy married, Jaira and Eilastra had a heart-to-heart. Eilastra told her all plans she and Jaira's father had laid for her with the union to the Vastra family. Within two generations, they'd hoped to align the Morgansteen family with the royal house. None of Oberon and Titania's sons had yet married, but were expected to settle down in the near future. Harhassus and Eilastra Morgansteen knew the timing would not work for the near future with *their* daughter, but perhaps a well-positioned grandchild might be bred and trained specifically to hook a fey prince.

Given Titania's position, a changeling child would kill that dream. How could Jaira be upset with her mother for mourning a hope she'd engineered for their family?

Eilastra asked the relevant questions. *How far along are you? Are you absolutely certain? Do you hope for a boy or a girl?*

Then Eilastra asked a more pertinent question. "Does Remy know yet?"

"No," Jaira said, shaking her head.

Eilastra bit her lower lip and met her daughter's gaze. "So, your plan is to get involved in court as a way to mitigate fallout once Titania learns that you've birthed a changeling?"

Jaira slowly dipped her chin and signaled her assent. The Queen was well known to be a hater of changelings; the only half-human, half-fey she tolerated where those she could control and were results of King Oberon's indiscretions. The King of the Summer Court had the power to open the gates between the worlds, and he sometimes visited the realm of man... which infuriated his wife to no end.

Sidhe were known to love far and wide, and to have rather loose morals when it came to monogamy. However, the queen had her own very specific set of rules when it came to her honor, and even the most sexually deviant fey who'd been attached by marriage only dallied with the permission, and often the joint engagement, of their spouse.

The only changelings who were allowed in Titania's sight were those who had earned special privileges due to some great act or another. The half-breeds at court kept mostly to themselves and formed a private clique within its halls. Tolerated at best, they jumped to please the queen and retain their status, but few of the méith fraternized with them for fear of displeasing Titania.

"Perhaps she can be reasoned with? Maybe I can ingratiate myself to her and build a friendship prior to her learning what grows inside me?"

Eilastra almost laughed at the thought. "See, dear child? This is why we had pushed so hard to have you engage with the Court."

She sighed and waved away the past regret. "But there's nothing we can do about that now, but you should know that Queen Titania is a vengeful, cold-hearted bitch. She has much power, and the thing about power is that it too-often darkens the soul, even if just by degrees."

"Then what must I do?" Jaira asked. "For my part, I admit that I should have paid better mind to your requests that I accompany you to Faery Cairn and engage in court politics. I must ask for your guidance here."

Offering a melancholy sigh that seemed meant to accept that apology, Eilastra set her jaw. "Your father and I shall write to the court magistrates and record your husband as a Morgansteen."

Jaira's brows pinched, though her eyes nearly flooded with surprised gratitude. *Never before had a human been made méith.* "You would do that? Would they even accept it?"

"Perhaps it is fortunate that you've had so little engagement at court," Eilastra noted. "If we are lucky, the recorders may not be familiar with your name, *or your husband's*. There's never been a requirement on our legal documents to list one's species. I shall draft a letter tonight with your father. It will take Remy as an official heir and member of the family, provided your marriage remains intact. He will attach our official seals and send it via courier in the morning."

Eilastra took Jaira's hands in her own and squeeze them. This time, the emotion on her face appeared genuine. "Your father and I might not always agree with your decisions, however, it would be regrettable if any disapproval on our part impacted the child you now bear."

Before Jaira could respond, something made a noise from the nearby threshold leading deeper within the house. Both she and Eilastra turned to address whoever had been eavesdropping.

Jaira stared directly into the face of an adolescent wildfey. Their eyes met, and she knew that the boy had overheard her secret. Tilting her face back to her mother, she asked, "Are you and father now employing ellyllon? I did not think you were so progressive."

"Come in here, Arawyn," Eilastra called.

He did as commanded, with ears drooping slightly. "Apologies, Lady Eilastra. I meant no intrusion. Harhassus sent me to fetch a snack."

Eilastra explained to Jaira, "We could scarcely turn Arawyn away. Your husband came to us and asked if we would house him temporarily... and in secret. He apparently knows something very important, something that jeopardizes his life, and we are now pulled into this strange cabal of shadows. We don't know his secrets, and Remy warned us against learning them." She glanced at the young elf. "Arawyn was supposed to be fishing in the creek with your father."

Jaira knew Harhassus had always wanted a son, but Eilastra had never been able to carry one to full term. Jaira had never had a brother like her father had. Jaira was the only Morgansteen heir after her uncle had burned enough bridges to guarantee he'd not be welcomed back into the méith, even if he somehow managed to reclaim saibhir.

It's good that he's got someone to do son-type-things with... even if that person might never be Remy.

"I can only anticipate that you heard all that," Eilastra said to Arawyn. It was not a question.

Arawyn blushed and then nodded slightly. "I meant no offense, but I thought Lord Harhassus might want a report if he had guests."

Jaira cocked her head and turned her gaze back to her mother. Eilastra didn't respond to it. She glanced back at the boy, whose eyes suddenly ogled and he looked away, embarrassed to have been caught looking at her. Jaira knew that look. It had been the same one that teenage suitors had given her in the past.

Smiling, Jaira realized that the boy was smitten. He'd likely not been intentionally eavesdropping, but had more likely watched her with teenage fascination. That gave her insight on how to deal with Arawyn.

"Arawyn," Jaira said.

He turned to her inquisitively. Most redness had faded from his cheeks, though not all of it.

"You may tell Harhassus that his daughter is visiting. And may I ask you a favor?"

Arawyn nodded deeply and sincerely. He might have pledged anything in that moment if Jaira asked.

"Please, do not share my secret," Jaira requested. "Not with anyone. Not even with my husband... I plan to tell him... but later."

Arawyn nodded, and Eilastra dismissed him. They watched him depart and return to the Lord of the house.

Once he was gone, Eilastra turned back to her daughter. "Perhaps our letter will help your chances... our *family's* future chances... but you must still go to court and make yourself known." A warning look flash in her eyes. "But remember yourself. Even though it is a fine hall filled with rigid rules and glamorous, civilized folk... the Summer Court is a very dangerous place."

Trishana's wrists burned where her bonds bit into her skin. She'd been tied to a chair in some dark cellar, but she did not know where she'd be taken. Trishana could have been halfway to the unseelie, or hell... she could be in the Fomori Kingdom.

She trembled as the dark cloaked figure came closer. Trishana didn't know his name, she didn't know what he wanted. He'd refused to speak no matter what questions she asked him. *How much time has passed since he took me? Days? A week?*

"No... No, please," Trishana whimpered as he took another step toward her.

Below the low hood of the monstrous sidhe, Trishana spotted a grin. It was the first emotion she'd noted on his behalf, and it made her blood run cold.

"I can't—I can't take it," she cried, and then screamed for help. Her throat was already ragged from previous attempts.

With every step, terror welled within her. Whoever this fey was, he'd tortured her daily since abducting her from the hotel. *What-*

ever else he was, he had to be aes sidhe. He'd previously done nothing more than rest a gentle hand upon her to fill her body with torment. He did not just wrack her with pain, but he also invaded her mind.

Trishana writhed within her ropes, rasping the already-red flesh, feeling them burn. But it was nothing compared to what this monster was capable of.

The fiend reached one hand toward her, and he stepped slowly, heightening her fear with anticipation. *Slowly*. Step. *Step*.

Trishana shrieked as the elf's fingers grazed the skin of her forehead. "What do you want?"

For the first time, her tormentor spoke. "I just want you. *All of you*. Your obedience... Your *soul*."

With a crackle of power, the dark maven unleashed a fresh wave of pain. Trishana howled as every fear and insecurity rolled through her mind, picking up speed and dark energy like a tidal wave. A lifetime's worth of pain, regret, night terrors, and irrational fears congealed at the forefront of her thoughts like a bad egwyl meddwl trip, the mushroom that could thrust one's psyche into either the best of the overlap between the aither and dreamspace, or the worst of it.

When she could take it no more, Trishana yielded. "I'll do whatever you want! Just make it stop!"

The torturer relented and stepped back one pace.

Cold wetness sheathed Trishana, and she shook as her body resisted the shock that threatened to overtake her. Glancing down, she noticed that capillaries beneath her skin had ruptured and she'd sweated blood.

"Just... No more... Make it stop," Trishana begged.

Beneath his dark hood, her abductor tilted his head quizzically. "Excellent progress. I nearly believe you." And then he stepped toward her again.

She screamed before he even touched her. Her ears barely registered his words.

"You've almost surrendered enough that you might become useful to me." And then the pain began again in earnest.

Fuerian stomped through the Vastra estate and into the large chamber typically reserved for family gatherings, such as business meetings or celebrations. He pushed his way through the door unceremoniously and walked toward the head of the table, where two others waited for him.

He felt confident in his demand for today's meeting. Partially because Gareth had straightened out his issues at the mine and got it running again.

Gareth had also gotten his pushers quietly deployed into the Haunts, where they resumed their apothiks trade, guaranteeing a renewed income stream. His issues being dealt with returned him to a position of strength and bolstered his overall mood.

The space was far too big for the three sidhe who'd gathered there. The trio could have met in the drawing room, library, or any number of other rooms; however, the place was important for its symbolism. This long hall was where family business was conducted, and it was governed by strict rules the family had put in place ages ago—it was a sanctum of business and no persons other than family were allowed within its hallowed walls.

As Fuerian pulled out his seat, he squinted at the she-elf across from him. "Loitariel," he greeted her disdainfully. He turned and spotted Margrave at the patron's head chair, where Juriahl should have sat, given the current state of family politics. "Should I assume that your husband will not be joining us for this mediation?"

Loitariel's eyes were hard like flint and her jaw stiffened. "Juriahl is away on some pressing business."

That move by his cousin irked Fuerian, but he should have anticipated it. Denigrating a rival by not even bothering to appear in person was a brilliant move. Fuerian would have done something similar if he was in Juriahl's position.

"And just what kind of business is that?" he countered.

Loitariel tilted her head. "The kind that is *none of yours*."

Fiery tension rose between them like static in the air before a lightning strike. Both looked to the large seat between them where Margrave sat; his job was as mediator.

The old elf appeared very tired, world-weary. He leaned back on the padded chair with every joint relaxed, nearly slack-jawed. Margrave's eyes were closed. Clearly, he would not be the one to defuse the situation.

Fuerian grimaced and got to the point of his complaint. He'd lodged it via the standard process half a year ago. The Vastras had extensive internal systems in place; sometimes they were the only things keeping the family from waging war on each other. As long as there were rules which applied equally, and could be exploited evenly, then their shadowy game of house politics could continue.

"My *cousin*," Fuerian hissed at Juriahl's conspicuous absence, and then glanced at Margrave, "and even my dear uncle, are in arears on a debt they owe me. The family is obligated to act on a matter that was decided nearly one year ago and which has since been ignored. For what purpose? I can only speculate."

Loitariel shot him a pinched gaze. "What are you talking about?"

"House Vastra decided on this measure after the duel and after my broken engagement with the Morgansteen girl."

"A duel which you lost," Loitariel snipped, provoking a nasty look from Fuerian.

"Regardless of the outcome," he said, "I had discovered elements of dishonor in the whole engagement, all of which led to the Morgansteens damaging my reputation. Whether Harhassus intended this or not is open to speculation, but his daughter certainly intended to harm my name... *our name*."

Fuerian saw Loitariel gathering a head of steam, but cut her off before she could launch into some kind of defense for Juriahl's inaction. "I remind you that we initiated a vote, and the family decided to act on its behalf. This is not merely a defense of my personal honor, but of the Vastra name. We agreed to inform Harhassus's creditors of the family's inability to pay back any current loans and pressure those parties into investigating the Morgansteen's accounts. I paid dearly for the information which revealed they were broke. It will only take one lender to call in their debt and others will rush to follow and not be the one left to hold the empty bag."

Loitariel scoffed. "So, your plan is to bankrupt a titled Lord—one who could perhaps be a future ally? This sounds like simple vengeance upon someone who wounded you publicly."

Fuerian shot her a hard glare. "Absolutely, it is. This is what happens when you fuck with the Vastras." He raised an eyebrow at Loitariel, challenging her. "Juriahl is obligated to fulfill this obligation to me and he has failed in doing so. Perhaps he has not prioritized this act out of spite for me... perhaps not. But it's undeniable that I am owed this obligation and Juriahl has failed to deliver it."

"I think you are more concerned with getting your friend, Gareth Morass, reinstated as one of the méith." She sneered at him. "Without an opening at the king's table, such a thing could not happen."

"Intentions aside, the vote was made," Fuerian snarled. "The obligation exists."

The she-elf studied him for a moment. Her eyes locked onto a spot at Fuerian's neck. Her eyes sparkled as the light caught a glimmer of the filigree chain at his throat. "What jewelry are you wearing, there?" she asked, her voice sounding frigid. "Show me the charm at your neck."

Fuerian's chain dipped below his neckline, keeping what dangled there hidden behind his tunic. "No," he said flatly. His tone bordered on amusement.

"Show me or I will have your head," Loitariel growled the words.

"I will not explain my clothing and accessory choices nor disrobe for you. Barter for a plaything if your husband fails to satisfy you. But we are not here to discuss baubles and fashion." His voice rose and his fingers dug into the table.

"Enough!" Margrave yelled. His eyes had opened wide, and he glared from face to face. "Do not think that I've been asleep this whole time. My eyelids may be heavy, but my ears still work exceptionally well."

Margrave turned to Fuerian. "You are correct in your request. The matter has long-since been decided. You are owed this obligation and it is grossly delinquent. Juriahl should have acted on this ten months ago."

Glaring at Loitariel, Margrave continued. "Because the matter is so far in arrears, I shall see to it personally. Will that satisfy you?" he asked Fuerian.

Fuerian nodded stiffly, giving his venerable uncle a kind of seated bow. "I would be honored and satisfied with that outcome."

"Then I shall meet with our friends in the banking industry over the next three days, or as soon as appointments become available." Margrave looked from one to the other and then rested his hands on the table. "If this is matter is concluded, I have better uses of my time than to navigate whatever quarrel you two have."

Fuerian stood. "I agree, and we are of a like mind. Profit is wasted on my continued presence here." Locking eyes with Margrave, he bent slightly at the hip, and then turned to Loitariel. He rolled his eyes at her and then departed with a grin.

Chapter Ten

"So, uh, what should I expect?" Remy asked Madadh as they crept through the trees that surrounded Fuerian Vastra's mine. The war party departed as soon as he had returned to the Fianna camp, bound for the remote location.

Madadh raised a brow. "Have you not seen a mine before?"

"No, not that," Remy said. "But I haven't seen wolf shifters before. The other day... Your arm... That was the first."

Madadh had turned his face back into the breeze, in the direction of their target. He didn't meet the duelist's gaze. "Then... just try not to freak out. Terror is a normal reaction." And then he strode toward the clearing that surrounded the mine, removing the bulk of his clothing as he walked.

Evening had drawn down a shade of color near the horizon, but it was not full dark yet. Madadh emerged from the woods wearing only confidence and a pair of eyes that burned with righteous indignation in full view of the Fianna at his back, and any of Fuerian's guards at the front.

Not breaking his stride, Madadh bent as if buckling with pain. His limbs shook and contorted, elongating and shifting into a larger lycan form. Teeth lengthened and muscles swelled as they bulged; hair blossomed and grew to cover the thick hide.

Remy forced himself to swallow and hold his ground. The creature Madadh had become appeared exactly as Arawyn had described to him. But hearing the description of a lycan and seeing one were very different things.

Madadh glanced back. His amber eyes locked with Remy's gaze and reassured him that the man was still in charge of the monstrous body. And then Madadh thrust his chest out, pointed his eyes at the sky, and howled.

All around the mine, wherever the trees provided cover, other Fianna took up the call, filling the air with a siren warning. Remy blinked and then forced himself to the tree line, only now realizing that those pack mates who'd accompanied them had followed Madadh's example and were now in their wolf-like shapes, as well.

In the clearing beyond, a road spiraled downward, terminating at a sheer face of stone where the mineshaft opened. Crude machinery and tools lay haphazardly in the perimeter, most being hand operated, though a few newer magitech items sat idle.

Hearing the lupine call, a pair of sidhe guards came from the mineshaft. They sounded the alarm almost immediately and readied bows, launching them at their opponents. One arrow went wide, the other struck wolf flesh, eliciting a snarl before the beast pulled it free with little effort.

Remy caught up to Madadh, who walked confidently on his hind legs, glaring daggers at the guards. The other Fianna swarmed down the slope on all four legs. They came from every side, hitting the basin's deepest point at the same time.

Meaty thumps caused growls of annoyance wherever fey arrows struck hide. A cluster of sentries shouted as their enemies crowded around them, shrugging off what would have otherwise been fatal wounds on smaller tuatha or humans.

The slavers shrieked as they began to die, falling to lycan claws. Screams turned quickly to gurgles and sprays of blood painted the stacked crates and equipment pools.

Following Madadh, Remy whirled when he heard a door swing open where it was concealed. A hatch, inset to the scrubby ground, flipped open and a small group of sidhe fled.

Remy recognized one of them. *Gareth Morass.* He touched the side of his temple, touching the small scar that puckered there from their last encounter.

"Madadh!" Remy yelled, but Gareth and his elves weren't launching a sneak attack. They were running, and Gareth was in the lead.

The lycan leader spun and leapt into the fray, raking one elf with his razor claws and then opening the next sidhe's midsection as if dumping out the contents of an envelope. The gruesome package spilled bulbous tubes of gray and pink, packed with liquid crimson that splattered the dirt.

Madadh chased the others, snapping one elf in his jaws and rolling him to the ground.

Gareth barely looked back as his fellow slaver begged him for help. He'd already slashed the tether of a horse and mounted it.

He tore his eyes away and spurred the steed to its maximum speed, slipping away before he'd be forced to take any chances.

Remy watched him go and felt certain that the elf hadn't noticed him. The duelist couldn't fault him for that. His observational capacity certainly must have diminished in the face of rampaging werewolves.

Howling victoriously, Madadh wiped the blood from his muzzle. Some of it, at least.

The Fianna leader motioned for Remy to follow, and he complied, rejoining Madadh at the mouth of the mine.

As several of the other Fianna patrolled the edges to ensure that they'd cleared out any resistance, those near the mine's entrance shifted forms, retaking their human figures and letting the lycan features melt away. One of the patrolling wolves retrieved clothing for them and distributed it just as a naked human male emerged from the shaft, towing a gang of humans.

Remy eyed them quizzically as they walked from the subterranean opening. He recognized them-not their individual faces, but he knew what they were. He'd seen unseelie slave gangs before... in the bowels of the Winter Court.

"What are you?" Remy asked the emaciated slave at the front of the line.

Like the rest, his feet were shackled to his neighbor, and he wore a slave's brand upon his face. "D-ddiymadferth," he stammered, as if this had been drilled into him by some harsh task master.

Remy shook his head. "No. You are *not* worthless, friend."

Once the prisoner seemed certain he was not about to be struck for answering incorrectly, he straightened. "They call us the Light-starved."

Setting his jaw, Remy stretched his lips thin. He nodded slowly.

Two more Fianna emerged from the tunnels, one dragged a half-mauled sidhe. The other led out four additional work-gangs, chained in a row just as the first had been.

"Where are the children?" Madadh asked.

The Fianna scouts shook their heads dourly.

"There is one." He rushed over to the diminutive form in the rear of one chain of slaves. Madadh paused and cocked his head. "A powrie?"

Whirling on the wounded elf, he seized the sidhe and dragged him to his feet with surprising strength and shook him. "Where are the human children? We were told your mine had purchased many stolen children."

"You don't know?" the elf asked as Remy found a ring of keys attached to an elven corpse nearby.

With blood dribbling down his chin, the elf spat to clear his mouth. His spittle was vibrant red. "You *ought to*. From what I hear, it was your kind that took the last ones... but... you know... rumors. Besides, more places than just this one buying ddiymad-ferth these days."

At the mention of the slur, Madadh shook him so violently that Remy wondered if the man still retained some of that lycan strength, even in this form.

"Who else is buying my people?" Madadh demanded.

The elf's head slumped, however, and blood leaked across the soil, spilling out from inside the guard's pant legs. He likely had an arterial wound give way below his clothes, which worsened by the interrogation.

Madadh growled and tossed the body to the dirt, turning to find Remy unlocking the shackles. As Remy inserted the key, the redcap raised his hand sheepishly, as if asking for permission to speak.

"What is it, powrie?" Madadh asked, still sour from losing the potential answers he'd sought.

"My name's Hobin," he said, pausing to bend down and rub the raw, red wound where the ankle cuff had bound him. "I heard some of them talking about it all. We came from the unseelie to replace the last batch of slaves. Lightstarved ain't as strong as run-of-the-mill folk, ya know... But they mentioned they needed slaves, and they had to be human, and they didn't *need* to be strong. In fact, it was preferred that they weren't... ya know... easier to keep the weak ones compliant."

Madadh tilted his head. "Why would they want the weakest of us?"

Remy grimaced. He'd figured it out. A dark memory resurfaced. He'd filled the Unseelie Queen's wedding feast with iron fillings and detonated an akashic bomb to scatter ferrous shrapnel into his enemies' flesh, nearly wiping out the entire Winter Court the moment Aderyn Corff had tricked the spider queen's consort into lifting his oath, allowing the Death Bird to take flight.

"They need slaves who can collect iron. It's highly illegal, but that probably means it's all going to terrorist cells or to some other plan Rhagathena is cooking up," Remy said.

Hobin shook his head. "That's just it, though... Iron mining is hard work. They had us scraping fungus off the mineral deposits instead. That's it."

Remy and Madadh traded a confused gaze. The latter confirmed, "That's it?"

Hobin nodded.

"But no other mention of where the children had been taken? We've been searching for leads on many of them over this last year and finally learned they'd been transferred here." Madadh scowled as he rubbed his chin thoughtfully. "It seems Oddur beat us to them."

Remy's brow arched. "But they're rescued, at least. Isn't it good, no matter who freed them?"

Madadh shook his head. He spoke with subdued volume. "There is a war brewing, Remy. And Oddur is not rescuing kids. He is collecting potential soldiers." Catching the confusion on Remy's face, he explained, "He means to make them like us... More warriors he can mold into his image. Even the young can make formidable lycans."

"He wants the Fianna to wage war against the sidhe?" Remy asked.

Madadh's look soured.

"Oh." *He wants war for control of the Fianna first.*

A pall hung over the scene for a few moments as prisoners passed the keys around and freed the remainder of them. Madadh stepped aside to coordinate logistics for assimilating the Lightstarved into his caravan.

"Where are my shoes?" Hobin wondered aloud, and then he spotted them sitting atop a few stacked crates off to the edge of a staging area near a line of trolleys on a mechanical rail. They were too high to reach, and he asked Remy, "A little help?"

The duelist walked with him. "I know a redcap, you know."

Hobin shrugged. "Not all redcaps know all other redcaps, Mister..." He trailed off, inviting an introduction.

"Remy"

"Mister Remy," concluded Hobin.

"It's *just* Remy. And my redcap friend is a pretty famous one."

"But still."

"Redcomb. Maybe you know him?" Remy asked.

"Actually, I *do know him*."

Remy wasn't sure if Hobin was being sarcastic or not at first. He furrowed his brow.

"No, seriously. He's my cousin on my mother's side. You weren't lying. He really *is* famous."

They reached the crates and Remy reached on his toes until he could collect the iron shoes that powries preferred to wear along with their traditional forward-slouched hat. He turned them over to the smaller tuathan and then looked past the crates, and found a refuse pit.

His stomach turned at the sight. Several human bodies lay there, decomposing with the trash and lying amongst old food stuffs, latrine waste, and other cast-offs.

A woman's corpse clutched a child, refusing to give up the embrace, even in death. They'd been left to rot together.

Anger rose deep within Remy's core. His nostrils flared when he remembered the leverage Fuerian Vastra had over him.

As a child, Remy Keaton awoke in the faewylds owning nothing but a name and his dagger. His memories had been wiped away, but Fuerian had proved that he knew parts of them—he'd even promised to return those memories to him if he would only comply with his whims and leave Arcadeax. Remy had refused.

"It's a pity Fuerian Vastra wasn't here," grumbled Remy, turning back to the powrie as Hobin clamped his shoes back on.

The duelist caught sight of a stamp on the crates. It read, *Stór Rúnda*. "What do eggs have to do with anything?" he wondered aloud.

"Huh?" asked Hobin.

"Eggs. I know that place. It's an egg farm, but the owner has nothing to do with the Vastra family."

Hobin shrugged. "They didn't feed us any eggs, that's for sure... Not even sure it qualified as gruel. But the crates were all empty when we got 'em. It's what we loaded the fungus in. Probably just reusing old boxes."

Remy's gaze narrowed at the containers.

"Whatcha thinking, big guy?" Hobin asked as Madadh called out for them to join the rest. They were leaving the area with all the freed slaves.

Remy took two steps toward a supply cache, which had several jugs of lantern oil. He retrieved them, began spilling the flammable liquids over the filled crates, and growled, "I'm going to burn it all."

Anya's wheelchair rolled into the foyer entrance of Kent's duplex. She heard voices coming from within the second unit as she navigated her chair near the door to take a look. It hung ajar about the width of a fist.

Beyond, she spotted Jaira, whose back was turned to the entrance. She spoke to someone further within the apartment whose voice Anya did not recognize.

As Jaira turned slightly, she caught Anya's gaze and motioned to let her know there was no trouble. Then Jaira opened the door and waved her in.

"Is everything all right?" Anya asked.

Jaira nodded.

"You know you went into the wrong door, right?" Anya teased as she reached for her chair's motivator. Jaira and Remy had stayed with her for the last several days, but she knew Remy wasn't comfortable bringing Jaira back to the cottage yet. He'd said that it felt too... vulnerable.

That human has stirred up some new hornets' nest, I'm sure of it. And he's playing it cagey, too.

Inside, Anya spotted a diminutive creature wearing metal boots and sitting on the couch. Kent had seen to it that the place was furnished even when it had sat empty.

The aithermancer arched an eyebrow at her friend. "A redcap?"

Jaira sighed. "I'm afraid my husband has taken up collecting."

"Of powries?"

Jaira rolled her eyes. "No. There's also a tylwyth teg." She gave her friend a thin-lipped smile and shrugged. "I got the sense that Remy intends to take this apartment since Kent had offered it."

As they spoke, Hobin had slid off the couch and bowed to Anya. "I am at Remy's disposal. He saved my life, you know. My name is Hobin Gwarchae,"

Anya studied him for a few moments. "Of course you are. And where is Remy, anyway?"

Jaira said, "He went out to fetch today's yellow journal." She told Anya about the attack at the maginarius and how it resulted in Remy delivering some fugitive ellyllon to her parents' home for safekeeping after the maginarius was razed by vicious creatures.

"No wonder he'd rather have you in the city," Anya noted.

Hobin picked up the story with a tale of his rescue by a bunch of disheveled, and mostly naked humans accompanying Remy, who helped him find his boots. "I'm beginning to think he really *was* the guy who helped my cousin get revenge on some orcs back in the unseelie. I totally thought he was shitting me."

Both of the she-elves cocked their head at him, not quite certain what he was talking about. Neither had ever heard that particular tale.

A moment later, the door closed with a click that startled Anya. She craned her head to find Remy closing the door. He carried a sack with some foodstuffs and a rolled bunch of folded sheaves that made up today's printing.

"Oh, good. I see you've all met," he said.

"And how you've been busy," Anya quipped. "So have I."

Remy nodded. "I got a lead about the Fianna after the Ollscoil Maginarius and tracked it down. Turns out, they've been looking for the lost human children. Although I'm not entirely certain anymore that it's connected to the missing aes sidhe."

Anya briefly recounted her quest through Ionad Import and Export's records. "It's no surprise that Fuerian Vastra is connected to the purchase of humans."

He noted, "I learned all that today, as well. I also know where many of the children went, but they're beyond anyone's reach, at present." Remy glowered. "I'm not sure how I feel about that, but it's got the Fianna riled up." His fists tightened around the daily report. "And for good reason."

Remy passed her the paper, which reported on the attack at Ollscoil Maginarius.

The front-page article included quotes from several Frith Duine members who claimed they'd overheard humans talking about launching a terrorist attack on the school. The anti-human group claimed its numbers were increasingly on the rise and that the humans had erred by launching such a brazen attack. Ochara offered no comment on the matter, as it was currently under investigation.

Anya looked up and caught Remy smiling at his wife. Jaira hadn't noticed him yet, where she had a hushed conversation with the powrie.

"She looks good, right? Jaira's practically glowing," he mumbled to his friend... the cripple who was practically his sister.

Anya shook out the paper and turned it to the duelist standings. "It's probably that new lotion I gave her," she lied for Jaira to cover for her. "Or maybe you've just been away too long and are all pent up. I see you were busy in Saibhir Gaoithe and put some ribbon seeker in his place." She turned the paper for him to see the write-up.

Remy nodded gravely, and Anya understood why. He couldn't disconnect his duelist appointment from the death of Anya's brother.

"Whatever is happening... However, it's all connected, it's giving me a sinking feeling."

Anya nodded, but Remy looked suddenly very tense.

"There's more," he told her. His voice brimmed with warning. "I'm moving into this apartment, and Hobin will help me keep it safe."

The powrie gave them a wave from the kitchen where he'd joined Jaira.

"I gathered as much already," Anya responded.

Remy shook his head. There was clearly more. "Someone should stay close for *your* sake... I spotted Gareth Morass. He's been released, somehow. Probably a bribe from some sidhe with money. He's likely to have a bone to pick with you after your testimony put him away."

Anya gritted her teeth and then cursed. "Fuerian Vastra," she put a name to their mutual guess.

Behind them, Jaira began making a meal for them all to share. With Anya nodding her agreement to join them for a meal, Remy crouched and whispered for her ears only. "I spotted crates from Stór Rúnda, which I'm pretty sure is one of Xander Kent's companies. He's always been generous and fair in my experience. I think someone in his enterprise is corrupt. I'm sure he'll want to know about it if we can find the name of an employee."

Anya remembered seeing Kent's name in Ionad's records. She said nothing, but Anya nodded. "I agree. I'll look into it."

Hobin's legs dangled in the chair as he sat at the table in Remy's new apartment. The powrie noted the furnishings had not included one of the taller, but narrower chairs made to accommodate the little folk and made a small judgment against Xander Kent's decorator for the oversight. The fourth chair had been removed and set out of the way to make room for Anya's mobility seat.

"This really is good," Remy said of the food.

Hobin had helped Jaira cook while the human and aithermancer were deep in conversation.

When Remy looked at her, Jaira told him, "It was mostly Hobin. I'm sure you've figured out by now that I'm a rather poor cook."

Remy slurped up another mouthful of food as he looked at their diminutive guest.

Hobin casually waved away any accolades. "It's all in the seasoning, to be honest."

"Well, whatever you did, this is pretty good," Anya agreed.

"Thanks. I mean, it's no repayment for my rescue at the mine, but I'll take it," said the redcap.

"You really have nothing to repay," Remy told him. "There is no debt and you're free to go whenever." His expression soured as if the human had suffered from old memories. His voice turned darker. "I have a severe dislike of slavery."

"I understand." Hobin nodded. "But my people take debts like this very seriously, and I'd much prefer to stick close until I can return this favor. Please, don't refuse and hurt my honor."

Remy looked skeptical, but he did not reject the request. Finally, he sighed and told Hobin, "Fine, I guess. It's not like you'll take up too much space."

Hobin smiled. "You won't regret it... Besides, it's not very safe for a single powrie to be out on his own in these parts... or *any parts,* for that matter."

"It's not just dangerous for redcaps," Remy said and explained his findings at Ollscoil Maginarius.

Then, Remy grimaced. "I've spared you the most gruesome of the details, but it was a total slaughter... And one the Frith Duine thinks they can pin on my kind."

Anya raised an eyebrow. "How on earth could it be like that?" she wondered aloud. "You're saying that none of the much vaunted aes sidhe, guardians of Arcadeax's arcana, couldn't do a single thing against these... what did you call them, the fáelad?"

"They used some kind of weed. I know little about it," Remy said with a shrug. "Probably comes from the unseelie or from the faewylds. Arawyn told me about it."

"The redcaps are unseelie, right?" Jaira asked.

"We are," Hobin told her. "But I don't know much about weeds, aside from the kind we like to put in our pipes at the end of a long day harassing orcs."

Remy returned to the original topic and noted, "You could always join the Court of Thorns. Bend the knee to Queen Maeve. The wildfey kingdom contains far fewer sidhe than other tuatha."

Shaking his head, Hobin said, "I don't think that's my path. Some of my kin have gone to the faewylds already, but it's not a popular idea among my kind."

"Wait." Jaira remained unclear. "Why can't just you go back to the unseelie?"

"Powries are hated there because we honor Wulflock's memory with our footgear. He gave us permission for it because of our greatest ancestor, Ystyfnig's actions to defend him in the Infernal Wars. He gave us explicit permission for the iron shoes."

Hobin scowled. "We fought in the True Winter King's defense as proud members of the court, but when bitch Rhagathena came to power, she cast us out."

"Like what happened with the trolls?" Jaira asked.

The powrie shook his head. "When she first came to power, Rhagathena demanded we surrender our iron shoes to her. We kindly told her to go fuck herself." He winked at Jaira. "Trollkinds' loyalty goes even further. They revere Oberon's brother as if he's some kind of family leader. Almost religious about it. Trolls are."

Remy's brow furrowed. "I thought the redcaps were pretty steadfast in waiting for Wulflock's return as well?"

Hobin shrugged. "We are. But we're pragmatic about it. I dunno... Some of us might have lost faith in the return of our king. I *hope* in it, but my *faith* is in what I can see and touch." He threw them a lopsided grin as he looked over his group of friends, noticing things about each of them. In particular, his eyes rested on Jaira and did not move away when something niggled at his nose.

Powries were a goblinoid race, a feral halfling species of tuatha. He smelled it on her. Hobin didn't need to be told she was with child; the subtle aromatics in her hormonal state were plain as day.

Remy scooped another plateful from the main dish.

"I dunno," Hobin admitted. "A lot of my kind get more religious once *their* kids are born, too. Maybe it'll change for you once—"

He didn't get the chance to say any more when someone kicked him below the table. His eyes turned to Jaira, who gave him a stern glare and a subtle tilt of the head.

Oh! He does not know...

Remy turned his eyes to Hobin. "What were you saying?"

"Uh, nothing," Hobin said. "Just that I'm glad to be here, or anywhere else besides that mineshaft." He flashed Jaira an awkward grin and decided he would keep her secret.

Remy rubbed his eyes as he opened the door of the apartment and blinked with surprise. He found a line of porters and other delivery persons carrying packages as they arrived. At the front of the line stood Xander Kent.

"Sorry for such an early morning arrival," Kent said as Remy yawned, "but I'm glad to see you're making use of the apartment."

"What's all this?" Remy asked, craning his head to look over the crowd.

"I thought I'd deliver a bunch of supplies. You know, food, sundries, and whatnot." His lips flattened. "Partly, it's an apology for needing you to accompany me on another journey so soon after the last one."

Remy flashed him a quizzical look. He knew Kent hated traveling abroad, except when it was absolutely necessary. Mainly, it was because he took such a hands-on approach to managing his many businesses.

"You don't need to do that," Remy said as the delivery crew entered and put away their items, stuffing the pantry. "I mean, it's why you pay me."

Kent held up a hand, refusing to hear another word on the topic.

"So, what's the reason for the trip? Where are we going?" Remy asked.

Kent's expression was unreadable. "I received a call to report to Faery Cairn... A summons from Oberon himself. Again, I apologize for such short notice, but we ought to leave at once."

<<<<>>>>

Chapter Eleven

Jaira was not pleased at losing her husband to work quite so soon after his return, especially since she eagerly expected his return. Remy tended to come in like a tornado, impacting everyone's lives in the process. However, that was often the exact thing that she liked about him. Sometimes, lives needed a good disruption.

Not sure what to do with herself given such a rapid turn of events, she paced near the table for several minutes, trying to come up with a revised plan of action. She felt Hobin's gaze track her from the corner of her eye. Remy *had* instructed him to watch over her.

Apparently, the redcap's vow had some kind of transferable property. She wasn't quite sure how best to utilize her powrie shadow just yet. She frowned. *I'm already scorned by the usual gossip-mongers... I wonder how fraternizing with an iron-wearing redcap might affect that?*

Someone knocked on the door, and Jaira traded a quizzical glance with Hobin. Remy had been gone only a couple hours after making arrangements to ensure all his needs were covered in his absence. Lunchtime was creeping up, but Jaira had no plans for guests today.

She walked toward the entrance, assuming it could be Anya. When she opened the door, Jaira discovered a messenger carrying a letter addressed to her. He wore a tunic gilded in the colors of the Summer Court.

Jaira greeted him and furrowed her brow as the courier handed over the folded billet. It was addressed to Jaira Morgansteen, and the address written belonged to her parents.

"Apologies, ma'am. Your parents told me where the message could be delivered and I was instructed to place it in your hands rather than leave it for retrieval," the young he-elf told her.

She thanked him and then watched him bow and depart. Her fingers trembled at the potential in her hands. It had come from Oberon's Court, which meant it was probably of a response to her parent's petition for Remy to be recognized as the Morgansteen heir and gain his place at court.

Jaira stared at the closed and sealed response for several long moments, prompting Hobin to ask, "What is it?"

"My future," Jaira said flatly. She still stared at it. As long as she did not open it, that future remained exactly as Jaira had hoped.

"Are you going to open it?" Hobin prodded again.

She frowned and finally broke the wax seal, scanning the letter as she held her breath. Jaira stiffened and dropped the letter, letting the paper flutter to the ground as she tried to hold back tears. She reminded herself of her need for oxygen and sucked in a lungful. The effort nearly made Jaira cry but her inner resolve hardened.

"Bad news, I take it?" Hobin asked.

Jaira nodded slowly, mechanically. "It is the response I expected, though not the one I'd hoped for."

"Tell me how I can help." Hobin's eyes brimmed with compassion as he met her gaze, although they ringed with something malicious as well. *Vengeance? Resolve, perhaps?* Jaira had no doubt that the powrie would commit violence on her behalf if it would help remedy her situation.

She sighed. "I'm afraid there's not much you can do. I've already made plans to visit the Court. This merely escalates my timeline. I'd wished to tell Remy about it over the next couple days..."

"And to also tell them about your... *condition?*" Hobin interjected.

Jaira nodded again. "But as of now, time is of the essence. This letter means the Court knows my husband is not sidhe, or even tuatha. It could indicate that the queen may be behind the letter, or perhaps someone close enough that they've guessed her disposition." She briefly explained to Hobin how her decision to marry a human could impact the future of her entire family if it felt insulting to the changeling-hating queen. "Once my pregnancy becomes visible to all, I will have lost the ability to influence any decisions to the contrary."

Her voice had wavered more than she'd hoped as she spoke, but Hobin nodded.

"Then we must go to Faery Cairn at once," he said.

She shook her head slightly. "I must go. Alone."

His brow pinched. "But you cannot go without an escort. And I told Remy that I would watch over you."

Jaira's gaze was steadfast, but firm. "I am trying to influence opinions for the better. How well do you think I can do that with a redcap as my escort?"

Hobin grimaced with a shrug, acknowledging what she told him. As a race, the powrie were not ignorant of how they were perceived.

"Don't worry. I have a new task for you. Although... Remy has an additional secret that needs a guardian. Gather your things. I will have you protect my parents and their, uh, ward," she told him. "We leave immediately."

Trishana shuddered as the black maven pulled the hood from her head, unblinding her. "I... I will behave," she implored her captor, voice wavering. It warbled with pain at the thought of learning another "lesson."

"I know you will," Hymdreiddiech told her. "I have something new for you."

Trishana shied away, fearing the nature of any new thing from such a harsh educator. The last thing that he had showed her was what it looked like and what it felt like to be flayed alive. The entire experience had been a working of magic, but that did not mean the experience was less real. It was intensely memorable. There hadn't even had a point to the lesson except to deepen her fear of him.

The lesson before that, Hymdreiddiech had unshackled her, claiming he would let her go free. But he offered her a choice, do her best to escape and earn double the punishment if he could find her again within four hours, or submit to her daily reeducation. She chose submission.

If I'd tried to run, what horrors might he have visited upon me?

Trishana trembled as she waited for Hymdreiddiech to instruct her. He could reach her anywhere, would find her anywhere if she managed to get away. And yet... he'd also *chosen her*. An elf with such power... And she was special enough for him to invest his effort. She'd not wanted to admit it, but the black maven increasingly owned her mind, body, and soul.

"Say it," Hymdreiddiech growled lowly.

The first thing she'd learned was the mantra. "I am yours to command."

"Good," he said, stretching out the vowels of the word. "I have a gift for you... something real."

She tried not to flinch when he dug into his pockets and then produced a small mirror. He offered it to her and unbound her hands.

Trishana took it in hand and gazed at her appearance. Only fleetingly did her mind address smashing the glass and using the jagged edge to cut her own throat and escape this hell. *No, Hymdreiddiech was too fast for that. He controlled all. He* was *all. There was nothing left but obedience to the black maven.* It was a thought she would never address again for fear that Hymdreiddiech would know she'd had it.

As Trishana took in the sight of herself, she remembered she was once a proud she-elf. She had once worn cosmetics and fine clothes even though she belonged to the working class. Trishana had been a knockout, a beautiful sidhe, something she'd often used to her own advantage when negotiating.

But now?

Bruises marred her cheeks, and her stringy, dirty hair looked only fit for a gutter. This monster, *her* monster... her *lord and master*, Hymdreiddiech had completely unmade her. Who she was, what she looked like? It did not matter. Only her obedience did. No other options remained.

Trishana regarded the reflection quizzically. The sight of herself Caused her no sorrow. It did not make her feel *anything*. Such minor inconveniences as disappointment or malaise were completely swallowed up by the constant buzzing of fear in the back of her mind.

She was broken. And Trishana knew it. But recognition of that fact had zero bearing on her new outlook.

"What do you see?" Hymdreiddiech asked her.

She worked her mouth wordlessly.

"I require an answer," her master told her.

"The flesh. Flesh that is yours to command," she repeated the mantra.

"Shall I instruct you again about truthfulness?"

Panic shot through Trishana's guts like an ice shard spell cast by an aes sidhe. "No. I tell you no lies. I could not."

Hymdreiddiech regarded her for a long moment. "I accept your answer. Elaborate upon it."

"I see who I am. *What* I am. I used to paint my face in order to highlight my beauty. But beneath that was this flesh you see now," Trishana said. The words might have caused her pain two years ago. Hell, it might have hurt her opinion of herself when she was still incarcerated—at least she'd held onto the hope of recovering her previous stature at that time. *But now?*

"Excellent," Hymdreiddiech hissed. "You are very special to me, aithermancer."

A surge of excitement rippled through her as he affirmed her, and Trishana turned her face to her tormentor. *Special?* The way he'd hurt her, broken her, and reduced her to nothing? He had completely unraveled her perception of self. Trishana had no hope except for the pain to end... but if she was somehow *special? What did that mean for her?*

"I know your thoughts," Hymdreiddiech told her. His voice sounded like gravel tumbling down the hill.

Trishana's eyes widened with a slight tinge of panic.

"There is no magic in it... I have *engineered them*. This whole experiment has been about *you*. I had to unmake you in order to ensure you are ready for what is next—I intend to make you a critical part of my operation."

Trishana tried not to sound excited by the prospect. She desperately wanted to ask him *ready for what?* But she'd been reborn as something... new. An acolyte devoted to a cruel master who so easily gifted either pain or nothingness. Instead, she repeated the mantra. "I am yours to command."

"Good," he reaffirmed her. "In that case, I will show you my use for you."

She dared to turn her eyes up to the hooded sorcerer who'd bent her to his dark will.

With the flick of his wrist, the minor incantation he cast undid her bonds and made the tight ropes fall as limp as mid-summer gossamer. It hung there, and he bid her to rise.

Trishana did as instructed. It was all she ever could do, would ever do.

"Follow," he commanded.

Hymdreiddiech led her to a hallway that connected to another room. At the beginning of her captivity, Trishana might have scanned the corridors looking for weak points, noticed the interdiction vault attached to the akashic drip line, searched out possible escape paths. She no longer did. Her eyes fixed on the back of her dark lord.

He led her into a different room. This cell had one piece of equipment within. A large coffin-shaped apparatus that opened upon hinges on one side. It was made of metal, with windowed ports upon the sides for visibility and access. Heavy latches dangled from the top half of the contraption, and wires led from it to the wall. An akashic drip line powered it, too, and she noticed an aither cord tethering it to an interface at the wall.

"Do you know what this is?" he asked.

Trishana shook her head. "I can only guess that it has something to do with the aithersphere?"

"You are correct," he said.

Something deep within her core rejoiced at pleasing her master. Hymdreiddiech told her, "In another life, you were a master of the sphere. I am not entirely without skill at aithermancy. However, I have need of an advocate... someone I can *trust*."

The way he looked at her made her inner-most self melt. His glance smoldered greedily, partly lust mixed with pride and girded by that simmering rage. "I am yours to command."

He regarded her skeptically for a moment. "Several learned sidhe have theorized that cutting off one's physical abilities can improve an aithermancer's potency... This is designed to do exactly that, to atrophy your physical form but amplify your astral self. This bit of magitech was made especially *for you*."

She turned her gaze to Hymdreiddiech.

"You were already on the verge of omnipotence in that realm. With this machine, you will be *a goddess... my* goddess."

He took one step closer to her and placed a hand on her face, almost lovingly. Hymdreiddiech bent lower and placed his lips near her pointed ear.

He was so close that Trishana could feel his warm breath on the nape of her neck. "Will you let me do this thing to you? Will you let me turn you into a goddess?"

Rather than repeat the mantra, her eyes met his. Some deep, primal part of her yearned to blurt out her willingness. Her eyes met his. The base depravity of her soul clicked with his primal urges, as if he'd unlocked something deep within her. "I... I will do *anything* for you."

He tilted his head. "Why?"

Without hesitation, she insisted, "Because I love you, my lord." Even as she said it, Trishana wondered at its truthfulness. This fiend had beaten her, abused her, and reduced her to nothing. And yet... Deep down, she believed that he had saved her. *And now, he wants to make me a goddess? He wants to unlock the one thing that has been my identity, the skill that I have been the most gifted at my whole life?*

"I want you to prove it," the dark maven said, his low voice rumbling. It ignited a deep heat far within her—an arousal that Trishana knew no other way to express.

She sank to her knees, pulled aside the folds of his robe, and removed his cock before wrapping her lips around it. The warmth of her mouth encouraged the flow of her captor's blood and made him hard.

Trishana worked her head against his waist, feeling his bulge choke her, limit her air. But it was nothing compared to the torture of his lessons... And she was giving pleasure, damn it! And that brought *her* pleasure.

Her mouth drooled, stickiness wetting her chest as she bobbed her head forward and backward. Hymdreiddiech barely responded... until he did.

When he finally engaged with her, he laced his fingers through the tresses of her greasy hair and interlocked them behind her pointed ears. He said nothing when he'd finished, but she felt the sudden burst of hot cum shoot down the back of her throat and she swallowed it down.

Hymdreiddiech had not been the first she'd performed this service for. In a world so often dominated by males, she'd learned this skill early and used it to bend he-elves to her whims when it suited her—or when it was profitable—or whenever the fuck she felt like it. But Trishana had been more willing for *him* than for any other... For the elf who had dominated her... taken her power and then given some back to her.

She sank back onto her haunches. "I hope that I have pleased you, my lord."

Hymdreiddiech looked down at her. His face looked neither more nor less endeared to her than normal. "You have proven yourself worthy," he told her.

Trishana blushed slightly. Somewhere in the deep recesses of her mind, she wondered if she ought to receive some reciprocal pleasure. She buried that thought. It was not her place to have desires. It was only her place to serve... Hymdreiddiech's lessons had taught her that much.

The dark maven's eyes had never wavered from hers. With one hand he raised her up and then guided her to the machine.

Trishana wiped the hot semen from her chin and looked at the contraption more closely now that she'd come to the thing's threshold. Her eyes flitted up to the top and those latches. In the center was a hasp where someone could attach a lock, ensuring that whoever resided within this akashic sarcophagus could never escape... At least not back into the physical realm. *Only through the aither port... and that port was everything for a sphere-goddess.*

She turned her gaze to Hymdreiddiech.

His eyes had still not broken away from her. His words came as a forceful whisper. "Get in."

Trishana knew that she had no choice. "I am yours to command."

Xander Kent caught the expressions on the faces of upper casted nobles as he strolled the corridors of Lord Oberon's castle at the heart of Faery Cairn; they were haughty glances. At first, he assumed their glares were meant for him since he walked through the inner sanctum of the court but was not méith. Then he realized their disdain was for his bodyguard and duelist... the human.

He'd spotted Remy casually checking his mystic dúshlán blade as they walked through the seelie capitol. The dagger had not glowed. *Oh, but what if it had?*

Kent smirked and then halted Remy at the threshold of the door, where his meeting with Oberon was to be held. The human paused dutifully and waited outside, giving Kent and the king their privacy.

A steely-eyed bodyguard glared at the elf as he entered.

The room contained a utilitarian office space much like any other, except that it was far grander. Stock items were inlaid with filigree and many objects were unnecessarily plated with gold. Oberon sat in a comfortable chair and welcomed the business mogul as he arrived.

Kent bowed low at the center of the room and then took the seat offered by the king. He waited for Oberon to begin the conversation. The summons had not described what the king wished to speak to him about, but Kent had a few good ideas.

"Zendamourn, please, wait outside," Oberon instructed his guard. The elf nodded stiffly and then exited, likely posting up adjacent to Remy Keaton.

As a savvy businessperson, Kent had made a great number of deals throughout his life and it earned him vast amounts of wealth. It could be that Oberon wished to extend him entry into the méith class. Kent would find that offer acceptable, even if it was never something he'd directly pursued nor thought he could attain... But it was hard to argue with an offer of eternal life, good so long as one retained the favor of the king. *Even despite its implication of golden handcuffs.*

Of course, the possibility was just as likely that his business dealings had earned him the wrath of the Lord of the Summer Court, or some other ranking member of the court, and Oberon wished to see him dead. For all his skills, not even Remy Keaton would be able to prevent that.

Kent remained calm and collected in his chair while the king studied him. He assumed that most people were unnerved by such an examination. Kent was not like most sidhe, though, nor even like most tuatha. By his nature, he was a betting man, and if the collective sum of all his gambles led Xander Kent here and to his death, then so be it. However, this whole charade might be nothing at all like either of the two outcomes he expected, and so Kent waited in silence.

Finally, Oberon grinned. "So, you are the elf who dared hire a human?'

Kent shrugged. "It was really no big deal. The man is incredibly talented, and I've always known that some problems require brute strength in oder to overcome... And the Sons of Adam are, by their nature, a hardier folk."

The king tilted his head but nodded his agreement. "That is certainly true. Though I have found that they are also much like flowers. They tend to blossom in the sun for a season, but afterward, they wilt at a speedier pace."

"Ah, but in that season..." Kent trailed off as he noticed Oberon steering the conversation away from business. Oberon stared into space, as if remembering something... or someone. *Probably one of his many human lovers.*

The king broke away from his reverie and then regarded Kent. "But you are more than just the elf who hired a deadly outcast, regardless of his talent. You are the sidhe who has done what the mavens could not."

Kent's jaw tightened, and he closed his mouth. The king hinted that he knew one of Kent's deepest secrets.

Oberon blinked at him as if waiting for a response to his statement.

The entrepreneur sucked in a deep breath and then sighed before cracking a wide smile. "So, I am found out, then?"

Nodding, the king explained, "My scouts have been searching for the owner of the rogue akasha factory for some time. We've been aware that many small power plants, much like yours, own various contracts with different cities and districts that supply them with akasha. Of course, that merely muddied the waters as we searched for you. But you know this, correct?"

Kent grinned again. "Guilty as charged, my lord."

Oberon smiled, happy that he'd finally solved a mystery that had puzzled the crown for some time. "Of course, none of those companies were capable of creating the stuff. The method of *developing* akasha has been a long held secret, and creating it in any form has been a secret held by Suíochán Naséan... But again, you must know this if you somehow uncovered a way to manufacture it."

Nodding to confirm all the king's suspicions, Kent still remained uncertain if he would leave this room alive. *But if not... Oberon could be warming up to an offer. Shall I roll the dice?*

"I learned the method almost accidentally," Kent told him. "As a smart businessperson, I've not always had to plow where I have harvested. Many years ago, I was put onto this path by an anonymous contact from the unseelie... To this day, I don't know his true identity, though I believe the aes sidhe may have been a former maven, perhaps some defector in hiding from the Radiant Tower."

Oberon stroked his chin as he listened. He nodded as if the suggestion made sense; many former mavens, if rendered ina aonar for dishonorable reasons, fled to the unseelie to escape the judgment of the Solais Cloaks.

Kent continued, "One point of fact, however, I do not manufacture the akasha," he insisted. "My true role in the trade is as a middleman. I own the distribution network, the lines that deliver the fluid to consumers. I also own the delivery company that contracts with many of those smaller operators who supply smaller boroughs and rural communities. But I will admit that I do know the trade secrets... and I am aware of how the stuff is made. If nothing else, I'm at least honest."

Tilting his head, the king both smiled and narrowed his gaze at him at once, and Kent was not certain how to interpret the expression.

"Why not also make it? It seems you could gain more profit."

"But assume more risk," Kent said. "Besides... I cannot. It requires the participation of a talented aes sidhe and I don't have a scrap of arcana within me. My highest and best purpose is as a middle-person... a well-paid one."

Oberon's expression took a furtive angle. "If I asked for the knowledge on how to create the raw akasha, would you give it to me?"

Gulping, Kent felt relief that the king hadn't demanded it, nor asked him in the olde tongue. The mavens and the throne had a series of political checks and balances; one of them had always been a division between Oberon, a powerful sorcerer in his own right, and the secrets of the Radiant Tower. Oberon's magic was different than that of the mavens, though Kent didn't know all the details, but it was meant for a different purpose—something vastly different from how the mavens plied theirs. Though it was imagined by many that the magnitude of Oberon's pure mystical ability exceeded all the aes sidhe combined, though nearly all of it was consumed with safeguarding his kingdom, creating a balance between the throne and the tower... But if Oberon had access to a storage pod of arcane power?

Kent answered with a lie. "I'm afraid I don't even have access to the method. It was written down and given to the third party who creates it in secret."

Oberon chuckled at the answer, and Kent assumed he'd asked the way he did to let Kent slither his way out of what could be considered a rude question.

The king asked, "Prior to beginning your business venture, were you aware that the mavens controlled one hundred percent of the akasha trade in my kingdom?"

"Of course, I was. But they were too small-minded. Had they consulted with someone like me I would have demonstrated how greater distribution leads to innovation and capitalizes on the desire of the non-arcane fey to such a degree that it could be greatly monetized *and* advances in magitech would bloom, creating immense leaps forward in comfort, industry—pretty much every field." Kent sat back in his chair. "I think the mavens were just too scared to do it. They feared that giving every-day commoners access to magic somehow lessened their stature."

"You are convinced of this?" Oberon asked.

"I am."

Oberon locked eyes with him. "I think you are correct."

Kent blinked. *I don't think I'm going to die today, after all.*

"It was very clever of you to shield your many dealings in the industry within Tógdraío Holdings, and then again via many other shell corporations... Stór Rúnda, I believe, is the one that handles your distributions." Oberon smirked. "Who would have thought an egg farm might have anything to do with distributing akasha?"

Kent merely shrugged again. He'd been able to stay one step ahead of the mavens for years, now, creatively swearing those he contracted with to secrecy with the olde tongue. But even before the Tower's Agents of Gray could ferret him out, the king's investigators seemed to have uncovered all of his secrets. *Almost all of them, anyway.*

Asking direct questions, Kent kept his posture carefully neutral. "You have demonstrated your ability to piece together all the details, my king. What is the next step?"

Oberon leaned back in his chair. "You're ambitious. I like that. Look around my office and tell me how many akashic ports you see. How many of them did you spot between the front gates and here?"

"None," Kent said.

"And not for lack of requests. I meant it when I said you've accomplished something that the mavens could not, *or would not*. And because of that, there are many rural homes in the middle of nowhere that are more technologically advanced than the heart of the Summer Court." Oberon tilted forward, leaning over his desk.

"I want you and your company to install your systems here and throughout Faery Cairn."

Kent blinked with surprise.

"I've had a long history of distrust with the mavens. They are... necessary. But even though I am king, they continue to check my power over even the simplest of things. Your assessment of them is correct, I think; they fear losing their high standing. Perhaps there is no malice in their decision to withhold akasha from the Court, but their short-sightedness has progressed beyond inconvenience and I'll not stand for. How soon can your company install akasha drip lines here?"

"I can make it my highest priority," Kent told him, and then speculated on a realistic timeline.

"Excellent. That was the answer I was hoping for," Oberon said. "Prioritize the most important places within the castle and then move on to those places that cater to the nobles who are méith. I'll expect you to communicate with my majordomo. He will send word to you soon."

Kent nodded and gripped the arms of his chair. "Is that all, my lord?"

Oberon nodded. "It is. You are dismissed... Actually, wait. I should note that I want the mavens to be the ones actually supplying the akasha for the system you will build here. I'm sure you understand... Politics and all."

"Of course. You need to keep the peace with the magi," Kent said. He flashed Oberon a grin. "And if they continue believing they can control the flow of it to you in the meantime, even if another source is readily available, then that serves your needs perfectly, my king."

A slow, matching grin spread across Oberon's face. "If the Tower continues to dither, there may be room for continued conversation on supply matters in the future."

"Thank you," Kent told him as he rose. "I'll get to work right away."

Chapter Twelve

Remy walked into his apartment fatigued from his return journey. Kent had been in a chipper mood and was eager to make good time back to Cathair Dé.

Something about the door felt wrong as he took the knob in hand. The mechanism didn't feel right... as if it had been broken.

Remy had barely stepped through the door when he spotted the stranger there. In a flash, Remy pulled his blade. The dúshlán didn't glow, but the intruder's eyes lit with both terror and surprise.

"Who are you? Where is my wife?" Remy snarled. He called, "Jaira? Hobin?"

The intruder, a young human, nearly jumped out of his skin at the sight of the renowned duelist drawing on him. Remy took stock of him and realize he was not a sidhe. He was young, barely a teen, and a rumpled blanket lay on the couch where he'd obviously been sleeping. Dirty and wearing animal skins, Remy assumed he was one of the Fianna by his dress.

"Please," the young man insisted. "No one was here when I arrived. I'm just a messenger!"

Remy's eyes narrowed at the words' possible implications. If they'd been delivered with more malice, they could have been a threat.

The messenger pointed to a scrap of paper on the table. "Is that important?" he asked hopefully.

Angling the tip of his dagger at the intruder, Remy stepped forward and forced the messenger backward to keep a space cushion. "What does it say?" Remy had no intention of taking his eyes off the man until he'd sorted out where Jaira was.

The messenger's cheeks reddened. "I, uh, cannot read… But I *can* track any kind of animal through dense woods."

Remy heard the embarrassment in his voice, and the attempt to cover it over with a boast. He decided to take him at his word and scooped up the note. It was in Jaira's flowing script.

Dear Remy, urgent business has come up requiring my presence at court as a méith noble. The timing is inconvenient, but I shall return as soon as possible and will plan to stay with my uncle in Daonra Dlúth. I brought Hobin to my parents for now. My mother can explain in more detail… With love, Jaira.

He knew that Daonra Dlúth was part of the metropolitan area surrounding Faery Cairn and he'd just passed through it recently. Daonra Dlúth was also home to Suíochán Naséan, a tower and sprawling campus belonging to the mavens. Its grounds split the border wall separating Daonra Dlúth and Faery Cairn.

"Morrígan's three faces," Remy cursed mildly and sighed. "If I'd have known, I might've stated in Faery Cairn with her."

"I don't much pretend to know what your letter said, but that's not the message I was sent with," the other human stated. "I was here two days waiting, though, and I'm eager to get home."

Remy met his gaze.

"Madadh told me not to return until I'd delivered it," the human continued. "The Fianna have called an official moot, a meeting between its factions."

"Like a peace talk?" Remy asked.

"It's more than that, but I'm sure Fian Bairn's attack on the maginarius will be discussed... I'm not old enough yet to vote, which is why Madadh sent me to fetch you."

The duelist nodded. "I'm assuming I'll have no privilege then, either?"

Shaking his head, the younger Fianna told him, "No... And you are invited only for the purpose of witnessing the proceedings. Madadh wanted you there as his guest, which is a rare occurrence, indeed."

"But why? Internal Fianna politics aside, I'm not sure what good it might do besides streamlining our conversations."

The youth held Remy's eyes. "You are our conduit, sir."

Remy arched an eyebrow. "Conduit?"

"Our connection to the sidhe. You have contacts and abilities that the Fianna lack. You have a voice amongst the fey, one that cannot be drowned out by even the Frith Duine."

Remy sighed again. He hadn't asked for any sort of role, honorary or official, but he understood Madadh's position. With the rising human-hatred that the Frith Duine fostered, the Fianna needed as many allies as it could muster as a matter of self-preservation. "All right, fine."

The youth nodded and motioned for him to follow. "I feared you wouldn't return before it ended, but here you are. The gathering is happening soon and we must hurry if we are to arrive in time."

He paused and looked at Remy. "Actually... Before we go, you should empty your pockets."

Gnub snorted in the evening air. The orc didn't like the smell of things in the seelie.

Mists poured into his group's location from the trees and enveloped their small camp where they'd set up tents and made a fire. Gnub had been picked from among his kin to accompany Syrmerware and Rharzal, older cousins of his, on their mission.

Their aim was straightforward. Kill the Betrayer for the glory of Winter and to advance an orc to the Rime Throne. The delivery of slaves had been enough to get them past the customs troops at the dividing canyons, but they'd have to keep hidden until their true objective became available.

The unseelie agents only knew that the human, Remy Keaton, was in the area. They simply needed to watch and wait for an opportunity to strike.

White fog rolled through the glade they'd set up near; their horses grazed on the grass. Gnub grumbled as he picked over the cold rations. His traps had yielded no prey, and Gnub preferred his meat warm, and if possible, still wriggling.

He glared at the three elves in their company, resenting them for not grimacing at the food they'd brought from their home. Gnub knew the foppish one of the three was the queen's personal attendant, Chokorum. Gnub had worked with Andrathan before, a sidhe who had a reputation for whipping lightstarved into line and putting down slave insurrections—he'd been picked for the team in order to keep their cargo in order. But the last elf Gnub only knew by reputation. She was either Arcenae or Eilrora and she was aes sidhe. Gnub did not know how to identify between the twin sisters. It might not have been possible even were they not twin sisters... All the elves looked alike to the orc.

"Has the queen been updated on our present location, Eilrora?" Andrathan asked her.

Arcenae nodded slowly. "My sister will know where we are. Even across the realms and beyond Solstox, she can sense my presence. There is no place I could go where she would not be able to sense me and know what I am feeling."

Andrathan snatched another handful of whatever they were eating. Gnub wasn't sure what it was; he'd never cared for the foods enjoyed by the sidhe.

"Well, tell Eilrora to pass along my thanks to Rhagathena for getting us the good stuff. I've never eaten so well while in the wilderness," Andrathan said with a grin.

The aes sidhe glared at him. "That seems a waste of my talents," said Arcenae.

"Queen Rhagathena did not choose the meal-plan," Chokorum said flatly, and Gnub mulled over the two's disposition. Neither seemed to care for Andrathan, likely because he was a working class tuatha and not one of the queen's pets, spoiled by the relative comforts of Arctig Maen. That made Gnub approve of him all the more.

Of course, Gnub would snap Andrathan's neck in a heartbeat if it would curry favor with the Winter Court and earn him higher standing within their ranks. Just because Gnub identified with him didn't mean he wanted to *be* him.

The orc shook his head and glanced back to his cousins, who were arguing about some hypothetical nonsense... whether Wulflock or Oberon would emerge victorious in unarmed combat.

"Yer both wrong," Gnub growled at them, drawing irked looks from the two other orcs. "If you could pit them against each other, then you ought to include Indech, king of the Fomorians."

The orc brothers looked at each other, and then at Gnub, and shrugged. "Well, obviously, I'd have to go with Indech," said Rharzal, and then the horses shrieked in the grassy opening. They whinnied with a guttural panic, as if wounded, and then all the animals bolted for the trees.

A blast of fire erupted and ignited the grass. Flames lapped the sky with an oily tinge, flashing with unnatural hues, as if conjured by alchemy or magitech.

An arrow zinged out of the billowing mists, narrowly missing Gnub and lodging in the log nearest him. He recoiled from the fire, realizing its light was how he'd been spotted.

"Away! Scatter," snarled Rharzal.

A hound bayed somewhere in the obscurity and voices barked out directions. "That way—unseelie invaders!"

"Shit," Syrmerware barked. "We've been spotted."

Gnub didn't see which way anyone had gone in all the chaos, but assumed each one had fled different directions, which would make it easier to escape.

All major cities had some kind of outpost meant to police the king's interests. Usually, they were filled with lazy fey hoping to get fat off an easy military appointment and were rarely called on for duty this deep in the kingdom. Apparently, the leader of Cathair Dé's patrol force possessed ambition.

Gnub's sidhe companions would have an easier time escaping than the orcs. There were no orcs of summer and Gnub hoped that whatever garrison had been sent after them caught one of the elves, rather than his kind. *Andrathan was the least needed at this point.*

A way off, Syrmerware shouted a reminder. "Meet at the waypoints," and then the voice faded between the dark distance and the huffing of Gnub's lungs as he sprinted through the trees.

His first objective was to escape, to get as far away from the hunters as possible. Only then would Gnub consider his other needs: food, shelter, and water. Afterward, he'd find his way to one of the locations they'd established as a regrouping spot in case of emergency.

Gnub bit his lip impatiently as he fled alone and into the darkness. *Aderyn Corff has earned a temporary reprieve.*

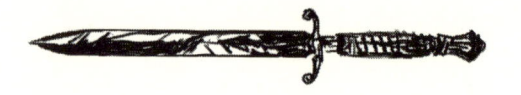

Remy lost his guide somewhere between the thick woods and crowded trees. The young Fianna had simply slipped away, but their destination had already become apparent by the glow of flame light.

Ahead, the trees loomed tall and the dense, leafy canopy blocked much of the light despite it being midday. Remy was not certain exactly where they were, though he knew they were only a short ride from Cathair Dé and in the opposite direction of the Madadh's caravan. As urban as the Arcadeaxn cities sprawled, the woods of remained as wild as ever.

There was no technology here. Though, technically, the aither was everywhere, nature refused to let magic or machine tame it. *A strange triumvirate,* Remy mused.

Against the large fire in the clearing up ahead, Remy spotted many bodies moving as shadows before the light. He got only five paces further when sentries, invisible only moments prior, halted him and pointed crude spears at his chest. They were both in their hulking, lycan forms, and both stood a head and chest taller than Remy, who was less concerned with spears, and much more focused on the talons that held them.

"My name is Remy Keaton," he said, holding his hands up submissively. He repeated the words that his guide had taught him. "I was invited to this moot as a guest of Madadh, leader of Fian Faolchú."

"No silver," growled the first wolf.

"None," Remy said, suddenly glad for the foresight of the messenger who'd had him remove any groats and silver pieces from his purse. Both denominations were made from the metal, which would have insulted the moot ceremony.

The lupine guards growled, but let him pass. The second of them pointed the way to where Madadh stood.

Remy headed toward the fire and noted that he'd arrived just in time for the proceedings. The bodies of a gathering crowd had just begun moving towards the clearing's center and Remy joined them.

As he grew closer, Remy realized it was not one large fire, but three of them. Together, they formed a triangle of space at the center of the space. Within that geometric area stood five figures. Crowds gathered behind two of them, arrayed on the flat sides of the triangle where they pressed in to listen.

Madadh stood next to a female figure who wore a thick belt with a pouch at her hip. Remy had seen her before in the Fianna camp. Her eyes were dark and hard, and her posture angled defensively for her leader. *There's more to her posture than devotion to her leader,* Remy thought, tilting his head as he scanned her. *Leader and lover.*

The other duo of individuals had no crowd at their back. There was kindness in their eyes and they looked as if they regretted being there. More heavily muscled than the first, one of the pair hung half a step back and looked warily at the fifth solo creature across the space. *An alpha and a subordinate... A tribal leader and their guardian?*

Unlike the others, the lone person was already shifted into his lycan form. He bared his teeth contemptuously as he scanned the grounds. *This must be Oddur.*

Remy pushed his way through the knots of Fianna. He traded glances of recognition with many of them. Several of them Remy recognized as freed slaves who bore the puckered scars that marked them as lightstarved; they'd fattened up somewhat these last many days and looked much healthier. Defiant passion replaced the previous despondency he'd seen in their eyes.

Turning a circle to ensure the assembly was gathered, Madadh glanced momentarily at Remy. He made no overt response to him, but Remy knew that he'd been spotted.

"As leader of the Fianna, I call this moot to order," Madadh stated in a loud and firm voice. "Recognized are Oddur of Fian Bairn, Madadh of Fian Faolchú, and emissary Sheera who represents Sbrintiwr of Fian Fèidh."

The meek-looking Sheera bowed slightly and looked as if she wished more of her pack had shown up like the others had.

Madadh continued, "Oddur, you have no appointed second."

Oddur growled. "I need none. If this moot breaks down into trials of combat, I shall fight it myself."

Remy gulped. He suddenly understood how werewolf politics worked. *Words first, and failing that, they'd resort to violence.* That Oddur refused to be in his human form did not bode well for any conversational outcomes.

Madadh's second curled her upper lip and shifted into her ferocious lycan form. Remy blinked at the terrifying sight. He had seen her before, eviscerating sidhe guards when the Fianna had set the lightstarved free from the Vastran mine. The belt she wore was a ready identifier, and he noted the bands of stretchy webbing between sections of leather that allowed her not to snap it.

"Easy, Scathach," Madadh told her, gently placing a hand on her arm. "This is no place for one to lose their composure." He cast a sidelong glance at Oddur.

Scathach's nostrils flared, but she reverted to her human form and held her temper in check, clothing now tattered to rags, which exposed distracting sections of her naked flesh.

Oddur's pack was smaller than Madadh's, but they held themselves differently. Remy recognized their posture, the confidence that burned within their eyes. *The Fian Bairn had trained for battle... These ones are warriors.*

"We are here to adjudicate the incident at Ollscoil Maginarius," said Madadh.

Oddur sneered. "Fian Bairn only recognizes it as a morale failure by Fian Faolchú."

A low growl rumbled in Scathach's chest.

Oddur continued, "We warriors exacted justice against the tuatha at the Maginarius. That Fian Faolchú did not join the attack is egregious to us. We went to great lengths to secure the dallineb weed which inhibits the aes sidhe's powers."

Remy's eyebrows arched. Everyone knew about dweomer root, which blocked spell casters abilities as well as interfering with imbiber's connection to the aithersphere, and it had a distinct flavor, and any aes sidhe dosed with it knew so immediately. It was so widespread that the mavens only ate and drank from trusted sources, foods certified as *iontaofa*. The yellow mavens were in charge of the dietary regulations governing it, and there were stiff penalties for intentionally dosing aes sidhe with the stuff.

He'd only ever heard rumors of other verbena reagents that could interfere with spell casting, and then remembered that Arawyn had told him about the stuff on their flight from Ollscoil. *Apparently, the Tower wanted to restrict widespread information on the stuff. Any knowledge about how to make a maven vulnerable was considered dangerous by them—when the effects of dweomer root came out, they'd successfully lobbied to install iontaofa, which carries a death sentence for violations.*

"The dallineb weed ensured our success without a single death in my clan," Oddur said. He tossed a bundle of it into the center of the meeting space as if punctuating his words.

Anger flared in Madadh's eyes. "Six of my clan mates were killed in that attack," he snarled.

"Then they should not have attempted to stop our slaughter." Oddur raised his voice.

"You used silvered weapons on your kin," roared Madadh. "Where you even got blades forged of alchemical silver is beyond my reckoning, but that you did it demonstrates your premeditation."

Oddur kept his composure, although Remy felt certain he spotted a smug grin on the Lycan's long muzzle.

"Then you should have sided with Fian Bairn," Oddur spat.

"And break our oath with Suíochán Naséan? You have endangered us all by instigating your war, Oddur! The mavens will hunt us, possibly even *all* humans, not just the fáelad."

"Then the unchanged humans had best join our ranks because war is coming whether you like it or not. Besides, I pledged the oath against violence to the High Maven Selashiuhl. Since her death, another has taken her place. Fian Bairn does *not* renew its oath to the corruption of aes sidhe and their so-called Radiant Tower. We did the Fianna a favor by culling the forces of our enemies before they could be indoctrinated against us."

Oddur scanned whatever faces he could see by the flame light. "The Frith Duine have been active within the aes sidhe, and especially at Ollscoil Maginarius. The university was a hotbed of hatred; they were training their students to hate us. The headmaster was a brother to Elethiel Ciníoch, the very sidhe who formed the Frith Duine." Oddur spat at the name.

Remy suddenly remembered the face of the tortured school leader he'd found with Captain Ochara. The victim bore a striking resemblance to the firebrand stirring up hate in Cathair Dé's market... The elf with the birthmark at his neck. *The elf who'd spied on Jaira and me to some ill-defined end.*

"Whether we like it or not, war is coming... It's best if *we* wield the tip of the spear," barked Oddur.

"Not if Fian Faolchú has any say," growled the leader of the Fianna. "We still lead, and Fian Bairn will submit."

Oddur stiffened as if bracing for a welcomed challenge.

"Here is my ruling," Madadh insisted. "Fian Bairn will release the children you have taken from the slavers. I have invited a guest who can deliver them to a human friendly orphanage for care, or you can surrender them to one or both of the other tribes." He glanced aside at Sheera. Sbrintiwr's representative.

Remy's stomach plunged when he noted her body language. It said... *nothing*. And that made him nervous.

Madadh either hadn't noticed or refused to pay it any visible heed. "Furthermore, you will surrender your scald for one year, ensuring you can create no more fáelad in that time. I will not abide by you converting disenfranchised youth into our kind and launching further attacks. As to whatever pack mate who used silvered weapons and killed members of Fian Faolchú go, our rules are clear. Surrender him or her and we shall cut the sigil from his body, casting them out of our assembly and rendering him human."

Remy looked from Oddur to Madadh. The way he'd used a specific pronoun at the end suggested Madadh knew exactly who had killed his pack mates.

"No," Oddur said flatly. He brushed away a patch of shaggy fur at his chest, exposing muscle-rippled hide and a mark made of raised scar tissue. It looked something like a brand upon the flesh, only more decorative. "Though you can come and claim it if you'd like to try."

Both Madadh and Scathach's figures blurred with motion as they shifted into their lycan forms.

Oddur withdrew a sheathed blade from where it hung at the belt on his hip. He slid the scabbard off slowly to reveal the silvered knife. Alchemical silver was stronger than the elemental metal which could be destroyed with repeat use and blunted easily because of its malleability—this was fey craftsmanship, and something requiring skill in magic to achieve.

All except for Fian Bairn's members gasped at the insult and at the blatant challenge. "Perhaps it is time for a change in leadership of the Fianna," growled Oddur. As he did so, many of his pack mates shifted forms and drew forbidden blades of their own.

"More defiance of the rules!" snarled Scathach. "You cannot issue a ritual challenge of leadership under these conditions. It will not be recognized!"

Oddur hissed at her. "Fuck. Your. Rules." He annunciated each word sharply so there was no mistaking them. "Either surrender rule of the Fianna to me, to Fian Bairn, or you shall rue this day forever."

Both Oddur and Madadh turned to Sheera.

She slumped visibly. "Sbrintiwr has made it clear in the past that Fian Fèidh wishes little to do with the bickering of the tribes. We remain in the faewylds and refuse to enter the argument," Sheera said. She blushed, knowing that her refusal to render a verdict would cast them all into disarray.

Still gripping his knife, Oddur and his warriors postured as if to fight their kin. "No longer are we Fian Bairn," he decreed. "We are simply *the Bairn*."

"You cannot just walk away from this. You cannot secede from this body," Madadh said.

"Watch me," Oddur said, and then he looked past Madadh and at the remainder of the gathered Fianna. "Any of you who wish to follow the path of vengeance, of righteous war against our enemies, you are welcome with the Bairn… But choose soon, before it is too late."

Smiling as broadly as a venomous snake who'd already injected his poison, Oddur and whatever Bairn were present turned and left. For a long moment, nobody, nothing, made a sound. Even the pyres which lit the moot seemed to crackle in quietude.

Madadh shifted back to his human form and snorted a hot blast of air through his nose. He muttered, "Well, that could have gone better. But at least now all our fears and suspicions are confirmed."

Adjacent to him, Scathach nodded solemnly and Remy pushed through the crowd to join his friend.

At the rear, a dull murmur rose as the Fianna whispered amongst themselves as to what all of this might mean.

Before addressing Madadh, Remy crouched at the center and retrieved the dallineb weed where it had been tossed. None of the Fianna paid him any mind, and none appeared to assert any ownership over the bundle of dried stalks and so he slipped it into his pouch.

He turned to Madadh and gave the Fianna leader a sympathetic look. "I'm not sure why you brought me here to witness all of this, but tell me how I can help. It sounds like trouble is brewing—and division amongst the humans can't help."

Madadh merely shook his head. "I don't think that you *can* help. But I needed you to see it for yourself."

"See what?"

"To see that Oddur was right about one thing, at least... war is coming. But not just against the aes sidhe—Fian Bairn... *the Bairn*—makes war against *us*, as well."

Jaira stepped out of the hired carriage that brought her all the way from her parents' estate to Faery Caern. She wasted no time getting there except for what was required to travel there. As soon as they'd hit the borders of Daonra Dlúth, Jaira had dispatched a message to her uncle requesting a later visit and told him of her desire to stay a few days while she attended matters of court.

In truth, she had only met her uncle, Talathan, the previous lord of House Morgansteen, twice, and both were when she was young. Jaira had only met her aunt by marriage, Kasianna, one time in passing.

She was not certain how they might all get on now that she was an adult and married, but she hoped for it to be cordial, despite the fact that they'd long ago squandered all the wealth Jaira's grandfather had built up. They had been forced to abdicate the title to Jaira's father in order to retain any semblance of stature. If anything was cause for a deep-seated grudge amongst the sidhe, it was losing méith to another.

Her aunt and uncle were no longer méith. To the best of her knowledge, Jaira's relations were not even saibhir... but that was an issue for later.

The entire ride she had reached out with her senses, those secret arcane abilities that gave her the ability to parse the future. She'd been unable to arrive at any conclusions. Oberon's castle was such a place of power and so filled with high-level players at politics that too many variables remained. Perhaps if Jaira was trained in using her abilities, she could sift through the potential outcomes, but in order to keep her secret, getting training was impossible. Her visions resulted in so many options, each cascading outward in a dizzying array of realities, that it gave her migraines.

Presently, Jaira stood at the tall doors leading to the main castle where the activities of the court happened during most days. Being méith provided her access to all the trappings of high society. At any given time, Oberon's palace played host to members of that class.

Feasts occurred regularly, wine and other drinks flowed, dancing and gossip happened on a regular basis... especially the gossip. Behind those doors was a political battleground where lesser kings were made, where deals and alliances formed in alcoves, and, very often, in secluded bed-chambers. Rulers of lower realms cut their teeth across all spectrums of this domain, and Jaira's ears rang with her mother's words. *The Summer Court is a very dangerous place.*

"Are you, uh, not going to open the doors?" A voice from behind Jaira startled her.

Jaira turned and blinked. She stood inches away from the most eligible bachelor in all of Arcadeax.

Oberon's eldest son grinned back at her. He was as gorgeous as any sidhe could be and looked every bit like a youthful Oberon, though his grin was perhaps more roguish and a playful mischief flashed in his eyes.

"My apologies, Prince Tanaquill," Jaira said, her eyes noting the stray touch of lipstick and makeup on his collar. It had undoubtedly been left by some earlier playfulness of another.

"Please," he said, "I prefer to go by my nickname... I'm certain you know it."

"Prince Puck," Jaira began.

He shook his head. "*Just* Puck. I'm not much for formality. Neither is my little brother." Puck looked around in all directions as if searching for him and then gave up with a shrug. "If you should find Prince Kenna, simply call him Mustardseed. He'll much prefer it."

Jaira blushed and then caught the mischief in Puck's eyes as he examined her.

"If you made it this far past the guards, then you are a noble fey." Puck squinted. "But I can't say that I know you."

"We've only met once in passing and you were... preoccupied," Jaira said. The last time she'd been here was to receive the Dagda's blessing from Oberon prior to the duels her father sponsored. Puck had been chasing a few silly she-elves who'd been throwing themselves at him. The last she'd spotted Puck, the prince was sneaking away with all three of them, and Jaira had known that at least one of them had been recently engaged.

She looked at him and that grin. He was gorgeous, but the longer she looked at him, the more Jaira thought he couldn't hold a flame to Remy. *Puck is supposed to be talented in many skills, but I'm pretty sure Remy could kick his ass if he wanted.*

"And what brings a pretty méith to this particular doorstep... And follow up question, what could stop her in her tracks on the threshold?" Puck tilted his head. "Third question... Is there some way I can help?"

The longer Jaira looked at Puck, the more of him she saw. There was sincerity in his words. Maybe it was that the owner of the makeup had slaked his lusts for long enough that his compassion could come through, or perhaps his reputation as a rake was greatly exaggerated. *Or maybe this exact sort of charm is how he's bedded so many of the eligible she-elves... and many who aren't?* Jaira shook away the jaded skepticism and decided to trust him. She'd need *some* kind of advocate at court, and he *was* offering to assist her.

"I... It has been a long while since I've been to court and I'm not quite sure how to proceed," she admitted as Puck opened the door and invited her into the building's halls.

"Well, come, then. You must accompany me as my guest." Puck wrapped an arm around her waist and escorted her within.

Jaira nearly pulled away and then recognized the gesture as more familial than predatory. She sensed Puck was being genuine and a kind of pressure formed in her head similar to the arcane foresight that had caused her earlier migraines. It was like her subconscious had sorted the best potential outcomes and attempted to steer her on this course.

Puck waved and greeted several of the folks who meandered the expansive corridors. Jaira noted that at least a few of them were changelings and her opinion of the prince elevated.

A few minutes after navigating the bending passageways filled with comfortable furnishings and fine art, they arrived at the entrance to the main hall of the Summer Court. Beyond the next set of doors, Jaira knew she would find the Gilded Throne set upon a dais and many rows of pillars that stretched to the ceiling, where balconies opened from private galleries. Just beyond this point lay the seat of seelie power.

She gasped slightly and swallowed down her nerves.

"You're right," Puck said, reacting to her noticeable balk. "First, we both require a drink." He snapped his fingers and a nearby servant hurried forward with a tray containing a decanter of gold liquor and two glasses.

He poured himself some and began pouring a second for Jaira. She held up a hand to stop him. "I... I can't."

Puck caught the way her hand brushed against her stomach as she protested.

"Oh... I... *Oh*." Recognition sparked in his eyes as he connected the dots. He did not look away as Jaira's gaze turned onto her feet and she bit the inside of her cheeks.

"Wait." He lowered his voice. "Am I the only one who knows?"

She gave him a brief nod, but then shrugged. "Well, almost. There are only a few who know my secret. You will keep it for me?" Her voice pleaded.

Puck sighed and nodded. Then he chuckled as he admitted, "At least *this* secret is one I'm experienced in sharing... Though it's a first when I'm not more, uh, intimately involved."

As he stared at her, something clicked between them and he smirked. "We are two of a kind, I guess." He laughed again. "And I'm just now realizing I don't even know your name."

"That is why I am here. My name... It's all because of what goes on some slip of paper somewhere and who it might upset," she told him. Her voice verged on panic as she began to explain.

Puck's brows furrowed. "I can't imagine anyone could be so angry with a simple name that it could worry a noble of the Summer Court."

She still hadn't disclosed her name, but as Puck sipped on the golden liquor, Jaira told him everything. Pregnancy details. All about her husband, including his job and species. The refusal to certify her marriage by Summer Court officials. Her fears over losing méith and, even worse, earning the wrath of Titania for birthing a changeling.

The prince blinked at her. "Wait, I *do* know you. By rumor, at least. You are Jaira Morgansteen—the noble who married the human duelist. *They say your husband is very good,*" he said admirably. He followed it up with an affable smile, but kept his voice low. "Hopefully, you've noted how I treat my half-blood siblings already. I'm very much in favor of seeing my mother's opinion shift on this matter."

"Thank you," Jaira said, finally exhaling fully and sucking in her first comforting breath since entering Faery Cairn's borders.

Puck smiled broadly and offered her a slight bow. "I will help you, and for no cost. I know, I know... not very fey of me, but I feel like your husband and I would hit it off well." His expression took on a slightly rakish edge. "I mean, I can see that he has impeccable taste in women, much like me, and I might be a touch jealous."

It was Jaira's turn to grin. "I shall tell him you said so."

He nearly laughed at that, but held up his hands as if to stay her tongue. "No need. I have a feeling he knows as much already."

"You know," Jaira admitted, "there was a time when my mother had once hoped to engineer a suitable match for you."

"Oh, yeah?"

"You are clearly a few decades away from settling down, and Lady Morgansteen had hoped my broken engagement would have remained intact but resulted in a daughter who could be of interest to you."

Puck laughed and tossed his empty glass to the nearby servant. Startled by the impertinence of it, he lurched forward to catch the drink ware, bobbled it twice, and barely managed to snatch it before it could shatter on the floor.

"Wait. If I recall, you are engaged to Fuerian Vastra?"

Jaira nodded.

"That guy is an idiot!"

They shared a laugh together.

"*We* would have made a better pair than you and *he*, and I'm afraid I've missed that opportunity. Regardless, I will help Remy Keaton for your sake, Misses Keaton-steen." He blended the names, recalling the reason for her visit.

"You think you can overturn the decision against Remy being named heir?"

"Fey, no," Puck admitted. "But I believe I can share a secret with you, and if Remy is as talented as you say, then perhaps he can earn such a thing from my father. Tell me this." The prince's expression turned suddenly serious. "Is you husband good at finding lost or stolen things?"

Jaira nodded slowly, confidently. "I was kidnapped between dueling matches, taken by a supernatural creature, the creation of an evil sorcerer. All others had given up hope, but Remy tracked me down, destroyed the enemy, and rescued me before handily defeating the vaunted Fuerian Vastra, accomplished duelist." Her words describing her ex-fiancé dripped with sarcasm.

Puck smiled as he said, "Perfect. Then first we must take a turn through Court. Forget what the gossip mongers might say. Their words don't matter—you just need to be *seen*. Regardless of what they say, we want them to be talking, *and about you*... And then comes the second part of the plan..."

Chapter Thirteen

Remy was already in a foul mood as he tromped through the center of Cathair Dé. He didn't know enough about their inner workings to know how to deal with the Fianna schism, and he wasn't sure he had any say in their politics, anyway. In the past, Madadh had offered him a place among their numbers and Remy had rejected it. The cost of admission was too high, as far as Remy was concerned.

The only thing the duelist knew he *could* do was get a bite to eat and try to think on the topic. Perhaps what the Fianna needed was a fresh perspective.

With his wife out of town, there wasn't much choice, anyway. Remy decided to swing by one of the food carts and grab lunch. He frowned a moment. *Thoranmir loved these carts.* And then he put that thought out of his mind; focusing on the past didn't help his present.

Maybe I should drop in at the Morgansteens' later and collect Hobin and Arawyn? It seems as if most of the danger has passed for the ellyllon, aside from perhaps needing to testify for Captain Ochara... But how can we do that without admitting that humans were responsible for the carnage—*the Tower already knows what, who, the Fianna are, so we can't blame it on wolf-monsters without implicating humans.*

Remy desired justice, but he found himself at a crossroads. If he gave up the truth to Ochara, it would not punish only Oddur's clan. *I've already seen that there are Frith Duine within the peacekeepers' ranks.*

Lost in thought, he bumped shoulders with someone hard enough to whirl him on his heels. Quick as a flash, he reached for a weapon in case this was a precursor to any follow-up attacks.

After all, he was close enough to the open dueling grounds that some ambitious ribbon seeker might have instigated a duel prematurely.

The other person he collided with practically mirrored his movements, also spinning and reaching for his weapon.

Remi locked eyes with Fuerian Vastra. The elvish fop also appeared startled to have encountered his most hated foe in the open market. A collective gasp rippled through any nearby bystanders. Their feud was well known, and any folks within their vicinity backed up as quickly as possible.

For several moments, the human and his nemesis stared at each other. The rising tension was thick enough to be felt even by those too obtuse to have seen what happened. A dull murmur of anticipation rumbled across the area. The fighters may not have been in the open dueling grounds, but that did not mean they could not duel. It simply meant that if one party issued the challenge, it could be declined. Of course, that would result in rumors and plenty of speculation, but it would also result in a bloodless afternoon.

Fuerian *always* had the option of declining, as he did not currently hold dueling credentials. But that status, or lack of it, was what the whole system was based on, anyway. If he refused to defend his honor with a challenge, regardless of the location it came in, he would lose face. And given the tenuousness state of his current situation, such a thing could ruin him.

Onlookers whispered amongst themselves and trading small, impromptu bets. The last time these two had met at the public duels, Remy had drawn first-blood and embarrassed the haughty elf. Certainly, Fuerian must be keen to publicly correct that outcome. Everyone knew how Remy had promised to one day kill Fuerian for ending the life of his best friend.

Both potential combatants stared daggers at each other; the hate was palpable. With nostrils flaring and curled lips revealing bared teeth, they sized each other up. Neither made a move against the other, however.

"Remy Keaton," snarled Fuerian. "Funny that I should meet you here. I had meant to ask you if you knew anything about these raids that have taken place at my mines recently?"

"Nothing rings a bell, but it sounds like someone is doing good work," Remy quipped dryly.

Fuerian continued, "Surely you know that I employed a number of human slaves because of the presence of iron ore within this mine?"

"Employed is a funny word to use when you really mean slavery."

Quirking his mouth, Fuerian relaxed his posture, seeming certain that the weapons for this duel were words. Remy remained uncertain of that, however. His shoulders remained tense and his gripped wrapped around his dúshlán in one hand and around the hilt of his sword with the other.

The human had long suspected Fuerian was a part of the dream hallow operation in the area. It had mostly fallen apart after Gareth Morass had gone to prison. But Remy had seen the elf at the mine and knew Gareth was out.

Fuerian continued, "You can tell whoever is behind these attacks that I've traded out my human workforce for good. The dregs my fey have pulled in from the Haunts are equal to the task," Fuerian told him. "I've got quotas to reach, after all, and they are a compliant workforce." A twinkle shone in his eye and the elf lowered his voice. "It seems an easy way to shorten the distribution channel, don't you think?"

Remy knew the Haunts. It was the worst district in Cathair Dé. Structures had collapsed there for decades. There, roofs caved in upon themselves and building foundations crumbled to rot, often falling in on themselves and crushing all those poor souls living within those dilapidated walls. Most places in the Haunts housed those tuatha strung out on dream hallow or any other various apothiks. Those who weren't—those who *chose* to live there—were scary in altogether different ways.

"As long as the work remains relatively simple and I supply the apothik junkies with enough scraps to find their next high, my business ventures will be fine." Fuerian taunted him. "Although you might take note that the Frith Duine has taken a keen interest in the deaths that these raiders caused. The killers were ddiymadferth by all signs... And the Frith Duine seem like the civic group best equipped to petition Oberon and demand justice from this crime. Several of those dead were Frith Duine members who were in my employ, you know."

"Why are you even here?" Remy snarled at him. Above all else, Remy knew that Fuerian loved to brag. The wealthy jerk had already divulged useful bits of information to him through taunts, but the he-elf was an endless fount of schemes.

Fuerian shrugged. "I'm merely about town on business, searching for a new aithermancer. It appears that mine has gone absent." A moment of consternation crossed Fuerian's face. Releasing his grip on the hilt, he took two steps closer to Remy, who did not relax his posture. Fuerian raised his hands, and he seemed almost genuine to Remy.

Lowering his voice, Fuerian told him, "You know, we would make far greater allies than we would enemies. There would be great profit in it, as well. If my reputation could be saved, I might even be willing to give you what I promised you prior to our first duel. Under different circumstances, we might even be friends, you know."

Remy spat. His angry, wet wad landed at Fuerian's feet. The wicked sidhe had tried to sell him back his birthright, the memories and life he'd forgotten upon his entry to Arcadeax when Remy was a child.

Remy had made his choice that day, and no amount of bartering would let Fuerian return Thoranmir to life.

"Fuck you, Fuerian Vastra. I've seen how you treat your friends. You left Gareth Morass to rot in prison, not that I mind your decision on that score." His fingers wrapped tighter around his dúshlán.

Something crossed Fuerian's face. Remy's comment seemed to have actually hurt the elf. Fuerian shrugged, and then reset his face to a placid, stony expression. "I suppose you are right. Though you are not much better. I seem to recall that your friend, Thoranmir Shelton, has also suffered because of his choice of friendships. Although he's in *the ground* rather than alive and behind bars... Although Gareth was recently paroled due to my efforts."

Blinded by his rage, Remy drew both his dagger and sword from their sheaths. His subconscious collected the data Fuerian shared. His mind flagged it while his body reacted, triggered to violence by his enemies taunts. *So, it was Gareth Morass I saw at the mine... And Gareth would have passed on to Fuerian if had he seen me there... which he apparently hadn't.*

Remy waited for the official challenge from Fuerian, some verbal desire to make this duel official. He clutched both sword and dagger in either hand and, seething, snarled wordlessly at Fuerian. But his opponent did not draw.

Instead, Fuerian Vastra merely smiled at him with an ugly, taunting sneer, and then he slithered backward and into the crowd. He left Remy friendless, alone, and with no vent for his rage.

Striding confidently through a lush, verdant field, Anya looked down at her legs as she walked—something only possible in the aither, where a person could bend certain laws of reality. She flexed her powerful legs as she inhaled deeply.

Crouching into a low stance, she leapt vertically, careened into the sky, and paused her momentum once she was high overhead. Anya floated, fixed in place high above the heather outside Cathair Dé. The grassy area was real, even if the rules of physics were not—or parts of her.

She was keenly aware that her phantom limbs only existed in her mind, but she didn't care. Right now, everything about her was an invisible construct, a projection of her soul, her mental energies, her aithermantic abilities. But dammit, sometimes it was just nice to take a stroll.

Anya wished that was all it was, however. She was out on business, even if she allowed herself to take pleasure in it.

The aither was a kind of astral realm that could be manipulated like a lucid dream. It was theoretically endless, and yet it also overlapped fixed points in Arcadeax, meaning anyone in the sphere could find secret games, advertisements from companies, and connect with stores of knowledge and records from businesses by astrally visiting those locations... But it also contained places that were *not real at all*.

Oberon had created an entire gallery devoted to art, artifacts, and other historically significant pieces that were destroyed or lost in the Infernal War. The pieces were created from the knowledge and memories of those tuatha aged enough to have a direct recollection of them. As contemptuous as it was, those méith fey horded things of beauty, this was one way the Summer King had earned the favor of regular folk and made those collections available to anyone with an aither connection.

When Anya turned her eyes toward Faery Cairn, she could see that museum simply by thinking about it. If she so desired, she could make it there in one direct leap and arrive within moments. She blinked a few times and looked away, letting the image of the place dissipate with the ease of thought. She knew only few aitherspace travelers had the skill to do exactly that and with such skill and ease, but any person could be taught the basics. Her skills merely allowed her to traverse the sphere more quickly than most—just as most folk could walk, someone could always run fastest.

Anya turned her gaze to the countryside and then flew in a direct line. She had very little knowledge about the location she had wished to visit, but Anya had enough curiosity and knowledge to make her search.

The last they had chatted, Remy had shared the name of a company their mutual employer owned. Xander Kent's business,

Tógdraío Holdings, owned many sub companies. Most recently, Kent had traveled to usurp a company in Saibhir Gaoithe known as Fuinneamh, which was one of the business subsidies of Suíochán Naséan and run by the Brown Mavens, which everyone knew weren't really mavens, anyway.

Fuinneamh had contracts with Saibhir Gaoithe to distribute the akasha to its citizens; Kent had been giddy about taking possession of their infrastructure—but he wanted their contracts—without those the physical networks to distribute it was of little value.

Although Fuinneamh had automatically owned those contracts because they were a part of the Radiant Tower, they didn't bother keeping up with their demand and hadn't yet realized that they no longer had a stranglehold on the market. Anya suspected that, at some point, the loss of business would eventually catch up with Avrylatoris, the leader of the maven's Brown caste who managed their business holdings.

When Kent's Tógdraío Holdings took over, his first order to Anya was to dismantle Fuinneamh's aither strongholds in that area. Whomever had set up their sphere presence in that area had been a real amateur.

As a good employee, she'd accessed those strongholds and removed any information about Fuinneamh. The stronghold was attached to a *place*, but everything else about it in the aither could be repurposed, and so she'd stripped it down and remade it more to Kent's specifications.

As she had *redecorated*, Anya found a closet labeled "Akasha Creators/Competition." Curious about what information was stored here, she'd sifted through what scraps Fuinneamh had collected.

Data in the sphere was analogous to both reality and to dreams, which also closely matched each other, but not perfectly. A dreamer might look at a painting and experience a memory or even a dream within a dream. Anya found a set of still images and motion states that functioned like interactive dreams and came across an image with a stamped wooden box in the background. Looking closer, Anya discovered it was branded with the logo of Stór Rúnda.

Anya knew there was no information about creating akasha. She had been unable to find that data in *any* corner of the aithersphere, and she'd looked.

She found it amusing that Fuinneamh *had* paid at least some attention to Kent's rise. But Fuinneamh's suspicion wasn't fully accurate—as far as Anya knew, and she knew a lot, Kent distributed the stuff, but he obtained it from a third party who was its creator, and only that secret source knew how to make it, aside from Suíochán Naséan.

Like most business people, Kent had diversified widely, but Remy had specifically mentioned one named Stór Rúnda. There were any number of plausible causes for old crates to be present at the Vastran mine, but Anya hated having to shock things up as coincidence... *Too many damned coincidences.* Especially when those things directly overlapped the mystery she'd taken over from her brother.

The more Anya thought about it, the more Remy's crazy conspiracy theory sounded plausible. *Someone else employed by Kent could be working against the otherwise ethical elf's aims from within—and if that was true, he or she probably worked for Stór Rúnda.* It did not take much research to learn the general location of the Stór Rúnda egg farm. Without an exact heading, she'd taken to a manual search and from her vantage point in the aither-sky, it did not take her long to find it.

The nature of the aither allowed people of Anya's talent to enter a location's aither-place, usually called a stronghold when connected to a physical location, from any door. However, it was considered polite to enter via the front door. It also reduced the chances of triggering any advanced security measures.

Anya chose the front gate. Before entering, she walked a full loop around the stronghold and eyed it suspiciously. Something about this entire set up felt... *wrong*. She was Tógdraío Holdings's chief aithermancer, and if *Stór Rúnda* was truly one of Kent's, then why was it not under her direct management? She'd never known the egg farm had a stronghold; it hadn't needed one... It was *just an egg farm*, and not even a huge one. That thought made her pause, and she was glad she did.

The longer she waited, the more she recognized the familiar markings on the stronghold. The way it was constructed, the thickness of its walls in general, and the layout alarmed her. *I know this place's maker as surely as I could recognize a famous architect's buildings... This is the work of Trishana Firmind... but she was supposed to be in prison!*

Anya crept toward the edge and spotted the place's security. Typically, Trishana half-assed her constructions, but not this time. She also realized this was *all new*. Either Trishana had significantly upped her game, or this place hid something massive—something significant.

And then, hiding near the rear edge of the place, Anya spotted her. Trishana walked out the front door, paused and looked around, and then rocketed into the sky much is Anya had done previously. Only Trishana had done it faster, with more grace and seeming ease than even the legless elf.

She'd never been able to do that before. Anya grimaced and prayed that her nemesis would remain gone while she snuck inside. Creeping up to the doors, she tried them, and they opened to... *nothing*. There was only a pulsing void—a blackness within.

Anya knew that could only mean one thing. Trishana was physically located inside Stór Rúnda if she could come and go from a place protected by an interdiction vault.

She stared into the empty space, certain more than ever that Kent had some kind of traitor in his employ. *It's the only reason an egg farm needed Oberon-level security!*

After taking a gigantic sigh to steel herself, Jaira pushed her way into the main hall of the Summer Court. Jaira could feel the glares of the other ladies at court as clearly as she might feel hot rays of summer sunlight beating down on her at midday.

She walked alone through the Grand Hall, avoiding the center aisle which led to the throne. It was considered bad taste to walk upon that carpet, except to cross it, unless one had official business with the throne. Instead, she meandered through the knots of she-elves who gathered to view the art, gossip, and wait for the next scheduled daily activity. Jaira knew there was a schedule somewhere, but she'd never bothered with it.

Most méith living in Faery Cairn and its surrounding cities spent much more time at Court than those sidhe of the more remote locations. Of course, the pompous upper class sidhe typically considered any noble who lived more than a half-day's ride from the capital to be a backwoods hick. Jaira fell firmly into the "hick" category. There were ways to avoid that stigma, such as spending a full week at Court once per quarter to keep relationships alive. Her mother, Eilastra, had done her best to encourage Jaira to that... But Jaira had historically refused, and now regretted it.

She moved between the different stations where pieces of art were displayed. Jaira's keen ears picked up the hushed whispers even as she felt méith women's furtive glances at her. *No doubt they are talking about me... the "human lover."*

Jaira arrived at a trio of statues. She felt a tingling at the forefront of her mind as her seer visions beckoned her—called out for her to see, to experience, something important.

Gritting her teeth and controlling her breathing, Jaira managed to suppress it, much like swallowing down and refusing to vomit when overcome by a nauseating illness. Of all the times to be overcome with her future-sight, this ranked among the worst. Steadying herself, she sucked in a breath of cool air and regained her composure, proud of the progress she'd made in learning to master the aes sidhe talent.

Jaira turned her gaze back to the statues. They were marvelous and impeccably sculpted. She stared at them for several long moments, recognizing Puck's visage was one of them. Behind his marble effigy stood a tall she-elf wearing a crown. Queen Titania was even more recognizable than the prince. The third figure was similar in age and stature to Puck, and Jaira assumed he was Mustardseed. Though the two brothers looked strikingly similar, their personalities were vastly different, she'd heard. Puck played the rake while his brother preferred quiet company and a good book.

She stood there staring, her ears still twitching as they picked up further hints from the gallery, words that sounded much like Jaira's name as the ladies prattled on about her with none mustering courage enough to actually engage her. After a few more moments, Jaira heard the gasps ripple through the room as Puck emerged from the Royal entrance nearest the Gilded Throne. He descended the dais and made a line for her, grinning ear to ear.

Perhaps slightly louder than necessary, he called out to her, "Jaira, my good friend! I am so glad you could answer my invitation! I hope your husband is well."

Jaira turned to him, all smiles. "Puck! It has been too long." She grinned as Puck took her hands in his. They both had to stifle any laughter as they heard the gasps of shock from the snobby she-elves who looked on.

They stood together for several more moments, examining the artwork together and letting Jaira be seen. More quietly, as if he spoke for Jaira's ears rather than those of the other méith, Puck asked her what she thought of the sculpture.

"It's lovely," Jaira told him.

"Isn't it, though? Jairu Odendes made them; my father commissioned them. He, uh, pissed off my mother, enraging her to such a new level that he needed to make a grand gesture." He shrugged sheepishly. "I'm not entirely certain that she's forgiven him yet. I'm sure mine is the *only* family with such drama?" He spoke sarcastically, begging no response from her.

Jaira laid a finger on the faces of the sculpted likenesses. "Jairu Odendes is a true master. There has not been one like him in centuries."

"He is. And my mother forced my father to commission more statues at great expense," Puck told her. "I do not think the king's indiscretion will provide me a new half-sibling or anything, but it will give the court a new point of pride. Odendes was commissioned to sculpt the likeness of every head of a méith family as a reward for their continued loyalty." The smile he offered at the thought did not reach his eyes and he shrugged, saying, "Perhaps once all these statues are made Titania will allow the artist to remake the one he did of Oberon... and even allow that icon to join the figures of the royal family."

Before Jaira could ask what happened to the original, one of the she-elves from a nearby gallery strolled nearby. "My dear Puck, I see you have continued making friends in every segment of the population."

"You know me," he told her. "I'm a friend to all and intimately acquainted with all creatures who live within the bounds of the Summer Court."

"Indeed." She postured like a snake, spitting words like venom. "You've always seemed very willing to engage with *every* resident from the Selvages to the Wooded Rim... including everyone from noble to harlot alike."

Puck merely grinned. "Indeed. What can I say? I like everyone, and most of them like me." He winked at her lasciviously and put an edge into his voice. "Perhaps you might ask your husband about that."

The she-elf nearly gasped at Puck's veiled implication of secret homosexual debauchery. Jaira wasn't quite certain how deep the insult ran, or if Puck was suggesting his knowledge was more *personal* of origin. The massive doors opened again, interrupting them. A he-elf strode in. Something about his presence hushed the nobles gathered at the hall and all eyes turned to the sidhe.

As the offending female noble took the opportunity to flit away and back to her group, Jaira asked Puck, "Who is that? He is no méith by the look of him."

Puck shook his head. "He is not."

As Jaira stared at him a moment longer, she spotted a strange discoloration at his neck. He did not move with the grace of the high-ranked caste, though he displayed the confidence and deliberation of a predatory animal. *He moves like Remy.* "I think I know him."

"He is from your city, so that stands to reason. That is Elethiel Ciníoch, the newly appointed governor of Cathair Dé." Puck locked eyes with her. Something in his expression communicated that he understood what stakes were at play. "He is the leader and one of the founders of the Frith Duine."

"What?" It was all Jaira could do to keep from raising her voice. "Why is he here?"

"Business with my father," Puck told her. "He's been to the capitol many times in the last several months rallying nobles to the Frith Duine's cause and building sympathetic alliances. He just needs one thing now to earn his request."

"What's he need? What is his request?" Jaira asked.

Puck eyed her. "He and his party are working to remove all protections the sons and daughters of Adam have in the seelie... If he gets his way, they'll be even worse off here than in the unseelie. At least the Winter Court will let them live as slaves. Ciníoch wants blood."

Jaira nearly gasped.

"As to what he needs, that is very simple. He's hoping to barter for a boon, promising to secure what was stolen from my mother." Puck looked at Jaira seriously. "Provided you can get my father to agree to it, he is chasing the exact same thing you must help your husband find."

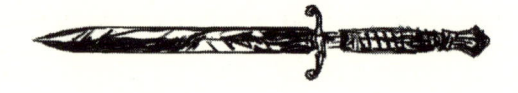

Loitariel turned with surprise as one of the house servants interrupted her work to announce a guest. She set down the papers that her husband would have normally been tasked with dealing with.

"Presenting Andrathan Elixodyr for Lady Loitariel Vastra."

Lady Vastra blinked dumbly as the servant whirled on her heel and went to the drawing room. Loitariel followed and blanched when she spotted the familiar figure. She still had to figure out how to reconcile her situation with a secretly murdered husband, the duties of leading in his stead given such a tenuous position, and the litany of secrets she'd devised... *and now this?*

No, no, no... You can't be here—not now!

As the servants either departed or silently melted into the background in case they were needed, one slightly overweight male sidhe crossed the room and leaned in to offer a familial kiss on the cheek.

"I can see you are doing quite well with your lot in life, niece," Andrathan said.

Loitariel scanned the room and made a mental note of each servant who was present. She would have to wipe their mind, and sooner rather than later, to ensure that no knowledge of their meeting escaped this room. The aes sidhe grimaced; some of these had already had memories tampered with and the mind could only tolerate so much meddling before it turned inward on itself and fell apart.

With a sigh, she turned to those sidhe in attendance who might overhear snippets of her past. "I need you four to stand in the corner. Please, do not ask questions, all will be explained after this meeting. If I need service, such as a refill of my tea, I shall ask you for it."

Each of the attendants nodded and, with a bow, did as she requested. Servants of House Vastra were anything if not obedient.

Finally, Loitariel turned to her guest. "Uncle," she greeted albeit with a cold tone.

"I can imagine you're wondering how I tracked you down?"

"That, among *why* you might take such a risk," Loitariel stated. "You're not supposed to be here. You jeopardize things I have worked so hard for these last few decades."

He kept his voice low. "I come so you can pass news to Glirien."

Loitariel bit her lip. *So, this is the contact Mithrilchon told me to expect—I hadn't guessed it would be my uncle.* "What does the Blue Maven need to know?"

Andrathan gandered at his niece's comfortable surroundings. "It looks like your work has brought you comfort." His words came as a mere observation and not a judgment. "I bring news, and I sent word as my presence near you was convenient."

"*Convenient?* We've not seen each other in *almost two decades*," Loitariel said.

He shrugged. "I was called into duty... I had to go." His gaze turned suddenly sincere. "I recognize how difficult this all may have been for you... being left in the care of the Tower's maginarius as a child, your last living relative disappearing, but I can see you are better for it—and it appears that you have begun your own legacy."

Pursing her lips as she listened, Loitariel asked him bluntly, "Why have you come?"

His serious expression not breaking, his eyes found hers. "Do you know why I disappeared?"

"Only bits and pieces. I know you are in the service of the Radiant Tower," she said flatly. "You are an Agent of Gray, one of the Tower's spies."

Andrathan nodded, confirming something she'd always suspected, but never known for sure. "And I know you are, or at least that you *were*, equally yoked to their cause."

She did not flinch away from his gaze.

"Then you know my level of commitment. You know why I had to leave you there as a child. I'm sure that could not have been easy for you." He swallowed. "It was difficult for me, too."

Loitariel's face remained expressionless.

"I won't bother asking for forgiveness, nor will I bother explaining myself. I'm certain you understand that when a High Maven recruits you to a task there is little room for denial." He sighed and looked at his feet. "But I'm uncertain our paths might ever cross again, and I needed to pass on a message."

Loitariel guessed her uncle had been deployed to some task for Suíochán Naséan long ago. She'd always thought her uncle had died a decade ago, and was barely keeping up with her shock.

Keeping his voice low for the servant's sake, Andrathan told her, "Agent Magryys sent me undercover in the unseelie. There are many of us Grays sent widely about and each on various missions, not all of us are in Summer."

"And what was your mission?"

Andrathan's lips stretched across his tight jaw. "I was sent to watch over different aspects of the Winter Throne's dealings. All Grays are trained to break cover and report if we discover plans of such realm-shattering proportions that the mavens and Oberon need to prepare. If it is possible, I am to remain in position."

"And you have stumbled onto such a plan?"

"A cataclysmic level event?" He swallowed. "No… And my cover remains intact, but I have a secret the mavens must know."

Her eyes pinched at the brow, but she motioned for him to continue.

"You may remember that several years ago there was an incident at Solstoxx, a conflict that created what is now known as the Iron Bridge?"

Loitariel nodded. "Queen Rhagathena's forces detonated an explosive device which littered the crossing with ferrous material."

"A ferrobomb," Andrathan confirmed. "The harvesting of iron is something under my purview in the Winter Court. I am taskmaster for a group of Lightstarved, a chain-gang populated by slaves capable of handling the stuff."

Tilting her head, Loitariel searched him with her eyes. She took in his expression, his body language. *Everything he's said is true.*

"*That* was not a cataclysm-level event. Neither is the news I bring now, but I did not have an opportunity before to get word of Winter's plans to the Tower. But this time, I knew a window would present itself and I sent word to the local Winter Hunters garrison to create the opening I needed."

He looked her over for several seconds before smiling warmly. "You look good, and I am happy for your success. I sincerely hope it continues. Please understand that you are more than a convenient tool for me to send a message. You are all the remains of family for me."

She nodded, her face softening.

At that, Andrathan continued, "I think that original assault has never ended, at least, the Spider Queen's plans never ceased their momentum, even though it was not her who detonated those ferrobombs."

Loitariel looked at him confused. "Wait, what do you mean by that? How do you know that? Her purpose was not to seed the bridge?"

He shook his head. "Rhagathena may not have seers in her employ, but she does have a few watchers skilled in chronurgy, which is how she was able to, at least, view what happened. The explosions were caused by Aderyn Corff when he rebelled. Rhagathena's would-be assassin set them off, destroying her entire invasion force." His gaze met hers once again. "You likely know him by another name. The Corpse Bird's name is Remy Keaton, and he's set up a whole new life in this part of the realm." He paused. "One does not escape such a life. Certainly, there have been rumors?"

She nodded slowly.

Time magic was one of the arcane arts forbidden by Suíochán Naséan. Chronurgic watchers could rewind time and view events unfold, though they couldn't affect what they saw—not anymore—all the spells known in that field of magic had long since been destroyed in the *Tempus Exterminus* purge... Rewinding time was much similar to traveling the aithersphere and observing interactions from a distance. Though it *was* possible to travel forward or backward in time in a more real sense, no aes sidhe had been talented enough to do so since the Infernal Wars when both Oberon and Wulflock agreed on the skill's cataclysmic potential and destroyed all knowledge of how to enact such a spell. Of course, they'd had to assassinate every aes sidhe knowledgeable enough to do so, making sure those secrets had truly passed.

Loitariel's jaw set. *Too many converging circumstances surround that ferrobombing, and all are things the Tower has worries about—what he knows must be important!*

She confirmed, "I know of Remy Keaton."

"As I said, my role is as an overseer of slaves, specifically those who can touch iron. I sometimes work with an orcish slavetaker named Syrmerware Kathwesion."

Recognition sparked within Loitariel's eyes. The orc was well known in all the realms, particularly for his ruthlessness.

"There was an... altercation not far from here. I had tipped off Oberon's troops to the presence of unseelie agents near Cathair Dé's outskirts; you're likely aware that Summer troops near the southern Horn of the Selvages have an understanding with the slavers out of Vale Rhewi who skirt the Solstox edge." Andrathan shrugged away his digression. "Anyway, in the confusion my party scattered so I could slip away. I've got to return to my service before it arouses any suspicion. But this information was too potent not to risk passing it onward." He paused and swallowed. "And I'd also hoped to see you one last time."

Loitariel nodded slowly. "Tell me what else you can, then. I shall relay it."

"I fear that another attack is coming. This time, however, it may come from within Oberon's own court. Rhagathena may be engineering another ferrobomb, but I think it is being built right here, in the seelie... right under the mavens' noses."

"What makes you say that?" In truth, Loitariel's stomach had flipped. Everything he'd told her so far was verifiable truths, and if he'd risked so much to come and see her, then there truly was a grave danger.

"I was with Syrmerware Kathwesion who delivered a troop of lightstarved just recently. It was composed mostly of humans and delivered to a nearby mine with more iron veins than naught. A mine owned by the Vastra family." He stared at her several moments, not needing to remind her that *she* was now Vastra.

"No. It is not," Loitariel hissed. "It is owned by *just one* Vastra, and not by the family. *Fuerian*."

Andrathan nodded. "His mine is filled with the stuff, and there is little reason to purchase a collection of lightstarved out of Winter unless you intend to harvest the stuff—hiring locals would be cheaper if not for the iron."

"But the mine was cleared by the mavens," Loitariel said. "Surely, that means that—"

"Think about it," her uncle insisted. "Work this through as if it's a problem of logic. Each of the divisions within the Tower have specific duties—and even *I* keep up on the basic changes at Suíochán Naséan."

She grimaced but worked through her uncle's concerns aloud. "Normally the Browns are in charge of weights and measures, but because it is ferrous, it falls to the Violet Order. The Violets would be responsible for certifying anything tainted by iron. The High Maven is Amarthanc who is the newest, and youngest of the High Mavens—only a few years older than I am, actually."

Andrathan made a rolling gesture with his fingers, urging her to continue the trail of logic.

"Amarthanc is a zoemancer, like most Violets. She specializes in healing... which includes necromantic arts. Amarthanc replaced Selashiuhl who died under mysterious circumstances."

Andrathan nodded. "Suspicious for sure, which makes me loathe to take anything she says at face value until she's proven herself."

Loitariel returned his nod. "You really think the danger is this significant?"

Her uncle sighed. "The only thing I know is unseelie forces have used that cursed metal in the past... And Fuerian Vastra has a known deposit of iron... *And* he has access to Oberon because of his méith status. I can't say anything more beyond that with any certainty. But there exists a certain amount of risk, and Suíochán Naséan ought to be informed."

"*Maybe I ought to just kill Fuerian,*" Loitariel wondered. *But would that stop all of his potential machinations? No... I have to get to the bottom of it, first.* "Thank you, Uncle," she told him stressing the last word.

He bowed. "I wish that we could arrange to see each other again with any certainty. But the unseelie is not a place that allows folk the pleasure of planning for tomorrows."

Loitariel bowed to her kin in response. And then Andrathan departed with haste. As she watched him go, she caressed the swollen abdomen that held her future. *I think I shall call him Andrathan if it is a boy.* It wasn't as if Juriahl could argue over the decision.

She turned to the cluster of servants waiting in the corner, summoned them closer under false pretenses of duty, and then obliterated any recollection she'd had any visitors.

Chapter Fourteen

Trishana Firmind shivered in the cold air. Her skin gleamed damp and cool in the confines of her cell. She knew the door to her cell was not locked; neither were the doors that could return her to the outside world. There was no longer any need for restrictions.

The stone block-work walls revealed she was in a basement of some kind, but she had known that ever since her master had taken her. Behind her, the tank hummed with the power of an akashic drip and the promise of returning her to the glorious aither. Trishana had spent every waking moment there since Hymdreiddiech had locked her into the metallic womb—a contraption promised her new heights and a life of possibilities she'd never before experienced... And it did not disappoint. *I don't need this crude flesh husk, anyway.*

She hunkered over a small table with an akashic lantern. The work of her master was too important to rely on candlelight. Using a series of tools, Trishana wrapped parchment thin sheets of titanium metal around and even more delicate contraption. She did not need the skills of a master crafter to know that she was helping construct some sort of akashic trigger. Imbued upon the thin sheaves of metal that crumpled with her touch, arcane sigils necessary for an incendiary spell had been imbued. Those sheaves, when crumpled, held their form as sure as lead solder.

Trishana molded the malleable sheets around a thin vial. The glassine tube was a closed loop where the material had been super-heated to encapsulate the raw akasha inside. Two wire leads protruded through the mystic glass battery. One of them she attached to the engraved, metallic foil.

A shadow darkened her doorway, and she turned her eyes upward to Hymdreiddiech's form. She spotted him there, watching her work. As she wrapped the crude, cylindrical detonation device with a thin wire to complete it, Hymdreiddiech approached and picked it up to inspect it.

The thing was no bigger than her pinkie finger. Around her, burned chunks of char littered the floor, showing all the test variations that she'd set off already from within the aither. He smiled at her while he examined it and whispered, "Good."

She practically melted inside. The only thing she lived for now was his approval.

The device was a simple one. The akashic charge it enveloped activated its inscribed flame spell. Many variations of this exact item existed, especially in the homes owned by the wealthier sidhe but who wanted to keep the air of tradition alive; with the simple activation of the spell, the otherwise smaller versions of these created a tiny spark that could light an oil-burning luminary, a fireplace, a stove or oven. But this version was different, much larger and more violent, but fast burning... And it was not connected to an activation spell. This was tethered to an anchor point in the aither. Those discarded bits of slag that Trishana had already triggered, she'd switched on from within the safety of the sphere and of her isolation chamber. These could not be accidentally activated; they were as secure as they were sure.

Hymdreiddiech looked at her. "You believe this is ready?"

She nodded slowly and kept her head bowed. "It is, my lord. I built it off the information you provided to me... A crude re-creation of what ruined the Iron Bridge of Solstoxx."

His lips curled up. "Excellent. Then let me show you what we hope to accomplish." He took her hand in his and led her through the underground maze.

After several twists and turns, past the whirring interdiction vault, Hymdreiddiech took her to a room where a motley collection of lightstarved worked upon a statue; it was a finely crafted figure of Oberon. Their workbenches were covered with tubs and casting material along with other evidence of a master forgery artist making recreations of the statue.

Wordlessly, the humans toiled. Already, the Summer King's likeness had already been recreated several times by the half-starved artisans. They wore chains at their ankles, but another creature's affixed him to the wall near the back. A black-eyed dwarf snarled at Trishana and Hymdreiddiech. He shook his shackles.

The dwarf's workbench was cleared except for a few spell craft reagents and several small statues, each the size of a paperweight.

All appeared to be impeccable marble creations. A block of the stone sat nearby.

Trishana knew dvergr were nearly identical to the coroniaids, the race of above-ground dwarves, except for their complexion and those black eyes that had almost no sclera. The creature's eyes were all cornea. Most of the subterranean species never saw daylight and even an overcast afternoon caused their exposed skin to blister. Unlike the coroniaids, the dvergr where master crafters and excelled in using magic and raw skill to bend earthen elements to their will.

"This is what you should know about our plan." Hymdreiddiech turned to Trishana and then tapped upon one of the Oberon forgeries. It rang hollow. "You are the link, the trigger, and you will help me remake Arcadeax."

"I am yours to command."

They turned their attention to the lightstarved who worked upon one of the likenesses. The forgeries were made of a much cheaper material, plaster and some kind of concrete, which distinguished the authentic piece from the fakes. The faux art lay on its belly with an opening in its back, where the workers poured a collection of black powder and jagged iron shards.

Hymdreiddiech handed one of the ddiymadferth the detonator that she had made and with the hollow figure half filled, he tucked it into the hole. A few minutes later, the form was packed solid and one of the lightstarved smoothed a patch over the entry point before the team stood it up.

The black maven tapped it again and, now filled, it sounded no different from any other solid figure. He turned his eyes to the dvergr who put up a false front, growling at the spell caster. Despite their blackness, Trishana could see the fear in the tuatha's eyes.

"Employ your craft, dvergr," Hymdreiddiech said with a voice like gravel. When the creature did not immediately comply, he asked, "Must I give you another lesson?"

The short, bearded figure wilted and averted the aes sidhe's eyes. He stammered, "I... I am yours to command."

Moments later, the dvergr reluctantly complied, though his slowness may have been because of the focus required by his skills. The block of marble at the dwarf's workstation seemed to relax, wobbling like tallow that had begun to rend, and then the creature used a simple dipper to scoop from it like warm wax. He applied it to the figure in glopping clumps. Before he was done, he smoothed and polished the statue to perfection and then released his spell. Solidifying, the skin of marble enclosed the statue.

Trishana nearly gasped in amazement. The recreation was indistinguishable from the original.

Hymdreiddiech took a small brush and painted black Xs over Oberon's eyes to mark it and prevent confusion among the slaves. He tilted the figure back and forth and shook it, feeling its weight. "This will pass any tests the mavens might put it through upon delivery." He snapped at the lightstarved, "Prepare the item for its final trial to ensure its efficacy."

Trishana tilted her head at him.

"And now for the fun part," he told her. "You get to destroy King Oberon."

She'd never seen her master *amused* before. "I am yours to command," she replied.

Hymdreiddiech took her by the hand again. He led her back to the warm, comfortable seclusion of her aitherchamber. It was both sarcophagus and womb, and was now the only place she truly felt comfortable.

Hymdreiddiech told her, "I shall return when we are ready."

The aithermancer crawled into the tomb-like bed. Her mantra, "I am yours to command," was swallowed up by the clanging metal of the locking closures... And then she slid back into the serene darkness, followed by the light of aitherspace.

Jaira slipped through a door and meandered through the back hallways of the castle... *Oberon's castle*. She spotted an innocuous door at the end of a hallway.

On either side of the closed entrance she spotted a patch of discolored stone, obviously marred by a thousand years or more of nameless sentries who had leaned there after posting up for long shifts as they denied entry to any but the royal family. She smirked. That it was currently unguarded was undoubtedly Puck's work.

Jaira open the door and slipped within. The inner halls were, at first, rugged and unassuming. If she hadn't known better, she might have been anywhere between the border of Daonra Dlúth and the interior of Faery Cairn. After the first turn, however, the decorating style turned far more elaborate than even the grand hall and those corridors surrounding it which only the méith had access to, and *that* decor had been meant to impress the nobility. This place's grand-ness, which nobody else would even see, seemed a likely sign of Titania's base-line expectations for comfort.

A writhing knot of nerves jumbled around inside Jaira's gut like a playful Cù-sith pup. *The thing about Cù-sith is that they get violent as soon as they grow too large to handle.*

She ignored her trepidation and pressed onward, keenly aware that she'd accessed the inner sanctum of the royal family. Well, *almost*. Puck had disclosed that the most private sections of the keep, those areas where *only* the royal family could go, lay deeper within—that included bedrooms, a drawing room, library, several living rooms, and a dining hall that was too-seldom used for merry making. However, this section of the castle was not open to the public... *not even to méith*. That meant she risked running into *her*.

Jaira turned a corner, scanning up and down the hallways in search of her target. And then a low voice barked at her.

"What are you doing here, Miss?"

Jaira stopped in her tracks, frozen. She pushed on her nerves, grateful that the voice was male rather than female. *If Titania had found me, all would be lost.* The she-elf turned sheepishly. "Pardon, I must be lost."

The sidhe, who stalked closer, examined her with intense, scrutinizing eyes. He scanned her while he approached and tilted his head as if unfamiliar with her.

And why should he know me? "My apologies. I'm fairly new to court. My mother has tried to get me to spend more time here, but the distance is great and I'd been reluctant up until recently."

The elf drew to within two paces. Jaira recognized the medallion pinned at his breast. It marked him as the king's direct majordomo. "Then I shall escort you away. You cannot be here."

Jaira paused. "Actually, I was hoping I could gain an audience with Lord Oberon."

The valet stifled a laugh. "I'm sorry, but he does not have a habit of meeting with lost, insignificant girls." He turned and pointed. "This way."

With her face taking a darker expression, Jaira said, "That's not the way that I hear it."

The elf's face showed his shock at her brazenness. Obviously recognizing his jaw had gone slack in the face of such acrimony, he shut his mouth hard enough that his teeth clacked. The valet seized her by the arm. "You have great gall, offering such impertinence *here,* of all places."

"Of all places?"

"In the home of Queen Titania—where her ears might overhear your insults," he hissed.

"Then I shall lower my voice," Jaira said, barely louder than a whisper. Now that the king's personal servant was so close, she whispered, "I have news for the king. I can help him reclaim what has been stolen... Find the objects which were recently taken from him."

The majordomo's eyes boggled as he looked at her. He blinked and then said, "I have no idea what you're talking about. The throne does not entertain wild rumors." The tone of his voice indicated he was lying, and he jerked her by the arm to try to force her to move.

Jaira refused to budge. "How will the nobility react when Saol Nua is canceled... When the King's Feast is discontinued and the méith go without their ambrosia?"

Glaring daggers at her, the servant spat, "Vicious rumors continue to worm their way through court, I see."

"You really *should* take me to Oberon. I know more than you might think, and I offer the best promise to reclaim that which was stolen."

The majordomo stared at her in silence for several seconds. And then Jaira began ticking off items on her fingers, listing the contents of the raided carriage, details provided by Puck.

She noted the strange flowerpot with a shriveled stub which was somehow important to the queen, three well-known pieces of art, and then she curled in thumb to make a fist. "And of course, the thieves took the most important item—the absence of which could cause the méith to revolt in a civil war—they took the Dagda's pot. Someone has stolen one of the two coire ansic... *the source of all ambrosia*."

Jaira felt keenly aware that she'd have never gotten this far without the prince's help. *Thank the gods that I made friends with him when I did!*

Swallowing hard, Oberon's servant set his jaw and then turned in the opposite direction. He spoke with no emotion. "Follow me. I shall escort you to the king."

The king's majordomo slipped inside an unassuming office door and left Jaira to wait several moments. Those moments stretch into minutes. Just when Jaira felt pangs of panic, thinking the whole situation a lost venture, the servant reappeared, quickly opening and shutting the door behind him.

"King Oberon will see you. However, he only has a few minutes to spare. He has much important business to do with the Council of Mavens and must depart shortly. However, if you have any actual knowledge regarding this... *incident*... he would be eager to hear of it," the servant told her.

Jaira bowed politely. Gone was her previous insolence. "I shall take what he will give me," she said.

Apparently appeased, the majordomo opened the door and let her pass. He remained outside in the interests of privacy.

Jaira found the King of the Summer Court seated at a relatively normal business desk. The room was comfortable and well apportioned, but not nearly as lavish as even the hallways, which made her guess that Titania did not venture inside here. It was altogether... functional. Utilitarian.

A smile played at the edge of Oberon's lips. "I guess I should have expected nothing less than this from the wife of the only human to ever achieve duelist status."

Jaira smirked. "We make a clever pair like that, my lord."

"Following the dueling standings is a hobby of mine." His expression now replaced with one of genuine amusement, Oberon sat back in his chair, relaxing. "What is it that I can do for you?"

Jaira told him. She explained how anti-human sentiments were set against her and Remy and how she wished for him to be legally recognized as her husband and as the heir to House Morgansteen with all the rights and privileges that accompanied such status.

The king's brows furrowed. "I can see that you are passionate about this... And certainly you are clever to get all the way into my office this way." He crossed his arms over his chest and leaned forward. "You know, your mother approached me many years ago to inquire about interest in a future union with one of my sons. Even then, she insisted you were cunning. We discussed an introduction to Puck, my eldest. Perhaps you met him?"

Jaira shrugged and downplayed any connection. "Only in passing."

"The conversation was never revisited and, since then, you have since grown up and moved on to other pursuits. You know, your husband was here only days ago. He and his employer. The meeting went well, I think, though I did not meet him directly.

Everyone without Adamic prejudice seems to speak well of him," Oberon admitted.

His words brought Jaira hope.

"I'm to understand from my servant that you have some pieces of information that you'd like to barter with to earn your husband's inclusion into your official family house. He says you want him to become part of a méith line, which seems obvious." The king stared at her hard. "I don't know how much you are involved in your family's inner workings, but from all accounts, it looks to me as if House Morgansteen is on the verge of falling out from the méith caste."

She gasped, her hope faltering. "What do you mean? How is that possible?"

Oberon flashed a thin lipped grimace. "Méith means something. It is a higher level of breeding, and with it comes a set of standards for conduct. One of those includes a certain level of financial stability. Unfortunately, several of your father's creditors have approached me and asked me to back the debts he has incurred so that, when they call them in and he is unable to, or is unwilling to pay, the crown will alleviate their loss to some degree. When this sort of deficit is passed to me, it automatically de-elevates the offending party from nobility. It is very much the opposite of how Summer Court nobles are expected to act."

Jaira nodded slowly. "Who is calling in these debts? Perhaps they can be reasoned with."

Frowning, the king listed three banking institutions, all of them friendly to Harhassus's business opponents. "Also, there are complaints from houses Vastra and Cinìoch."

Rolling her eyes, Jaira said, "Of course, they would come from my ex-fiancé and his accomplices. He and Elethiel Cinìoch have been buddying up ever since that political climber got elected and then formed the Frith Duine." She sighed. "I didn't even know that House Cinìoch was méith."

Oberon gave her a smile that barely touched his face. "You ought to have spent more time at court."

"I know, I know."

"Liquidation will occur to forcibly pay his debts," Oberon said. His voice remained apologetic, however. "Unfortunately, the proceedings have already begun so that the next time Court is in full session, the door is open for the creditors to come calling."

Then he winked at her. "However, I can grant a reward that may be enough to pay off those debts. Of course, your family name will probably suffer regardless... Not just because creditors raised an issue to the crown in front of all, but it will put a spotlight on your... human dalliances." He smirked at a thought Jaira was not privy to. He confessed, "I do understand that sentiment. However, my wife will be a key figure who will set herself against your family. You ought to be prepared."

Jaira nearly deflated. "It might be a relief, in fact. If it was up to me, I would avoid Court altogether. If Remy and I could simply live in peace in some small burb and enjoy each other, that would be ideal. Possessing a noble title is more burdensome than I particularly care for... This was always my father's dream rather than mine. If Arcadeax would simply let us live in peace, I would be content."

Oberon looked off, far and away. Wistful, he mentioned, "I know how you feel; that would be nice if such a dream were possible." He swallowed the lump in his throat. "For many of us, however, our role in the universe is too important to set aside."

Finally, he fixed her with his eyes again. "You are certain your husband can reclaim my items?"

"He is the best there is, my lord. Were it not true, I would have chosen Puck for myself—and I would have managed to claim him," she asserted, before hissing, "It would have been an enormous upgrade from Fuerian Vastra."

Oberon chuckled for a few moments. "Then make it so. Your family's financial salvation depends upon it. I don't care about the rest of the items, only the bowl." He made hand gestures to give her an approximate size and shape almost equal to her torso. "That is the one item that I care about; every other item could be lost or destroyed as far as I'm concerned, although attempts to reclaim them are appreciated. But without recovering coire ansic, the Dagda cauldron, there is no redemption for House Morgansteen."

Jaira bowed her agreement. "I understand."

At the rear of the room, the door opened silently and the king's majordomo gestured it was time for Oberon to depart for his next piece of business.

"It was lovely making your acquaintance, Daughter of Morgansteen. For your sake, I certainly hope you can deliver on your promise." And then Oberon departed.

Before taking Jaira's arm, the majordomo provided instructions on how to contact the king once she had recovered the bowl, and then he released her through the doors leading back to the Hall with its myriad galleries and trappings for the nobles, returning her to the lesser world of house politics and gossip.

Trishana's astral form hovered in the aither. For all intents and purposes, she was able to fly in the sphere, much like Anya Shelton, who had always held an edge over her. Regardless of her jealousy, Trishana had found other ways to build her business to surpass the competition when her talent was insufficient. It had allowed her to build a reputation equal to Shelton's.

But now that her master had given her the incredible apparatus which held her body while she ventured abroad without it? She was more powerful than ever before—perhaps the most powerful aithermancer in existence!

She reveled in that fact as she watched the lightstarved humans complete their task. They'd mounded a pile of fine sand at the base of a gully and set the completed statue upon it. The silica grains allowed them to easily level the figure.

Oberon's visage gleamed in the sunlight. The smooth marble coated every last scrap of the statue. It was even more beautiful in the daylight.

Say what you will about the dvergr, but their craftsmanship is impeccable.

Hymdreiddiech's slave may not have created the design, but his ability to skin the sculpture with a layer of silky-smooth stone was a work of art in its own right.

From her vantage, Trishana detected her master. In the aither he glowed with a faint aura as most of the powerful aes sidhe did; their power existed in both realms and it radiated in the overlap.

Hymdreiddiech was not looking at her, at least, not directly. But she felt the dark maven's spirit was with her—she and the master had grown close enough that they were one. She knew what he wanted to see for this demonstration.

As the lightstarved finished packing sand around the statue's base, she felt for the aithermantic trigger. A thin strand of silver trailed off, connecting to the tiny piece of magitech like a thread of gossamer silk. Had she not known where to look for it, it would have been invisible. Using her power, the aithermancer summoned the line, pulling and stretching the tether so that it lengthened and reached her hand as she beckoned.

And then she pulled it taught, holding it steady and slack-less.

The humans below had no idea. They finished their work in diligent silence... *But her master?* She knew what he wanted. He stood far away, watching the gully with vicious, expectant intent.

Trishana knew what a successful test looked like in his eyes. She said, "I am his to command," even though no one could hear it but her.

She jerked the cord, and the statue detonated in a cloud of fire. The conflagration erupted in a maelstrom of stony shards and ferrous shrapnel. Flechettes of marble and iron tore the slaves to gory chunks, charring them in the explosive flash, which mushroomed out of the gulch and then shrank back into a haze of smoke and blasted earth.

From the safety of the aither, Trishana descended and set her feet upon the blackened soil, tiptoeing over the shredded remains of the lightstarved victims. At the center of the sooty cloud, not a scrap of the statue remained.

Oberon had been thoroughly destroyed, and Trishana could only cackle with mad glee.

Chapter Fifteen

Remy strolled through the marketplace, eyes scanning one way and then the other. The diminutive redcap followed after him.

"What am I doing here again?" Hobin asked while munching on a skewer of meat he'd gotten at one of the vendor booths. He complained, "Arawyn was going to teach me to play fidchell."

The duelist didn't even glance at him. "Plenty of time to learn games later. Besides, I seem to recall you insisting you needed to honor some kind of debt to keep me alive or something?" He'd collected the powrie earlier and figured an extra set of eyes wouldn't hurt, especially given the local tension with the Frith Duine.

Hobin shrugged. "Do you even *have* a fidchell set?"

Remy threw his hands up. "Not sure what Kent's got lying about the apartment. You can look for one later... Look for Ochara, *now*. He's supposed to meet me this afternoon."

"Fine, fine," Hobin grumbled.

They walked a few more paces. "Oh, there he is." Hobin pointed to a he-elf.

"That's not him."

"Oh! Oh, there he is. That must be him." Hobin pointed the other direction at another sidhe male.

"Still not him," Remy said, realizing that the redcap had no idea what the fey constable looked like. "You know what, never mind. Just... watch my back in case anyone with bad intentions approaches."

"You got it, boss."

It only took a few more minutes strolling the market to spot Captain Ochara. Remy closed the distance, and the peacekeeper began looking at some random booth's wares. The human feigned interest in something else nearby the elf.

"Is your witness safe?" Ochara asked, not looking at Remy.

Remy nodded. "He is. Should I be worried?"

Ochara shook his head. "Not even remotely. His existence didn't even make the reports."

Turning to regard the man, Remy's brows pinched.

Remy asked, "You didn't mention that you had a living witness who could testify that it was monstrous beasts who tore the maginarius apart and murdered those people?"

"I did." Ochara kept his voice low. "But that's not the version that left the precinct. Someone else went over my head with a revised report, which claimed all evidence pointed to disgruntled humans."

"Frith Duine?"

Ochara nodded slowly. "Got a while mess of them in my employ... One of them must've revised the reports. They stepped over me and put their 'findings' in the hands of one former magistrate who I've only ever known to be corrupt in his verdicts." Ochara set his jaw with a scowl. "I had hoped for the best when he'd finally stepped down from his post last year... But he got went and got himself elected governor."

"Elethiel Cinίoch," Remy hissed.

"One and the same," Ochara said. "He's a proper méith bastard, too, and one of the original crew who founded the Frith Duine."

Remy frowned with a shake of his head. "Shit." After a moment passed, he mumbled, "At least that kid doesn't have as much to worry about. Thanks, Captain."

"Maybe not... But everyone *else* does," Ochara said. "And it's just Ochara, now. Asshole pulled some strings... Elethiel Cinίoch demanded I side with him and join his ranks. I refused. I'm no longer an officer."

Remy's jaw tightened, but there wasn't much he could say or do.

"Now, if you don't mind, I'm out and about looking for work, and it's not good for my resume to be seen fraternizing with a human and... *that*," he glanced to Hobin, "thing."

"Oh, before you go." Remy caught him. "Do you have any friends in the bastille? I'm trying to check on a few things."

"You're thinking about Gareth Morass and Trishana Firmind? I know you were connected to both of them, as was Anya Shelton. Seems they were both exonerated. Released with full pardon." Ochara offered a wry smile. "Watch out for those corrupt nobles. Their pockets reach into places where justice will not."

Remy nodded and then watched Ochara depart. Grumbling expletives beneath his breath, Remy turned to leave and practically tripped over the elderly Hazimon.

They collided with only light impact, though the human nearly toppled the old dryad. Remy glared down at Hobin, who shrugged... The expression was clear—*you were supposed to have my back.*

"What? She didn't seem like she intended harm," Hobin groused.

"Quite the contrary, mister redcap," Hazimon said. "I came with a report... or perhaps it is a warning. A caution meant for all of Arcadeax, I suppose."

Remy stared at her. Many folks believed the old elf to be a simple, insane figure who haunted the marketplace with her wild rants. "What is it, Hazimon?" He didn't think she was crazy, but still... The old woman seemed like she might crack at any minute.

"Don't you hear the crow's call, Remy Keaton? It cries out, speaking your name."

He cocked his face at her. "What?"

"The crow. It has returned, and this time it brings its mate. The white bird. Corax and Gwyn."

"Who told you that bird's name?" Remy demanded, trying to keep the heat from his voice. Corax had been his pet bird when he'd gone by his assassin moniker, Aderyn Corff, in the unseelie. Corax was destroyed in the explosions at the Iron Bridge when Remy had escaped from Winter several years ago. Nobody knew that detail, and none alive knew Corax's name.

"Gwyn is Corax's mate," Hazimon said.

"No," Remy snapped at her. He'd never spoken of Corax to anybody. He spoke very little about *any* of his time as Aderyn Corff. It was a dark past that he did his best to distance himself from.

Hazimon stared at the human like *he* had lost his mind.

"Who told you?" Remy repeated.

"Why... Corax told me," replied the dryad.

Jaira stood outside Hawk and Hems, a shop on Middle Street in Daonra Dlúth. Her uncle, Talathan, had owned it for many years, ever since losing the title of méith to her father years prior. For some reason, high above the entrance, Jaira spotted a large pile of bricks stacked upon an overhead platform over the door.

She smirked at the reference on the sign. Talathan's nickname had been Hawk for as long as she'd known him; though she didn't know him that well, her father had always spoken well of his 'Brother Hawk,' despite how poorly the elf had done in the world. The store also sold dresses, hence the Hem. Her aunt, Kasianna, didn't have a similar warm mention in the shop title, Jaira noted.

Jaira knew Kasianna even less than Uncle Hawk. She primarily knew only her reputation as a stern shrew who'd grasped at her former glory and was willing to do anything to regain her former status.

Talathan spotted Jaira through a window and smiled at her. He waved as she headed inside, certain that her letter must have reached him.

Eyes darting left, Jaira read a sign warning ne'erdowells. *Thieves will not be tolerated. If found, you won't survive until prosecution.* Three bricks were drawn next to it.

Jaira's eyebrows rose, but she entered, regardless.

Her uncle greeted her affably and caught her apprehensive look at the hinged platform. "Just a little thievery deterrent. We had a rash of problems for a spell and we had to find a creative solution."

Jaira smiled nervously at him, but soon forgot about it as they exchanged pleasantries. She shared how the family was doing, area gossip, that sort of thing.

"I heard you were married," he said. "How is that going?"

"Well," Jaira said. She kept it simple, unsure of how much he'd heard.

Uncle Hawk nodded with a smile. The elf could obviously take a hint. He showed her around the store. Its shelves were crowded and contained all manner of items, from expensive pocket watches and magitech to dried foodstuffs, taffies, and ladies' clothing. "We hafta keep the Hems in Hawk and Hems," he joked.

Jaira spotted her aunt across the way. She stared at a few robed individuals. Their cloaks were a kind of beige canvas and trimmed with the flashing tinted for their order. They were maven initiates, the freshest of their order, and likely just recently released from some maginarius or another to seek membership in Suíochán

Naséan, whose Radiant Tower loomed in the distance, dominating the Daonra Dlúth skyline.

"We must be ever watchful of their kind," she groused as she pocketed a few coins from their purchase and then watched them go.

Before long, her aunt, Kasianna, arrived at her uncle's side. "It is time we closed," she whispered to him. Absentmindedly, Talathan moved off and locked the door behind the last shoppers. Kasianna waited silently, seeming to glower at Jaira while he did so.

Eventually, her uncle ushered them upstairs and into the apartment where he and Kasianna lived. His wife showed Jaira to a small guest bedroom, where she deposited her sparse travel items. In her haste, Jaria had left with little beyond a small satchel and the gown which she'd not donned until before exiting the hired carriage in Faery Cairn. The carriage she'd hired wouldn't retrieve Jaira until the following morning.

So far, her aunt had treated Jaira with a brusque indifference that made her eager to leave. If she'd not needed a good night's rest in the interim, she would have hired a second carriage that could have traveled overnight. Jaira also recognized that it would seem rude of her to pass by and not have paid her kin a visit, and if Oberon's report on her father's creditors came to pass, the Morgansteens would need family more than ever.

"Are you still living on the estate?" Kasianna asked in a jaded tone.

Jaira didn't meet her gaze. "I did until I was married. I moved out afterward."

"Right," Kasianna said.

Her uncle joined them in time to overhear. "Oh, yes... The big house. I grew up there, you know."

Nobody had any comments. A coldness filled the air.

Her uncle plowed forward, heedless of the room's temperature. "I remember that magical period... The months following our nuptials."

Kasianna scowled at her husband and then left the room.

Talathan pursed his lips with amusement as if he knew what her reaction would be, but he had pressed ahead anyway.

"I really don't mean to case any trouble," Jaira told him.

He chuckled. "Truth be told, Kassi used to be hot as a Summer Court tart... But ever since we lost status, she's grown as frigid as an unseelie grindylow." His jaw tightened. "Perhaps it's a cautionary tale... Be sure you pick the right horse before you put the bridle on it."

She flashed her uncle a knowing grin. Hawk's resentment for his past choices had always been something her father had hinted at, but she'd never heard him say so directly. "I am certain of my choice, and I have already made it," Jaira said confidently.

"Good," he told her. "Then we must go to supper." He offered his niece his arm and escorted her the short distance to the area nearest the kitchen where the table sat.

Uncle Talathan pulled a chair out for Jaira, obeying all the aspects of social decorum for a caste he'd been ejected from now for many decades. In the doing, something seemed to shift in him and he glowed because of it.

Trying to make small talk while her uncle retrieved a small roast from the oven, Jaira asked her aunt about the mavens. "You'd mentioned something about those aes sidhe initiates earlier." Jaira's curiosity was genuine, and she let it show in her voice. "What did you mean when you said we had to watch them?"

Kasianna pursed her lips. "Those maven arcanists are both a caste of sidhe and also transcend classes. There are some who think Suíochán Naséan's power exceeds even that of Oberon." She paused for several moments while she chose her words carefully. Kasianna spoke with an honesty that only family was capable of. "What I meant earlier was that we must be ever mindful of who... and *what* the aes sidhe are. They have many varied powers. Some of them are forbidden. And if a seer is located, the tower will pay a high bounty for them. All citizens of Daonra Dlúth know this—most have heard tale about what to watch for to identify one... the money they promise is enough to change one's stars."

Jaira regarded her words for several moments. She could really only ask one question without rousing suspicion. "How much are they offering?"

"One hundred gold marks," Kasianna said.

Gulping, Jaira remained silent. *That's a decade's wages for most commoners... those of the Oibrithe middle class, and still significant enough for a Saibhir to take note.*

Kasianna looked Jaira over speculatively. "Any person who puts the mavens onto a seer could earn a tidy sum... All who live in the tower's shadow know this." She worked her jaw as Talathan cut the roast and served them both. "Your father has written to your uncle often. Perhaps you did not know that, but he shared some... interesting details," Kasianna said, as if toying with her. Her voice lowered somewhat. "I've read everything Harhassus ever sent, you know."

Jaira's brows pinched with confusion.

"Your father mentioned that his business ventures took a significant turn for the better since you began consulting with him regarding them in your teenage years." Kasianna's gaze narrowed as she gauged Jaira's reaction. "It seems like he thought you were quite the luck charm, although it's maybe proved too little too late. Several of his earliest investments soured or slowed while you were still young. It's tough to dig out of a hole that deep without *help*."

Jaira felt what Kasianna was hinting at... *She thinks she knows my secret.*

"Is it normal for noble fey to let an untrained daughter help make business decisions—and what is the real likelihood that you could have guessed so many good ones?" Kasianna asked. Her words brimmed with accusation.

"I'm not sure I follow," Jaira told her. And then Jaira held her arms stiff at her side, willing them not to move as a dinner roll hit her square in the face and bounced off and onto her plate.

Kasianna had thrown it at her. She watched the young she-elf's reaction as if searching for signs of prognosticative ability... But Kasianna didn't heed Jaira's lack of reaction. She watched for body language and judged the lights of Jaira's eyes.

The shrewd aunt grinned and her hard eyes glinted as if she'd earned some kind of knowledge in the encounter.

She suspects I am an aes sidhe seer!

Talathan came nearer as he spotted the dinner roll rocking on his niece's plate. "What's happening over here?"

"Oh, nothing, my dear," Kasianna told him. "Just us girls telling secrets."

"Not really secrets," Jaira said. "In fact, there's nothing much to tell. Sometimes we think we know things and they turn out to be mere conclusions we've leapt to."

Talathan looked from once face to the next as he handed a plate to each of them and then took his place opposite them. Shaking his head, he muttered, "I'll never figure out you she-elves... If I could, I'd have written a book and made a thousand marks."

Kasianna sipped from her goblet as she fixed Jaira with eyes that peered just above the cup's rim. "Not a thousand, my dear... more like *one hundred*."

Oberon arrived at the entrance to Suíochán Naséan from the Faery Cairn side. He said nothing. He made no demands, he merely *arrived*. Upon doing so, his four personal guards, Zendamourn, Galucard, and Idrolmos, along with his sluagh thrall, peeled off and stood at the gates of the Radiant Tower.

The tower guards, all members of the Solais Cloaks, recognized the seelie king. The Solais Cloaks were warriors of the aes sidhe who would never gain the rank of maven, but they were employed as the private forces controlled by the High Mavens. Their cloaks, trimmed with ribbons that shimmered with the shifting colors of the spectrum, readily identifying them. They stepped aside at Oberon's approach and bowed deeply.

Through the unadorned stone tunnels, Oberon's footsteps echoed as he walked through. Wherever he passed a maven, they stopped what they were doing and bowed, allowing him to pass without impediment. Oberon found Mithrilchon's chamber in short order and stormed in.

The White Maven looked up from his studies. He didn't rise or bow or show any deference. "Oberon," he said, flatly greeting the king.

Oberon took a chair as if he were any other visitor calling on a friend. "Mithrilchon," he responded in like kind.

"What brings you to my corner of the kingdom... I am quite busy working on our mutual problem, as you can see," the maven said.

"I remain concerned," Oberon told him. "Saol Nua is not far off, and I grow impatient. Every four years we pick a location of interest—we began this practice at the maven's suggestion many decades ago and now, *now*, my bowl has been stolen."

Mithrilchon grimaced and set aside the manuscript he'd been reading. "Coire ansic *will* be found in time. I have a half dozen of the cloaks searching for it. They are my best sidhe."

Oberon tilted his head. "Are they? Because as good as the Solais Order are, the cloaks were not good enough for admittance to the order of mavens, so why should they be the ideal tool to search for something as important as the Dagda's Cauldron?"

Mithrilchon held his gaze for a long moment before sighing. "The Order excels at certain *martial* attributes. They were trained to be mavens, sure, and never quite reached their intended potential, but they are trackers, warriors, skilled wielders of the blade. Their talents are *other* than what mavens possess, yet also employ the abilities of an aes sidhe."

The king scowled for a long moment. He understood the rationale, but he disliked that they'd produced no leads thus far. "I want mavens looking for it too. Interrogate every relative of the caravan drivers. I don't care what it takes." He levied a withering gaze at the High Maven. "This could cause a civil war, and without the ambrosia, we are *all* mortal."

Mithrilchon swallowed and nodded. "I shall dispatch a second and third team from the Solais Order and shall give them each a maven liaison." He met the king's eyes and reassured him. "We *will* find it before the festival. I can assure you of that."

Oberon remained ever suspicious of the Tower and its masters. As much as their missions aligned, they'd also sparred frequently throughout the years. The king's brow knit. "You cannot possibly know that unless you possess the talents of a seer."

His suspicions had grown these last several decades that the maven corps had been playing loose with the law. There were rules that governed the assembly of wizards—laws laid down for good reasons and in response to ancient grievances.

Shifting into the olde tongue, the language of magic, Mithrilchon said, [I assure you that I have no ability to foretell or see futures... If any of those under my control or employ have the ability to prognosticate, I am not privy to their abilities.]

Mithrilchon tilted his head as Oberon chewed over words spoken in a language which could not be used to speak falsehoods. "My lord, is there something that has bothered you enough to darken my door?"

Oberon gritted his teeth a moment, and then he nodded. "I am dispatching another agent to search for the item. You are aware of my other seekers?"

"You have three other teams of talented hunters looking for coire ansic." Mithrilchon steepled his fingers as he spoke. "They are composed of bounty hunters and talented warriors. Shall I list their identities?"

The king shook his head. He wasn't here for a pissing match or a comparison of spy networks.

"There are also the Frith Duine," Mithrilchon noted. "Their influence has grown wide, and I'd wager my marks on *them* locating it... if I was a betting sidhe, anyhow. Talent may be low, there, but they cast the broadest net."

Oberon forced his face to remain neutral, despite the maven's admission that all their deployed talents paled in the face of random luck. "An additional request to join the hunt came to me from one of the nobles, and not a well-known one, either."

Mithrilchon rose one eyebrow.

The king continued, "It worries me that knowledge of this has leaked. The more who know that Saol Nua is in jeopardy, the more tenuous the situation becomes." He held Mithrilchon in a stern gaze and spoke with equal firmness, "Fix this."

Nodding deeply, the maven said, "We shall do our best."

"I require more than your best. Fix this soon... or else." Oberon's eyes blazed and recognition of the king's warning flared in Mithrilchon's eyes. If Coire Ansic was not present at Saol Nua, he'd see the White Maven executed and replaced. Oberon noted the understanding on the elf's face. Both elves understood the stakes—if the méith revolted, Oberon would make it a point to take his frustration out on the elf.

"At some point, a cataclysm will finally overtake us all, anyway," Oberon admitted, "but I will work hard to ensure many more generations will pass before that happens."

"You fear the prophecy?" Mithrilchon asked. There was no insinuation of weakness in his words; they were not an accusation.

Oberon stated, "A dragon is the only thing that could ensure destruction of the realm. It has long been foretold."

Mithrilchon nodded.

"You are one of the few who know what actions were taken against the pendragon. You are among those who know what transpired to keep her influence limited and beyond Arcadeax."

The maven stared shrewdly. "But the prophecy remains... If a dragon eats of the ambrosia, that will usher in the worst of the apocalypses—the end of days."

Mithrilchon's words hung in the air for several long moments as Oberon mulled them over.

"I know *all* the prophecies. I am responsible for many of them," Oberon reminded him. "But my fear is that with so many events spiraling out of control, we cannot contain the next Cataclysm. Preventing destructive outcomes are why I formed Suíochán Naséan more than two millennia ago. You exist *for this very reason*," Oberon said. "Too many scenarios whirl around us, gaining in potential destructive power and increasing exponentially by the day. These tremors are precursors to a dragon's arrival. If you do not take these threats seriously—if you are not focused on the danger that a dragon represents—then it may be time a new leader directs the Radiant Tower. Are we clear?"

A tense silence hung thick and palpable. "Crystal, my lord," Mithrilchon said.

"Good," Oberon said. He stood, sliding the chair back from his haunches. Moments later, he collected his dedicated guards to himself and departed.

Jaira said her goodbyes to her uncle. Talathan gave her warm regards and messages to pass on to her father. Her aunt was polite, though Jaira sensed a kind of hungry jealousy about her. She felt tempted to reach into the stream of time with her senses to see what the potential futures might reveal about *the now*, but she resisted the urge.

The trio descended the creaky steps that led from their upstairs apartment and to the storefront below. "My carriage should be here at the beginning of business hours," Jaira told them. She squinted into the distance. "I see it now, actually."

"Yes, yes," Talathan said absentmindedly. "I suppose it is time for us to open up the shop for the day."

"I believe I see it approaching now," Kasianna told her from where she could see out the large display window as she worked the ropes for the blinds.

Wearing her traveling outfit, Jaira slung the duffel over a shoulder as the sounds of hoofs clopped outside on the streets. "Then I am off. Thank you, Uncle Hawk."

As soon as she stepped outside, a note of warning shot through her—a cold light behind her eyes demanded she leap out of the way. It was so strong of a sensation that her body reacted of its own accord.

Jaira dropped her carry bag and darted to one side just as the bricks crashed down, streaking toward Jaira with the unerring force of gravity. The weights smashed the boardwalk, splintering it, and flattening the duffel she carried.

As she looked up, shock written across her face, Jaira turned to her uncle. He appeared as flabbergasted as she was. Then both faces turned to Kasianna, who shot Talathan an apologetic look.

"Oh, dear, I'm so sorry," she fretted, though Jaira picked up on notes of falsehood that perhaps only she-elf ears could register, males seemed ever-oblivious to female in-fighting. "I must have pulled the wrong cord while I was setting the shades!"

Talathan hurried over the bricks and checked over his niece, the whole while apologizing profusely. "We must replace your dress with one of those on our racks. Come... Come pick out any one that you like."

I'm not staying one moment longer, not with that murderous bitch trying to sniff me out.

Jaira looked past him and kept her eyes on Kasianna. Her aunt's eyes pinched shrewd, verging on amusement at her experiment.

"Thank you, but no," Jaira said flatly, still not breaking eye contact with Kasianna. "I have other dresses." And then she got into the carriage and departed for home.

Chapter Sixteen

Jairu Odendes worked a polishing cloth over the marble statue he'd recently completed. The elf was known as the great statue maker of his day and he took great pride in his attention to detail. This piece, much like the others, was a tastefully sculpted nude, which had been the most popular style for the last two hundred years.

He felt the shadow pass over him as someone darkened his doorway. Odendes looked up and found a she-elf there. She seemed nervous, but the artisan knew that was normal whenever fans of his art found him. After all, he was the master artisan and being in the presence of greatness often had a swooning effect on people. Especially pretty young art students.

The elf was pretty, but she also looked too old to be a student. There was no naivety in her eyes, though he detected a glimmer of hunger.

"How may help you, Miss..."

"Miss Verda," she said, ever-so-slightly stressing the *miss*.

Odendes could tell that she was lying about her name. He suspected she was not used to having an alias. Fibbing about her name made it more likely that she was here for reasons related to *him* rather than his art, and he adjusted his groin with hopeful anticipation.

"Well, *Miss Verda*," Odendes said, "what brings you here today?"

"My master sent me to interview you. I work for a very wealthy individual who wishes to remain anonymous, at least for now."

Ah, so that explains the pseudonym. He tried not to pout at the lost recreational prospect. "What mission did he send you on?"

"He is a regular member at the Summer Court and is of the understanding you were commissioned for numerous statues to be made for the king."

Odendes nodded. "I expected that word would will out sooner rather than later. In fact, I'm just finishing up one of those statues right now."

"May I examine it?" Verda asked.

Her enthusiasm sounded genuine to Odendes. The sculptor motioned toward it, giving her free rein to look it over.

"It's marvelous. My lord and benefactor would much like to order similar sculptures, not so many as the Court, mind you, but he often invites others to view his collection and always strives to remain in vogue." Verda smiled with a coy gleam playing at the edges of her eyes.

Maybe she is *here for some extracurricular fun, as well?* Odendes found himself wondering how he might pivot her in that direction before the end of their meeting.

"Anyone who is anyone knows that all trends in fashion and art come out of Faery Cairn. Well, from the mind of Titania, to be specific."

Odendes flashed her a knowing grin. "That much is certainly true." He looked over his current piece and then at the block of marble at a nearby station, which he'd planned to begin working on today. "I am afraid that I have many more pieces yet to make for Oberon's court, and I'm uncertain when I can begin taking new orders."

"My master is a very patient elf," she told him, eyeing the current piece. "I recognize this noble. He hails from House Treanna in Te Sástacity, correct?"

The artist nodded. "You are correct. So far, I have completed nine other statues." He listed those names. "And I have a couple dozen more yet to do."

"That is quite an impressive feat," Verda said. "Please tell me who those other méith are... I would love to see them once finished." Her voice verged on flirtation.

Odendes listed them without giving her reasoning much thought. He was too busy staring at how the elf's tits threatened to bust out of her dress and he wished for some sort of jarring. Maybe the cord that laced the two halves of her bodice-style garment would snap and they'd spill out and unto glorious purpose... *Well, lascivious purpose, anyway.*

Perhaps she would volunteer as a model for me. After all, I am known for accuracy and my attention to detail—one must get all his facts in order before beginning. He shook his head to clear the fog from between his ears and he recognized that she'd been speaking.

Odendes blinked at her while she finished thanking him and then turned to depart. The she-elf left, and he muttered to himself, "Damn it. I gotta stop getting so carried away... Maybe I'll see her again?"

"Maybe you should get Anya to help us," Hobin told Remy as he set the foodstuffs on the counter.

"We don't need to bother her," Remy said as he unwrapped a bread loaf and located a knife. "Besides, I've not seen much of her these last few days, except in passing. I just know that she was working on something big."

Hobin arched an eyebrow. "Bigger than feeding the most handsome redcap west of the Selvages?"

Remy chuckled as he shook his head. "That's what *I'm* doing. You could always help, you know."

"I can't reach that high. But I would like to point out that what you made yesterday was... Well, I wouldn't call it food."

Ignoring Hobin, Remy said, "I asked her what she was up to, but she said she needed to verify a few things before she could tell me more."

"And *I've* got to suffer your cooking because of that?"

Suddenly remembering he had it, Remy withdrew the bundle of dallineb weed from his pouch and laid it on the counter. "Careful, now, or I'll hide this stuff inside your sandwich and see if it has any negative effects on redcaps, too."

Hobin leaned against the counter and sniffed, sticking out his tongue at the musky aroma. "Blech."

"Arawyn called it dallineb weed. He said this is what Oddur's fáelad used. I guess he lit several of them and screened the place with smoke for several hours before the attack. I hadn't heard of the stuff before, and Arawyn only knew it because it was in one of the mavens' libraries at the Maginarius."

"That makes sense. Mavens would want to restrict that kind of information, I suppose." Hobin took a seat.

Remy nodded his agreement. "Look what they did when folks discovered the similar effects that dweomer root had on them—they engineered the entire iontaofa dietary laws for anyone entertaining mavens."

"What is ion-ta-ofa?" Hobin annunciated the term he was unfamiliar with. Redcaps were not known to host suppers attended by mavens.

"Any place serving iontaofa guarantees, under penalty of death, that their foods contain no dweomer root," Remy explained.

The redcap stared at Remy as the human did his best to slice bread and spread condiments on it.

"How is it you can be so skilled at sticking that sharp pointy object into living creatures and yet this loaf of bread represents a serious challenge?" Hobin chuckled.

The duelist glared at him over the shaved beef he was struggling with and pointed his knife at the smaller creature. "Come here, and I'll show you," he teased.

As the door opened with a metallic *click*, both Remy and Hobin looked up at it, discovering Jaira who walked through it. Something in Remy's eyes shifted from an ever present worry for his wife which settled into relief at her return.

Remy rushed over to her and embraced the she-elf. "Morrígan's three faces... I was worried when I got here and thought you might have run off and into danger without me."

She shrugged. "I kind of did... Just not the kind you're used to dealing with."

He cocked his head. Jaira glared at the powrie, as if communicating nonverbally with him. Remy couldn't pick up on anything in particular and he assumed it was related to her stashing the redcap at her parents... But he knew there was something *they'd shared*. Remy knew she wouldn't keep secrets from him, and if Jaira thought he needed information, she'd give it to him.

Hobin kept grinning at her, though, finally prompting Remy to ask, "What? What am I missing?"

"You'll never believe how bad this guy is at making sandwiches," the redcap told her.

She scowled with an expression that verged on playfulness. "Oh, I would believe it." Jaira headed for the kitchen. "Here, let me help."

To everyone's benefit, she took over the travesty that had been Remy's attempts at the culinary arts. The whole time, the powrie watched her.

Jaira held up the bundle of dallineb weed and wrinkled her nose. "What's this?"

Remy explained, "It's the stuff Arawyn told me about... Knocks out aes sidhe abilities for a time."

She eyed him and its proximity to the food. "And you were, uh, planning to poison a redcap with it?"

Remy shrugged. "I was considering it."

Hobin frowned. "So, are you going to tell him yet?"

"Tell me what?" Remy asked.

Jaira turned on her heel and pointed the knife she held at Hobin. "You can keep your trap shut, ya little goblin."

"Sheesh," Hobin said as he stared at the knife. He held up his hands in surrender. "You two deserve each other, you know."

Remy repeated, "Tell me what?"

Jaira sighed as she completed the first sandwich, placed it on a disk of parchment paper, and flopped it on the table before the redcap. It nearly unmade itself with the gesture, but Hobin slid the thing back into a manageable stack of deliciousness. The diminutive tuatha licked his lips and then began systematically devouring the human-sized portion.

Sucking in a deep breath, she closed her eyes and re-centered herself as the sandwich shut Hobin up. "How much about my trip did my mother tell you?"

"Eilastra said very little, in fact, and this rotten little redcap refuses to say much about anything. I assume you swore him to secrecy—with ears like that he can't be *this* ignorant."

Through a mouthful of food, Hobin mumbled, "You underestimate the levels of my stupidity, good sir." He swallowed. "Besides, we powrie take our secrets seriously."

Jaira nodded. "You know I went to see my aunt and uncle."

Remy tilted his head and frowned at her. He knew the story went so much deeper than that. "That can't be the reason you went all the way to the capital."

"No," Jaira admitted. "And I only just missed you, it seems. Oberon himself said as much."

Remy blinked at her with surprise. "You... you talked with Oberon? King of the Summer Court?"

"I did. And apparently he's heard of you and is impressed with what he hears."

The human touched the tips of his ears and glanced at the floor. "Even though I'm—"

"A son of Adam? Of course, dear. Everyone knows that... It's only a few of the more cantankerous fey who take issue with it," Jaira told him.

"So, what was your mission then? What was such urgent business that you had run off so quickly?" Remy asked.

Jaira's jaw set, and then she unlocked them as if by sheer force of will. "I came across some snippets of information that I needed to deal with. Legalities and other nuances of Court that needed addressing from a Morgansteen representative."

"And this was something your father could not deal with?" Remy asked. He watched his wife's reaction to that question and realized the answer from her expression. "It was something Harhassus doesn't know about." He did not phrase it as a question.

"Correct. It goes deeper than that, but I'll spare you the details. Regardless, my parents are in trouble, and I have found a way to save my family's legacy from ambitious creditors and noble asshats. Even more, include you in it."

Remy worked on cutting bread for his own meal, tore the loaf into a ragged mess, and then set it all aside. He glanced sidelong at his wife and realized this conversation was more serious than he'd first thought.

The way Jaira held him in his gaze communicated something deeper than he'd realized. *Up until now, I haven't been a real part of this family... Not truly... Not in the eyes of the Summer Court.*

Jaira seemed to have realized what he'd picked up on. She explained, "Titania would never allow a full human in her court. She barely tolerates the changelings as it is, and I'm led to believe that the Frith Duine have established a presence there. I made good inroads with the king and asked Oberon if I could solve his most pressing problem for him in exchange for legal recognition of our union."

Remy blinked at her. "That's... that's a huge step forward for the rights of humans in Arcadeax. What that kind of thing would signal is huge." His words trailed off.

She nodded in return. "You should hear the task."

"I'm not interested in killing for the benefit of any throne or crown," Remy told her. "You know I've had my fill of that." As his wife, he'd shared more details about his gory past with her than any other—he needed her to know truths rather than gossip and exaggeration.

Jaira shook her head slowly. "I think you would do this one for free, given that the Frith Duine are also trying to curry his favor by accomplishing the same task."

"What is it?"

"Locating a few stolen objects," she told him. "Really, it's only one object that he desires. The rest of the artwork and trinkets that were stolen are things Oberon couldn't care less about. It's just stuff, and mostly his wife's stuff."

Remy raised an eyebrow, intrigued.

Jaira told him about the Saol Nua festival and its moving location. She explained the ambrosia, its connection to long elven lives, and how it factored into the méith nobility. "If this legendary item, the Dagda's Bowl—"

"Coire Ansic," Remy interrupted her with the item's name.

She nodded. "If it is not discovered by the time of the festival, it could result in civil war amongst the sidhe nobility."

Remy grinned. "But if I can recover it in time I might earn such favor that Oberon would engineer a tidal shift in seelie sentiments because of it?"

"Exactly," Jaira said. "But you'll have to act quickly. Not only are the Frith Duine attempting the same thing, and their reward would be much worse for humanity, but Oberon has likely dispatched mavens as well as other royal hunters." She looked him full in the face. "You *must* be the first to find it, Remy."

He nodded.

"Bah," quipped Hobin through his last bite. He brushed crumbs off of his chest. "It'd be even better if he was the second and *I* was the first."

The couple stared at him, silently signaling him to elaborate.

"It's not the entire court chasing this thing—just a few social climbers. That means they're keeping it all hush-hush. And if they're keeping it quiet, that means it's a big, fat secret." Hobin's grin practically glittered. "And didn't I already tell you? We redcaps are serious about our secrets."

"Do you know something we don't?" Jaira asked.

"Not exactly. But the powrie are good at *uncovering* the secrets of *others*, too... And if the Court is still in the dark about this one, at least most of them, then it means they've kept a tight lid on information thus far. It means you have some time to operate."

"Sure," Jaira said. "But how does that help us... And what does it have to do with *you*?"

Hobin grinned broadly. "Everywhere you go in Arcadeax you'll find the little folk. Even if you can't, you know, actually find them, we're there—and the wee fey will talk to each other more often than we're likely to chat with you bigger folk."

"You think you can find out information about the lost treasure?" Remy asked.

Hobin nodded. And then he walked toward the door. "Give me a little time, but I've got to go alone. Some of my kind get real cagey around you tall ones."

Remy stared at him skeptically.

The powrie merely winked in response and then turned to Jaira. "I'd tell you both more, but you know... secrets and all. Although I'd *love* another sandwich when I get back, but I have no idea when that will be. Probably the middle of the night."

Hobin had to reach up, and stretch to grasp the door closed by its handle. But then he shut it behind him.

Glancing at his wife, Remy noted, "He was acting weird. Are you being blackmailed for sandwiches by a redcap?" The whole idea was so absurd that he did not push it any further. Especially not when she changed the subject given their sudden privacy.

After several days apart, she pressed her soft lips against his, fumbled for the closure of his pants and shoved him toward the bedroom. It was the perfect resolution for any conversation, and Remy forgot all about any sandwiches of his own.

Andrathan skulked along the road, trying to act as casually as possible, though he knew that his demeanor, and even his gait, gave him away to small degrees. He'd become so assimilated with the winter fey that he'd forgotten the mannerisms of his original people. At his core, his heart had fealty to Summer—to Suíochán Naséan, specifically—but his body belonged to Winter.

A traveler passed him going in the opposite direction. Andrathan nearly gave a two-finger salute common to the unseelie sidhe, but swapped that for a friendly nod at the last moment, only remembering it by chance and just in time.

Further down the road, he plodded along when a stone whizzed out from the trees and skittered across the ground near his feet. He paused in his tracks.

It happened again, and this time he heard where it broke free of the leaves ahead. Whomever lobbed stones at him, hadn't intended to hit him. They hadn't been pitched nearly hard enough for that. *Which means someone is trying to get my attention.*

Andrathan hurried over to the dense foliage and peeked beyond the tangled bracken, spotting the familiar shape of a boot print stamped upon a face.

"We thought we lost you," growled Syrmerware Kathwesion.

"Yeah, well, I figured you'd all gotten yourselves killed," Andrathan muttered back at him, pushing his way into the greenery that hid three orcs and two unseelie sidhe. "I see you've all survived."

Rharzal looked the elf over apprehensively. "You sure took you dear sweet time finding us."

Andrathan shrugged. "Thought I'd lie low a few days. You know, catch a few sights, terrify the local children, bed their she-elves and stomp on their pets." His voice trailed off for a few moments. "Their food really is rubbish."

Gnub chortled at the rear behind Rharzal. The orc warlord let his ire go and focused his anger on his kin, instead clubbing Gnub with a backhand.

"Why are you still here, anyway?" Andrathan asked. "I figured I wouldn't find you again until I was well past the borders of the selvages."

"We never left," said Syrmerware, "We aren't here to *just* deliver slaves—"

Andrathan grinned. He'd kept his ears to the ground and his contacts in the fortress of Arctig Maen had been right all along about there being more to this than a simple delivery gig.

The slavetaker's brother interrupted him. Rharzal hissed, "Because we are springing a trap... And it'll be all that much easier with one more in our crew."

Odessa Cócaire sifted through the produce where she stood in front of the small market stall in the woodland village of Vail Carvanna. She had been sent to fetch items in the town for her employers at the Fyndrolker estate where she played governess to Donnalia, a once precocious girl now in blooming into the earliest stages of her teenage years... A girl who was, unbeknown to most, also Odessa's daughter.

She'd been allowed to remain in the girl's life under the strictest of confidences. Lord Ylamenor Fyndrolker, Donnalia's father, was a titled lord; he was not a forgiving elf... But he *was* able to give the child a life Odessa never could. Even if Fyndrolker mostly kept her secluded, embarrassed at the girl's hearing impediment. Odessa wondered how that might play out once Donnalia was old enough to attend court.

Taking fruit and filling her canvas bag, she paid the vendor and then stepped into the street.

Maybe Ylamenor will have a change of heart? No... He's never altered a belief in his life. Most likely he'll arrange a marriage to some other noble's child... Or worse, to some withered, old noble himself. As long as the méith live almost forever, I fear that...

So lost in thought was Odessa that she nearly collided with the dirty and bloodied elf who staggered through the dirt street and toward her. Odessa gasped as he lunged for her, grabbing her shoulders with a hand on each side; he shook her with urgency.

"A report must be sent. We are under attack, I tell you!"

Odessa looked both left and right and then beyond the elf. The woodland village remained as serene as ever. "What you mean, under attack... by who?"

The elf's unfocused eyes seemed to narrow and return to some semblance of lucidity. "Monsters," he told her. "My entire caravan was destroyed. Only I was able to get away. But they were more than monsters, huge wolf-like things... When they first attacked, *they were men.* Ddiymadferth surged out of the trees on either side of the road and attacked, stealing all my cargo—a load of ddiymadferth children collected on request of the Radiant Tower. They also took the food and other items and killed my other traveling companions."

He spat on the ground with disgust, cursing all of humanity. "Three of those damned *things* transformed into beasts before my very eyes."

Odessa merely stared at him, wondering what he expected her to do with that information. She had heard many rumors of missing human children, but it didn't garner lots of attention as the topic was barely noteworthy to most sidhe. *Attackers were probably the families of those who'd been abducted... I would have done the same.*

"Make haste, girl," the elf snarled. "A message needs sending, and as soon as possible! My brothers in the Frith Duine must know, as does the Tower. I have contacts at the capital."

Odessa frowned. She had at least one good human friend and sensed trouble brewing for Remy Keaton. "Not much way to send any quick communications from Vail Carvana. I suppose you could hire a messenger. You don't suppose this monster is still looking for you, do you?"

He grumbled something barely audible at her while shaking his head. "I said this was *urgent!* Where is the nearest aither connection I can use?"

Odessa practically laughed in his face. "Out here? *In Vail Carvana?* We don't have any of that fancy stuff out here. It's too tiny to have attracted any of those kinds of vendors. No akasha either." She shrugged.

Of course, she'd been lying through her teeth. They had akasha, just not a steady drip system like in the cities; an elf supplier arrived weekly to top off any supply tanks of those who'd opted to install it in their residence. At least one home in Vail Carvana had an aitherport, as well... the Fyndrolker estate, but she had no intention of telling him that.

Besides, Ylamenor would not want some random outsider using his private systems.

"Dammit," the wounded elf groused. "Where is the closest place I can find one?"

Odessa pointed at the hard-packed road leading away from the town. "That way. If you're on foot, Cathair Dé is about a day away if you walk briskly. Best of luck to you, sir."

"That's it? You will not give me assistance or loan me a horse?"

She looked at him skeptically. "Do I look like an elf of means?" Odessa scanned him up and down. Raising her voice just loud enough so that her fellow locals could overhear, she said, "I daresay even if I had a horse, this looks like a clever ruse to part a fool with her belongings. Now, as I said, *good day*, sir. I really must be off."

The abused elf scowled at her, but she did not care. She turned her back on him even as she heard him rant at some of the other citizens of Vail Carvana, searching for any kind of aid.

Odessa felt confident that she'd seeded doubt enough to keep any others from giving the elf access to anything so valuable as a horse, and only the staff at the Fyndrolker estate knew that Ylamenor had an aitherport. The only concern she had was that the self-professed Frith Duine member might find another member of his group. Beyond the fact that they hated humans, she did not know much about them except that their influence was growing... And this story would only encourage it.

Odessa quickened her pace and hurried toward the house. There she'd be able to send a message to Anya through the aither. She knew that the sister of Thoranmir Shelton, her deceased would-be suitor, would be able to relay it to Remy... And she had to be quick about it. Whether or not a human attack was true, members of the Frith Duine would be able to voice their complaints to the throne.

Ylamenor is supposed to walk the orchard with his gardeners this afternoon, she thought. *That should give me an opportunity to sneak in and borrow the aither connection today.*

Chapter Seventeen

Fuerian stepped inside his apartment and pressed a button on the wall where it had been mounted. The toggle activated a spell built into the magitech, switching on the lights throughout his apartment. The luminaries flickered to light, blazing with active akasha.

He allowed himself a momentary grin at the irony of it. The bulk of House Vastra's generational wealth had been built on lighting their communities; while bringing light to the masses had earned them their first fortune, organizing collectives and using strong-arm business tactics had allowed them to keep it and even make it grow... for a time. And now, Fuerian embraced the present technology and worked his way beyond his family history.

"Hello Fuerian," said a cold, feminine voice.

Nearly jumping out of her skin, the sidhe whirled, half expecting to find the recently missing Trishana waiting for him, possibly hijacking his aitherport in the darkness. Instead, he found Loitariel.

"It's far too easy to gain access to you now days, maybe you need better quality locks," she said, her words ringing with a murderous tone. "Perhaps it's high time you invested in a replacement for... what was his name, Naz?"

His doors were safeguarded by the most secure smithing on the market. *She'd have to be a safecracker or a fucking aes sidhe to get past them... I know too little about this interloper,* he realized.

Fuerian narrowed his gaze at her and then glanced down at her hands. He half expected to see her holding a weapon of some sort, perhaps one of those blunderbuss scattershot casters... *She'd have filled one with iron filings, no doubt.* But he found her hands were empty.

"What are you doing here? This is my private home."

A smile played at the edges of her lips. "Why else do you think I would be here?" She stood, the curve of her pregnant form becoming more obvious while on her feet. It made her a slightly less imposing figure.

Fuerian's eyes darted to the sword mounted on the wall. He was good with the blade. One of the best, actually, and the duelist rankings in the journals placed him in the top ten blade fighters in the kingdom, as if that meant anything; Remy Keaton had beaten him in the tournament, and his unknown friend had managed to draw first blood on the sidhe when he'd taken the field.

"So predictable," Loitariel hissed at him. "You won't be able to keep all your secrets forever, and adding the murder of a pregnant she-elf would be a big one. I doubt even *you* could keep it for long."

Huffing angrily, Fuerian crossed his arms over his chest as if putting away his hands signaled his willingness to engage with words rather than active violence. Of course, that was a ruse... He was always ready to do violence. He was good at it.

Fuerian half-growled, half-sighed as a sign that she ought to continue with the conversation, but that she should get to the point.

"I know your secret, Fuerian Vastra. I know how you finagled an iron mine out from Harhassus Morgansteen and have been working to convert it into a profitable enterprise that benefits *only you*, as opposed to the family."

"Iron mining is illegal," Fuerian told her. "This mine is a liability, nothing more. While I am obviously trying to make it profitable, there is no risk to House Vastra—the family voted upon this at the very meeting your marriage into it was revealed."

She looked down her nose at him. "Correct. And all of that was engineered to fill your pockets with coin and cut House Vastra out of it."

He smirked at her in response. What she accused him of was perfectly well and good. It was a legal play where business was concerned, and Vastras were ruthless in that field, even to their own... especially to their own.

"So?"

"So... You are gambling with the House's status," she snarled. "Harvesting iron is a capital offense—perhaps one idiotic Vastra would escape execution by the fact of méith status, however prison would be assured, along with the entire de-elevation of rank for the culprit's family. *You are fucking with everyone else's livelihood, you little shit!*"

"What you say is true only if I am actually harvesting iron." He let the vestiges of a grin escape his control. While it wasn't his primary export, he'd harvested *a little* of the stuff; it was an obligation he incurred for his deal with Hymdreiddiech, but there was no way anyone could prove that.

Her lips curled angrily upward, exposing her teeth. "That's exactly what you are doing. And while you may have tricked the rest of the House of your fortuitous position, your use of the family as a shield while you to harvest that damned ore *will* be made known and they will *not be happy*."

"Yeah, well, maybe you don't know the Vastras as well as you think you do," he spat back at her, even though she was fully correct. "Besides, this is the kind of confrontation better suited to an *actual* Vastra." He sniffed. "Is Juriahl too busy trying to learn his numbers and letters, or has something else caught his attention?"

Rage overtook Loitariel momentarily. "If he was still—" She caught herself and smoothed the hems of her garments as Fuerian tilted his head, perking up his ears. And then a slow, devious grin played ever so subtly at his lips. He knew his composure had that particular tell, but he did not care. *I think I have learned something new.*

Loitariel took a fresh approach. "The next meeting of House Vastra shall prove an interesting one, indeed. You bribed Amarthanc at your iron audit, which is an attempt at safeguarding the family, however poor. But you will be found out, and I will ensure you become ina aonar."

Fuerian let his smile broaden even further as he held her in his gaze. She could have only known *that* if she had some connection to Suíochán Naséan. He had not told anybody about the bribes to the High Maven of the Violet Order. *That's now two things I have learned... And now, it makes sense how she got in here.*

The noble's hand slid up to his throat, and he clutched the amulet he wore, pulling it up so that Loitariel could see it. He wanted her to know how he was insulated from her magic. Revealing it shifted the balance of power. And Fuerian was always happy to dominate others through his use of it, whether subtle or blatant.

Loitariel's eyes widened as he did so, revealing even more of their whites. It was exactly this reaction that he'd hoped for, and his eyes glanced back to the blade mounted within easy reach. Through his cocky smirk he asked, "Tell me, wizard... Did you kill Juriahl with your magic, or did you use more conventional means? Yes... I think you're right that the next meeting of *my* house will be very interesting indeed."

The she-elf's expression could not have looked more rattled. *So, it is true-my cousin is dead. Excellent news.*

And then her gaze narrowed to daggers at him. "No, it was *you* who killed Juriahl." Her words seethed with venom and Fuerian felt the subtle push of magic against him as she infused them with the force of magic, but their influence dispelled under the protection of his ward.

"What are you talking about?" Fuerian snarled. And then he understood her meaning. *Loitariel wasn't bothered by my charm's warding ability—she doesn't know her husband wore a fake... It must be in the hands of Juriahl's killer! Whomever killed him must've stolen the forgery to set me up.*

Grimacing, Fuerian held up his hands, hoping to talk. There were many potential opportunities for them both to integrate this new revelation into positions of profit and power. Several ideas stitched together in the back of his mind, forming so automatically that he could focus on grooming the widowed aes sidhe.

While he lifted one arm, the sudden movement of his sword hand made the intruder panic. As automatically as his mind schemed for personal gain, hers must have been geared toward defense—and Fuerian's hands, whether holding a blade or not, were the most dangerous things in the room at that moment.

Although his amulet awarded him against direct magical attacks, it did not prevent environmental changes. Loitariel summoned a flash of light, ten times more brilliant than the akashic luminaries, momentarily blinding Fuerian. He shook his head to clear his vision, and once his eyes had cleared, he realized that Loitariel had fled.

With Juriahl dead, the title would fall back to him, regardless of Loitariel's marriage to him. Loitariel clearly understood how Fuerian had everything to gain from killing her outright, making escape a priority.

But Fuerian didn't want *everything*. He wanted so much *more*... And even now, a new idea solidified in his mind and that broad, devious grin returned to his face.

Loitariel hurried out beneath the darkened sky. She'd stop by the Vastran estate only shortly in order to grab a sack that she'd prepared for exactly this sort of contingency and to set a few contingencies in play to explain her absence.

The moment her husband had died, Loitariel had assembled a bag containing a great deal of coins, some basic supplies, and most importantly, she'd added a full kit of magical reagents in case she'd needed to call upon her aes sidhe training and embrace her arcane talents in order to protect her life and that of her unborn child.

Loitariel had hoped to never need to flee, but she was a stickler for preparedness. Contingencies were something that Mithrilchon had drummed into her and his other apprentice, *now his only one*, Agarogol.

Thank the Dagda for my foresight.

She hurried out into the night. It had drawn long. By now, most reasonable sidhe with jobs, families, and run-of-the-mill concerns had retired for the evening.

Clambering into a carriage owned by her deceased husband, Juriahl, Loitariel signaled the driver to make all haste for one of the transport lines on the eastern edge of the city. He knew better than to ask questions and he cracked the whip, driving his team of horses to the lady's destination.

After arriving, her driver dropped her moderately heavy luggage on the boardwalk. Loitariel turned to him and drew him close.

Startled by the move, the he-elf blushed as she pulled against him. Loitariel was so close that they might have kissed purely by accident.

"My lady?" he asked, with cheeks growing redder by the moment.

She said nothing, working the first parts of the spell in silence, something only possible by incredibly talented mavens. Loitariel was, after all, only a few years junior to Amarthanc the Violet who was the youngest aes sidhe to achieve the High Maven status.

The driver continued stammering. "I, uh, understand that women in your condition... That is, I mean, as the pregnancy goes into its sixth month, the mother begins to feel, uh, certain urges." He swallowed as Loitariel fixed him with an intense gaze. "I mean, I've thought about it, but I just don't think that it's right if we—"

She interrupted him with a few words spoken in the ancient tongue of magic, giving him a command. [You will forget everything about today. You will not remember anything and if someone compels your memory with magic, you will bite off your tongue, first to stall, and then find the nearest object and attack your interrogator. Die with honor; keep my secret.]

The spell bound man blinked and then nodded slowly. His demeanor changed as he fell fully under her thrall.

Loitariel slipped a handful of coins into the elf's palm and wrapped his fingers around them. Continuing in the ancient tongue, she insisted on one last set of directions. [Find the nearest pub and drink to your limit. Then have one more drink for the road before stumbling home on foot.]

With a monotone voice, he answered, "Yes, my lady." He turned and departed. He left her with a vacant expression plastered upon his face. The darkness of the stables and the silence of the night quickly enveloped her.

Among the shadows near the barns, and by the transit station, she spied several greedy faces watching her. Loitariel had been too close to her driver for them to be able to discern what had happened, and she imagined she looked like an easy target. She was an obviously pregnant woman left alone and abandoned with a carriage and horses. Any cut-purse worth their salt would be tempted beyond reason.

Loitariel played into that scenario and leaned against the wagon, looking distraught, as if she'd been abandoned by her ward. Using some of her magic, she pushed an aura outward from herself, a mystic augmentation of that belief.

A trio of dirty elves approached—they were not even bruscar—these were casteless. They wore cocky faces, but the glimmer of mischief in their eyes revealed their evil intentions. Loitariel was a quick score to them. She represented nothing more than meat and money.

Loitariel pretended not to watch as they moved toward her, but she knew they had drawn knives and clubs as they came near. Playing her part, she glanced at them and jumped as if suddenly startled.

"Oh, thank the Dagda—I am in need of help."

The elf in the front grinned. His wide, foul smile indicated his poor hygiene. He reached down and grabbed his crotch, adjusting it and signaling he was comfortable with the worst sorts of actions anyone could visit upon a pregnant woman. The leader gripped his rust-spotted dagger.

Looking into the elf's eyes, Loitariel frowned. "No, you certainly won't do." Her voice shifted with a rumble. [Burn with dark fire and suffer pain, I cast upon you Brigid's flame,] she growled in the high tongue.

Immediately, the would-be rapist and robber collapsed. He writhed in pain, as if set ablaze by some invisible fire that neither of his two companions could see. The flames provided no illumination, no heat, no damage to anything or anyone around him. Only aes sidhe could even see them.

Of the companions on either of his sides, one's face darkened, and he turned his eyes to Loitariel with murderous intent. She knew his thoughts. It wasn't magical or anything, but his expression was obvious. Where the earlier elf had failed, he intended to succeed. By contrast, the other sidhe dropped to his knees to check on his downed companion.

Loitariel tilted her head and looked at the one who'd stalled. "You," she said after making eye contact with him and noting the worry on his face. There was compassion there, and she hoped his life of crime was something he'd been forced into rather than one chosen willingly. "I'm offering you a gift—both wealth and a chance for a fresh start."

The remaining murderous elf pounced upon her, snatching Loitariel by the wrists and pinning her against the carriage. He snarled, "I'll give you a gift, you little whore. I'm going to take everything you got, and then I'm going to kill you to keep you quiet."

She met his gaze and furrowed her brow at him. Before she could cast a spell and dispatch him, the he-elf screamed. Blood spilled from his parted lips and then he shuddered, trying to take in more air to continue his screeching. But he could take in no more. The elf whirled, suffocating on his own blood as it filled his lungs.

As she turned, Loitariel saw the look of panic frozen on the remaining elf's face. He'd plunged his dagger upward and between the ribs of his companion. Moments later, the enraged elf finished choking on the fluid in his lungs and then collapsed to the ground, spilling bright pink fluid—blood that had been intensely oxygenated where it pooled in his chest. It spilled out and all across the ground.

Loitariel's eyes met the whelming look of panic that threatened to overtake the remaining sidhe. "Look at me. Look at me," she reassured him.

The elf complied. Her spell forced him to... mostly. It was suggestive magic—she could not have bound the will of anyone who lacked compassion.

"I'm going to give you a gift in exchange for your help. Can you drive this carriage?"

Still dealing with the shock, he nodded. "I have driven one before."

"Good. Good." She reassured him with the lie that would help break his shock over the deeds he just performed.

Loitariel's first priority was to preserve herself and protect her child. "I'm on the run from a wealthy elf... A former lover who wants to murder me and kill my child." Using a small bit of illusion magic, she made her face appear as if bruised. She summoned a falsely swollen eye ringed yellow and blue.

The would-be savior stepped closer to her and laid a hand against her cheek to examine her. "What did that beast do to you?" He gasped. "It's just like my mother all over again. Tell me how I can help. I'll kill him, if you want me to."

"I need to get away, fast and far. And I need to keep it quiet. Can you do this in secret?"

Her new driver nodded resolutely.

"But I just need to get to the next city with the transit hub. Can you get me there by tomorrow during the day, just as they might open for business? He owns this carriage and it may be recognized by one of his spies. I can travel anonymously from there to my next destination. I—I have to keep shedding modes of transport and altering my name lest he find me."

He nodded his understanding and then hedged slightly. "You said something about a gift? I mean no disrespect, but I *am* mighty hungry... I mean to help, but I need some help in return."

"Of course. You may keep this carriage and the horses. Start your own business, become a taxi, I do not care. Sell the horses if you like or even eat them. They are yours to do with as you please once we part."

The dirty elf nodded, helped load her luggage into the wagon, and then they were off.

Remy stalked through the central hub of Cathair Dé. Hobin hadn't returned in the time-frame he'd given Remy and Jaira, and so Remy began investigating on his own.

The morning had drawn long, and he had plenty of important business to do yet, including a planning meeting with Kent. His patron had, more and more, scheduled upcoming meetings with suppliers and vendors as he worked on whatever secret project he'd negotiated with Oberon. But the duelist understood that he'd had it pretty easy so far as work went, up until now. Some patrons insisted their duelists be available at almost all hours.

Remy had just come from two of the information brokers who he knew operated in the city. The first one hadn't heard of the king's lost caravan of loot and Remy had not divulged what its contents were. That broker had made out better than Remy and now had a new rumor he might potentially sell.

The second contact had turned the human out on his heel. The inside of the information broker's small shop, which doubled as a pawn dealership, had a sign that plainly read *No Humans*. A second poster affixed below it was of the Frith Duine symbol.

Swearing beneath his breath, Remy noticed that several of the marketplace vendors had a similar shingle hanging from their tents' hardware. *Their campaign has begun in earnest, then.* He realized that the Frith Duine's sympathizers were organized and maintaining solidarity by denying service to the sons and daughters of Adam.

Sighing, Remy spotted Hazimon near her usual place and he went to her. Dropping a few coins onto her blanket, he asked her if she'd heard anything about the King's lost shipment.

Hazimon's face pinched gravely. She motioned him closer and Remy crouched down nearer her blanket, where she displayed her trinkets.

"Of course, I have. I always pay attention to news of Titania's failures," she told him, beaming proudly.

Remy blinked with surprise. He knew she had a sustained hatred of the queen, but he hadn't quite expected her to have access to such a good rumor. From the corner of Remy's eye, he spotted Hobin slipping through the edge of the market. He quickly stood and shouted to the powrie and waved him over before crouching back down to the elder dryad.

Hazimon's gaze narrowed at the redcap who approached.

"Don't worry," Remy told her. "He's with me."

She nodded and then continued just as Hobin arrived. "The caravan raiders are tuatha wildfey and they have taken their claim to Winter. They have to keep off the main roads and travel in secret, but my spies know its location. In fact, they are just about to cross the Iron Bridge."

Remy's eyebrows rose. "How can they get over the forsaken ferrous shards? Are they that brazen?"

"The bridge is open now that the iron has been removed. Several smugglers are using it lately. It's become all but abandoned and someone picked it clean of iron—for what purpose, I cannot say. I assume it will become public knowledge over the next several months, and the courts will return a garrison to either side... but for now, at least, it can be crossed freely."

"Where did you hear this?" asked Remy.

She smirked at him. "Few tuatha care to speak to an old crone, but the animals still whisper to the green elves... And they're not nearly as prejudiced. They still make their homes amongst the trees, both young and old."

"You can talk to animals then?" Hobin asked her.

She looked down her nose at him. "I could do a hell of a lot more than that, if my body were ever restored." She looked down at her gnarled fingers. "I can't even make the right shapes of my hands for the somatic gestures, though."

"You're an aes sidhe?" asked the surprised redcap.

Hazimon's eyes blazed. "What I am *predates* that word."

The powrie gulped, and Remy thanked her, tossing her another coin for her troubles. Standing, he pulled Hobin several steps away and asked him, "What did you find out?"

Hobin looked back and then glanced hesitantly at the withered lady. "If her information is correct, then it is all good news. My cousin currently operates in that region. If I leave straightaway, I can get to him in time and he can help locate the thieves before they get beyond his territory. Surely Redcomb will help."

Remy nodded. "Do it—go to him. Just tell me what you need."

"Some coin, probably? I used what I had yesterday, and I may need more yet for bribes, plus coin to hire a shuttle to ferry near enough to my cousin before the thieves get away."

The human pulled out his purse and weighed it in his hand. He shrugged and turned it over—all of it.

Hobin arched an eyebrow. "The shuttle won't be cheap, man. No other tuatha will want to ride in a carriage with a redcap."

Grimacing, Remy withdrew a second pouch and turned it over as well. Hobin's brows pinched. "Is this all? I'm not sure I can—"

With a sound that was half growl and half sigh, Remy began reaching into his pockets. Then Hobin broke with laughter and gave the human a playful shove, which didn't even budge him. "I'm kidding. I just wanted to see if you'd actually do it."

Speaking very seriously, Remy said, "Securing this treasure is worth everything I've got." He bit his lower lip. *Especially if it keeps the Dagda's pot out of Rhagathena's clutches. The Winter Queen has had to barter for ambrosia out of Wildfell and the Court of Thorns throughout her entire reign—giving that monster eternal life would shift the balance of power firmly out of Oberon's hands.*

He momentarily reflected upon his mission from many years ago, when he was sent to kill Queen Mab. Rhagathena wanted to prop up Queen Maeve, who promised to provide easier access to trade—but *this, ambrosia,* was what Rhagathena was after. Remy knew Mab demanded steep terms in order to keep the Rime Throne supplied, and the Spider Queen did not share her blessings, except with a handful of close confidants, including her majordomo and a few other advisors.

The old spider had enough reasons to want Mab murdered *without* the ambrosia factoring in, and Aderyn Corff was the tool she'd employed to kill her. Not that it worked out in the unseelie's favor. Mab had died by Remy's blade... But the wildfey queen had flipped the script on Rhagathena. Remy couldn't even begin to imagine what sort of toll the Briar Throne extracted from Rhagathena, now, after the fallout from the assassination which Mab had seen coming.

"I suspect that, if you and your cousin cannot capture the bowl in time, it will be sold to the Winter Queen," Remy said, establishing the stakes.

Hobin spat. All powries had an intense hatred of Rhagathena. "I'll get it done," he promised, and then scampered off just as Remy heard a familiar whining sound.

Turning, he found Anya approaching in her akashic chair. The legless elf wore a very stern expression.

Remy tilted his head, and Anya spoke at a low volume. "I just got a message for you via the aither."

"In the aither? Who, or what, could that message be?" Remy was famously a luddite when it came to anything involving that realm.

Anya's eyes remained hard and cold. "Come with me, and I'll tell you everything. It came from Odessa."

A long shadow lay cast across the street, perfectly outlining the shape of the Radiant Tower. Kasianna walked through the silhouette and into the storefront.

She was supposed to be minding the shop today while her husband worked his second job, but she'd closed for an hour in order to run this errand. Talathan took occasional gigs as day labor for one of their supply distributors; the extra income was often necessary to make ends meet.

Kasianna swallowed as she looked around. Her eyes met the shopkeepers as she slid within. She'd been here on several previous occasions. While Hawk and Hems Catered sundries for folk of all classes, this store was far more elite.

The gallery of high-end items was not large, but the collected value was immense, mostly including pieces of art or historical significance. Paintings hung on the wall or stood propped on pedestals. A glass case contained fine watches and other mechanical pieces, including newer magitech and akashic batteries. Upon one rack of garments hung very fanciful garments.

She let her fingers trail through the furs of a fine coat she'd once owned. Kasianna scowled through clenched teeth. *This is probably the last heirloom I have that's worth anything.*

"What do you have for me today, ma'am?" the he-elf near the front asked.

"A rare book," Kasianna told him.

He scowled. "I don't deal in those sorts of things. They never sell well."

"Come now, Hareleth. You know me better than to offer you something of no value."

His worked jaw for a silent moment, and then Hareleth motioned for her to show him what she had.

Kasianna withdrew an ancient book from her satchel, drawing a curious gaze from the shopkeeper. "This has been in my family for many generations."

She paused a moment, suddenly unsure about turning it over. *If he is one of those spies for the tower—an Agent of Gray—this could all go very badly.*

He cocked his head and let his eyes scan the ancient title. Already read, it rendered Kasianna's fears moot; it was too late to withdraw, now.

The book was not a massive tome. It was bound in leather, though its gilding had worn off through the ages. "The Veil of Ash... That sounds very ominous." Hareleth paused for a moment and then looked at her with wide eyes. "Wait a minute. Is this *that* Veil of Ash?"

She nodded slowly. "I am no aes sidhe, and so it's of little value to me, but I am aware there are only a handful of original copies that predate the Infernal Wars. One is owned by the White Maven, another is lost in the unseelie, most likely, and I believe Oberon owns a copy. The Tower uses it for... the obvious reasons, I suppose, which goes far beyond what history it records."

Kasianna decided his reactions were real. *So, not likely an Agent of Gray... Not unless he's an excellent actor.*

Hareleth began leafing through the pages, using care not to damage any of them but searching their text for a specific marker. "I know what you want, and I can assure you that it's there. This edition includes instructions for the Chronurgic Surf spell... The only piece of chronomancy permitted by Suíochán Naséan after *Tempus Exterminus*, when Oberon and Wulflock wiped out the chronomancers and then destroyed any other documents teaching time magic."

Hareleth chuffed as he found the page he was looking for. "Yup. It's here." He licked his lips and then looked up at the she-elf. "It's a rare book all right, but I'm not sure what I can pay you for it... I've also got to verify with the Court that it's even legal to own this. It's a lot of risk for a transaction since it's a gray area for forbidden magic."

Kasianna scowled. "I was hoping for funds sooner rather than later." She locked eyes with the shopkeeper. "You and I both know how much this thing could bring. Even if it's *not legal*, it would still fetch a great amount through... *unconventional* channels."

He set his jaw but nodded. "All true, but that still makes it risky for me, and that risk brings the value down."

"I am aware," Kasianna stated.

Raising his eyebrows and shaking his head, Hareleth stared at the potentially illegal, but very rare item as he decided a price for her share. "I can give you five gold nobles for it."

Kasianna chuckled. "Come now, that's ridiculous. This is one of, what, maybe four existing copies?"

Hareleth sighed. "*But the risks...* I know you're aware of them. It's probably why you didn't go to a rare book dealer. Plus, I've still got to find a way to sell it." He rubbed his jaw as he stared at the thing.

She waited for his answer while she drummed her fingers on a handbill lying there. Kasianna picked it up and read while Hareleth considered his offer.

"Best I can do is eight nobles."

Shifting her eyes to him, she demanded, "Make them marks, and we have a deal."

Hareleth grimaced at the suggestion, but finally nodded. Gold marks were only a slightly higher denomination than nobles. "It will take me a little while to come up with the rest, but I can give you those five nobles today. Come back in a week, and I'll settle up the difference."

She nodded and let him slip away to collect her funds. Kasianna's eyes scanned the paper she still held. It was a public announcement from the Tower reminding the public to alert Suíochán Naséan of any suspected seers. Their Solais Cloaks would collect and interrogate any sidhe found to possess those talents. Further, the handbill promised a reward to any person whose information turned out to be accurate.

Kasianna smirked at the flyer as Hareleth arrived and deposited four medallion sized gold coins with a small hole punched in them, nobles, and a small bag containing eighty silver coins. He added a gold mark, a wafer shaped, stamped gold unit.

"Five marks, as promised."

"For now," she corrected and reminded him, "you still owe me three marks."

He nodded. "And you will owe me discretion regarding the transaction."

She nodded and then handed him back his handbill. "You think this is true?"

"The reward? Probably. Although I think the Tower wants us to think that it's a point of civic duty to turn in any foretellers." He raised his eyebrows. "But if you have any actual information, I know a guy who'd likely pay even more."

Kasianna's smile broadened. *Definitely not one of the Tower's Agents.* "Oh, really?" She glanced over her shoulder and spotted a familiar wagon parked across the street. Talathan labored there, picking up sacks of grain and other heavy products before delivering them inside the opposite storefront. Guilt whelmed in her gut at the temptation of selling out her husband's kin. It overpowered the rage that dwelled there, but barely. That simmering heat in her core resented Harhassus and his family for taking what should have been hers. Well, Talathan's.

"That's very interesting," she said simply.

Hareleth met her gaze. "One week at least. Give me the time to gather your remaining funds."

She nodded and then departed, sneaking out the front door while Talathan hurried inside the opposite shop with a load. Kasianna rounded a corner and then quickened her step for a block before slowing again.

A large group of tuatha, mostly sidhe, had gathered on the nearby corner and were shouting. Several members of the mob broke away and affixed flyers to poles that held aither connection lines and akasha tubes out of the way of city traffic. With large block letters, the top of the prints read *Frith Duine is the Future*.

One of the elves in the cluster pointed at Kasianna. "That one—she's connected to the human lover!"

A knot of surly looking fey approached. Menace burned in their eyes.

"What? What are you talking about?" Kasianna snapped back at them.

"I saw her," shouted a faun. "She was with that human lover, the she-elf from court who married the human duelist."

Kasianna rammed as much ice into her glare as possible as she stared him down. "I don't know what you're referring to, you stupid puck, but if you take one step closer, I shall scream and you'll meet my husband, who's in that shop over there. And *he* is a trained duelist," she lied.

Her harassers paused a moment.

"I do not have any connection to humans or those who consort with them," she snarled. "Now, leave me be."

Before she could turn, the faun's nostrils flared. "Your husband is such a good fighter that he can take all five of us?"

She hardened her gaze at him like unseelie ice. "It won't matter. But I will assure you that he will kill *you,* israddol." She hissed the last word of the insult.

The group disbanded, deeming her either truthful or too dangerous to cajole any further. And then Kasianna hurried back to her store and got resumed her work.

Chapter Eighteen

Four sidhe stood below the stoop of Remy's apartment. Three wore peacekeepers' badges.

"We have it on good authority, Mr. Keaton, that you harbored a witness who saw everything that transpired at Ollscoil Maginarius," said one of the three detectives.

From his vantage, Remy easily looked down his nose at them. It worried him that each of the sidhe enforcers also wore a button bearing the Frith Duine sigil. It bothered him even more that they'd brought the fourth person. Remy knew the sidhe and recognized him as a reporter for the local press. He'd taken an interview from Remy after the duelist's victory at the amphitheater.

No idea how they found out, but they probably want to spin Arawyn's existence to implicate humanity in the slaughter of the aes sidhe. If they were able to get their hands on him, they could likely intimidate him into falsifying his story, or else they might kill Arawyn outright. The best-case scenario is that I'm the bad guy in the story, and the worst case is that I'm directly implicated.

One elf narrowed his eyes at Remy. "I seem to recall you were already at the site of the murders when we arrived."

Remy twirled the newest ribbon affixed below his duelist pin. "I've got a pretty good alibi," he quipped with a nonchalance meant to influence the journalist. "It seems to me that this case was already closed and that Captain Ochara had all the facts. It seems some tuatha didn't like his findings and a few powerful fey decided they wanted to revise those details." He grinned and added, "I mean, *not you*... You guys don't really give me any impression of power."

The detectives stared at him with pinched faces and smoldering eyes. Remy could feel their hate for him... *For his kind*.

"I feel I'm hitting pretty close to home on this. What happened at the maginarius was a tragedy, but it will not be solved any time soon, and not by members of the Frith Duine. They are absolutely who is driving this entire investigation. Terrified little hatemongers who can't stand the fact that some of us have slightly different ears. Maybe if they weren't so paranoid about their own length and girth—" Remy egged them on.

"How dare you!" snarled one of the elves. He stepped forward, reaching for his blade, but Remy was quicker.

In a flash, the duelist's dagger was out. Remy's dúshlán gleamed in the light, but it did not glow.

"How's this for a headline?" roared the angry sidhe. "Ddiymadferth insults constables and is taken into custody for his connection to the Ollscoil slaughter."

Remy sneered, satisfied at how he'd provoked the nasty response. *Getting them to look like fools is the only better story I can give the reporter.* "The problem is, that's inaccurate. If you take one step closer, the headline is going to read 'Asshole Constables Harass Human and Get Themselves Killed.'" The way he enunciated the tone of those words expressed his absolute sincerity.

Behind his opponents, the reporter's brows rose, and he jotted some notes.

The trio grumbled amongst themselves, wondering how to handle the human. They'd arrived with such confidence and bravado, but Remy had tipped them on their ear.

Remy growled at them, driving his point home. "Allow me to give you a suggestion. Run back to your Frith Duine masters and tell them they cannot intimidate me. Furthermore, you can tell that corrupt judge and political pretender, Elethiel Cinίoch, that if he needs another peek at me in the nude, he doesn't have to sneak up to my window again. If he's so desperate to compare cock sizes, he can make an appointment. I'm happy to oblige."

Another grin appeared on the face of the journalist.

Flabbergasted, the detectives each shook their heads, turned, and departed.

"Can I quote you on all of those things?" the reporter asked Remy.

"Just as long as you get them correct and in context," the duelist said darkly. Remy sheathed his dúshlán hard enough that it made a sound when the hilt snapped in place.

Nodding, the journalist seemed to understand the implied threat of misconstruing Remy's words. He gulped, nodded, and then also left.

Remy watched him go. Then he gave it a few more moments, taking in long, calming breaths. *Between this and the Frith Duine shit-storm about to erupt at Faery Cairn, I've got to talk with Madadh before someone else does something stupid.* And then he, too, departed.

"I've got to go. I'll be back as soon as I can."

Jaira heard her husband's words as if at a great distance; the door clicking shut seemed to echo.

She'd heard him just beyond the entrance to their apartment and dealing with some constables. Jaira's world seemed to tilt drunkenly. A sharp sensation pressed against the forefront of her mind, demanding to be acknowledged. Insisting to be let in... a vision demanded she yield and experience it.

It was an aggressive, brutal feeling as the potential future unfolded, revealed itself to her; it came on much like a migraine. Jaira had no choice except to let it in. She was untrained, and as far as she knew, this was her only aes sidhe ability. *Don't they have some sort of name for that,* she wondered absentmindedly.

Regardless of her naivety, she'd experienced this before. This was the way a seer saw futures that were unavoidable without direct intervention. What she was about to see could be changed, but only if she acted quickly.

Normally, she saw myriad images, moving pictures sprawling out throughout time, tied like gossamer strands of spider silk and woven into a web. One could traverse any of those lines and trim the tangents, engineering outcomes that were already foreseen. *But when they came like this?* There was no avoiding what she was about to see—however, she *could* change it in real time.

Jaira tipped onto her side, allowing the vision to overtake her.

She watched as if from a distance, hovering behind Remy. He was in a small village, a place Jaira recognized, though she'd not been there often.

A thousand iterations of him arriving in the town blossomed to life and marked the first point where she could alter the tides of history. And then they unfolded in glorious magnification.

Crossbow bolts skewered her husband, tearing open his throat as great gouts of blood arced into the sky. Bolts of magic slammed into Remy's chest, stopping his heart with elemental force. Enemies leapt out of the shadows, gang tackling him and holding down the human duelist as they skewered him with blades. In some of the visions, the enemies placed him in shackles and dragged him east... *To the unseelie lands.*

Jaira gasped as she realized that these were all Winter fey.

Wiping tears from her eyes, she rolled to her knees and shook off the fugue, regaining her bearings. Jaria wasn't entirely certain how long she'd been transfixed by the vivid images. She did not merely watch the visions; she'd experience each one and endured the pain and trauma of each of them as if they'd been her actual reality.

Slowly, Jaira placed one tentative foot onto the floor and then the next. The pain of the headache still throbbed in the background of her mind, like the afterglow of her mental anguish. But with that came an open portal through which she could begin parsing the different potential outcomes of those actions not yet committed.

Jaira swallowed and staggered, still searching for avenues of action that might rescue her husband from a fate worse than death—and on the heels of his death loomed a shadow. A darkness that had plagued her all her life. In that black future she saw the inevitable: the dark shadow maven who could collect her the moment Remy was out of the picture.

It was not mere self-preservation that motivated her. Jaira knew she loved Remy—she was tied to him, heart and soul—she was bonded by blood and the secret child growing within her. But she knew if she did not act, and do so immediately, her husband would die.

Remy's horse quickened its pace as the duelist left the city behind. He kept the mount moving at a reasonable speed, but did not urge it to a gallop. If he was being watched, Remy did not want any onlookers to jump to the worst sorts of conclusions: that he was somehow guilty of whatever rumors were spreading and now rushed off to speak with his fellow conspirators.

And yet, that's not far from the truth. Remy was painfully aware that it *was* humans who had committed the atrocity. Biting his lip, he understood the mavens were responsible for terrible things, but he also knew that did not give him the right to sit in judgment over them. After all, many of the Bairn's victims had only been students, and many were young.

He sighed again, remembering what Arawyn had told him about his peers attempting to kill him, merely because he was the *wrong sort* of sidhe. The more he thought about it, the more Remy felt conflicted. *Maybe Oddur has a point?*

Remy shook his head, refusing to arrive at any definitive answers. The only thing he *was* certain of was that *Madadh's Fianna* were not the perpetrators of the crime. In fact, they had attempted to stop the Bairn and paid for it with grievous wounds.

"I need to shut this whole thing down," he grumbled as his horse trotted into the edge of Baile Dorcha. The town appeared to have recovered since a band of roving unseelie fey, displaced by the mad queen, Rhagathena, had overtaken it. His lips flattened at the assorted memories.

"I guess I just hate when the underdog is bullied." Remy tried not to think of the young boys, brothers who he'd attempted to rescue from the monstrous orc who had trained him. The orc tried to replicate Remy's training upon them, using the same brutality that had turned Remy into an unseelie killing machine. Both boys died, horribly and painfully. They had both been innocent, taken as human slaves. The boys refused to be molded into something vicious and terrible—into what Remy knew he was deep at his core.

Remy swallowed. He knew he had to protect those who were innocent. If he let the incident at Ollscoil spiral out of control, a lot of innocent sons and daughters of Adam were going to get killed, *or worse.*

He scanned either side of the road as he went through Baile Dorcha. The small dale had mostly repopulated and both businesses and residential homes had sprung back to life. *At least that's something. Tragedies can be recovered from.*

Remy left the village behind and then spurred his horse to quicken it. It wasn't long before he arrived at the woods where he could find the Fianna. One of Madadh's scouts emerged from the wood and took the reins of the mount, leading it around on a different path. Madadh's community was large enough that they were ever conscious of spreading out and dispersing footsteps, minimizing direct evidence of how to find them.

Madadh greeted Remy and motioned the duelist over where a few of the women devoted to Madadh worked at preparing arrows, sharpening blades, and performing a variety of other tasks.

The female warrior who had been at Madadh's side during the moot gathering looked up. "Are you reconsidering Madadh's offer and here to join with us?" Scathach asked Remy.

He locked eyes with her and shook his head. Remy felt reasonably certain Scathach was Madadh's primary mate, but he could not tell for sure. He felt the eyes of many people on him as he joined the leader's circle.

Madadh seemed to catch the seriousness of Remy's expression and he dismissed the others nearby. The females cast reluctant glances towards the non-Fianna male, but obeyed orders.

"Is something bothering you, my friend?" Madadh asked.

Remy nodded slowly. "We have to talk."

Although humans were, on average, more heavily muscled than most of the sidhe, that did not mean there were no burly elves. Two of them blocked Hymdreiddiech's way forward, and both rested heavy hands upon the hooded stranger standing in their midst.

Hymdreiddiech allowed them to stop him before he could access their inner sanctum. The Frith Duine had rented space at one of the unused buildings in Daonra Dlúth where he'd gone on other business.

"Don't make us repeat ourselves, *friend*," stated one of the door persons. "There are no hoods allowed here."

The other sentry explained, "We've got to see your ears if we're going to let you in."

Hymdreiddiech did not bother trying to disguise himself. He let the well-practiced arcane veil fall and then slid back his hood. Beneath it, the human hating elves clearly saw him for what he was: an elf of sharp teeth and malevolent eyes. They were red, burning with rage in the light and the contrast made more apparent by his excessively pale hair layered over the top of his nearly snow white skin. But the albino elf's ears protruded through his mane and he was allowed to pass.

Taking a seat near the back where he would draw fewer gazes by nature of his noticeable condition, the aes sidhe, *the black maven*, watched. For the first few minutes of the gathering, the Frith Duine welcomed new members. Hymdreiddiech raised a finger and exerted a small modicum of power, encouraging the subconscious of all those gathered to overlook him. It was easy magic, especially when all the present minds had already succumbed to their weakness: to hatred.

Their hatred differed from Hymdreiddiech's. The Frith Duine's was irrational, and unfounded, which was different than his.

My *hatred is strong—it is devoted to religious zeal... to my true master, the ancient prince who is yet to come... The dark one who has not yet been revealed.*

An area businessperson stood and lamented the presence of humans who sometimes came into his shop. Two more similar stories were shared, along with the report of humans attacking a caravan in the south near Vail Carvana. Hearing about actual violence perpetuated by humans had the sidhes' corporate hackles up and their blood boiling.

It did not take long before two of them were shouting, each egging the other on and encouraging their friends to commit random acts of violence against the ddiymadferth. A trio of them departed immediately, hatred bubbling out of their eyes with clear intent. *The first short-eared bastard they could lay their hands on was going to die tonight.*

Hymdreiddiech leaned back in his chair and watched. Listened. *Any group with such vast reserves of hatred and ignorance could be useful to my lord.*

And then another businessperson stood... One who was familiar to Hymdreiddiech.

The chairperson of the group tried to regain some sense of structure for the meeting. "Really, my fellow Frith Duine, this is the last story we can share tonight. We still have club business to get to... There's plenty of time for us to engage in purging our streets of the filth once we've seen to matters of decorum."

"You all know me. I've been here since beginning, but I'm not super active or vocal." The elf shopkeeper turned as he spoke, and Hymdreiddiech allowed the man to meet his gaze, lifting the arcane misdirection. Hareleth and Hymdreiddiech locked eyes.

Hareleth stammered for only a moment. "I wonder how dangerous things may become for all of us. I don't know if humans have magic abilities, but I believe that, if so, they are not nearly as adaptable or varied as our aes sidhe... But I heard from a group of our own how a she-elf with connections to the human-lover—you all know of who I speak—visited court lately. There are... things that lead me to believe the ddiymadferth may have access to a seer."

A moment of stunned silence rippled through the room. Hymdreiddiech leaned forward eagerly, his seat creaking only slightly beneath his weight.

"I, uh... I just wonder about things." Hareleth swallowed. "It seems as if the stakes may be increasing." He paused and fidgeted as if not quite knowing what he wanted to ask, or how he wanted to ask it. Finally, Hareleth said, "I guess I'm just worried. Violence is coming, and if anyone here knows how to bypass the abilities of a seer, I'd really like to get their suggestions."

Hymdreiddiech stood, his feet pushing against the chair, making its legs scuff the ground. The sound made everyone turn to look at him. "There are certainly ways to defuse their abilities." He grinned at Hareleth. "I shall come to you when it becomes clear such a rare occurrence as a bona fide seer proves a reality."

Then Hymdreiddiech turned and left, grinning to himself the whole while.

Yes, the Frith Duine seems like a hotbed of activity and an excellent opportunity to engineer outcomes in my favor. I'm certain they will prove themselves useful.

"I can't help but notice that your numbers have grown," Remy told Madadh.

"That is certainly true," the Fianna leader told him. "I don't think it's just limited to this region, either, but I think it's everywhere." Madadh blinked, realizing that Remy wasn't privy to his inner thoughts. He explained, "The attacks, I mean."

"Which attacks?" Remy's eyes narrowed.

Madadh tilted his head. "Everywhere we go, the human haters, the Frith Duine, have been quick to abuse humans. Sometimes they attack us outright, sometimes they engineer situations that can result in nothing but a fight. Humans are finding strength in numbers and are seeking us out regularly."

"And the Bairn?" Remy asked.

Madadh set his jaw. "I assume it is much the same for them, although I think they enjoy seeing the violence, regardless if it bolsters their numbers."

Remy gazed across the large encampment. It was larger than the last time he visited the Fianna and was roughly twice the size of when he first met them so long ago on the road. He asked Madadh, "How many of them have you converted? I mean, how do you make them into shifters, into lycans?"

"The process is only painful in the beginning." Madadh raised an eyebrow. "Are you reconsidering my offer?"

"No. I'm just trying to gather all the details and make sure humanity is not mustering for a war," Remy told him.

Madadh shrugged. "The three Fianna tribes possess a special power, and we can use it to increase our ranks of warriors." He motioned toward the vast assembly gathered in knots throughout the towering trees. "Some of them have accepted this gift, others are reluctant. But the nature of this gift cannot be *forced* upon humans against their will... at least, the Fianna do not force it upon any."

Remy held Madadh's gaze. "But could you?"

Madadh did not flinch from the duelist's hard eyes. "We *would not*," he insisted.

Nodding, Remy assumed that was as good of an answer as he could get without causing offense. Besides, he had every reason to trust his friend.

"We have built our numbers to make certain that we can combat any army that Oddur and his Bairn might raise. Our numbers grow to keep him in check, and I hope that Sbrintiwr and the Fian Fèidh are also increasing ranks of fáelad to keep pace with the tides of power."

"Fáelad?"

Madadh nodded. "It is what we call ourselves... what we call the power. A form that has many names. Lycan. Shifter. Wolven... *werewolf.*"

An uncomfortable silence stretched between them. Remy rubbed his jaw thoughtfully. Finally, he broke the quiet. "Dammit. So you're certain that Oddur is building up his forces?"

"I am."

Remy grudgingly admitted, "Then you're probably right. There is no other way to keep the Bairn from instigating a full-blown war without building up another force equal to his. Your tribe is keeping him in check... mutually assured destruction and whatnot."

One of Madadh's scouts interrupted them momentarily and whispered into the tribal leader's ear. When done, Madadh nodded to him and dismissed the man.

The scout glanced back at Remy with a sheepish look and then hurried away. Remy wanted to ask what that was about, but Madadh continued their conversation.

"This strife with the Bairn cannot not last forever. It is the way of the fáelad for power to rise and challenge itself, becoming something new in the process. If Oddur contests my rule of the Fianna during rituals and I lose..." Madadh swallowed uncomfortably. "If Fian Faolchú falls or if he unseats me at moot, the Bairn will cut down every tuatha in their bloody path until only one remains."

Remy snapped, "Yeah, well, he made it very clear that the Bairn are no longer part of the Fianna, so that shouldn't be a problem, right?"

Madadh said nothing.

"Right?"

"That is not the way of the fáelad. Some of us may be monsters, sure, but we are all still human. The sons and daughters of Adam know that we are all connected... whether we like it or not."

"Dammit," Remy growled. Anger twisted in his gut, evoking emotions he'd not had since prior to meeting Jaira... really since before escaping the unseelie. "I'd really hoped that might work."

Madadh worked his jaw sympathetically for a few moments. "Do you really think war with the fey might be averted?"

"It has to be," Remy insisted. "I have seen the courts' armies lay waste to new and rising powers. The moment Oberon thinks the Fianna, the fáelad or whatever, are a threat to his kingdom's stability he will lay waste to every human he sees. We've got to change the sidhe's thinking. They must believe we mean them no harm." He looked around at the group again. "You do not have nearly enough fighters to stand against Oberon, not if every one of you were a lycan, and you made peace with Oddur and formed an alliance tomorrow."

The Fianna leader smirked knowingly. "Oh, you silly Adam... You think this is all there are of us? This is just my *personal* tribe."

Remy blinked rapidly. "How many of you are there?"

Madadh winked at him. "Enough."

"Fuuuuuucckkk... I'm just trying to help you, you know."

"I know. But you are *still* not Fianna." Madadh shrugged, then smiled. "But you are a friend to the Fianna. That is why we feed you."

Remy glared at him and promised, "I'm going to stop this war."

"And you have a plan to do this? A *good* plan?"

"I'm in a place to curry favor with Oberon. He has... something he needs was stolen, and he's asked me to retrieve it for him in exchange for a high price. This will earn me the king's friendship... his respect, at least. The only problem is that the Frith Duine are after the same thing." Remy kept the details light. Madadh wasn't the only one with information he did not want to share fully.

"Perfect, so retrieve this item and then use your time with the Summer King to explain the situation." Madadh sat back as if it could be done so casually. He peeled off a strip of venison from a nearby roast cooling on a table and then licked his fingers.

"It's not so simple. I don't know where it is. But I'm looking. I mean, I have allies looking... There is a plan." Remy cringed his own words as he heard them. They did not brim with their usual confidence.

"And what if that does not work? What if the item is not found, or if the Frith Duine discover it first?"

He sighed. "Then I'll have to come up with something *different* regarding Oddur. I assume he can't be reasoned with."

In the trees nearby, a crow called loudly. Blinking, Remy locked his gaze on it, unsure exactly how long it had been perched on that branch. He stared. There was no mistaking the bird for who it was. *Corax.*

Without moving his head, Madadh's eyes shifted from Corax to Remy. "Is that a friend of yours?"

"Morrígan's three faces... I hope not." Remy bit his lip and then explained to Madadh how he'd once lived his life as Aderyn Corff, the famous assassin of the Winter Court.

"This could be an omen from the gods," Madadh said, keeping his words reverentially low.

"I will not..." Remy whispered, staying one step away from making an oath to himself... to Arcadeax. "I left that life behind when I crossed Solstox. If I can do anything to avert this conflict without having to... embrace the man I used to be... I will do it."

Madadh watched Remy from the corners of his eyes. An irony-tinged smile blossomed on his face. "My respect for you continues to increase, Remy Keaton." He shrugged. "But I dare say that would be the case even if you embraced the call of the corpse bird and assassinated Oddur. Sacrificing one life to save all our people seems a good trade."

Remy shook his head as he hung it low. And then he turned his eyes back up to the branches. As easily as Corax had come, he'd disappeared.

Blinking, the duelist sighed. "I've got to go. There are plenty of things I can put my efforts towards instead of yapping out here in the trees."

"Yapping with friends rarely results in words returns void." Madadh grinned.

Remy rolled his eyes. "You're starting to sound like a philosopher. Now, where is my horse?" He spotted the man who'd taken his mount earlier and signaled him to bring the horse.

The Fianna member approached him and apologized. "I cannot do that, unfortunately."

Remy narrowed his gaze at the man. "And why not?"

He frowned sheepishly. "My scout honestly did not recognize you when you came. He assumed you were another transient come here to stay. You see, people keep coming to us and when they come—"

"Where in the hell is my horse?"

The man hung his head, shoulders slumping. "I'm afraid we ate it."

Remy merely stared at him, though Madadh tipped over onto his side with laughter at the miscommunication.

"What do you mean, you ate it?" Remy shouted.

"There are so many of us now. We are hunting the grounds as much as we dare, but every day more of us arrive than before and it is our duty to feed them."

"Then go to the market!" Exasperated, Remy pointed in the direction from which he'd come, although he nearly grinned at Madadh's infectious amusement. "They have one at Baile Dorcha, for fey's sake!"

Madadh stymied his laughter and crawled back to his feet. "I can pay for your horse, my friend." He tried to wipe the smug grin off of his face. "I am truly sorry."

"Really, man, it's a lot easier to send someone to the market than to butcher every passerby's mounts."

The Fianna leader withdrew a small pouch of coins for compensation.

"Bah. Keep your money," Remy growled. "It's just a horse." It was not the first time Remy had lost a horse because of the hunger of a friend, not that he wanted to make a habit out of it. "People don't always think straight when they're famished. Use your money to buy more supplies for your people. It's not so far home that I can't walk."

And then Remy set out on foot, keenly aware of how many people were grinning at his back, amused by the circumstances.

Chapter Nineteen

Now on foot, Remy approached the edge of Baile Dorcha and appreciated it for what it was. Baile Dorcha was a charming little village, home to perhaps two hundred individuals. That meant it hosted fewer residents than the nearby Fianna encampment.

"Now I feel kinda bad for recommending they come clean out the local market," he mumbled.

Flowers bloomed in many of the homes' planters. Some had fresh paint and others had new steps, shutters, or trim; the recent upgrades were a mark of the new crop of fey who'd moved in to revitalize the "suddenly abandoned" village. The village was a cluster of perhaps fifty mostly-wooden structures.

He moved past the first few houses and kept to the main road. It bisected Baile Dorcha evenly with the center occupied by the only three story construction. Buildings on either side were the only businesses in the area, mainly catering to agriculture, travel, and the few places of commerce.

Sidhe children ran through couple yards as he passed, playing under the watchful supervision of their mothers. Remy smiled at them. He'd always had a soft spot for kids.

Rounding the corner of the market where the road turned, a sudden blast of fire and a gale force wind blasted into him, throwing him from his feet and smashing him into the home across the street. Fire splashed off the house's exterior, setting it ablaze in an instant.

Lying in a heap beneath the rubble of a smashed door and a wall, Remy groaned. He shook off the dust of crumbled plaster and stood, clapping his body to shed the debris.

His clothes had been singed from the flame, but Remy remained otherwise unburned. *Undamaged* was a whole other matter, and he stretched, rolling his shoulders against the pain of being slugged across a road and halfway through a house with elemental fury.

Remy's nostrils flared. *That can only mean one thing... I'm being attacked by a spellcaster.*

Behind him, a wall groaned and Remy cast a backward glance. The force of the impact had snapped several of the home's load-bearing beams. An interior wall buckled, slowly shifting as the house began to cant.

He looked around feverishly, but did not know the house's layout. Remy only knew it was all about to come down on his head and so he dashed forward, through the flames, and out the hole in the front where there had once been a door... *And where I'll find my attacker.*

The first face he found was the ugly, snarling visage of Syrmerware Kathwesion—the slavetaker who'd once tried to collect him after Remy escaped from Rhagathena's control. The orc had tried to brand Remy's face, but wound up with the ever-burning ferrous boot print instead.

"So, you found me at last, Syrmerware Kathwesion," Remy sneered. "You're not supposed to be here, not in the lands of Summer."

The orc snarled one word in response, "Ddiymadferth."

Remy realized there was a second orc who looked much like Syrmerware, only without the puckered, pink and ruined flesh affixed to an even uglier face. He, too, snarled, and then stepped forward.

Eyes narrowing at the creature, Remy noticed the orc was not dressed as a spellcaster would be. He wore bracers at his forearm which Remy knew inhibited the somatic hand motions often required for advanced spells, like the one that had flung him across the intersection.

The human's eyes darted around the nearby surroundings, searching for any aes sidhe or other tuathan sorcerers. Behind him, the ruined house made a cracking sound and then, with a loud sigh, folded with a thunderous echo and a *whoosh* as the sudden expulsion of air fanned the flames into a raging inferno. The heat licked Remy's back, and he smelled the fire, but he didn't dare take his eyes off the pair of orcs.

On the periphery, people screamed and several fled. Certainly, the burning mound of timbers would spread flames to adjacent homes without intervention.

As the second orc stepped forward, a local resident rushed into view, headed for the home, likely trying to rally residents to combat the flames. Syrmerware's peer grinned wickedly; the sidhe misjudged the greatest of the nearest threats and the olive-skinned orc drew his blade in one fluid motion, slashing the bystander's throat.

The orc brought the blade to his lips and licked the blood from it, casually stepping into the street and introducing himself. "I am Rharzal Kathwesion, Warlord and Chieftain of the unseelie Kathwesion clan. I am named high general of the Winter Army and..."

Remy's eyes continued searching as the boastful orc proclaimed himself by every title imaginable. *I've got to find that spellcaster before he or she wrecks this entire town.*

"... soon to be consort of Queen Rhagathena, Ruler of the Rime Throne and the unseelie, Lady of Arctig Maen, and Anansi of the Spinefrost Ridge, mistress of the N'arache-folk."

Remy's lips turned up in a smile when he spotted a face he *did* recognize. Chokorum, the Spider Queen's sidhe lackey.

"So, you are Rhylfelour's cheap replacement... I can see they've scraped the bottom of the orcish barrel for you and even had to dip into the diasporan orc families for talent. I can't blame 'em after I destroyed the demonsbreak clans." He winked at Chokorum. "It looks like they trust you so little that they sent you with a babysitter."

Rharzal snarled at him, but Remy did not react. He knew how to get under orcish skin. Remy quipped, "Funny thing is, whenever they sent *me* to kill someone, they didn't make me take a governess to ensure the job got done."

And then Remy spotted the aes sidhe hiding in the alley nearest the market—and just in time. The winter elf finished a hand gesture and then snapped his wrists, locking them in completion as Remy drew his sword and sprang into action.

The sidhe female flung fireballs at Remy, one after another, hurling them with the speed of a carefully trained athlete. But Remy was faster; he darted out of the way of each flaming sphere. They whistled past his ears, warming them as they passed, and collided with the homes beyond.

"Shit," Remy roared, not sparing to look behind, but knowing that much of the village had just been lit up. And then the flames became a lesser concern as the two orcs got on either side of him, flanking him.

The brothers brought their swords to bear, hacking and slashing with timing and precision that moved and flowed more like a dance than random strikes and thrusts from brutish orcs.

Drawing his dúshlán in his other hand, Remy deflected and parried their blows, whirling between them and keeping his feet underneath him as he moved between his opponents. He could not escape them, but could make them reposition while he edged towards the market and maneuvered them into place.

From the corner of his eye, Remy spotted the spellcaster beginning another enchantment, probably something meant to slow or stymie the human and allow Rhagathena's new champion to deliver a killing blow, earning even greater fame. At the other edge of his peripheral vision he saw the flames roaring high.

I've got to take that elf out, and now!

Rolling through the same sequence of maneuvers, Remy suddenly changed up his attacks and went the opposite direction.

Rharzal snarled as he struck with extra force. Remy anticipated the flow of the battle as it shifted. The orc champion's blow hit with enough force it knocked Remy's dúshlán free as he blocked.

The human grinned, outplaying the orc. He whirled closer into Syrmerware, driving a fist right into the middle of the orc's tender scar. As Syrmerware reeled in pain, Remy snatched Syrmerware's dagger from his belt. In one motion, he turned again, safely beyond the reach of Rharzal's weapon—but not for lack of trying—and Remy threw the enemy's blade at the aes sidhe.

She saw it coming, just in the nick of time. Dropping the spell, the caster lunged out of the way and the dagger buried itself in the planks of the wall where the aes sidhe's chest had been a moment prior. The spell blew back at the caster, reversing summoned power back at her with arcadeaxn fury that manifested its ire with smoke, green flame, and other miscellaneous side effects.

Remy watched her flee, but knew she'd be back once she shook off the effects of a botched spell. He glanced back at Chokorum, but the majordomo remained motionless and almost looked bored.

I guess he's just here to watch. Good... One less enemy to— Then another elf stepped past Chokorum and drew his blade. *Shit.*

The caster was down for a few minutes, but Remy still had two very angry orcs to deal with, plus whomever this sidhe newcomer was.

Morrigan's three faces... I really wish I still had my horse.

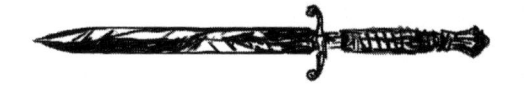

Gnub leaned over the ledge of the rooftop at the tallest building in Baile Dorcha. He squinted against the glare but grinned at the burning buildings across the way.

"Looks like the fun's about to begin." He chuckled, watching the shadows play across the street as his orcish kin and the other attackers did battle.

He took a quick visual stock of his setup. Against the knee-high wall he'd laid six different crossbows, each one cocked and loaded with bleeding tipped quarrels. They had three razor-sharp blades at their head in order to rip open a wound that could not close before their victim succumbed to exsanguination. Even if the shot did not strike true, the tips had been poisoned, so the slightest nick would slow a victim.

Gnub scanned the half dozen readied weapons. He beamed with pride, having personally modified each one—their rails had to be filed down so that the tri-tipped projectiles could slide freely along them without catching. These bladed tips were brittle, unlike the sturdier broad-heads of arrows which could be sometimes reused, or the pointed, narrow tips of regular crossbow bolts, which could punch through even plate armor within certain ranges.

He'd prepared to give himself five good shots at their prey if he needed them: the first was meant to take down Aderyn Corff's horse, and the rest were there as backup. "No idea why the ddiymadferth isn't on his horse, but I don't really care... One extra shot, in case I need it."

And Gnub intended to take it as soon as a shot presented itself. His cousins' instructions had been explicit and clear. Gnub was only supposed to kill the mount and unseat the human, allowing them to isolate him and make an honor killing.

Gnub grumbled an admission, "Fat chance I leave you the glory and the throne... If killing the corpse bird is the ticket to the Rime Throne, then *I'm* going to take it."

He sneered for a moment and then took a clear position at the center of the flat roof. Three stories high, he had a perfect vantage to shoot the human. Gnub was a seasoned warrior. With Aderyn Corff unaware, his first shot would not miss. *And if my cousins have a problem with that, I've got two shots apiece left over for each of them.*

Sighting down the center rail to check his aim, Gnub spotted arms and legs flailing just past the corner of the lower market building. He just needed the ddiymadferth to clear the edge and give him an unobstructed shot.

Something nearby made a clicking sound, but Gnub ignored it, focusing on his target. A faint smell like sulfur reached his nose and a musky smell wafted nearby, something like swamp odor and incense. He ignored it, certain it was some kind of akashic lighter device—probably a timed beacon for whenever business operated inside the structure that he camped upon.

"Closer... closer," he murmured. "Come on, you little bastard. Show your face." Gnub moved his finger from the weapon's body and to the trigger, grinning with anticipation.

Remy grimaced as the unseelie he-elf rushed toward them. As good of a fighter as he was, Remy knew he couldn't take all three at once. He'd been lucky to hang in the fight as long as he did; Syrmerware Kathwesion was no slouch as a fighter and his brother had proved himself as a top tier opponent. If this third warrior was anything like the others, it would be over soon, and not in the human's favor.

Syrmerware snarled, recovering from the attack on his weakest point.

Remy dug the tip of his sword into a pocket of sand near their feet and flicked it upward into the slavetaker's eyes, buying himself a few more moments. He snatched his dúshlán blade from where it had fallen and then turned to make his escape.

Sprinting toward the alley the aes sidhe had disappeared into, Remy hoped to lose his opponents in a foot race. Shoving his enchanted dagger into its holder, he yanked the throwing dagger free as he passed. *Just one problem... not enough alleys in this village to get lost in.*

He'd only gone past the dagger mark when he found the adjacent buildings in flames. Broken bottles lay near the base of each of the growing blazes. *The spellcaster must have brought alchemical flame with her, too.*

Those flames barred the avenues Remy might otherwise take, funneling him in the loop back toward the main road. The best he could hope for was to split his attackers, separating them into more manageable chunks. Losing them entirely became an unlikely scenario.

Hearing footsteps of his pursuit, he accelerated around the corner, spun on his heel and then went back the way he'd come. The maneuver surprised the elf who'd given chase and Remy aimed the swiped dagger at him.

The surprised elf tried to dodge out of the way by getting close to one of the walls, but he only hemmed himself in as Remy released and let the dagger fly toward him.

Remy watched the blade sink home. It had not been a clean shot, not with the elf trying to dodge out of the way. But it had caught him in the shoulder and pinned the sidhe to the wall. Remy knew he could not delay, given the odds, and he darted back out the mouth of the alley, hoping to further upset the orcs with a few tricks. *I've just got to stay alive long enough to find a mount—ideally, whatever kind these assholes came in on. If I can scatter the rest, I can outpace them and get back to Cathair Dé.*

A moment of concern for the locals rippled through him as he neared the mouth of the alleyway. The orcs had already proved their willingness to slaughter the residents, but the fires had scattered most people, minimizing that concern—and creating a whole host of new ones.

Emerging from the alleyway at full tilt, Remy spotted both orcs waiting for him at the other side of the horseshoe-shaped alley. Across the road, he spotted an opening between two buildings. One of them was on fire, but there was enough space for him to clear it and, given his present speed, the orcs would be hard-pressed to corral him again.

And then Remy heard it. A voice cried out, a familiar voice. *Jaira's voice...* And Remy skidded to a stop... out in the open. Vulnerable.

"Whatcha doin'?" Her crystal clear voice rang out on the rooftop.

Gnub shook with surprise as Jaira startled him. Still holding his crossbow, he turned to find her holding a spellcaster's wand that she held pointed at him.

"Get out of here," the orc growled, eyes glancing down at his weapon. "Stay and I will kill you."

Jaira understood his meaning. He had limited ammunition and did not want to waste any event on her. To him, she looked like easy prey, a weak elf who'd just stumbled into his assassination attempt.

Gnub turned back to the unfolding scene below, unwilling to be distracted.

"I'm going to use this thing on you," she insisted, infusing her voice with as much menace as she could muster.

"No, you're not," Gnub said without turning back to her. "You are no aes sidhe... I can tell because you're holding that damned thing incorrectly."

Jaira smirked. "You really think so? So confident, aren't you, Gnub? So certain that your plan to kill Aderyn Corff will work... That you'll curry favor with the Winter Court and depose your cousin as general and earn the Rime Throne for it."

Slowly, he turned back to her. "How do you know my name?" His brow knit as he reassessed her as both a threat and as an aes sidhe. "There is no way you could know such a thing. Not unless—"

"You are correct." Jaira smiled at him. "Not unless I was a seer. You've never told anyone about your ambitions. Always been a good little orc, doing as you're told and letting your clan mates take the best shares of any spoils. Until now, anyway."

Gnub sneered, but it was not a mirthless act of defiance. It bordered on a genuine smile and his amusement reached his eyes, making them sparkle.

"But it will never work," Jaira insisted. Her voice lowered slightly. "I have seen your fate, Gnub Skrarranzak, and it is not good."

He leveled the crossbow at Jaira. "How does it unfold?"

"First, you should know that your plan worked."

Gnub raised his brows. Pleasure spread across his face.

"But also it does not. Your arrow struck true. You killed Aderyn Corff, your people's greatest traitor, but that does not depose your kin. It does not steal Rhagathena's hand. In fact, you never see the unseelie again. You never leave this village. Rharzal kills you before you can get away and you die in the agonizing flames your cousins set at the base of this building. They curse you as you die and then laugh about it over mugs of ale later."

The amusement on Gnub's face faltered. "You lie. Seers do not know absolutes, and I will kill the orcs first, and *then* the Corpse Bird."

"You are correct in something at least, orc. We see all the potentials. I have seen a great many possible futures, and in each one where you managed to kill your enemy, the result is the same. Whether you die by fire, by blade, or poisoned by the queen's majordomo, every eventuality results in the same thing: a dead Gnub."

He stared at her for a moment, his face twisting into a mask of both disbelief and apprehension.

Jaira knew she had him... And then her eyes darted to the road below and she spotted Remy fleeing the flames of the alleyway.

It wasn't much, but it was enough for Gnub to recognize that he'd been distracted from his mission. He turned, crossbow in hand, and reacquired his aim when Jaira leveled the magic wand at him and activated it.

The thing did not need to draw power from her. It had its own magic, and lots of it. It sucked from the akashic battery rather than her inner reserves of arcana. Lightning erupted from its tip, ensnaring the orc and roasting him with the power of a storm.

Gnub collapsed. His skin blackened and peeling like a fish baked too long over hot coals. Gnub convulsed only momentarily and his limbs broke at the joints where the fully discharged wand's electricity had fried them to cinder. Boiled blood burst from pustules rupturing on his blackened lips and he died groaning.

And then the aes sidhe who'd set all the fires below snatched Jaira from behind, wrapping her sharp fingernails over Jaira's throat. It was barely all Jaira could do to scream with surprise, and then she shouted the only thing she could think of. "Remy!"

Chapter Twenty

Remy turned his eyes up and spotted Jaira. He still held both weapons, not yet surrendering himself as easy prey for the two orcs who approached cautiously. On the rooftop, the winter sidhe clutched his wife from behind, holding her like a shield while the spellcaster hedged closer to the edge of the rooftop.

"Jaira?" Remy cried out.

"It's me, Remy. They got me... I'm sorry. I'm so sorry," her voice bordered on sobs.

Remy hardened his core, refused to immediately give up and die. He knew better than anyone how creatures with arcane talents could trick their opponents into giving up without a fight—and whoever this aes sidhe was, she'd already proved herself competent at magic—and that could include illusions for all Remy knew.

Syrmerware and Rharzal approached, one foot at a time, each making sure that their next step was defensible.

"Aderyn Corff," Rharzal cried out. "You will come with me."

"Why would I do that?" Remy asked, not recoiling, but also not yielding.

"Because if not, Corpse Bird," Syrmerware hissed, "we will kill your woman." The slave taker shot Remy a nasty glare. "Perhaps I will brand her face before we leave this town," he said. "Not because I want to collect her as a slave, laws prohibit it... but this one is just for fun."

The way Syrmerware glared at him told Remy everything he needed to know. *If I surrender, that bastard will mark me before we ever reach Hulda Thorne... But torture or not, if they've really got Jaira, there's nothing else I can do.*

Rharzal grinned at him, taking several paces to one side so that he could flank the human. "You are to be a gift for the queen. Your head is the price for my ascension, and I wish to deliver you to her alive so she can watch you die."

Remy noted that he did not mention arriving at the Winter Court undamaged. Just the one condition... alive.

Turning his eyes up to the rooftop, Remy cried out to Jaira. "Is that really you?"

From behind, the aes sidhe squeezed her clawed hands around Jaira's neck and answered for her. The winter sidhe hissed at him. "Of course it is, you fool. Cease your gambling and submit. You will come with us back to the Winter Court so that our queen may preside over your execution."

Remy raised his weapons toward each of the two approaching enemies, one on either side. He pointed his sword, gripped in the dominant hand, toward Rharzal and the tip of the dúshlán at Syrmerware. "Not so fast. I'm not going anywhere until I verify this is not some trick, an aes sidhe deception meant to disarm me."

He glared at each of the orcs. "Let's face it, assholes. Without it, neither one of you are a match for me one on one."

"That's why there are two of us," Rharzal growled at him.

The human tilted his head and shot him a threatening look. "For now. Now that you've pissed me off, give me two minutes."

Rharzal paused mid step, making Remy assume the orc was not as stupid as he looked. The much heralded general of the Winter Court army motioned for the spellcaster to let her captive speak.

"If that's really you, Jaira, then tell me something only I would know."

Jaira called out, "I love you, Remy Keaton."

"That doesn't provide any new data."

"No. It does not," Jaira stated flatly. There was no trace of fear in her voice and Remy's guts knotted—any normal person would be freaking out. *What the hell is going on here? Is this an illusion? Or maybe she's not in any real danger?*

"Answer the ddiymadferth, or I will rip out your throat," threatened the aes sidhe. "And then he will die, too, but more painfully."

"What guarantee do I have that you let her live, even if I surrender to you?" Remy asked.

"You have none," Syrmerware grinned deviously. "But if I mark her face, I'd want her to live and age with her reminder of today."

Remy still had no idea what was happening. He could only chuckle in response. "That's not the kind of answer I'm looking for, you idiot."

"An oath in the old tongue," Rharzal said, trying to move things along. "If that would satisfy you, I would make such an oath."

Still pointing his swords at the orcs, Remy flared his nostrils with anger. If he became oath bound, there was nothing he could do to affect a later escape. But there was no way he would allow them to harm Jaira, not if he could help it.

Just as long as that is really her. I need proof before we start invoking ancient magic.

"Tell me how I stole you away from Fuerian—that day I snuck you out of the garden. What did I give you as a signal that I waited for you?" Remy stared at the image of his wife, still uncertain if it was her. Only three people knew the answer to this question: Remy, Jaira, and the gardener's daughter.

Jaira—or her image—said something, but too quiet for Remy to hear it.

"I can't hear you!" *She'd better not be speaking quietly on purpose. I'll not let her sacrifice herself for me!*

The aes sidhe gave her a shake by the throat. "Louder, israddol. Speak up or you shall *both* die."

Jaira said something again, but Remy still could not hear it. He blinked at her, focusing on his wife's face. As she spoke, still too softly, her eyes met with his and she was smiling. *Smiling!*

What the hell is going on here?

In response to Jaira's husband's question, she answered in a whisper. "I know something you don't know."

Her captor bared her teeth. "What are you talking about? Speak up, I can barely hear you."

"Then you must come closer." Jaira's voice was barely audible.

"I'm right here—there's no way to be closer without crawling inside of you, foolish seelie."

"I know," Jaira said, this time its normal volume. "I just needed a couple of extra seconds. And your closeness helps me do this—"

Jaira snapped her head back and cracked the thick of her skull into the aes sidhe's nose, making her release the grip on her throat.

As the she-elf screamed and clutched at her face, blood poured from her ruined nose. She reeled backward and immediately summoned magic to her aid, intent on forming it into something deadly and useful—something that would obliterate the insolent elf noble before her husband's eyes and shift the tide of the battle.

Jaira glanced back down toward the streets and watched Remy spring into action against his two enemies.

And then the aes sidhe glared at Jaira. "Why can I not summon my magic?" Her voice bordered on panic.

"You don't smell that? I was prepared for you, Arcenae. Oh, yes... I know your name," Jaira said. "It's almost as if I can see the future, and that's why I set the dallineb weed up here and lit it before you ever arrived."

"Seer," her enemy hissed. Arcenae yanked a dagger into each hand from the sheaths at her belt. "I shall kill you here and now—if you have smoked the rooftop, then *you* cannot access any magics, either—you cannot know what happens next."

Jaira kept her face calm. "But I don't need to. If you'd been listening, you would know why." She whispered a string of words again, too quiet to be heard.

"Infuriating, insolent elf," growled Arcenae. "You are unarmed, and I am trained with the blade. The moment you try to snatch one of those crossbows, I will plunge these daggers into your back and twist them between your ribs. *Death will come slow for you.*"

Jaira winked at the impotent spellcaster and spoke at a louder volume, keeping the female focused on her.

"I *said*, 'I know something you don't know.'"

"That you're about to die?"

Jaira shook her head. "No. In fact, I know many things you don't know. Presently, the most important of those is the name of a human woman you've never met... and neither have I. Her name is Scathach."

Arcenae arched an eyebrow, and then the clawed hand of a lycan reached around from behind her and Scathach tore out the winter fey's throat. Arcenae spun as she fell, face locked in horror and surprise; she turned up her eyes to the growling fáelad. Blood leaked out all across the rooftop, creating a deep pool of unbroken crimson, and then the aes sidhe's eyes rolled back and the hands that clutched at her throat fell away, splashing in the dark blood that poured from her.

Behind Scathach towered another werewolf.

Jaira steeled her nerves. Although she'd seen these creatures in her future-sight visions, they were terrifying to behold in person.

She turned to both of them, finally allowing the panic to reach her eyes. "You have to save him. You have to save my husband!"

Anya took a swig of water from her canteen and checked the akashic battery on her mobility chair. She'd stashed several extras on the shelf below the seat, anticipating she would need them.

The harsh sun beat down on her as she piloted the chair along a dirt path in the countryside outside Cathair Dé, but she was determined to complete her mission. In the heat of the day, Anya smelled the foul odor of chicken manure and the pungent smells of cut feed as it fermented in the sweltering temperatures.

Over the rise of the next hill, Anya knew she'd find the location of the interdiction vault that blocked her from visiting in the aithersphere. She could think of no reason for there to be one at Stór Rúnda unless one of Kent's employees had gone rogue—and certainly they must have if the farm was playing host to Trishana Firmind... *Anya* was supposed to be the aithermancer for Tógdraío Holdings, Stór Rúnda's parent company, not that two-bit hack.

She kept near the outgrowth of trees as she maneuvered through the property and trusted that the chair's wheels would keep their traction. It was a top of the line model and could overcome most terrain outside of stony hills or deep gulleys.

Anya crested the rise and spotted Stór Rúnda. The egg farm sat on the outskirts of a rural village not far south of Cathair Dé.

Long rows of crude, slat buildings stretched into the distance. A short distance from them was a squat, wide bungalow which Anya recognized as the business and operations center for the company. She knew it had to house the interdictor. If she got inside its range, she'd be able to access the aither and gain the full run of whatever secrets the place might hold—of course, that was not without risks.

If Anya were discovered by an enemy who suspected she was up to no good, there might be dire consequences. She sucked in a breath and steered for the place while hoping to find an aitherport conveniently located where it might be easily accessed with her aitherdeck. But even if not, she just had to get close enough to be within the vault's reach; inside Anya's pockets were a few pharmacologicals that would let her enter the aither even with no tech... but she hated doing it that way—apothiks always gave her a splitting headache and a monstrous hangover that put her out of commission for days.

One of her wheels hung in a rut and she momentarily panicked. Then she set her jaw and rocked back and forth until the wheel caught enough purchase to overcome the obstacle. Anya kept pushing forward, recognizing that her foolish stubbornness was a family trait; Thoranmir had it, too, and it had gotten him killed.

What drove Anya most was the fear that, because of Kent's new connection to Oberon and his potential access to the Court, someone in his employ was engineering a serious amount of foul play... perhaps even an attempt to assassinate Oberon.

Well, that was her second most powerful drive. Anya felt in her gut that whatever was going on here was connected to the disappearing children and the abducted aes sidhe. She wanted to complete her brother's quest on his behalf.

Anya knew Trishana was involved, but she had to know *who else* if she was going to make any accusations. She'd have reached out to Remy, but had been unable to cross paths with him for several days now, and her impatience hotly rivaled Anya's stubbornness.

Her chair moved across the lawn at a brisk pace and Anya sighed with relief, knowing she was almost halfway to her goal—the second half was her journey home. She steered around the edge of the bungalow, scanning it quickly for any sort of aither access so that she wouldn't have to dip into her pockets and use the egwyl meddwl she'd stashed there.

And then Trishana Firmind stepped around the corner. She looked awful, slightly emaciated and with none of her makeup or fashionable clothing. Hygiene had apparently taken a backseat to everything else happening here.

"Well, well, well," Trishana said. "What a surprise? Look who's come for a visit? My old *friend*." Her words dripped with venom and she stepped around to take Anya's chair by its handles. Trishana disconnected the power lines on the chair with a grin.

"Come right this way," said Trishana as she pushed her rival, giving her no choice. "The master has been away a few days now... but I will make introductions as soon as he returns."

Trishana escorted Anya to the doors and then steered her within, closing the door behind them.

Remy crossed blades with both orcs. He lunged toward Rharzal, blocking and parrying, and then positioned himself on the opposite side to avoid retribution from Syrmerware. Foresight and clever footwork kept him from becoming an immediate victim of the winter fey's double team.

Still, Remy did not know how long he could keep it up. His eyes glanced over Rhagathena's majordomo, thankful for the he-elf's refusal to enter the fray. If one more opponent came at him, either the aes sidhe above him, or the elf he'd pinned to the wall in the alley, the tides would shift and do so quickly.

Remy ducked a blow from Rharzal and then slashed at the orc, hoping to disembowel him while keeping tight inside his guard. Rharzal leapt backward just in time, creating enough separation that the human's dúshlán sliced through only the leather of his belt. It clattered around the orc's feet while the two brothers regrouped against the human duelist.

Running from the alley and holding his blade in high guard came the wounded sidhe male. Blood poured from the elf's shoulder, but the wound was superficial. Remy glanced at him. *It must've hurt like a bitch to pull himself free of the dagger.*

"Meet Andrathan," quipped Syrmerware. "He's killed far more ddiymadferth than any other tuatha I know... even if they were all weakened lightstarved."

And suddenly, Andrathan erupted in a red mist and a splatter of gore as the massive, bulky shape of a werewolf dropped atop him. Madadh's lycan form crushed the fey creature like a gooze-melon, both landing atop of Andrathan while also raking him head to toes with his terrible, jagged claws.

Madadh crouched within the middle of the garnet splatter. He'd shredded the unaware warrior before any was aware of a threat. The leader of the Fianna flared his arms wide, brandishing his talons, and roared a challenge at the two orcs.

Even Remy blinked at the brutal display of ferocity, but his enemies bared their teeth and shouted a bestial acceptance of the fáelad's challenge.

Rharzal withdrew a stoppered bottle from a pocket and bit off the cork. He used half of its contents and poured them over his blade before tossing the container to Syrmerware've.

"I met your kind before," the slavetaker growled. "Surprised it took you this long to show your ugly face."

Madadh roared in response and then leapt toward Rharzal. The orc champion blocked and then thrust his blade at the creature. Leaping aside, the Fianna leader grazed Rharzal with this clause, but drew only a little blood, given the orc's thick hide.

Rharzal laughed as if he enjoyed the fight.

Both orcs paired off against the defenders when the body of the aes sidhe smashed violently into their midst. The lifeless corpse arrived in the shower of blood and a spray of viscera that removed anyone's doubts who had survived the ordeal on the rooftop.

Magical reinforcements aren't coming for the attackers... and Jaira is evidently safe. The aes sidhe's neck broke upon the impact, though the she-elf's wounds were clearly visible where her throat had been torn out.

Remy chanced a glance upward and spotted a second werewolf. He recognized it as Madadh's second in command, the female lycan named Scathach—he'd seen her before in this form, and Remy assumed it was her that threw the corpse over the ledge.

Syrmerware took no such chances and refused to sacrifice an iota of his attention. He lunged forward, using his blade against the human.

Remy blocked everything the orc threw at him and glanced sidelong at his companion. Madadh winked in response as he and Rharzal traded turns attacking and defending. Neither landed a solid blow.

"See? This is why I didn't want everyone blabbing so much about my past," Remy grumbled. He lunged at Syrmerware with his sword and then reacted as the orc spun along the angle of attack, evading it while trying to plant his blade into Remy's back. The human brought up his dúshlán and blocked it before stepping back a pace.

Rharzal swiped at the Lycan.

"'Go to the market,' you said. 'It's a much easier way to get the supplies you need,' you said," teased Madadh.

And then Rharzal ducked beneath Madadh's broad defenses, slipped a taloned grapple, and came up within the fáelad's guard. With a baleful shout, he plunged his blade, polished with the alchemical elemental tincture, into Madadh's torso. It slipped easily through the toughened hide of the werewolf, shimmering with mystic fury as the silvered metal split muscle and bone.

Rharzal snarled as he ripped the weapon free, causing Madadh to collapse into a heap of panting flesh. Overhead, Scathach cried out, much similar as Remy assumed Jaira would if he fell to such a severe wound.

Scathach grabbed the ledge of the building overhead as if she might launch herself at Rharzal.

"No!" Remy shouted. "That's exactly what he wants—he's trying to draw you in for the same fate."

Ignoring Remy, the orc champion roared victoriously and pointed his blade at Madadh. "And now, wolf, you die."

Chapter Twenty-One

Scathach paid Remy no heed. She flung herself over the edge and directly for the wicked orc and his silvered blade. She snarled as she plummeted to the ground, aiming for Rharzal's throat.

The orc champion balked for a moment, not thinking the female fáelad would act so brazenly, so violently, and with such reckless aggression. Both Rharzal and Remy blinked in surprise.

Syrmerware seized the opportunity and sprang for Remy, trying to score a cheap blow during the distraction.

Remy blocked the orc's shot and then returned his blow before pressing his attack, forcing the orc back on his heels. The slavetaker reeled and leapt away, creating a space cushion. He sneered at Remy, disappointed his strike hadn't worked.

Rharzal shook himself free just-in-time to get a half step back from the lycan, just far enough to avoid being smashed violently as Andrathan had been. Regardless, he tumbled backward and had to kick his legs away to avoid the raging werewolf's claws; Scathach's swipe might have otherwise severed them at the knees.

Madadh's breaths came as a ragged, gurgling gasp. He got to his knees and then sank back on his legs, erect but barely. He was in no condition to do anything more than watch.

Behind Remy, Scathach slashed at Rharzal over and over as the orc defended against or dodged each blow. Scathach was fast, but so was Rharzal. With a roar, the orc slipped below a vicious stroke meant to cleave the orc's head and, twisting with a falling momentum, he plunged the dagger into Scathach's forearm before landing in a somersault and rolling away.

Scathach screamed. Her voice echoed, reminding Remy of those female slaves Remy had heard several years ago in Syrmerware's cages at Vale Rhewi. Her raw pain mixed with a lupine howl was something a person could never unhear.

Rharzal lost his grip on the blade as he went down, but the damage was done. He drew a short sword, which he wore strapped to his leg as backup, and slashed at the air with a challenge and sneered at the werewolf as she turned to face him. Her arm hung futilely at her side. It dripped red as blood pooled in the matted fur and spilled to the ground.

"You rob me of my kill, Wolf. *Now, I demand two.*"

Remy was too far away to intervene and realized Syrmerware had moved himself into the perfect position where he could intervene if the human attempted it. And then he heard a low rumble.

As Scathach stared down Rharzal, that rumble transitioned into something more recognizable. A growling sort of laughter. It came from Madadh. A moment later, Scathach joined it.

She punctuated their amusement with another loud shriek as she ripped the blade free. Blood still poured from the open wound and alchemical silver droplets fell with them, pushed out of her body by the lycan's advanced healing. The pool of crimson at her feet shimmered metallic.

The two orcs traded nervous glances, but Syrmerware tightened his knuckles around the blade in his hand. Between them, they still had another of those treated weapons.

Sucking in deep breaths so that he could rasp out a few sentences, Madadh spoke. "You don't get it... fools."

Syrmerware brandished his silvery sword. "We know of your kind. We know that the silver harms you, bypasses your thick hide with ease, that it hurts you beyond all measure—you cannot heal so quickly from us."

Madadh clucked and Remy wasn't sure if the sound was because of the sucking chest wound or if it was more of the fáelad's laughter.

"My kind is not alone in having such a critical weakness," Madadh said. Speaking seemed almost too much for him, and he swayed on his knees. But as Madadh stabilized himself, a massive grin overtook his face.

"What you fail to understand," Scathach snarled, "is that my kind is used to pain. Silver does not cripple us. Though we are weak to it, those wounds still heal at a natural pace; it mostly *just pisses us off!*" She flung the treated blade into the distance; it soared into the burning buildings and beyond reach.

The female warrior shifted the leather belt around her waist so that what dangled there became readily evident. She tore the fabric away from her pouch to reveal a clawed gauntlet made of blackened cold iron. She fit her hand into it and flexed the jointed fingers below the wicked metal claws.

"Syrmerware! Your blade," Rharzal demanded with an open hand, but his cousin was rooted in place. The overwhelming terror of the ferrous claws on such a beast transfixing him. His eye, inset at the boot print, twitched involuntarily at the promise of fresh pain.

"My arm will heal, but slowly. *Yours* will burn as long as you live, *if* you should you escape," snarled Scathach. And then she pounced upon them with such speed that they could barely react.

With a roaring strike, she slashed Rharzal across the face, raking all four iron claws across his visage in a diagonal pattern.

The orc champion reeled backward, staggering and tumbling off his feet, clutching his wound. Steam momentarily shimmered between the orc's fingers, floating away in tiny wisps as the warrior shrieked.

Scathach stepped toward the orc slowly, casually. In the blink of an eye, the battle's tide had turned, and she strode with nonchalance while Rharzal kicked his feet, pushing himself away from his enemy as much as possible.

Syrmerware shrieked at Chokorum, "Help us, you fool!"

The indifferent fey tilted his head and then simply stated, "No."

With his brother still screaming and trying to put more distance between himself and the wolf, he snarled at the majordomo. "What the fuck do you mean, 'No?'"

"I'm here to watch and bear witness of Aderyn Corff's death on behalf of the Queen. I am not obligated to render any sort of aid. It was not I who decided to battle these," he glanced aside at the two fáelad, "interlopers."

Remy did his best to hide his grin, even despite his worry for Madadh. The Fianna shuddered with every ragged breath.

Syrmerware turned his attention from Remy and back to his brother, who was moments away from being murdered by the hulking, monstrous form. He looked back and forth one additional time, weighing odds and trying to decide. Finally, he made one and lunged toward Scathach with his silver blade at the ready. He slashed the air, making her pull back momentarily, and then Syrmerware grabbed his brother and helped haul him to his feet.

Rharzal grasped vainly for his weapon, which had fallen into the dirt, and Syrmerware used a toe to nudge it into his brother's grip.

The slavetaker glared daggers at them all, including Chokorum, and then took a step back, silently signaling his retreat. He held the blade in a defensive grip, trying to ward off the lycan with her iron claws.

She took a step forward, not taking the hint and Remy walked to her side, keeping one step behind so he wouldn't interfere with her extracting retribution. And then they both froze in their tracks when they heard Madadh fall to his side, collapsing.

Syrmerware curled a lip, baring his teeth as he helped his brother retreat further backward.

Chokorum tilted his head, seeming to understand that this fight was over. It seemed in his best interests to join his own kind and flee back to Winter.

Remy hedged backward another two steps, making his way toward Madadh. Scathach did likewise, but more reluctantly. Both parties backed away from each other at seemingly equal speeds, and then they reached a large enough cushion of space that they turned and ran.

The wolf and the man hurried to Madadh's side.

The unseelie cut through the ruined village's buildings in route. Flames and falling debris hid their retreat.

Scathach knelt down at Madadh's side and applied pressure. She let her wolf form melt away and laid her second hand on Madadh's neck and stroked him. "It's okay. It's okay. I've got you."

A moment later, Madadh's shape withered and shifted back to his human shape, as well. Both were covered in blood.

Jaira burst out of the alley near the tallest building and ran to Remy. She leapt into his arms and he grabbed her, squeezed her tight.

A moment later, Jaira looked down at Madadh. "Is he going to be okay?"

Scathach looked over the wound. Madadh's eyes were open and glossy, but he remained conscious. He didn't try to speak; he could barely blink under his own power. "The blade hurt him badly, and healing will take much time. But we are hardy folk, and we have help nearby. There are several skilled medicine women at hand." Without looking, she pointed into the distance.

Remy followed her finger and spotted a growing crowd of humans emerging on the slope of a forest-covered hill in the close distance. And then his gaze caught on something else: a group of sidhe gathering.

The locals' soot-stained and tear-streaked faces hardened as they laid eyes upon the small group of humans and a solitary sidhe. Their homes and village was in ruins.

Remy felt their glares as if they were burning brands. They pierced him as deeply as any crossbow bolt might. "I think we've got to get out of here," he mumbled.

And then he heard something that hurt worse than the glares of those innocents who'd just lost everything.

"The Frith Duine was right," shouted one elf in the group.

Another voice called out, "Down with humans—down with ddiymadferth!"

Still another: "This is just like Ollscoil Maginarius."

"Up with the Frith Duine!"

Remy and his group did not stay long enough to hear them give further vent to their sorrow-bent rage. They helped Madadh away from the scene, only pausing to build a hastily constructed litter to transport him, and then they made for the trees on the hill.

Fuerian pinched the paper packet he carried in his pocket and reassured himself that it was still there. Its contents were not exactly legal, at least not for him, and he grinned from the shop window where he watched the main road.

He was not just an excellent fighter; Fuerian was a tactician. He was good at guessing the next step in any gambit, whether that be a game, wager, a duel... tracking his prey. Fuerian also rarely played fair.

Loitariel stepped out of a hired carriage across the street and stretched her legs. She handed a groat to the driver and Fuerian assumed by her gesticulations it included a tip in order for him to remain outside for her to return.

"A wise use of the money you stole from my family," he mumbled, and then watched her slip into the building.

Fuerian had sent several hired sidhe after her to track her movements. He'd insisted they not approach or. *She's aes sidhe—she could kill them in an instant if not prepared.*

They'd found the stolen carriage right after her rescuer delivered Loitariel to her first stop. *He* hadn't been off-limits for Fuerian's thugs; he did not survive.

Fuerian touched the thing in his pocket again and smiled, proud of himself and how he'd deduced where she was fleeing to: Suíochán Naseán. Because of that, and because of what she was, he also knew where her stops would be upon the way.

Above the bistro near the hired carriage towered a sign the read *Sylvan Sips and Savories*. And below was a smaller placard claiming their food and drink were iontaofa—they followed the dietary rules meant to keep aes sidhe safe.

Fuerian grinned and removed the packet of ground dweomer root from his pocket as he headed across the street and for the chef's door at the restaurant's rear. To beat a spellcaster, even a maven, he didn't need to know anything beyond where that aes sidhe would have their next meal.

The door clicked shut behind him.

Madadh gasped as one of the old women from his tribe smeared a kind of herbal paste into the wound at his chest.

The old lady gave the warrior a melancholy smile. "It will help draw out any remaining silver and speed recovery." She put a hand on Scathach's shoulder and told her, "I think he'll be okay, but it will be several weeks before he'll be walking, even. We will wait to transport him back to our camp until it's fully staunched."

Scathach nodded, and then the healer gave her arm a similar treatment to combat the silver sheen there.

Remy and Jaira sat holding hands just inside the tree line on the hilltop. Below them smoldered the remains of Baile Dorcha. Fire had destroyed a third of the village already and another third actively burned. In the distance, a cluster of various folks from Cathair Dé hurried toward the smaller Dale in order to help fight the fires.

The unseelie intruders, the ones truly responsible for this mess, had fled in the opposite direction of the incoming help. By the time the humans had gotten to the safety of the forest, they'd been unable to spy them any longer, but Scathach claimed they'd headed away, back toward Winter. Like most fáelad, she had a keen sense of smell and was an excellent tracker.

"Are they really gone, do you suppose?" Jaira asked.

Scathach nodded. "They are. At least for now."

"They will be back now that they've identified me, and now they know where I've made my new home. They—Rhagathena and her court—are not ones to forgive." Remy swallowed hard. "We'll see them again, I'm certain of it."

As the healer salved the nasty black and blue tear in Scathach's flesh, the she-wolf looked at Jaira as she got her wound wrapped with a bandage. "How did you know my name before we met?"

Jaira turned to Scathach. She blinked rapidly, trying to push any visual tells of her sudden panic away from her face. "I, uh... Maybe I heard it somewhere before." She shrugged. "A lady never tells all of her secrets."

Scathach returned a shrewd look and mouthed the word *secrets*.

The old medicine woman looked Jaira up and down, her eyes fixed to the claw marks at her throat where the aes sidhe had dug them into her flesh. "Nasty looking wounds," she told the elf.

Opening the satchel at her hip, she dug through a few smaller pouches and produced some herbs and reagents. "Chew on these," she said, offering them with outstretched hand. "They'll ease the pain and speed your healing."

Madadh's hand suddenly shot out and grasped the forearm of the medic. With grave eyes, he met the lady's gaze. "No... Pregnant... I smelled her."

Quickly retracting her hand enclosing the herbs in her fist, the woman shook her head. "Apologies. This has spikenard, and could make you lose the child."

Remy's eyes turned to Jaira's, wild with fear, enthusiasm, joy, and so many other emotions. "Is—is that true?"

Jaira nodded slowly. Her eyes were glossy, but brimmed with hope. "It is. I... I've wanted to tell you now for some time. I just did not know how."

Scathach gave her a kind of apologetic smile as she nodded. Still oblivious to the totality of it all, she nodded and again mouthed the word *secrets*.

Remy pulled her into a tight embrace and then kissed her. "I... I don't know what to say. I don't know—I don't know what to do. I mean, where do we go from here?"

"I think that from here, we can only go forward."

Epilogue

Oddur stood upon the log stump in the wooded glade where he'd assembled his tribe. There were many of them, and they'd gained new sons and daughters of Adam, either liberating them or attracting them as the Frith Duine increased their oppression.

Their numbers included the young and the old, but it also included many able-bodied fighters, men and women of breeding age. He held up a totem so they could all see it. A long, thin chain trailed off the thing, coiling to the ground.

"My Bairn," Oddur called out, "show them our power!"

Humans dispersed throughout the assembly transformed into the hulking forms of the bestial lycans. Both rage and intelligence burned within those forms' amber eyes.

Some of the newer folk recoiled, others stared with awe and admiration. None fled, though Oddur could feel general trepidation.

Behind the tribal leader crackled a large fire. Its dazzling flames glinted off the metallic totem, a disc of some unknown metal held by the three tribes of the Fianna—now the Fianna and the Bairn.

"We fáelad are either born or made," Oddur proclaimed. "This is the tool which does the making—though it is not without pain. For every blessing, there is a sacrifice. To earn this power, there is a cost, and that cost is to take the brand."

A murmur rippled through the crowd. Most of those gathered were newcomers to his growing group of nomads. Always the smallest of the Fianna, the Bairn had swelled too large to remain where they were and remain hidden from tuathan suspicion... but to move, he needed to secure his followers ability to protect themselves... to hunt for the party... *to fight like wolves.*

"I offer this power to you," he proclaimed, and tossed the thing into the fire, withdrawing it from the coals after several moments, pulling it by the chain.

Oddur used two swatches of leather to handle the hot items, and he dangled the elaborately crafted totem which now glowed red hot. The human nearest him, a man who'd been preparing some time to take the sign into his flesh, stepped forward. Bare chested, he nodded at Oddur, who pressed the thing against the man's torso.

The odor of burning flesh wafted upward and the man gritted his teeth and groaned against the pain. The noise turned to a growl and Oddur pulled the brand back, revealing the scald's ridges permanently marking his body. Raised flesh, puckered from the burn, formed intricate patterns in the reverse image of the totem's shape.

"Continue your growl... Let the wolf take you," Oddur urged.

The young man shuddered, his voice turning to a roar, and then his shape shifted. Muscles swelled and his face elongated to a toothy muzzle. Arms extended, cracking into place with fresh joint and sinew, claws lengthening as if daggers unsheathed.

Oddur nodded and then tossed the totem back into the flames. "Take your place with the other Bairn." He nodded to a cluster of nearby fáelad.

The lycan complied and joined his peers. He touched the area where his skin had been seared and sealed and then pulled his hand back from his hide. If there was pain, he did not indicate it.

"Now." Oddur grinned at the crowd. "Who's next?"

Men and women formed themselves into a line.

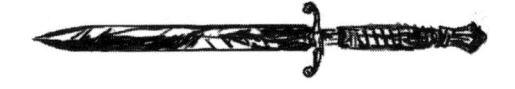

"You are certain of this?" Rhagathena growled at her advisor, the twin elf named Eilrora.

The aes sidhe nearest her nodded slowly. "I am, my queen. I felt my sister die."

Glaring at the winter spellcaster, Rhagathena tilted her head. "I know of the special bond you and your twin shared. If Arcenae has died, then how do you know that Rharzal remains alive, though wounded?"

"My spy told me," responded Eilrora. She held Rhagathena's gaze. "Your majordomo is unspoiled. However, Rharzal was defeated in battle and the slavetaker helped him escape. None else survived the encounter with Aderyn Corff."

Rhagathena growled as she bit her lip, her sharp teeth cutting into her own flesh. She spat blood, and then dabbed at the pooling redness with a silk kerchief. "And you are certain that the traitor also survived?"

The advisor dipped her head affirmatively. "Your hunters are presently making their return to Arctig Maen."

Rhagathena grunted animalistically and paced a few circles, agitated enough that her silk gland dribbled small splashes of webbing material to the floor. It was a nervous tick that belied how much rage she felt over the situation. But Rhagathena paid the silk splatters no heed. Chokorum's temporary replacement would clean it up later.

Eilrora had just lost her sister, but Rhagathena had lost something *more*... She no longer had access to knowledge gleaned through their psychic bond. She muttered several curses in the tongue of the n'arache people from her ancestral lands, lamenting the predicament.

Finally, Rhagathena turned on the spellcaster, wondering what more value the aes sidhe might bring to the Winter Court without that ability. *Useless things do not fare well below the Rime Throne.*

"Information and advice are always of value," Rhagathena said. "Tell me, who is this spy who provided your knowledge? I must know if it can be trusted."

Bowing low, the she-elf spoke plainly. "I was told it by a creature of the air. All the information until my sister's death I'd already known and everything that followed comes from the beak of a crow. A *white* crow."

Rhagathena steepled her fingers and leaned forward, eyes narrowing with glee. She hissed with pleasure. "Excellent."

King Oberon walked into his wife's favorite chamber. Titania lounged upon a chaise while she read a book and sipped wine.

"Are you enjoying yourself, my dear?" he asked her.

Titania ignored him for a few moments while she finished a paragraph and then sipped from her goblet before placing a bookmark at her page. Turning her attention to him, she said, "Of course, I am. There are few pleasures grander than a good plot enjoyed with a fine wine."

Oberon smiled at her, glad he'd caught her in a pleasant mood. Of course, he'd misread her in the past and sometimes her mood was merely a product of the wine. He made a mental note to bring her more.

"I wanted to discuss something with you," Oberon said. "I've just had a package delivered. Oddly enough, it was brought in by one of the mavens. This seems strange, does it not?"

"Which one?" Titania asked.

Oberon shrugged. "Outside of the High Mavens, I rarely pay attention to one wizard or another; they all look alike in their hoods and robes. I honestly don't even remember the color." He slid in next to her and placed his queen's legs over his lap while she swirled her wine.

The king looked over at her, and she met his gaze. "Thank you," he said simply.

"For what, my dear?"

"For the statue. The one of me which the mavens delivered. I had the servants place it with the likenesses of you and our sons in the main gallery."

Titania nodded slowly. "It arrived sooner than expected, but that is providential. I had asked the sculptor to hasten its delivery in order to motivate you to find our lost items. There are pieces amongst the art that I wish back... and as quickly as possible." Her eyes blazed with momentary fury, and Oberon was glad it had not been directed at him.

He took her hand in his and interlocked their fingers. "I assure you, Titania, that I am doing everything possible to reclaim the stolen treasures. Even you might be surprised by how many talented hunters I've dispatched to secure it."

A deep magic crackled in Oberon's eyes. "If we do not find it in time and the celebration of Saol Nua is ruined... All the Summer Court is ruined along with it."

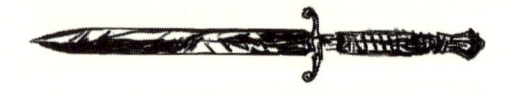

"Where is Arawyn?" Remy asked Eilastra as he took a seat.

Eilastra smiled and sipped her tea in the Morgansteen's drawing room.

Jaira sat close enough to her husband that the lengths of their upper legs touched. She held Remy's hand.

"We had not been expecting visitors," Eilastra said. "Arawyn and Harhassus have gotten on well." She took another sip and then looked over the rim of her cup at the married couple. With the tilt of her head, she quirked a smile. "I can see that you've finally told him about the pregnancy."

Jaira's expression remained placid, but Remy's eyebrows arched high. "Your mother already knew?"

"Of course, she did," Jaira said.

He stretched his lips into a kind of bemused smile. "I suggested we drop in on your parents for tea so that we could share the good news with them."

"I thought it was just for tea."

"Well... tea, and more," Remy said.

"That is still possible," Jaira said.

Eilastra nodded with a sort of regal, political smile. "I think that is a good idea. And I certainly think that Harhassus has warmed somewhat to this eventuality; it seems ever more likely after his time spent with Arawyn... an ellyllon. The other day I heard Harhassus correct a business acquaintance when he used the word israddol, even."

Remy took in a deep breath and then let it out. He hadn't even realized how much tension he was holding in his chest; sharing the news with his father-in-law had been a weight on him. Remy tried not to think about how the conversation *could* have gone, and he refused to entertain those words Harhassus had used in his dreams. Dreams in which everything Remy loved was destroyed.

Gulping, Remy actively rejected the notion that his dreams guided his fate, and yet somehow, he was still forced to entertain it.

Remy recalled his old mentor. Genesta had been an aes sidhe and a seer. Remy had been forced to kill her, though it was at Genesta's request. She'd often commented on his sometimes strange dreams, reminding him dreams were connected to destinies given by the gods.

Remy refused the notion of fate, though. *My destiny is of my own making.* His mouth upturned momentarily. *Genesta would have chuckled at that.*

Eilastra laughed at something Jaira had said while Remy was consumed with his thoughts. "You know what would be a delight? You should let Arawyn tell Harhassus. He's done such a good job keeping your secret so far—he's bit his tongue so often I thought we'd need to resort to an apothik solution."

Remy blinked. "Wait. What? Arawyn knows, too? Am I the last one to know?"

Jaira shrugged sheepishly. "I don't think Xander Kent knows, but Hobin does."

"You told *the powrie*?"

Both Jaira and Lady Eilastra laughed. Jaira looked at him with those sparkling eyes.

"Have some tea, dear," Eilastra said. "It will help calm you down."

Remy smooth his face and reached for the cup. As Jaira had told him right after he learned of her condition, *we can only go forward.* "Good idea. After these last several weeks, I could use some calm."

Hobin perched in the tallest tree he could find. It towered above the canopy of other greenery below, and he shielded his eyes from the brilliance of the sun, searching the roadway for a very specific carriage.

On his way back to the unseelie lands, he'd stopped and gleaned information from whatever sources he could, limited as they were for a powrie. He knew what he was looking for, at least.

From his vantage, Hobin knew he could spot either a sign that would lead him to his cousin, or perhaps even the very bandits who carried the prize. Below him sprawled the Selvages. They were a region of land stretching from the Solstox Canyons to the seelie and unseelie on either side.

Technically, the Selvages belonged to the faewylds, but Queen Mab had never asserted her authority or contested the presence of her neighbors, not even when they built garrisons there. It was unlikely that Queen Maeve would either; the new queen's rules had mirrored her predecessors exactly, which seemed odd given the rumors of Maeve's discontent for her aunt, which had blossomed into wholesale hatred, eventually resulting in a murderous coup.

Hobin had never paid much attention to political winds. Few of the powries had, and it had harmed them as a people group throughout the years. He put it out of his mind and resumed his search.

"Gotcha," he said, smiling to himself as he spied a distinct wagon.

He shimmied down the tree all the way back to the base and then scampered through the woods, hopping along as gracefully and as quietly as a deer, even despite his metal boots. He followed animal trails and detoured through a series of rolling hills that disrupted a large glade. Emerging on the other side, he spotted the carriage in the far distance.

Hobin had managed to get quite a way ahead of it, allowing himself time to hide and concoct a plan. *Perhaps I can ruin the wagon wheels unseen and cause a breakdown... Maybe I can steal the important piece for Remy and slip away unseen?*

He frowned as he wondered exactly how he could sabotage the wagon without being noticed. *If nothing else, I can gather more details about the thieves and then find my cousin. If I know how large their caravan is, we can bring overwhelming numbers and capture it.*

"Erp," Hobin gulped, feeling the weight of a weapon pressed into the base of his spine. He stiffened and listen to the words of whatever scout had found him.

"Where do you think *you're* going, little redcap?" The voice was a low, threatening growl. "Make one move and I'll gut you like an orc at the Spider Queen's bloody wedding."

High above the abandoned fortress of Canol Lár, a black crow descended to the shattered peak that overlooked the blackened rubble of the castle. The bird spiraled in its downward descent, cutting through the updrafts that came through the cliffs of the Solstox Canyons. Finally, it landed at the roost, built at the topmost landing.

A rival—the white crow—screeched at it, kicking small stones of debris and then attacking with its beak, pecking at the black. The two birds clawed at each other as they tumbled through the long abandoned nest. They rolled sidelong as they screeched and cawed, thumping against a sphere-like object and dislodging it.

The ancient, scaled egg, that of a dragon, rolled free of the roost and tumbled away, down into the courtyard of the abandoned keep and out of sight. Both birds hissed at each other and then continued their chatter and fighting until the black subdued the white.

Pinning her down, the black bird held the white crow until she calmed, slowing her breathing to normal. And then black released the white.

Neither moved for a moment.

The white crow blinked and bobbed her head, turning to face away from the black crow, and then the birds mated in the roost high above Canol Lár.

next is book 3:
Court of the Scorched Throne

Glossary

Aes sidhe – a class of magic wielding seelie fey

Aes sith - the equivalent of aes sidhe, but these fey are all wildfey

Aderyn Corff – "the death bird," a feared unseelie assassin who disappeared after defying the unseelie queen

Akasha – "magic in a bottle," a magic-based power source available to non-casters

Aither – a spiritual realm composed of pure thought and power

Aphay tree – a tree whose fruit erases memories

Apothiks - any variety of recreational apothecary-created drugs, often containing a magical reaction in addition to a physiological one

Arcadeax – the world of faerie-kind which coexists with Earth, the Infernal Realms, and many others

Bruscar – low class tier of Arcadeaxn society

Changelings – half fey, half human

Chronurgy - time magic

Coire Ansic - also known as the Dagda's pot or cauldron, or the King's Cup. It is a jar that regenerates ambrosia for the sidhe nobility; it is one of the most prized possessions of the Arcadeaxn gods

Coroniaids – often mistaken for dvergr who are the subterranean version, these are dwarves

Cù-sìth - a kind of hellhound

Cupronickel – a common metal alloy used so that no iron is present

Dagda – the chief deity of Arcadeaxn religious thought

Dallineb weed - a kind of incense that makes it difficult for spell casters to access their powers

Ddiymadferth – the chief insult among the fey: a derogatory word for human

Dream Hallow – a type of drug that causes euphoria and sends its users into the aither

Dúshlán – a kind of fetiche item given by Arcadeax itself, it is a boon for its recipient to right a great wrong with an act of vengeance

Dvergr – often mistaken for coroniaids who are the above-ground version of dwarves

Dweomer root - a tasty herb that blocks both arcane abilities and muddies connection to the aither

Egwyl meddwl - a fungus capable of freeing a person's mind and spirit to roam in an astral sense, accessing the overlap between aitherspace and dreamspace

Fáelad - what the werewolves call themselves for a term to include all of the lycans including branches of the Fianna and any others

Faewylds – any part of the world not claimed by the seelie or unseelie courts

Fetiche – Arcadeaxn magic that predates the aes sidhe; it is the magic of the gods

Fey – a word used to describe anything with Arcadeaxn origins

Frith Duine – a fey alliance dedicated to the eradication of humans living among them

High speech – also called the Olde Tongue and denoted by [brackets] when it is being used... oaths and commitments made in this language cannot be broken

Ina aonar – a house-less, ronin status for duelists who belong to no specific guild; also a name for excommunicated members of noble families

Iontaofa - a kind of dietary food law that applies to mavens and any vendor selling food or drink to the public with the guarantee that it will not inhibit aes sidhe abilities, under the penalty of death

Israddol - an insult used by some sidhe about inferior races of elves, especially the tylwyth teg; some Méith and Saibhir will use it as a derogative reference for lower castes

Maginarius (maginarium, pl.) - a kind of university for teaching magic to those with aptitude for it

Magitech - machinery and contraptions which can be activated through mystic means and powered by akasha

Maven – politically aligned mages who govern factions of magically gifted citizens

Méith – the elite class of the Seelie society

Olde Tongue - also called High speech and denoted by [brackets] when it is being used... oaths and commitments made in this language cannot be broken

Oibrithe – middle class of the Seelie society

Powrie - a goblin-like race of tiny unseelie creatures who wear red caps and have generally murderous intentions

Saibhir – upper class of the seelie society, but not méith

Saol Nua - a festival and feast Oberon puts on for his lords during which he distributes ambrosia to each house, granting the loyal sidhe functional immortality

Seelie – the summer court: one of the kingdoms of elves ruled by Oberon and Titania

Shade – a kind of animated corpse under the control of a necromancer

Sidhe – members of an elvish species of the fey folk

Shade - see Sluagh

Sluagh - a kind of walking dead creation, a reanimated corpse under control of one with necromantic skill

Solais Cloaks - an order of aes sidhe with martial training; these are warriors, scouts, and assassins working for the radiant tower and is a training path taken by aes sidhe who might never ascend to the rank of maven, otherwise... also called the Solais Order and readily identifiable by the cloaks they wear

Sphere - slang for "aithersphere" or "aitherspace"

Spherewalk - slang: to project one's conscious self into the aither

Teind – the "hell tithe" which rulers of Arcadeaxn realm must pay to infernal forces to keep shut the gates of hell

Tempus Exterminus purge - the campaign, ordered by both Winter and Summer Thrones to eradicate almost all sources of chronurgy

Trow – beneath the seelie and unseelie realms are subterranean kingdoms of under-elves which make up the autumn and spring courts

Tuatha – creatures or "people" native to Arcadeax; includes the sidhe but also other sentient beings such as fauns, dvergr, etc... can be a synonym for any fey creature in most contexts

Tylwyth Teg – a type of elf from the faewylds and considered uncivilized and barbaric by their seelie and unseelie counterparts; looked down on by other sidhe

Vantadium - a metal alloy made of vanadium and titanium so that no iron is present

Wildfey - residents of the faewyld; it also refers to the type of fey native to that region but living abroad (the Tylwyth Teg, etc.)

Wolfranium - a metal alloy made of tungsten and titanium so that no iron is present

Wulflock – the long-lost rightful king of the unseelie

Named Places of Arcadeax

The Seelie Kingdom of Summer

Cathair Dé, a mid-sized city

Baile Dorcha - a small village a short distance from Cathair Dé

Faery Cairn, the capitol city fortress

Daonra Dlúth, a large city that forms a ring around Faery Cairn

Suíochán Naséan, a tower and campus belonging to wizards on the wall between Daonra Dlúth and Faery Cairn

Vail Carvanna, a small woodland village

Te Sástacity, city (location not specific)

Saibhir Gaoithe, city (location a day's ride of Cathair De)

Cath Bua

Deisiúil

Inmhianaithe

Raidhse

Well of the Gates

Wooded Rim, the western edge of the kingdom

The Unseelie Kingdom of Winter

Hulda Thorne, a large city that forms a ring around a walled fortress known as Arctig Maen
Frosthorn
Iâ Tre
Gaeafdale
Icedinas
Spinefrost Ridge, mountain range on the eastern border. Home to giant spiders/driders known as N'arache
Eira Cartref
Coldhome
Vale Rhewi, mid-sized city located in the wastelands
Lloches Oer
Hestref
Gwylltown, small city
Wastelands, despoiled lands south west of kingdom
Demonsbreak Enclave

The Faewylds
Capitus Ianthe, a mobile caravan city
Wildfell, large walled city in the north region
Brakkholme, a small forest village near the rift
Draenen
Fiáin Vale
Clawdale
Fiacail
Dant
Crafangu

Canol Lár, an abandoned fortress left since the Infernal Wars

The Selvages, a series of rifts too deep to see the bottom

Horn of the Selvages, the southern reaches where the canyons end and mountains begin.

The Grinning Wood

The Aegis Bastion

The bottom reaches of Winter and Summer are both guarded by a towering wall erected via magic of the gods... below it lies the Fomorian empire. This is also known as The Iron Wall

Remy Keaton's story truly begins when he enters the seelie in *A Kiss of Daggers*. The sequel is, *Of Mages, Claw, and Shadow*, and the series will continue from there. To go back to the beginning, the prequel book, *Origins of the Fey Duelist* is available now. *Court of the Scorched Throne* and the rest of the series is due out soon!

Keep up to date and stay in touch with the author at this link: https://www.subscribepage.com/duelist

and add your email to be added to the newsletter list!

Legends and Lorecraft

Many authors have dedicated fan groups online. After publishing nearly 100 stories I wanted to build a place allowing me opportunities to engage with readers and engage more meaningfully than even my newsletter does.

Enter *Legends and Lorecraft*.

In an industry where publishers, platforms, production costs, and promotional fees eat up most of the revenue authors make from books, subscription services help creators writing. Folks often tell me "I love supporting writers," and this provides a way for them to contribute to a sustainable space for them to shape the future of my writing (whether they're a paid subscriber or free.)

Consider joining my readers community. Unlike the big publishers, *it is focused on putting readers first!* Members get early access to beta and alpha read projects I'm working on (which means they'll sometimes see early drafts—even before a story is done,) and there are tons of insider bonuses, plus amazing exclusives.

Take the first step towards adventure:

https://www.authorchristopherdschmitz.com/community

Also By Christopher D. Schmitz

Wolves of the Tesseract
1. Wolf of the Tesseract
2. Gate of the Multiverse
3. The Architect King

The Casefiles of Vikrum Wiltshire

Curse of the Fey Duelist: Origins of the Fey Duelist
Curse of the Fey Duelist: The Crow and the Troll
Curse of the Fey Duelist: A Kiss of Daggers
Curse of the Fey Duelist: Of Mages, Claw, and Shadow

The Seelie

Inmhianaithe

Faery Cairn   Suíochán Naséan

Daonra Dlúth

Deisiúil

The Faewilds

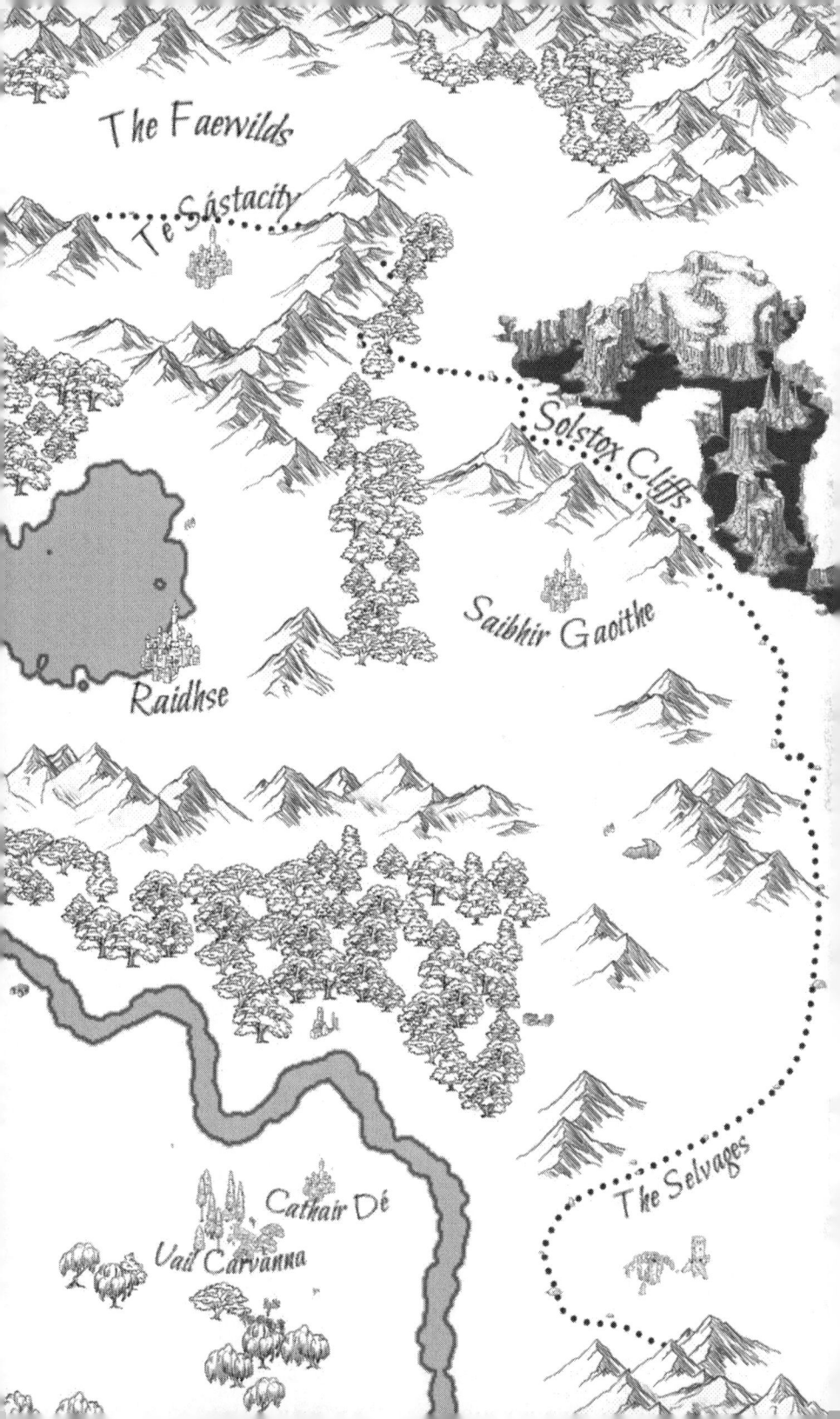

Te Sástacity

Solstox Cliffs

Raidhse

Saibhir Gaoithe

Cathair Dé
Vail Carvanna

The Selvages

Wildfell
Draenen
Fiáin Vale
Dant
Salstox Cliffs
the Selvages
Vale Rhewi

Icedinas
Clawdale
Crafangu
Faewylds
The Unseelie
Gaeafdale
Coldhome
monsbreak
nclave
Hulda Thorne
ylltown
Iâ Tre
Hestref
Lloches Oer
Eira Cartref

About Author

Christopher D. Schmitz is an indie author from the fly-over states who dabbles in game design. He has published award winning science fiction, fantasy, and humor. He's written and freelanced for a variety of outlets, including a blog that has helped countless writers on their publishing journey. On any given weekend, he can be found at pop culture and comic conventions across the USA or playing his bagpipes for people. You can look him up at:

www.authorchristopherdschmitz.com.

Made in the USA
Columbia, SC
05 April 2025